SCOTLAND, 1542:

*Amid a furious blood feud sparked by a
legendary and mystical stone,
a determined laird seeks peace. . . .*

Robert Maxwell, eldest son of the notoriously ruthless Red
Rowan, plans to set a new course for his irascible and war-
hungry family by making peace with the clan's long-
standing English rivals. And what better way to mark the
beginning of a new era than by wedding the Graham family's most precious lady? Peace always comes at a price,
and seducing a beautiful woman seems a small one to pay.

Incensed by her brother's scheme to marry her off to a
Scottish barbarian, Caroline Graham is shocked to find her
betrothed so pleasing to the eye. Nevertheless, she enters
into the arrangement with a determinedly icy heart and a
vow to resist her husband's every touch. But when she sus-
pects she's merely a pawn in her brother's ultimate plan to
destroy his ancient enemy for good—and to find and claim
the storied magical stone as his own—Caroline is torn.
Robert's bravery, loyalty, and charm have begun to melt
her resistance. Is it possible that her sworn enemy is really
the love of her life?

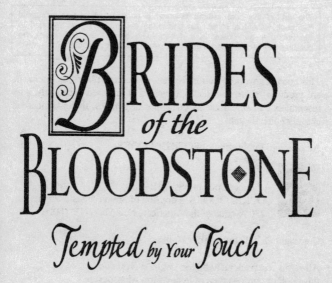

BRIDES of the BLOODSTONE

Tempted by Your Touch

JEN HOLLING

SONNET BOOKS

New York London Toronto Sydney Singapore

An *Original* Publication of POCKET BOOKS

A Sonnet Book published by
POCKET BOOKS, a division of Simon & Schuster, Inc.
1230 Avenue of the Americas, New York, NY 10020

ISBN: 0-7434-3802-7

First Sonnet Books printing January 2002

10 9 8 7 6 5 4 3 2 1

SONNET BOOKS and colophon are trademarks of Simon & Schuster, Inc.

For information regarding special discounts for bulk purchases, please contact Simon & Schuster Special Sales at 1-800-456-6798 or business@simonandschuster.com

Front cover illustration by Lisa Litwack; front cover photo credit: Bates Littlehales/Gettystone.com; back cover illustration by Gregg Gulbronson

Printed in the U.S.A.

To George and Jennie Miller
For summers in New York,
Pineapple-orange soda,
Rides on the car-lift,
Back scratches,
And being the best grandparents ever.
I love you.

In loving memory of
George Joseph Miller
1928–2001

Tempted by Your Touch

PROLOGUE

❧

Annancreag Castle, West March,
Scotland, 1482

Malcolm suspected the celebration had gotten out of hand, though he was no keen judge, having himself consumed large quantities of mead and whiskey. To his dismay, his bride had disappeared. *Again.* He was not surprised she'd been drawn away, for she was, in his heart and mind, the most beautiful woman to set foot in Annancreag and managed to command the attention of every male in her vicinity. And she was his.

Malcolm stood, swaying slightly, and peered about the great hall. Many of the Maxwell clan had already found their beds and were scattered about the floor, unconscious. He noted, with a satisfied grin, that the Graham party that had escorted Elizabeth to her wedding still got on fine with the Maxwells, in spite of their drunken state. Yes, this marriage was good. Many had been opposed to it. The feuding between the Maxwells and the Grahams had been going strong—flourishing, in fact—since Malcolm was a child. Murder, raid, rapine. A nasty state of affairs.

Malcolm had not only brought an end to the feuding, but was fortunate enough to have it come about through a love match. Ever since the raid he'd visited on Graham Keep two years ago he'd been in love with Elizabeth Graham. He'd seen her, standing at the top of the stairs, shrieking like a wildcat, sword clutched in her fists, and had questioned all he was.

He'd called the retreat and left, taking no prisoners and no plunder for himself (though he couldn't deny his men their rightful share). But the memory of her had been branded in his heart and he'd vowed to have her at any cost.

"Elizabeth!" he called, raising his voice to be heard over the fiddle and pipe music, and the yells of men gaming. A crash, followed by thrashing limbs, startled him. A rope had been thrown over the ponderous candelabra suspended from the ceiling by chains for the children to swing on. After a few tankards, some of the stupider men decided to have a swing. One now sprawled flat on his back amongst the platters of meat and bread.

Malcolm brushed the food off his sleeve and set off in search of his bride, more than ready for the bedding down. Though the betrothal ceremony had taken place a fortnight ago, Elizabeth had held him at bay, saving her maidenhead for their wedding night. The wait had been excruciating, but it was finally over.

The fuzziness began to clear from his brain when a circuit of the hall did not produce Elizabeth. Graham eyes followed him. The Maxwells were oblivious, immersed in their cups and sport.

"Elizabeth!"

Where was that woman? Malcolm left the hall behind, not giving another thought to the Graham men. He stepped into the courtyard. The walls were sparsely manned tonight—most of the Maxwells had joined the celebration. Malcolm's eyes narrowed at the man-at-arms walking the wall. Was it the whiskey, or was that man unfamiliar?

"My lord . . . ?" A hissing whisper from the shadows.

"Who's there?" The slur of his words dismayed him—definitely the drink causing his suspicion.

"Have a care, my lord. . . ."

Malcolm surged forth, surprising his spook and snagging a handful of rags. He yanked it around, out of the shadows and into the torchlight. It was the Musgrave witch.

He released her as if she were a viper and stepped back. "What are you still doing here? Skulking about?"

She'd arrived right before the wedding, bearing a mysterious package. An English hag, shrunken, wrinkled, and toothless. The entire hall had fallen silent, awestruck, as she relayed the legend of the Clachan Fala, the Blood Stone. They'd all heard it before, in one form or another—but apparently corrupted and incomplete. It had once rested in the scabbard that protected King Arthur's sword, Excalibur. The legend was not clear on how the Maxwells came into possession of it, and so Malcolm had always assumed it wasn't real. Rumors cropped up from time to time, that some Maxwell or Graham had discovered the stone, feeding the legend. Many Maxwells and Grahams alike still searched for it—raided and murdered each other under the mistaken assumption the other had it and kept it secret from them.

The witch revealed the stone to all, now nestled in an intricate gold setting. She told how the Lady of the Lake gave King Arthur the sword and scabbard, and how the scabbard, encrusted with precious gems, protected him from harm so long as he wore it. But it was stolen by his enemies. A knight from the north had come to serve the great king. He was of an ancient family that was to become the Annan Maxwells. He tried to recover the scabbard for his king, but was only able to retrieve the one stone. For his loyalty and efforts, the king gave it to the knight as a wedding gift. The knight's bride was of the Graham grayne that eventually settled on the Eden River. Through greed and treachery, the Grahams murdered the Maxwell knight, seizing the stone.

A witch, charged with the hiding and protection of the Clachan Fala, stole the stone through witchcraft, to keep safe until a Graham and a Maxwell of the proper graynes joined again in a worthy union. It had taken nearly a thousand years for an Annan Maxwell and an Eden Graham to come together in love.

The witch's audience had been enthralled—none could deny there was a force to the stone, a pulsing that filled the room. Malcolm had taken it in his hands and felt the power resonate in his limbs, had seen the wonder in Elizabeth's face as she looked upon him. And knew what she'd thought—had heard her words in his head. *We're worthy.*

He'd set the stone down hastily, unsettled that he'd heard her voice so clearly and yet her lips had not moved. Or had he? He'd been drinking even then.

And why was the witch not gone, having accomplished her mission? Why did she still slink about the shadows, watching?

"It's not for you," the witch said, plucking at his sleeve. "You protect it, keep it—for your son. He will be great."

She'd said that before—and yet he knew—he felt it in his bones—were he to take it into battle it would serve him as the sword and scabbard had served Arthur. He would *know* what the enemy planned. He saw it clearly, like a prophetic vision, his own invincibility in raids and battle—against the English. Knowing instantly what the opposition planned and countering before they could even execute it.

When he didn't reply, she said, "Mark me," and backed away, melting into the night.

He started after her and was grabbed from behind. He let out a shout and snatched reflexively for his sword.

"Whoa-ho, my lord! Have a care—'tis just me!"

Malcolm relaxed as his younger brother, Kinnon, accompanied by several inebriated Maxwells and a dozen Grahams—not so drunk—surrounded him. They shouted advice and encouragement on bedding a woman. Mostly silent, the Grahams exchanged strange glances with each other. Malcolm turned, peering into the darkness where the witch had been—but she was gone. Warnings rattled through his foggy head, but before he could do or say anything, he was bustled back into the castle and down the hall to the bedchamber.

"Elizabeth awaits you, my lord," one of the Grahams breathed in his ear.

Malcolm forgot his suspicions and thought only of his bride, waiting for him. The door to his chambers was thrown open and he was pushed through, into the bedchamber.

The bed curtains were tied back. She lay in the bed, covered to her neck by a fur blanket, her hair spilling over the bolsters like molten silver. The sight of her hurt—burned his eyes, made his heart ache. The Blood Stone—an enormous blood red ruby—swelled on a table beside the bed. It transfixed him, seduced him, reminded him of the witch's strange warning, but then his gaze fell on Elizabeth again, and it was forgotten.

He tried to say her name, but emotion choked him. Kinnon laughed, unbuttoning his doublet; someone removed his belt, his sword. Malcolm remained motionless, his eyes never leaving his bride. Awareness prickled the hair on his neck.

Something was wrong.

Though he'd left Elizabeth a maiden for this night, they'd already explored much together. There should be no cause for the terror glazing her wide blue eyes. She was not afraid of him.

But here she stared at him—eyes unnaturally wide, skin drained of color, mouth pinched. Her head shook—imperceptibly—but he stared so hard he caught it. She was trying to tell him something. Her eyes slanted sideways. Malcolm followed her look.

She was not alone.

Hidden in the folds of the curtains, beside the bedpost, stood a man.

Elizabeth's gaze darted to something behind him, her eyes widening further, the whites glaring at him. Malcolm whirled, reaching for his sword—but his movements were clumsy and his sword was gone.

The last thing he saw, before the sword pierced his heart, was Kinnon, impaled on the door. And the last thing he heard was Elizabeth's anguished scream, "No!"

1

Graham Keep, West March,
England, 1542

sixty years later. . . .

Sisters. As women, they should be compliant, deferring to their fathers and husbands. Should they lack both, then their brothers shall guide them and care for them. They should be grateful for his loving and kind protection; for the great pains he took in administering their future.

Unfortunately for Ridley Graham he was not blessed with such paragons of sisters.

Ungrateful, devious, argumentative, surly . . . well, one of them was surly; these were all words that described his sisters, but never compliant or appreciative.

Ridley paused outside the door to his sisters' bedchamber. He smoothed the fine whiskers of his beard thoughtfully, then adjusted the small starched ruff at his neck. It was nearly noon and he'd seen neither of his sisters nor his stepmother today. They were apparently closeted up together in their chambers, plotting against him. This avoidance did not bode well for what was to come.

It was their father's fault, Ridley knew. After Ridley's birth, Mother had suffered a succession of miscarriages. When finally she began birthing live babies again Father had come to view children differently. He loved and coddled his next three children. Never did they suffer the lash as Ridley had; never were they forced to bear Father's mockery or derision. And this was the result. Spoiled and petulant, believing they had some say in their future.

Ridley knocked briefly and entered before being granted admittance.

He paused again just inside the door to examine the scene before him. Fayth, Ridley's youngest sister, slouched in a chair near the fire. The light from the fire picked out the reddish strands in her hair, making it appear auburn rather than the drab brown it was. She looked more like a beardless lad in a kirtle than a lass overripe for marriage. Fayth's head swiveled around, her dark eyes narrowing on Ridley before turning dismissively back to contemplate the flames. Ridley's lips tightened. She'd not always been this bitter and unpleasant. When Father was dying she'd leeched onto some ruffian, claiming to love him—but Ridley knew she was scrambling to find a man of her choosing before Father died. Unfortunately—for her, that is—her paramour had been murdered in a raid. She knew the fate Ridley had planned for her and fought against it. *Insufferable little bitch.* He would beat that defiance out of her spine if necessary. But not now.

He turned, facing the other occupants of the room. Two women and a man.

"Father," Ridley murmured, bowing his head to Caroline's priest, Father Jasper Graham—a distant cousin on their father's side.

The tall, thin man approached Ridley, hands tucked into the sleeves of his fine green robes. "This is not what Lord Graham wanted—you know this." Father Jasper's head was long and thin like his body, the cheeks hollowed. His large eyes were haunted, as if he found no solace in God's calling.

"News travels fast. I only just left the messenger from Lord Annan." Ridley shot a hard look at his young stepmother, Mona, a small woman of dark, inscrutable beauty. Her black eyes held his, condemning. Then she put her back to him and resumed brushing Caroline's long blond hair.

"My lord," Father Jasper implored, moving in front of Ridley, blocking his view of Mona and Caroline. Ridley hated the priest. He'd always championed Caroline, because of the vocation she strove for. Like-minded confederates, they were. The priest was probably the only person who knew Caroline's thoughts.

"Caroline does not wish to wed. Lord Graham asked you to care for your sisters, see to their happiness. The Lord expects you to honor your father's wishes."

Tipping his head back, Ridley stared up at the priest, annoyed at the man's manner. How dare he attempt to call forth a higher authority. Ridley was the highest authority on Graham lands now. And he was sick and tired of the usefulness of the Graham women going to waste.

"I have a duty—as does every member of this family." He circled the priest and went to stand behind Caroline. Mona melted away.

Pale green eyes gazed at him from the mirror's distorted reflection, as if she had two faces, one slightly offsetting and obscuring the other.

"I am fulfilling my duty," Ridley said. "It is time you did yours. Alliances are essential for survival and I have but two sisters and many alliances to forge. You'll not deny me my right to give you away in marriage."

His sister was most unattractive—manly in every way, from her long face to her oversized body. She put on no airs, was aware of her defects, and yet still carried herself with an innate confidence that other, more beautiful, women couldn't feign. It was unseemly.

"Look at you," Ridley said, his lip curling. "You hag. You should thank me for arranging this marriage. Lord Annan is said to be a kind master. He has promised not to beat you and to allow you many liberties. The messenger said the ladies find his looks pleasing."

Caroline showed no emotion, her face serene, expressionless. He was sure she practiced it in front of the mirror, this look of a martyr, of the lamb going to the slaughter.

"You know what they call you? The Pious Graham Mare. He will not trouble you overmuch with his attentions. Perhaps he will get a few heirs on you, but he will surely seek his pleasure elsewhere."

"Who has called Caroline such a thing?" Mona asked, sliding back into Ridley's field of vision.

"Suitors, who want our wealth and name, and will wed a dray horse to get it."

"Oh, you are foul," Fayth hissed behind him. "If father were alive—"

"Father is dead!" Ridley nearly trembled with fury. "I am the master now. I hold your future in my hands. You will obey me, or you will be penniless."

"I choose poverty, then." Cool as water and fair as spring was Caroline's voice, like the Virgin herself addressing her people. "I will go with Father Jasper and enter a convent." She rose to her full, unnatural height, towering over everyone in the room except the priest. Father Jasper joined Caroline, placing a comforting hand on her shoulder.

Ridley shook his head, laughing at himself. He'd set himself up for that one. "Sorry, Carrie, you'll not get off that easily. You are to wed Lord Annan in a fortnight."

She stared down her nose at him, managing not to

look the least bit haughty. Only saintly. She did not speak.

Ridley grew impatient. It was always this way. Caroline could weigh him down in silence. He wanted to know her intentions and she would reveal nothing until she was ready. She was no saint, but a conniving demon.

"You pig!" Fayth spat. "You won't marry me off to the highest bidder. Father said I could marry as I pleased. He promised."

Ridley rounded on his little sister, as diminutive as Caroline was tall. Fayth's fists balled at her sides and her face flushed. She was the complete opposite of Caroline, unable to hide her emotions—or stop a single thought from escaping her lips.

Giving in to the urge that had plagued him for the past five years, Ridley slapped Fayth, knocking her flat. Mona screamed and Caroline gasped. Ridley whirled in time to catch the horror he'd surprised Caroline into revealing before she quickly masked it with calm reproach.

She went to Fayth and knelt beside her, speaking softly. Fayth's breath hissed through her nose and teeth, murder in her eyes. But she had shut her mouth. Perhaps force *was* the way to deal with her.

"Ridley, please," Mona said, taking his arm and steering him toward the door. "I will talk to them, calm them."

Ridley allowed her to lead him, smiling to himself. He looked down into his stepmother's beautiful face, her troubled brow, her deep velvety eyes. Always the peacemaker. He'd been in love with her since his father had brought her home and presented her to the family. She was a Musgrave and common, but still, he had seethed with jealousy, imagining her in Father's bed—the old skeletal frame of Hugh Graham rutting on her. It had made him sick. And mad with want for her. Now Father was gone. He could not marry his father's widow, but he could keep her as his mistress, if only . . .

"I know their manner vexes you," Mona whispered. "But you must not blame them. Your father indulged them and allowed their natures to grow strong. They'll be a match for any man and since their wit is sharp, perhaps they'll win respect, if wed to the right men."

"*Respect.* It is not their place to be respected. It's time for them to become meek and gentle in preparation for marriage. My rule is nothing compared to an irate husband's. They will be beaten dead within the first year of marriage. Caroline will certainly hold her own in a fight, but will end up the worse for it—mark me."

"You're right, of course. I will speak to them. I think this marriage to Lord Annan is a fine thing and Caroline will come to see that, too."

"Tell Caroline that if she refuses, I'll give her the poverty she desires. She'll live alone in the tower. Under guard. She can live out her days as a dried-up old nun if she wishes—but she will do it alone. I'll not even allow her Father Jasper."

Mona nodded. She started to turn away but he caught her arm.

"Tell her Lord Annan is a papist . . . and that she can bring Father Jasper."

"Aye, my lord." She strained against his grip.

He pulled her into the corridor. "You can save them both, you know." He dragged her against his chest, burying his face in her hair, inhaling the musky scent of her. "Tell me where it is and I will send them both abroad. I'll buy Caroline's way into the finest convent and Fayth can marry a plowboy if she desires. It's all in your hands."

She wrenched free, her face twisted in revulsion.

"You'll never have it, so long as I live and breathe!" She scurried back into the room, closing the door behind her.

Caroline stared at herself in the mirror, trying not to give in to the terror gripping her heart. She'd known this day would come. Though Father had promised her she would never have to marry if she didn't wish to, and Ridley had mouthed his assurances that he would force no unwanted unions upon them, she'd known Ridley was not to be trusted. He'd always been a sly boy. Ten years Caroline's senior, he had nevertheless been her hero when she was a child—that is, until she discovered how he despised his three siblings. Caroline, Fayth, and their little brother Wesley had all been close to each other and to their father. But Ridley had stood on the outskirts of the family; even Mother had rejected him.

For years it seemed to Caroline that Ridley was only biding his time, enduring Father's instruction and advice with a patronizing smile, waiting for the day he could take charge and do things his way. And now Ridley was Lord Graham. The day Father died Ridley had installed a reformed minister in the castle's chapel, displacing Father Jasper. He'd been trying to force conversion on Caroline. Wesley had capitulated, still retaining some residual hero worship toward his big brother, and wanting to believe everything was for the best. But Fayth and Caroline held out. And now they were both to be married off in political alliances.

Mona returned. She began twisting Caroline's hair into a thick plait. "Lord Annan is Catholic. Ridley says you may take Father Jasper to Scotland."

The silence drew out, heavy.

"It is true that some husbands are harsh," Mona said.

"But for most women matrimony opens a door to many possibilities."

"It didn't for you," Fayth said.

Mona's mouth thinned. "You're father's and my . . . relationship was not typical."

Caroline didn't know if this were true or not, but she did know her father had treated his children far better than his wives. Caroline's mother had cried incessantly for years, then one day just stopped, and never shed another tear. She stopped speaking or running the household. Caroline had been forced to take over while Mother spent her days in the solar, creating tapestries that depicted horrifying scenes of death and dismemberment. When she'd finally passed away, quietly in her sleep, it had been a relief to all, most especially Father. Caroline caught her lips trembling and tightened them. She would not cower from Lord Annan. She would not cry.

Mona leaned close and whispered, "Surely marriage is a better thing than remaining under Ridley's rule? He will force you to repudiate the true religion, else imprison you. Your new husband will allow you to worship as you please. His people say he is fair."

"He's a Maxwell," Caroline said. "The Maxwells loathe us—his people won't accept me."

"You can't do this," Fayth said, impassioned. Fayth had always thrown herself wholeheartedly into the feud with the Maxwells, but since her betrothed had been murdered by one, her hate consumed her. "Run away! I'll help you. Anything—*death* is better than sharing a bed with a Maxwell!"

The blood feud between the Maxwells and the Grahams had been thriving for generations. Caroline wasn't even sure what had started it, only that they had raided and murdered each other since she was a child. The

Maxwells were Scots—godless barbarians. Her husband would rape her and be unfaithful. She would live in a hovel, dress in rags. Hysteria churned in her gut, but didn't show on the surface.

Mona touched Caroline's shoulders. "This marriage will bring peace to the clans. No more raids, no more death. You will finally heal a wound that has been open and bleeding for three score years."

Caroline blinked.

Mona raised her voice, for Fayth's benefit now. "Besides . . . the Maxwell man Ridley holds for ransom is nothing as I expected . . . he seems quite civilized. He is Lord Annan's brother, Sir Patrick. I've spoken to him— he tells me Lord Annan is very honorable. The ransom Ridley set for Sir Patrick's return is too steep for Lord Annan. His brother's safe return is all he requested when negotiating the marriage."

Fayth snorted, then jerked, touching her bruised jaw gingerly. "How do you know?"

Mona didn't answer, but Caroline knew Ridley would tell their stepmother anything she wanted to know, being thoroughly besotted with her. Poor Mona. She should be the only one benefiting from Father's passing, but Ridley kept her like a prisoner.

"Just think," Mona said softly. "You will be the reason Lord Annan is reunited with his brother. An auspicious beginning, to be sure. 'Twill not be so bad. You'll see. A better lot than mine." Mona looked over her shoulder at Fayth, who had wandered back over to the fireplace. "And a much better match than the one Ridley has in mind for your sister."

Caroline sighed. Perhaps Mona was right. Surely ending the feud was a good thing. Lord Annan sounded like a reasonable man. She was allowed to keep Father Jasper.

And Ridley was right—she was no prize. Four-and-twenty this past winter, she was no longer young. Nor was she beautiful. Lord Annan would seek his pleasure elsewhere. She could continue as always. Perhaps children would be a comfort. Mona claimed Caroline possessed hips well suited for bearing many large children and that death in childbirth would not be such a danger to her as it was to most women.

Mona returned to plaiting Caroline's hair. What if this marriage did not bring peace? What if the fires of reform engulfed Scotland and her husband repudiated God? How would she be better off than under Ridley's rule? An idea occurred to her. Upon seeing her, Lord Annan would be as disappointed about the marriage as she was. Perhaps, if he were truly a reasonable man, he would be willing to renegotiate the marriage contract.

Perhaps . . .

2

Annancreag Castle,
West March, Scotland

Robert paced the length of the empty hall, hands clasped behind his back. It was strangely silent for midday. Trestle tables lined the wall, ready to be set up for the dinner hour. The air was redolent with the scent of pork, beef, and other game, roasting for the upcoming feast honoring the keep's new mistress.

Her party had been sighted from the tower nearly an hour ago. The entire castle had been in an uproar with last-minute preparations, but now, with her arrival imminent, they were all in hiding where they would watch the first meeting between Robert Maxwell, Lord Annan, and Caroline Graham, unseen.

Robert wished he could join them. A shadow passed over the sun and he raised his head to the high slit windows that lined the hall. They allowed in little light. Torches usually supplemented the sun's light, and the candelabra that hung from the ceiling was lit at dusk, but for this occasion Robert had commissioned fine glass lanterns that hung in place of the torches. As an Englishwoman, she would be accustomed to finer things than he could provide. His stomach turned again with unfamiliar nervousness. He wanted very much for his bride to be pleased with her new home and husband. He wanted her to feel immediately at ease, for them to become friends. He didn't imagine finding love in this union, but friendship, affection, respect, all were possible, and hoped for.

The clatter of hooves in the bailey brought him up short. He took a deep breath and started for the doors, rehearsing his greeting in his mind.

It wasn't his bride-to-be, but his little brother. Damn, but it was taking her a long time to climb the hill Annancreag sat upon. He'd hoped to get this confrontation with his brother over long before now . . . or much later—now was not the best of times. Alexander Maxwell strode toward him, face flushed from riding hard, red-brown hair escaping the club at his neck to fly around his face. He looked like a lion on the rampage. He looked like their father.

Arms folded across his chest, Robert said, "Good day, Alex. Come to greet Mistress Graham and give us your blessing?" He hadn't seen his brother in weeks—not since their last falling out over Robert's precarious truce with the neighboring Johnstone laird.

Alex stopped abruptly in front of Robert. "I came to find out if it were but a rumor—and here I learn it's true? You're marrying the Pious Graham Mare? Was that her party I passed outside the gates?"

Robert frowned at the cruel sobriquet. "Aye. Do not speak of her so."

"So it's true . . . ?" Alex shook his head in disbelief, as if he simply couldn't accept it.

"Aye."

"I cannot believe you would marry our father's murderer."

"Mistress Graham did not murder our father."

"Her people did!"

Robert gritted his teeth, weary of having this same argument with Alex and never getting anywhere. "What did you expect? Father murdered scores of Hugh Graham's people—it's amazing he lived so long as he did!"

Alex waved a hand in disgusted dismissal.

It was useless to try to make Alex see reason, so Robert said, "The betrothal is tomorrow morning and after the banns are said, we will be wed."

"Why?"

Robert sighed and paced away from Alex. "You know why. This really isn't a good time to discuss this. She will be here any minute."

"Thank the Lord! Then I am not too late!" Alex's footsteps echoed across the stones as he followed Robert. "You cannot marry a Graham. To bring one of their kind into this family is . . . is . . . well—it's blasphemous. Father would never forgive you."

Robert tried to find the calm patience he always practiced with his brother, but with everything else on his mind today, patience was in short supply. "Father is dead and I am now responsible for Maxwell lands and all the people on them. Far too much blood has been shed and property lost in the name of this blood feud. For my people's sake, I am ending it by marrying Mistress Graham."

Alex's hand cut violently through the air. "This will end nothing! Our sire's blood stains their hands! Grahams are treacherous—their word means naught. You saddle yourself with an ugly wife and for what? So she can betray you by supplying the Grahams with intelligence—by telling them how to hurt us—where our weaknesses lie!"

"Our weaknesses lie in illiberal fools who insist on murder and theft to avenge some slight they cannot remember! I do this for Patrick—as you are well aware.

You ken the ransom Ridley Graham asks is impossible for me to gather. With this alliance he has agreed to release Patrick immediately after the wedding." Robert lowered his voice and added, "And I will not tolerate any more insults to Mistress Graham. Are we clear?"

Alex's lips drew into a thin line as he obviously held back the rest of his diatribe. He inhaled deeply and some of the redness faded from his cheeks. "Forgive me . . . I'm most distressed." The apology was a surprise, even offered so grudgingly. Alex never apologized. He must be desperate to change Robert's mind to resort to such tactics as asking forgiveness.

Robert's brows raised in interest.

Alex slid an arm around Robert's shoulder, turning him toward the fireplace. Rowan, Robert's father, had been uncommonly tall, a trait he had passed on to his surviving children. But Robert was the tallest of the lot and now looked down on his brother, whose russet head was bent in thought as he led Robert across the hall.

"There are other women . . . beautiful women, who would be more than happy to wed the Maxwell laird. Women of good stock that would make fine wives—"

Robert shrugged off his brother's arm. "I have always known that my marriage must be political and I have long resigned myself to it—but I've not spent thirty-five years refusing the women father tried to force down my throat only to give in to you! This is a good marriage and it will end the constant raiding—the senseless death. And there are other aspects to the union between man and woman than what goes on in the bedchamber, Brother. Our own mother was no beauty and yet Father never had reason to regret their marriage."

This was the wrong thing to say and Robert realized it as soon as the words left his mouth.

Alex's skin flushed crimson. "Our mother was beautiful. How dare you compare her to that pious old nag? She was a fine woman—finer than any English whore!"

Robert couldn't remember the last time his brother had so infuriated him. His hand shot out so quickly Alex hadn't time to duck. He cuffed the redhead hard. "Jesus God! I don't care if Mistress Graham looks like a horse's ass, she's to be my wife and I'll not—"

A gentle throat clearing interrupted Robert's impassioned speech. His voice was still echoing through the cavernous and deathly quiet hall—or was it his words merely echoing through his mind? Alex, rubbing his ear, stared past Robert, wide-eyed.

Robert grabbed Alex's shoulder. "Is it . . . ?" His voice was little more than a rasp.

Alex nodded, a smug smile spreading across his face.

Robert's heart sank. *So much for setting her at ease.* The first words she heard from his mouth were him calling her a horse's ass. No point trying to explain, it would only make matters worse and introduce Alex's opposition to the marriage. He would give her no reason to change her mind.

He squared his shoulders and turned, fixing his expression into polite welcome.

A small group stood at the opposite end of the hall, just inside the door. As he advanced toward them he noted two were quite tall—one a man, a priest, by his vestments, the other, a woman. He paused, astounded by the woman's size. Though he immediately continued toward the group, the sharp eyes of the woman had caught his hesitation. Caught it and assigned meaning to it. Meaning he had not intended, for at that moment, he knew she was his bride.

Henry, Robert's steward, dashed through the doors behind the party, looking thoroughly bewildered. "My

lord," Henry wheezed, mopping his shiny pate. "Allow
me to present Mistress Caroline Graham." He waved a
hand at the tall woman and stepped back.

She was enormous. Not taller than he was, but then, he
was uncommonly tall. The top of her head was level with
his eyes. An unattractive headdress covered her hair,
equalizing their heights and preventing him from deter-
mining the color of her hair. Nothing of her body was visible, hidden as it was beneath a voluminous gray velvet
cloak.

It was her eyes that held him captive. A green so pale it
reminded him of firs sparkling with winter frost. Her eyes
were large and framed with lashes so blond that she would
appear lashless had they not been luxuriously thick and
long. Her brows were a bit darker, arching delicately over
the wide eyes, eyes that stared at him with surprising direct-
ness, without a trace of condemnation for his ugly words.

She held his gaze a moment longer, then dropped into
a curtsy, lowering her eyes. "My lord."

Robert realized he was gaping, that he'd not spoken a
word to her. He reached down, expecting her to place her
hand in his so he could raise her, but she didn't move. He
touched her shoulder briefly. "Prithee, rise."

She complied. Her hands, encased in fine kid gloves,
folded calmly at her waist.

"It is my pleasure to welcome you to Annancreag,
your new home. I hope you will find it comfortable and
come to love it as I do."

She inclined her head gracefully, a shadow of a polite
smile on her lips. "I thank you, my lord." Her hand swept
to the side, indicating a young man he'd not noticed. "This
is my brother, Wesley Graham, and my chaplain"—her
other hand glided toward the tall priest on her left side—
"Father Jasper." Standing there, with her hands spread,

she reminded Robert of a painting of the Virgin he'd seen once.

Robert exchanged polite greetings with the men, noticing that Wesley seemed markedly hostile. Robert had heard of Wesley—he was making a name for himself as something of a slippery reiver. Wardens on both sides of the border would like to string him up.

Robert looked for Alex, realizing courtesy demanded he introduce his little brother, and was relieved to find him gone. He was mucking this up admirably without Alex's help.

Robert nodded to Henry and a table was set up near the fire. "Come, have refreshment after your journey."

Mistress Graham, her brother, and the priest all followed him while the rest of her servants were taken to the kitchens where they would be closely guarded while they ate. Despite his desire for peace, he could afford to take no chances.

When they were all settled about the table with tankards of ale, Robert asked, "How was your journey? I trust your passage across the border was safe and unmolested?"

Wesley didn't reply, only glared at him.

It was Mistress Graham, sitting on his right, who answered. "Aye, my lord. Your men met us at the edge of your lands and escorted us. We thank you for your care."

"And I'll thank you to continue your care," Wesley said. He was a young man, mid-twenties, perhaps, with dark brown eyes, wildly curly brown hair, and a thin downy beard. He resembled his sister slightly with his thin, rather long face, but the resemblance ended there. He was of average height and, for a man, slightly built.

"Wesley, please," Mistress Graham said, but the priest raised his eyebrows and examined Robert closely, awaiting his answer.

"Don't *please* me," Wesley said. "You heard what he said—he said you looked like a horse's ass. I want to know if he plans to treat you like one!"

" 'Tis a fair enough question," Robert said.

Mistress Graham showed no sign that his words had wounded her. "Very well," she said in the same cool, polite tones she'd spoken in since he'd met her. Initially, he'd found her voice lovely, soothing, but already the controlled calm grated. He had no wish to hurt her feelings, or humiliate her, but what other effect could his words have had? And yet, she appeared genuinely unaffected. As if she didn't care one whit what he thought of her.

"Well?" Wesley prompted.

"Mistress Graham is to be my wife, and as such, she will be treated with dignity and respect. I will honor and care for her to the best of my ability. She will live in comfort and always be protected from harm."

Wesley looked insolently around the hall, snorting. He took a long drink of ale, but didn't meet Robert's eyes.

"And that is all that could be expected of you," Mistress Graham said.

Robert fought the urge to give her a cross look. It should also be expected that he not yell out his intended looked like a horse's ass. She *should* be insulted. "Mistress Graham—Caroline, I hope you'll accept my apologies for what you overheard . . . you know not all that came before and so what you heard was completely out of context."

Wesley propped his chin on his knuckle and stared at Robert with sarcastic interest. "Illuminate me on the context in which saying my sister's face looks like a horse's ass is a compliment."

"Perhaps it is a very fine horse," Caroline said.

Robert was startled into laughter. Caroline, however, appeared neither amused nor angry. She was . . . serene.

As if human emotions were beneath her. Robert's smile faded. He had concluded that her nickname was just some ridiculous misunderstanding. Perhaps she'd been teased as a child for being so long and it had stuck. Though she still wore her cloak, Robert was certain she was not fat. Her face was not unattractive, skin luminous and pale, and tinted pink from her journey. And her eyes—were arresting, the loveliest he'd ever seen. She had a wide mouth, but it was well formed, with a generous bottom lip—plump and pink. He'd then thought that maybe she was likened to a horse because of her teeth— but no. From what he'd seen when she spoke, her teeth were not overlarge. In fact, they were straight and startlingly white. Though not the most beautiful woman Robert had ever seen, she was nevertheless gentle to the eye. He was well pleased with his intended's appearance. Sharing a bed with her would be no chore.

But now Robert had to admit that perhaps there was some truth to the nickname. *Pious.* He slid another look at her and fancied she would look right at home with a golden halo painted around her head. The image conjured uneasy feelings that he could not name. He looked away abruptly.

Wesley glared at his sister, but she showed no sign of noticing.

"I find your sister's appearance most pleasing." When Wesley rolled his eyes in disbelief, Robert sighed. "It's true that I heard . . . rumors about her. But it's obvious that's all they were: rumors. Perhaps the horse analogy is due to your great length? For I can think of no other explanation."

Caroline gave him another of her detached smiles. "You are most kind."

Though nothing in her voice or manner indicated it, Robert felt she humored him—as though she assumed he lied. Irritation surged to the surface now. "I am being honest, not kind."

"Of course," she said.

"Aye—of course. I wouldn't lie. If I didn't like the look of you, I wouldn't say a thing."

But even his bluntness didn't surprise a reaction from her. She merely inclined her head.

The priest cleared his throat loudly.

Robert tore his gaze away from the pious Caroline with fathomless eyes.

"My lord," Father Jasper began. His expression had changed from the hard regard of before to a cheerful smile. It did a great deal to soften his skeletal features. "Lord Graham asked me to deliver the contract to you to be signed. It will be sent back with Master Wesley."

"Aye," Wesley said, standing. "I regret that I cannot stay to see my sister settled. I must leave on the morrow, so I hope we can settle this matter tonight. I'm expected to report that the betrothal is . . . binding."

Robert looked at Caroline, perplexed, but she was no help, blinking serenely back at him. It was understood that a betrothal was more binding than the actual marriage ceremony—which was no more than a formality. Indeed, many couples consummated their union after the betrothal. He stood now, understanding. Ridley wanted consummation. For they couldn't hold the ceremony until after the banns had been said. This was fine with Robert; the sooner Ridley was convinced of the marriage's permanence, the sooner he would release Patrick.

"I had planned to have the betrothal tomorrow, followed by a feast—but if Mistress Graham is not opposed . . . ?"

Caroline unfolded her long length from the bench. "We may proceed at your convenience, my lord."

Robert managed not to grind his teeth. Why did her polite acquiescence nettle him so? She was more than he'd hoped for and from all appearances she would be simple to get along with. He rubbed his forehead wearily. Lack of sleep must be the culprit. He hadn't been sleeping well since Father passed on. It hadn't affected him before, but his judgment was clearly faulty. Caroline Graham was exactly what Annancreag needed.

Robert turned to lead them to his chambers. To his surprise, Caroline laid a hand on his sleeve. He looked down at it. She had removed her gloves. Her hands were long and slender, delicate and white. He imagined they were also very cold.

"My lord, might I have a word with you, alone, before anything is signed?"

"Caroline," Wesley said, a warning in his tone.

Caroline gave him one of her beatific smiles. "Fear not, Wesley, I'll not try to talk him out of marrying me."

"Let us talk," Robert said, leading her to his chambers. This was encouraging. He felt an odd surge of hope. Perhaps there was something more to her after all.

Inside his chambers a fire blazed and wine was set out on the tabletop, quill and inkpot beside it. He offered her refreshment, but she refused, her hands clasped lightly at her waist. He poured a cup for himself and leaned against the stones of the fireplace.

"You wanted to speak with me alone?" he asked, watching her intently. The urge to see her remove the cloak and headdress like a butterfly shedding its chrysalis seized him.

She stepped farther into the room. Each step was measured, controlled—no rushing for this one. "It's about our impending marriage."

"Have you changed your mind?"

"No. My mind was never taken into consideration." The firelight played over her high cheekbones. Her eyes were clear, colorless. "What I fear is that this union will not mend the feud between our families."

He pushed away from the fireplace. "And if it doesn't?"

"Then we will both be trapped in a cold and loveless marriage."

"It is not required that we love each other. My only hope is that we can live together in harmony and friendship."

She paused several beats, her eyes never leaving his face. "You seem to be a reasonable man. I have a proposition for you."

"A proposition?" Intrigued, he set his wine aside and paced the room slowly, coming back to stand in front of her. "Very well. What is this proposition?"

"It has not escaped your notice, I'm sure, that I'm well past a marriageable age." She stood so still, like a statue, an ice queen.

"Are you warm? May I take your cloak?"

"No, my lord. There is a reason I've not been wed. My father promised my sister and me that we could wed as we choose—or not at all. I chose not to wed. I planned to enter a convent upon Father's death, but my brother . . ."

Robert's fingers were at her throat, deftly unhooking the cloak. He swept it off her shoulders.

No more than curious by his actions, she began to speak again. "As I was saying, my brother's intentions are noble and therefore I agreed to do my duty. However— Lord Annan? Is there a problem?"

Robert inspected her headdress. She backed away several steps. No, Mistress Graham was not fat. Nor was she thin, exactly. A partlet filled the square neck of her gown, not allowing him the tiniest glimpse of skin. Her gown

was plain, but very fine. Silk, in a soft mossy green that
set her eyes aglow. She was a big girl, with generous pro-
portions—wide hips, a narrow waist. The bodice of her
gown made it impossible to fathom if she even had a
bosom. Her narrow arms seemed very fragile. He thought
he detected a tremor in them, but her hands were clasped
placidly at her waist.

"Aye, there is a problem . . . this thing on your head—
I should like to see your hair."

She didn't answer him immediately, apparently considering his request. Then she reached up and pulled out
several pins, removing the monstrosity. She held it between her hands and began to speak again. Robert had
stopped listening. He returned to the fireplace and
watched her, rubbing his chin thoughtfully.

He'd not been wrong when he thought she would look
at home in a halo—for that was exactly what her hair
was—a golden crown that glowed warmly in the firelight.
It was plaited and wound about her head in thick braids
that glistened like spun metal. He had never pondered the
things he wanted in a wife, for they seemed obvious. A
competent woman to run the household. A godly woman
to see to the moral and religious education of their children. A strong woman who could bear children without
harm to herself. A firm and resolute woman to defend the
keep when he was away.

These were all qualities that were necessary in a lord's
wife, but apart from these he had never considered what
he desired in a wife—for himself, not for his people. Perhaps he had refrained from such imaginings because he
knew it would be impossible—that he would be opening
himself wide for disappointment and unhappiness. But
quite suddenly, as he stood before the fire, gazing at his
betrothed, he desired Caroline Graham.

"What say you, my lord?" she asked in that calm, untroubled voice.

He'd not been listening to her. He met her questioning gaze and that feeling of unease returned. Yes, her looks suited him, but her manner distressed him inexplicably. Though he'd spent little time in contemplation of it, he had still never envisioned such a cold union as he could foresee with Caroline. His own parents had shared a warm and enduring friendship, and he'd imagined he would find this as well.

But perhaps he was being hasty. He'd only just met the lass. She would surely thaw as they came to know each other. *He hoped.*

"Forgive, my lady. My mind was elsewhere. What were you saying?"

Completely unruffled by the fact he'd been ignoring her, she began again. "Rather than go through with a betrothal and marriage ceremony, why not handfast? Then, in, say, a year—or less, if our union has not brought peace between our families—we will be free to dissolve the union. I will enter a convent and you can remarry a more suitable woman."

"Handfast?" Robert repeated, brow furrowed. The only way for her plan to work was if they did not consummate the marriage. Though considered imperfect without the kirk's blessing, handfasting was nonetheless binding if the couple followed it up by lying together. "Why not just go through with the betrothal? What difference?"

She gazed steadily at him. "You know what difference, my lord."

He shook his head, turning his back on her. "No. Ridley will not release my brother unless our marriage is consummated."

"That is easily faked."

Robert turned slightly to look at her. *Not so pious as she appeared.* "You would lie?"

"The Lord accepts that equivocation is sometimes necessary." Her expression remained unclouded, but she had raised her chin a notch.

He came to stand in front of her, hands clasped behind his back. "But I want a wife—I need a wife. I fancy you. You'll bear strong children."

"A fine brood mare?"

He sighed. "I didn't mean that."

"Of course you didn't."

There it was again! She patronized him. Oh, one day she would make a venerable abbess—but damn it, he wanted her skills here, in his home. They held each other's gaze for a long moment. He wanted time to think this over, but time was currently in short supply. The fact remained that if he got her into bed, she was his, handfast or wed in a church—it mattered not. A betrothal was difficult to dissolve, whether consummation had taken place or not—but a handfasting, so long as the couple did not lie together, was a simpler matter.

He was not a cruel man. If she were miserable, he would allow her to enter a convent. But it was apparent she wanted no ties with him and to be unspoiled—and he intended to spoil her. Divorce might be the fashion in England, but to Robert, it was distasteful.

"What of my brother Patrick? What if Ridley refuses to release him when he hears of this?"

"Ridley wants consummation. This Wesley will believe occurred."

"But what about you? If we fake consummation, as you suggest, will that not prove problematic for you to explain later—should you choose the veil?"

She gave him another of her perfectly polite, yet empty smiles. "You would, of course, do the honorable thing and tell the truth. We could sign a secret statement so that later you would be free to wed again."

Since she was quite serious, he held in his incredulous laughter. He paced away from her, clearing his throat. When he was certain he could speak without showing amusement, he said, "Mistress Graham, does this . . . arrangement not seem a trifle one-sided to you?"

One golden brow arched slightly. "How so?"

How maddening! And fascinating. How could she possibly think he'd agree to such an extraordinary plot? He turned slowly, thoughtfully, so she'd think he truly considered it. No need to antagonize her. "Well, first I must change the terms of the original agreement with Lord Graham—an act that could jeopardize my brother's chances of freedom and destroy the peace I've worked so hard for." He paused, but unlike most women he knew, she did not take the opportunity to interject her arguments. She only watched him, calm, confident; as if her silence were a testament to her reason. "Next, I must willfully lie before God, claiming I am taking you as my wife, and promise to wed you proper before a priest sometime in the future. Third, I do not get to lie with you. And last, in the event I must give you up, I must also declare to the world that I lied before God and didn't bed my wife."

"Not to the world, my lord. Surely no one beyond the West March will take note."

He did smile, couldn't help himself. But she was not jesting. "Think you marriage to me will be so disagreeable?"

"I find you quite agreeable, my lord. But I am not suitable for marriage, as you will soon discover for yourself."

She was so self-possessed. He'd never met a man so

completely in control of himself, let alone a woman. She was untouchable, like a marble statue. He raised his hand to touch her, more out of curiosity than aught else, to see if her skin was hard and slick like stone. He trailed a finger down the line of her jaw, under her chin.

She blinked rapidly. Blood rushed to her cheeks. She took a step back, breaking contact. "My lord?"

She was warm and soft. And she had momentarily lost her composure.

He dropped his hand, studied her. "What do I get out of the agreement?"

"You're correct that if the peace fails I am the winner. But if it succeeds—I've lost far more than you."

"Explain."

She took a deep breath, as if bolstering herself for some unpleasant task, and tilted her chin. "If I do go through with this marriage, docile, as women are expected to be, what would I gain? I am surrounded by enemies, people who hate me because of my surname. I am your chattel, to do with as you please, to mistreat however you choose, to abuse if you wish. I will run your home, care for your people, bear your touch and your children, and stand by silently while you commit adultery. Any woman could do this as well as I. And truly, I'm not suited for it. I am difficult and prone to argue. I do not like being beaten and because of my size, you will find it a challenge. I tend to enrage those who attempt to discipline me." She smiled gently. "I think, in the end, you will feel fortunate indeed to have had the foresight to agree to my proposal."

Robert was speechless. She had described marriage as he knew it succinctly—but never had he viewed it as a woman might. Most unpleasant. But he had been judged unfairly. And he didn't like it.

He folded his arms over his chest. "No."

The corners of her mouth tightened imperceptibly. She averted her gaze. "Very well. After all, I am only a pledge."

He hadn't thought she could become colder, remoter, but she proved him wrong. She seemed to detach herself from the moment, staring blankly before her, awaiting her fate.

Damn.

He circled her, inspecting her stance, the golden hair—she smelled fresh, roses and rainwater. She didn't move, didn't acknowledge him. So, this was what it would be like. She could be cold *and* resentful. He didn't want her to feel powerless, to see herself as his chattel. He wanted a partner and companion. He was feeling slightly magnanimous and decided perhaps they could reach an agreement satisfactory to both.

When he was in front of her again, he leaned forward, placed a finger on her chin, forcing her to look at him. She didn't pull away this time, held herself stiff.

"Aye, Caroline, you'll have your handfasting." Her eyes widened slightly and he smiled. "My gift to you. But with this gift comes the understanding that when we pledge ourselves, you are the one speaking false. I do not make promises idly. If I vow before the Almighty to take you to wife, I mean to do it."

Her eyes narrowed. "If you choose to rape me, there is, of course, nothing—"

"I've never raped a lass and I don't intend to start now."

"I'm afraid I don't understand, then."

He let his finger trail across the silken skin of her jaw before stepping away. " 'Tis simple, really. If you wish to be a nun, then all you must do is resist me."

3

Caroline didn't know how to respond to Lord Annan's remark. Why ever would he say such a thing? He'd given her what she wanted, therefore she was loath to argue it further, and yet his assumption that this was a game unsettled her. She was still at a loss for words when he threw open the door and called for his incompetent steward, Henry, to fetch Wesley and Father Jasper.

He'd agreed and that was all that mattered. The rest could be managed. She'd anticipated various reactions from him, but in the end, she'd not expected him to grant her the handfasting—however, Caroline had never been one to let the odds stop her from trying. Battles had been won against incredible odds—and logic, calm, and reason were formidable weapons. The chattel speech had turned the argument in her favor. That one usually infuriated Ridley.

Lord Annan turned back to her. His mouth tilted slightly at the corners, the lines beside his eyes deepened. It was obvious he found the situation, and her request, laughable. It was also abundantly clear he was doing nothing more than humoring her. She supposed she should be thankful for that—an indulgent husband was preferable to a tyrant. And yet his confidence that she would be unable to resist him annoyed her. Such arrogance.

"Should we not compose the statement?" she said.

"Do you write?"

"Yes."

"Good. You come up with something and I'll sign it. But later." He smiled, smug. "No need for anyone to know but us . . . unless it becomes necessary, of course."

This was absurd. She wanted to explain that he should not view this as a conquest, but men were ever thick when it came to pride in their sexual prowess. To have such an unattractive woman show a lack of interest in lying with him must have been a blow. How remiss of her not to consider that. Her father and brothers had always been confident that every wench in the keep would welcome their advances and reacted with affronted anger when rebuffed. She did not wish to anger Lord Annan. This was all so very tiresome—how had she managed to bungle it? She'd meant him to focus on the convent aspect, to be repulsed by her wanting to be a nun. In the future she would be clear about her chosen vocation.

Lord Annan paced the perimeter of the room, arms folded across the considerable breadth of his chest. She had *never* imagined he would be larger than she was, so his size had been a shock. She quickly noticed he was a man of motion—full of energy. He did not stand still for long periods and seemed to think on his feet. He was silent, so she allowed her thoughts to wander—a technique she used for maintaining composure.

Much of Caroline's life had been spent ignoring derogatory remarks in reference to her appearance; she paid little heed to them now and they caused her no distress. She'd long since discovered there were facets to life other than the admiring approval of men. She had value and knew it, even if a great many people remained unaware. Even her father had teased that she would one day make some lucky man a fine dray horse. This troubled her not, for she spent many happy hours with her father, reading to him and playing chess. He had valued her presence in his life—had accepted her, faults and all—and this gave Caroline the strength and courage to accept the body God had given her. She'd long ago concluded that she was more suited to a life of contemplation than of matrimony. A life in which she would be appreciated for what she was, rather than denigrated for what she wasn't.

But she possessed little vanity and realized it was unrealistic to expect a man to be as forgiving of her faults as her father had been. Especially a man expected to share a bed with her. She knew beauty. Her mother had been lovely, Mona was stunningly beautiful, and even Fayth was pretty in a devilish way. Caroline did not blame men for seeing her for what she was—it was not their fault for desiring women like Mona, women who inspired poets to write verse, however poor, praising their beauty.

"Why do you wish to enter a convent? Have you . . . experienced God's calling?"

Caroline turned to face Lord Annan, who had moved behind her. He leaned against the fireplace again, his broad shoulders hunched slightly. It was ironic that a man so well built for war would be so intent on peace. In fact, his appearance was totally at odds with his behavior. He looked every inch the warrior—from his great height and muscular frame, to the close-cropped chestnut hair—silvered at his temples—and steely gray eyes. His clothes were well made, but simple, not cut in the current fashion. He wore no ruff at his neck. A buff leather doublet encased a powerful torso. The round collar of his white shirt circled a neck thick with muscle and darkly tanned. He looked ready to don his armor and ride into battle at a moment's notice.

"God calls on us all to serve him in our own way."

He straightened and walked around her again. She turned to follow his progress. His prowling was most disconcerting.

"Aye, but those who choose to enter a convent or monastery have been called upon especially to do God's bidding—to live without the comforts of the flesh." His Scots burr lent his deep voice a musical quality that caressed her ears.

"You must be aware that there are many other reasons for entering a convent."

He stopped in front of her. She resisted the urge to retreat. Would he touch her again? Her heart skipped a beat. She'd never expected him to touch her in such an intimate manner; the slow gentle pressure of his finger trailing across her skin had jolted her. She could still feel it, as if he'd burned her. She felt foolish for becoming as flustered as a hen—he was a comely man, certainly accustomed to touching women all the time. He must think his cow of a bride silly to react so strongly to the mere touch of his finger. And it only reinforced his belief that she would be helpless to resist him.

It would not happen again. Having experienced it, she could now prepare herself for any future unexpected touches from her husband, and respond appropriately. Indeed, she already anticipated that he might expect a kiss during the wedding ceremony and had planned accordingly. It was vain to think he would want to kiss her.

Surely if he had refused her offer of handfasting and insisted on consummating the union, he would not feel it necessary to kiss when rutting on her. Kissing was an act of passion—she had witnessed it many times—rutting an act of lust—or duty. Her husband would feel neither lust nor passion for her, and so would not bother with kissing. Nevertheless, it was only practical to prepare herself for any eventuality.

"Aye, many women who enter a convent don't like men." His gaze probed her. *Was she one of those women?* What did he care? What an odd conversation! Not at all what she'd expected.

"Yes, and some women, though they find men perfectly agreeable, are simply not suitable for marriage."

"You fall into that latter group, eh?" He was prowling again, arms folded across his chest.

She turned—not wanting her back to him. "Yes." Where were Wesley and Father Jasper? What was taking so long? She forced herself not to look at the open door. This was her opportunity to prove her determination to enter a convent and yet all she could think to say was, "I have much to offer the Lord."

He stopped in front of her again. He reminded her of an animal, stalking its prey, unable to get at it, but intent on it all the same. "In what manner are you unsuitable for marriage?"

She tilted her head back to meet his gaze. Unaccustomed to looking up to anyone but Father Jasper, she was again filled with a nearly overwhelming urge to retreat from him. "I—"

"Well?" Wesley entered the room, followed by Father Jasper.

Caroline seized the excuse to move away from Lord Annan. She went to the table to pour wine for her brother and Father Jasper. She felt Lord Annan's eyes still on her, as if he expected her to finish speaking.

"Mistress Graham and I have decided to alter our original agreement."

Wesley looked from Caroline to Lord Annan. "Your agreement was with Lord Graham, not with my sister. She hasn't the authority to negotiate anything."

Caroline had anticipated this and formulated an argument, but before she could give it, Lord Annan said, "The union will still take place, as agreed. But since Mistress Graham, as well as myself, are both involved, I think it meet that some provisions be open to discussion."

Wesley frowned deeply. "Very well . . . what provision has been altered?"

Lord Annan crossed the stone floor, coming to stand beside Caroline. He removed her hand from the flagon of wine she was preparing to lift and held it between both of his. For the second time since she'd met him he acted in a manner she could not possibly have prepared for. But she managed to school her expression for blandness, averting her eyes slightly to stare at a tapestry. She reminded herself that touching her would soon be his right—a right he apparently intended to exercise, but hopefully not force. His hands were very large and warm, engulfing hers. Her belly fluttered. She felt his gaze on her, but did not look at him.

To Wesley he said, "Since you must return to England on the morn, we've decided to handfast—this way we do not have to wait for the banns to be said."

"Handfast?" Wesley repeated incredulously. He looked at Father Jasper. "Does he speak the truth? Is it binding in the eyes of the church?"

Father Jasper studied Caroline with mild disapproval.

She'd not shared her scheme even with him (though she wished now she had), so he was trying to fathom what she had in mind. After a pause he nodded. "Aye, so long as it's followed with the church's blessing, it is all the same."

Wesley was silent for a long moment. "Ridley will be angry."

Lord Annan's hands tightened on Caroline's. She fought the urge to look up at him. She was too aware of his presence—she could smell him. He had bathed recently. He smelled clean and male—nothing like the men she'd grown up around, who either stank of sweat and stale beer, or tried to mask it with cloying floral scents.

"But," Lord Annan said. "If all the conditions are met—will he release my brother?"

Wesley's pause was telling and fear coiled in Caroline's belly. *She'd been so close.* Wesley scrutinized her, his mouth a thin white line. "I'm missing something here, aren't I?"

"No," Caroline said. Her argument was weak—they all knew it. Couples frequently lay together before and during the time banns were said. Caroline stared hard at her brother. He hated this marriage—he was being thick right now, but if he only thought about it, he would understand what she was doing. If she remained a virgin, there would be no marriage at all—which was exactly what Wesley wanted.

Wesley eyed her dubiously, but before he could speak, Father Jasper placed a hand on Wesley's shoulder, turning him away, speaking softly, earnestly.

Caroline let out the breath she'd been holding. Father Jasper understood. He would explain it to Wesley.

Lord Annan squeezed her hands and she looked up.

He watched her narrowly. "I hope I'm not the one missing something."

A threat? Her mouth went dry. He'd been so reasonable that she had forgotten for a moment they were enemies.

Wesley and Father Jasper turned back to them. Wesley nodded slowly. "Very well. A handfasting is satisfactory. I'll inform Lord Graham." He pointed a surly finger at Lord Annan. "Everything else remains as agreed."

Lord Annan's grip relaxed and one of his hands dropped away. "Of course."

Caroline wanted to pull her hand from his but couldn't think how to do it courteously. She'd never expected him to *want* to touch her! But that was not what this was about—it was a show, for her brother. He wanted Wesley convinced she would be cared for properly.

"Then I'm certain Ridley will release Sir Patrick." Wesley's gaze darted to their joined hands. "Shall we get on with it?"

"Father Jasper?" Caroline said, pleased her voice remained calm and steady. "Will two witnesses be sufficient?"

The priest nodded. He shot her a look full of questioning reproach and a touch of hurt. She wished she'd confided in him.

Lord Annan's attention returned to Caroline. Her eyes were level with his mouth. It was a strong mouth, the lips neither too full nor too thin, and set now in a hard, grim line. She met his gaze and noted the line of worry creasing the dark skin between his brows.

"I, Robert Maxwell, take thee, Caroline Graham, to be my spoused wife, before the eyes of God, and thereto I plight thee my troth."

Caroline could not look away from him without revealing her own anxiety and reluctance, so she repeated the words back to him, never dropping her gaze from his, concentrating on breathing evenly. When it was over, the men leaned over the desk, their backs to her, poring over the documents Father Jasper had brought. Wesley remained rude and unpleasant, but Lord Annan ignored his tone, focusing instead on his intent, and all progressed well.

Caroline moved to the fireplace, trying to be unobtrusive. Sweat trickled between her breasts, but a quick swipe of her forehead told her that her fear had not been visible. *Good.*

She couldn't believe it was done. It seemed absurd that something so momentous and life altering could be over in mere seconds. She gazed about at her new home. Annancreag was a crude structure—built primarily for defense, not comfort. But the tapestries that hung on the walls were lovely and kept the cold at bay. The lanterns hanging in both the hall and this chamber were some of the finest craftsmanship she'd ever seen. The furniture was sturdy and well made, but relatively unadorned. Her fingers trailed along the back of the polished oak chair before the fire. It was uncommonly large with a tall back and legs. Made especially for Lord Annan's great length. *Her husband.*

Her cheeks burned. Caroline turned back to the fire, confused by the rush of strange emotion she felt. If anyone noticed her flushed face, they would attribute it to her proximity to the fire.

All that was left was to wait. It could take months until the new-found peace collapsed, but Caroline doubted it would take that long. Barely a month went by that a Graham didn't have a falling-out with a Maxwell. And when things got ugly, Lord Annan would hopefully honor their agreement and release her.

Until that day, she must live as the lady of the keep. She was groomed for it. She had spent a year with her aunt, learning to run a household in preparation for marriage. Before retreating from the world, her mother had taught her many skills. And Caroline had spent several years before Father wed Mona running Graham Keep. She was well equipped to handle her duties and found she looked forward to them. It would keep her busy in the days ahead.

It wouldn't be so bad. Lord Annan might think this was some sort of game, but he would soon tire of the chase as men were wont to do when it got them nowhere and the prize wasn't worth the effort. And then she would be left to herself.

When the men concluded their business, Caroline was introduced to the housekeeper, Celia, who showed her to her chambers. It wasn't nearly as far of a journey as Caroline had hoped. Celia opened a door in Lord Annan's chambers, led her through a bedchamber, and into another chamber. Obviously a woman's room, it contained a loom and furniture adorned with embroidered pillows.

"Very nice, " Caroline said, turning in a circle. Other than the one they came through there was only one other door. When Caroline opened it, she discovered it led to a corridor off the main hall. Caroline closed the door, unease churning in her belly. Would she not be provided with her own bedchamber? Her mother and father had not slept together, and Mona had only shared Father's room to nurse him.

"Is there a problem?" Celia asked, her voice dripping with sarcasm. "Because if there is, 'tis doubtful it can be remedied."

Caroline turned to the woman, puzzled by her tone.

She'd never been addressed so by a servant. "I find these chambers more than adequate, thank you."

Eyes so blue they brought forth visions of a sparkling body of water stared back at Caroline. Celia's hair was black as coal. She was a small woman, with round hips and bosom, and a tiny waist. The type of woman that inspired lust in men—not poetry. And she defied Caroline's ability to pinpoint her age—thirty perhaps? She'd obviously been taking care of this household for some time and resented the intrusion. Caroline would have liked to assure her that the situation was only temporary, but that would not be proper. She also wanted to verify that she would be sharing the bedchamber with Lord Annan but since that was clearly the state of affairs, she held her tongue. He would find her more adequate quarters soon.

"Send for Father Jasper and my maid."

Celia sniffed. "I am your maid."

Caroline crossed the room to stand in front of the raven-haired elf. Celia took a step back, her eyes widening as Caroline towered above her. "I am grateful to Lord Annan for seeing to my needs, but I brought a maid. You will doubtless make yourself useful to me in other ways."

Celia's cheeks glowed and her eyes narrowed. Caroline watched the transformation with curious amazement. Graham Keep had its share of unruly servants, but they either found a way to tame their tempers, or found themselves unemployed with no references. Things were obviously quite different at Annancreag. Perhaps Lord Annan didn't flog his servants as Ridley and her father had.

Celia's lips trembled and twitched as though she held back a flood of bile. She lowered her insolent stare, fixing it instead on Caroline's chest, and said, "I will inform Lord Annan you are displeased with his arrangements."

Before Caroline could contradict her, the woman was gone. Caroline sighed. She'd feared the Maxwells would not accept her and this only confirmed it. How to deal with it? She couldn't go about dismissing Lord Annan's servants. She would have to speak with Henry, the steward, about the level of civility Lord Annan expected from the help.

"Caroline?"

Caroline turned gratefully at the sound of Father Jasper's voice. "Father, I'm so pleased you're here and I'm not completely friendless."

He swept across the room and took her hands, looking down at her with a sad smile. "You've heard then?"

"Heard what?"

Father Jasper's eyebrows rose, his expression pained. "Oh, why must I be the one to tell you!"

"Tell me what?"

The priest's lips thinned. "My child . . . your maid is leaving with Wesley—part of the agreement was that you brought no other Grahams into the household . . . and she is your cousin, however distant. You are only allowed a priest."

Caroline could think of nothing to say. She was stripped of family, of friends, set down in enemy territory, with a husband large enough to crush her. And the only thing protecting her was her husband's honor—a Maxwell's honor. Caroline glanced at the door, making certain it was closed. She gripped Father Jasper's hand and whispered, "What am I to do, Father? I confess that I'm terrified of Lord Annan . . . he has agreed not to consummate the marriage without my consent . . . but how can I trust a man who won't even allow me my maid?"

"Caroline," Father Jasper said, starting to place a hand on her shoulder, then withdrawing. "You must understand your husband's position. The Grahams and the Maxwells have been feuding since time immemorial. You cannot expect him to simply drop his guard and welcome the enemy in with open arms. Give him time."

Did her ears deceive her? Was Father Jasper defending Lord Annan?

"Am I a prisoner?"

Father Jasper laughed, but it was strained. "Of course not, my lady . . . but you can't go about unaccompanied—just as Lord Graham didn't allow you and Fayth to roam unattended."

Caroline crossed her arms and went to the loom. When Father Jasper spoke of Lord Graham, he meant Ridley, not their father. And Ridley had kept Fayth a virtual prisoner since Father's death. It hadn't been a necessary precaution with Caroline, but just the same, she'd not been allowed to walk or ride without an armed escort. For their protection, Ridley'd said.

She kept her back to the priest, for tears were coming very close to the surface. *Breathe deeply.* Her breath shuddered through her chest. The swish of robes alerted her to Father Jasper's approach and she quickly composed herself. She blinked rapidly and to her dismay a single tear slipped over her lashes. She quickly swiped it away, hoping her eyes were not red and over-bright. Foolish and weak—that's what she was being. *Bear up! It cannot be so bad.* This had been a woman's lot since the beginning of time and they bore it with dignity—as she would.

"I know you didn't want this marriage, but I must tell

you, now that I've met Lord Annan . . . I think it a good match."

Caroline turned to him, composed now, and smiled. "Why? Because he is a giant?"

Father Jasper clasped his hands in front of himself, trying to look saintly. "That will only make the more . . . intimate aspects of your relationship . . . er . . . more. . . . It will . . . uh . . . make you more . . . compatible . . . in the, er, biblical . . ."

"I think I understand, Father."

Father Jasper looked at her sternly. "Really, Caroline, you should blush when a man speaks of such matters in your presence."

"You're a priest, not a man."

Father Jasper didn't refute her words, but his mouth flattened with displeasure. "I will bless the marriage bed."

Caroline didn't bother reminding him the blessing was unnecessary and followed him into the bedchamber. At the bed, Father Jasper prayed softly in Latin. Caroline wandered about the room, inspecting the tapestries and furniture. The sturdy and functional construction of all the furniture was pleasing to Caroline, though it didn't enhance the room's appearance. But, she noted, other things had been done to soften the stern decor. Flowers in glass vases and woven baskets had been situated on cabinet tops and chest lids. Whoever had prepared the room for her had tried to consider her comfort and for that, she was grateful.

Father Jasper's voice died away as Caroline fingered the pale blue petals of the forget-me-nots. "Father? You have lived long—do you recall why the Grahams and Maxwells began this feud?"

Father Jasper turned, but didn't seem to be looking at Caroline. His green eyes were distant, sad. "I am old, aren't I? Some days it doesn't seem possible that I've lived so long, seen so much . . . but then I'll catch a glimpse of myself in the water and . . . well . . ." His eyes focused on her and he smiled. "It's always a surprise to see that old man's face."

"To me, it's a very dear face."

Father Jasper smiled. "The feud? Well . . . I'm not *that* old. It's been going on since before I was born, and I am nearly three score years. But it seems to have been . . . revitalized—infused with new hate, sometime shortly before my birth. Apparently, there was an attempt, such as this, to make an alliance and end the killing . . . but it was nothing more than a ruse. I cannot recall which clan was at fault—the Grahams, methinks—though I'm sure we claimed otherwise. But on the wedding night, the bride let in a raiding party and it was a massacre."

A chill traveled over Caroline's scalp. "How horrid . . . I wonder . . .?"

"If that is why you are allowed no servants?"

Caroline nodded.

" 'Tis likely some remember and wish to take precautions." He came to her, placing both hands on her shoulders. "Give him time. Gain his trust. He will allow you your maid, eventually." He stared at her for a long moment, then touched her cheek gently. "This is good."

She stared after him as he swept out of the room, wishing for a measure of his confidence.

In a dungeon, far below the warmth and light of Graham Keep, Sir Patrick Maxwell languished. It was an unusual state of affairs. Most noble political prisoners were kept in fine chambers above ground, well fed, and allowed some liberty. And so it had been for Patrick until the Graham laird had died. When the mantle fell to his son, Ridley, Patrick had been moved to the dungeons and denied even light. He was still fed edible fare and he managed to exercise himself by roaming the confines of his cell, but he'd had little contact with other humans.

Someone brought him food and left a torch to eat by outside the bars of his cell—but when it extinguished, there was no more light until the next day.

A bar was mounted high on the wall for chaining prisoners and currently, Patrick used it to pull himself up repeatedly. It passed the time and kept his arms and shoulders strong. The door above opened and shut. Patrick dropped to the ground. He felt around for his shirt and doublet, both stiff with filth, but dry.

Hands on the damp, moldy wall, he felt his way to the large wooden door. Flickering orange light lit up the small barred window. He gripped the bars, pressing his face against them.

"I demand to speak with Ridley!" he bellowed, as he did every day. Usually the female servant ignored him, and sometimes a certain young man would taunt him— had once even withheld his food, but not his water.

Today it was none of the usuals—it was the dark woman again. She'd come once before. A cloak covered her hair, cast her face in shadows. She pushed his plate through the slot in the door and fitted the torch in the sconce.

Patrick took the food and set it aside. Why had she come again? Last time she'd asked him questions about Robert. Though she'd done nothing to indicate she was sympathetic to his plight, nevertheless he felt she was a friend.

"Tell me," he said, sickened by the note of pleading that entered his voice. "Any word from my brother?" The chill air dried the sweat from his bare skin and he shivered.

The woman glided closer, but her face remained shadowed. "You're cold." Again he noted her voice lacked the refinement of nobility—a rough English border accent, pinpointing her heritage to somewhere in the vicinity of northern Cumberland.

"I'm fine—prithee—tell me of Lord Annan and why Lord Graham has not released me?"

"You'll soon be released. Lord Graham's ransom was too high for your brother to raise, but they've reached another agreement."

Patrick sagged against the door, eyes closed. *Thank God.* This nightmare would soon be over. When he opened his eyes again, he found the woman had moved closer. He could see the shine of her eyes—they were dark in color, the straight line of her nose, the curve of her lips, the jut of a stubborn chin. A curl of ebony hair peeked out of the hood.

"You have no shirt?" Her voice was kind, concerned.

"Aye—but a clean, warm one would be nice." At this point he was not above begging charity. The nights were cold, and when he slept, rats bit him.

She stared into his face for a long moment. Then she pulled the tie at her neck and swung the cloak off her shoulders. His breath hissed through his teeth. The dowager Lady Graham—the deceased laird's widow and a notorious witch. Rumor had it she'd bewitched Old Man Graham and had now cast her spell on the son.

Patrick had seen her before, from afar, and now that he was getting an eyeful up close, by torchlight, he couldn't say he blamed either father or son for his lapse. She was a vision. Blue-black curls, a fine figure, skin like cream. Currently, she stuffed the cloak through the food slot. Patrick helped her, tugging until it was through. She backed away from him, toward the stairs.

"Wait," he said, desperate for company. "Don't leave."

She hesitated at the foot of the stairs, her expression

hidden from him in the shadows. But he fancied she wanted to come back, to stay with him. Then she turned, resuming her ascent.

"When will you be back?"

She called over her shoulder, in a loud whisper, "Soon. I'll bring candles and warm hose . . . perhaps another blanket. And something to pass the time."

And then she was gone.

4

Fayth paced the width of her chamber. Twelve paces, from wall to wall. Turning on her heel, she crossed the room again. Where was Mona? She went to the window. The bailey was filled with the usual activity. The dinner hour drew near and most of the people would soon come indoors. Fayth chewed her ragged fingernails, waiting. She couldn't bear any more of the interminable waiting, the isolation, Ridley's self-righteous speeches about how a lady should comport herself. If she had to endure another day of it she would start screaming and never stop.

She turned cautiously at the click of the lock disengaging. Relief poured through her when Mona slipped inside and shoved a sack into her arms. "It's all here—take it and go—quickly, before Ridley comes and it's too late."

"Come with me," Fayth said, clutching her stepmother's arm.

Mona shook her head. "I must wait until Wesley returns—but you can escape—go!"

Fayth hesitated, hating to leave her stepmother behind to Ridley's machinations. Ridley could not force Mona to wed, could he? He couldn't exert the same control over her that he did over Caroline and Fayth. But, of course, that wasn't what Ridley wanted from Mona.

"I can't leave you," Fayth said, dropping the sack in a chair.

Mona's pretty features hardened. "I can handle Ridley. I'm here now, aren't I? He is easy enough to gull. But you must leave. He will see you wed to that old carcass, Carlisle. He means to do it; his mind cannot be changed—I've tried."

Fayth crossed her arms at her waist, gripping her elbows. "Maybe it won't be so bad? He's old . . . mayhap he'll die soon, then I'll be a rich widow—"

"Like me?"

Fayth stared at her stepmother. At eight-and-twenty Mona was not much older than Caroline—and rich widow though she was, she was a prisoner. Ridley would never let Mona go. Fayth would not be surprised to learn that Ridley had already raped their stepmother repeatedly since Papa's death six months ago. But she didn't ask—didn't want to know.

"But . . . surely Carlisle's son won't want me that way . . . won't be like Ridley . . ."

Mona shook her head briskly, opening the sack. "We don't know that. Besides, Carlisle is a hardy man with much life left in him. He still leads raids and hot trods as if he were no more than a lad—right in the thick of it. He's also a cruel man, with evil desires. Your wifely duties will be unbearable—and will quite possibly kill you, if you don't kill yourself first. Should you be forced to go through with this union I will prepare poisons for you that will kill him slowly, make it look as though he succumbed to an ailment. But I don't want to do that. Better this way."

Fayth's blood curdled at Mona's words, further protests dying in her throat. She had no idea how Mona knew these things, but the fact remained that Mona *did* know things and was always right. Fayth pulled off her kirtle, revealing boots and breeches beneath. Mona removed a male doublet and bonnet from the sack and Fayth quickly donned them, stuffing her hair up underneath.

Mona dragged her to the fireplace and smeared ashes all over her face, dusted her clothes, then stood back, inspecting the result critically. "You'll fool no one who takes the time to look closely, but at a distance you look to be a fair lad—just watch out for the demented ones— those that like the fair lads."

Fayth shrugged. "I've done this before and no one has discovered me. Not even Jack." Pain and loss for what might have been stabbed her heart, but she pushed it away. "Truly, men aren't as suspecting as you'd think. They see the breeches and that's as far as they look."

Mona still looked skeptical, but said no more. She pulled rope out of the sack. "Be certain you secure this well—I don't want to scrape you off the flagstones later. Are you sure this will work? Have you ever lowered yourself from a window before?"

"Aye, my lady," Fayth lied, affecting a broad local accent that drew a smile from her stepmother. She hadn't time to work out the logistics of it—she had to escape. Ridley planned to send her away any day now.

"Oh Fayth, I wish it didn't have to be this way." Tears glistened in Mona's eyes as she embraced Fayth tightly.

"Why must you go to Caroline? It's about the stone, isn't it? The one Papa married you for."

Mona pulled away, shaking her head. "I cannot tell you, but you should go to Caroline, too. Meet me there. Caroline will keep you safe."

Fayth's lip curled. "And join Caroline's hell? Living under the same roof with Maxwells? Never! They'd stab me in the back the first chance they got. Besides, I have other plans." And those plans involved rescuing her sister from the devil's lair she now inhabited. But Fayth couldn't tell Mona that. Mona had convinced herself that marriage to Lord Annan was the best thing for Caroline. That was Mona's way; if she couldn't fix things, she convinced herself that it must then be for the best. Not Fayth—she would fight to the death to avoid Caroline's fate.

Mona shook her head sadly. "Very well. May the Lord keep you."

When the door shut behind Mona, Fayth returned to the window and waited. It wasn't long before the bell clanged and the bailey cleared.

Fayth tied the rope around the base of a sturdy iron candleholder—it was chest high and would span the narrow window horizontally, allowing her to lower herself to the ground. Providing the candleholder supported her weight. She preferred to take her chances with the candleholder rather than with Carlisle—the odds were better. She climbed atop the cabinet below the window, then onto the window ledge. Hands clasping stone, she peered down.

It was a long way to the ground. Three floors. Her stomach seemed to drop the distance to the flagstones. She tilted her head up, eyes closed, letting the wind blow over her skin, clearing away some of the weakness that had seeped into her limbs.

She tied the rope firmly about her waist and slung the coil over her shoulder. Taking a deep breath, she situated the candleholder midway across the window, counting on the notch of mortar between the stones to hold it in place. She leaned back, her feet still planted on the sill, her upper body and torso outside. Cold wind pulled at her, trying to whip her cap off.

The candleholder held. Slowly, Fayth played out the rope, moving her feet off the sill. If all went as planned, she would just walk down the side of the wall. The stone the keep was built from was smooth, but Fayth could use the space between the stones for toe holds. She cast her foot about until she felt the tiny ledge. Gripping the rope tightly, she took another step. It was working! It seemed her luck was changing. . . .

The shriek of metal against stone tore her gaze away from the wall in front of her. She couldn't see the window anymore, just the ledge. The rope went slack and she plummeted. A scream ripped from her throat only to be silenced when she halted abruptly. She slammed into the wall sideways, the rope cutting into her waist.

She dangled there, immobilized by the pain squeezing her in half. Wind bit at her and she shivered, sending shards of agony down her legs. With a detached sense of horror, she heard herself whimpering. Her shoulder ached. She couldn't move her arm. The rope twisted about her shoulder, crushing it. Rope burns seared her palms. She realized what had happened—the mortar hadn't held the candleholder and it had slid down to the sill. Her weight dropping suddenly had cause the rope to cinch up, tangling tightly about her shoulder and upper arm.

Someone yelled below her. She clawed at the wall with one hand but couldn't right herself. The air wheezed in and out of her chest, rasping her throat raw.

"Fayth! God damn you!"

The shout came from above. She turned her face, peering upward. Her eyes watered, blurring her vision, but she could make out Ridley's bearded face.

"Pull her up!"

She was yanked upward and cried out as pain racked her.

"Gently!" Ridley bellowed. "Her arm is twisted unnaturally."

She began moving upward again, slowly this time. It still hurt, but she managed to keep quiet. Her face burned with a mixture of shame and frustration. She had failed. Ridley would imprison her in a room with no windows—never to see daylight until her wedding day. Sobs welled up in her chest but she fought them, refusing to cry. He wanted to break her—but he never would. She would run away from her husband if it came to that; she'd never stop running until she was free of them.

Hands grabbed her under the arms, pulled her through the window. The rope was removed and, though the pressure eased, the pain remained.

Someone held her. She opened her eyes and saw Ridley above her. He had Caroline's eyes, large and long lashed—but a pale blue rather than Caroline's misty green. In all else, he resembled Fayth more than Wesley or Caroline, who had both inherited their mother's rather long face. Ridley and Fayth had their father's round cheeks and sharp chin. These features were pleasing enough on a woman, but on Ridley, they looked elfin. He sported a pointed beard that he fancied camouflaged his little chin—Fayth thought it looked like a matted animal pelt. His chin was the only thing elfin about Ridley. Though not as long as Caroline, he was nonetheless a tall man, and well muscled, though lately he was going to fat.

Ridley clasped her to his chest, shaking his head in exasperation. "Why, Fayth? Why do you do these things?"

"Let me go." She pushed at him weakly.

He carried her to the bed and laid her down upon it.

"You stupid little fool—you would rather die than obey me?"

She turned her face to the wall, still fighting the urge to moan and cry. He grabbed her cheeks, forcing her to look at him. Fury at her inability to fight back choked her.

"Answer me! Would you truly rather die?"

"Aye! I'd sooner die than wed Carlisle!"

"You've done no more than buy time, lassie—I'll not send him damaged goods—but the goods he'll get, I assure you. When that arm is healed, you'll be wed."

She tried to spit in his face, but the pain was too excruciating and the saliva dribbled down her chin. He released her face, wiping his palm on the bed. Fayth couldn't turn her head, was too weak. Mona appeared beside him. She pushed at Ridley's arm and he stood, backing away. Mona knelt beside the bed and wiped Fayth's mouth.

"Drink this," she whispered, pressing a cup against Fayth's mouth. "It will help you rest."

Fayth's world was a blanket of black velvet—no thoughts, no dreams, no pain. She drifted about for a while, wishing to stay forever. If she woke something bad would happen, she couldn't remember what, didn't want to remember. But voices intruded—a man, angry, and a woman, placating. Both distressingly familiar.

Her shoulder ached. Her throat hurt.

"You helped her!" Ridley insisted. "You brought her the rope, the clothes."

"I did not! I have not the key and you know it."

"You needn't a key, you goddamned witch! You could have killed her—is that what you wanted? She is thoughtless and stupid—you know this as well as I! You don't give a length of rope to a half-wit. Had she a lick of intelligence that rope would have been her freedom. Not

Fayth. She managed to nearly rip her own arm off. I thank God she was discovered. What if she had fallen? Do you also believe death is preferable to a good marriage?"

Rustling fabric, light footsteps. "Don't you see how much she hates this marriage? Why do you force her? Don't you love her? Don't you love anyone?"

"You know I do." There was a long silence, then sounds of struggle. "Was it Father who made you hate the touch of a man? Give me a chance, Mona, you'll not regret it, I swear."

"Stop it!" Mona hissed.

Panicking, Fayth forced her eyes open. Ridley's arms imprisoned Mona, his face in her neck. Mona tried to ram her knee into his crotch, but he blocked her, laughing.

"Stop it, Ridley!" Fayth cried. "You disgrace our father! Our family!"

Ridley released Mona and backed away, flags of red staining his cheekbones. "You're one to talk about disgrace!"

Fayth tried to sit up, but her shoulder throbbed when she even lifted her head. Mona was at her side, lifting her, pushing pillows behind her so she was sitting.

"How bad is it?" Fayth asked.

Mona pressed a cup of wine to her lips. It was laced with something. "Mostly cuts and bruises, but your shoulder—displaced. I popped it back in place. It will be useless for some time."

Fayth stared at the embroidered coverlet, her vision blurring. How could she escape now? She was cornered, trapped into this marriage.

"Mona, leave us."

Fayth looked up. Ridley's pale eyes were on her, inscrutable. Turning back to Fayth, Mona mouthed, "I'll be back." Then she slipped out of the room.

Ridley folded his arms across his chest. He stroked the scraggly beard he was so fond of. "So you'd rather die than wed Carlisle."

Fayth swallowed convulsively as foreboding gripped her. He had something else in store for her—something she wasn't likely to enjoy any more than marriage to a cruel old man.

"Answer me!"

"It depends on how you plan to kill me! Perhaps being raped and beaten will be preferable!"

Ridley rolled his eyes, throwing up his hands. "How many times must I tell you, when a husband lies with his wife it is not rape!" He snorted. "You cannot imagine what it is like, little sister—you think to hate it, but once you get your first taste, it'll never be—"

"Shut up!" Fayth screamed. The effort was agony, but she didn't care. "How can you speak to me so? Oh, you are so vile! I loathe you!"

He grinned knowingly at her.

She sniffed, the heat receding from her cheeks. "If you think me untouched," she said calmly, "then you're a bigger fool than you look. You think Jack never courted my favors? You're blind. And only men lust mindlessly, like animals. Women keep their wits about them."

Ridley's eyes narrowed dangerously. "If you're no longer a virgin, you'd better tell me now."

This was not something Fayth had considered. It was true Fayth had allowed Jack to do little more than kiss her—but perhaps spoiling the goods was all it would take to free her. "And if I'm not?"

The silence drew out until Fayth became uncomfortable. Ridley never averted his eyes, staring at her, ruminating on her words.

"You bluff," he said finally. "But you can never be too sure, so I'll check myself."

His hands were at the waist of her breeches, unlacing them. Fayth screamed, slapping him with her uninjured arm, kicking her bruised legs into the air. "Help! Mona!"

He grabbed her hurt shoulder, squeezing until she almost fainted from the pain. "Are you a virgin, you little bitch?"

"Yes! Yes!"

The pressure of his hand increased. "Do you swear?"

"I swear!"

He released her. She sagged back onto the pillows, her head lolling to the side. Shards of agony radiated outward from her shoulder. "I hate you," she muttered, unable to turn her head or open her eyes. The pain slowly dulled, leaving her exhausted.

"Yes, I know."

A tear slipped unbidden from her eye, tracked down her face.

"Ah . . . she can shed tears." Ridley's voice was beside her. "You are a good girl, inside. I know it."

Fayth felt her face crumpling, her bottom lip trembling. Another tear escaped. Oh, how she hated him for seeing this! The wine Mona had given her—whatever was in it made her weak, unable to maintain control.

Ridley stroked her hair, as if she were a dog. "I'm sorry you lost your man—but he's gone now and we must look to the future. I know you won't believe me, but I truly want you to be happy."

Fayth squeezed her eyes tightly as the tears flowed, silent sobs shuddering through her.

"However, being an overlord makes me responsible to many more people than you. Though I have no heirs now,

I will, one day soon. I mean to pass a bounty on to them. For that, I need you. Don't you understand?"

When she didn't answer, he mopped her face with a rag. "Look at me, Fayth. Stop weeping and look at me."

She opened her eyes, but his round face was quickly obscured with fresh tears.

He knelt beside her bed, handkerchief in hand, wearing a look of indulgence. "Perhaps I can arrange another marriage. The groom is not likely to be as wealthy or influential as Carlisle, but there are other alliances. I know of one young lordling—your age, handsome, liberal . . . and I'll allow you to meet him before I agree to the betrothal."

Fayth blinked, certain she heard him wrong.

He smiled, eyebrows raised. "This pleases you?"

"Why? Why would you do such a thing? What do you want from me? You would never do me a good turn without expecting one in return."

He grinned, but it was false. "Aye, I would require a favor . . . a small one, and one you'd certainly enjoy."

Fayth smirked. "I knew it. Well, I'm not going anywhere, so you might as well tell me."

"Our stepmother has something that I want very badly."

"Oh God! You disgust me! Leave me out of this. I won't help you."

"Silence! Not that, you ninny. Mona comes from a long line of Musgrave witches. For centuries they have been keepers . . . protectors, of an ancient stone. The Clachan Fala."

"That's a myth—a story. The Blood Stone isn't real." She gave Ridley a narrow look. "That's why Papa married her, isn't it? What makes you think she's the keeper?"

"I know not how he found her, but he did. And it is no

story. The Clachan Fala *is* real—and I mean to have it. Mona knows where it is."

Fayth sighed. "Very well. But how can I help you? If the threat of you raping her hasn't scared the truth from her, nothing will."

Ridley stared at her for a long moment, his brow furrowed. "Why do you say that? I've never threatened to rape her. Has she said something to you about me? Is she frightened of me?"

"No, Brother. She speaks not of you—nary a word."

He scowled, exhaling loudly. "As I was saying. According to legend, certain . . . er . . . criteria must be met before the keeper of the stone will unveil it. Those criteria will soon be met. But Mona has her own ideas of who the stone belongs to. She means to deny me my right."

Fayth looked away from Ridley, down to her hands, clenched tightly in her lap. A small bud of hope bloomed inside her.

"What must I do?"

5

~

"The strawberries are to your liking?" Robert asked his bride, at first, for no more than something to say.

Caroline sat beside him, tranquil as ever, eating little, speaking less. "Delicious, my lord." She hadn't touched them—had no idea how they tasted. Two plump red ones perched on the silver plate they shared. Robert looked from his wife to the strawberries. She'd barely looked at him to answer—was once again fixated on the musicians entertaining them during the meal.

Trying to be an attentive husband, he'd cut up her meat and attempted to feed it to her. This was what he'd seen other newly wedded couples do. She'd removed the first piece from his knife with her fingers, and thereafter chose to feed herself. This did not go unnoticed by Robert's kinsmen seated at the head table with him, though Wesley and Father Jasper didn't seem to think her actions odd. The more inebriated the Maxwells became, the more they seemed to take offense at Caroline's serene silence.

"Since you are so fond of the strawberries, allow me to

get you more." He waved at a servant bearing a bowl of fruit.

She inclined her head, smiling slightly. "My thanks, but it's not necessary."

"Oh, but it is! If they please you, I shall shower you with them."

The servant brought him the bowl, filled with pears and strawberries. Robert set it in front of Caroline. Giving him one of her placid smiles, she chose a strawberry and placed it beside the pair on their plate. Then she turned her head away, back to the pipers.

Robert took a drink of ale, slamming his tankard down on the table. Ale sloshed onto his hand. How was he to live with this paragon when he couldn't even get through a meal with her? He wanted to make her angry, to make her show annoyance, or . . . *anything* that acknowledged him as more than another unpleasant presence she must endure. She was his wife, whether she liked it or not—he expected something more from her.

"Eat it. I want to see how it pleases you."

Wesley was seated on Robert's right and turned to look at him quizzically. "Why must she eat the strawberry?"

"Because she finds them so delicious, or so she said."

Robert had garnered his wife's attention now. One golden eyebrow rose ever so slightly. Her pale eyes were lovely, and yet devoid of warmth or emotion. How would they look, burning with anger or passion?

Father Jasper sat on Wesley's right. The priest leaned forward, eyes wide and anxious. "Perhaps she was merely being polite."

"Why?" Robert never took his eyes off Caroline—nor she him. "If she doesn't like strawberries, why lie about it?"

Frowning deeply, Wesley reached across the table, plucked a strawberry off the plate, and popped it in his mouth. "Oh, Lord, she's right." He moaned in mock ecstasy. "They're so delicious—give me more." He crammed several more in his mouth, until a thin stream of red trickled down his chin and into the fine hair of his beard. "Does this please you, my lord? I'm eating the strawberries—and I *love* them."

Robert only glanced at his brother-in-law. "It pleases me."

Wesley scowled and scrubbed his sleeve across his lips. "Leave her alone. She doesn't have to eat the strawberry."

"Why not?" Robert asked. "She claims they are 'delicious.'"

Caroline never looked away from him. Had he disconcerted her with his obstinacy? Who could tell? Nothing in her countenance or the way she held herself betrayed a single emotion—she even blinked slowly, as if everything she did was designed to portray polite disinterest. But he was suddenly sure that's all it was—a portrayal. He had seen her blush, seen that measured stare deteriorate into confused blinking. He vowed he would see it again—and more.

"Perhaps," Wesley said, "she ate one when you weren't looking and found them disagreeable. In England, we try not to insult our hosts—a foreign concept to you, I'm sure."

Caroline's mouth curved into a slight smile and she lowered her eyes demurely. "Please excuse my lack of manners. I cannot eat strawberries; they irritate my skin. My lord is right, I should have said so."

"Why are you apologizing?" Wesley said incredulously. "It is he who lacks manners." He shook his head, shifting in his seat to put his back to Robert. "Jesus God, who cares if she likes the strawberries?"

She delicately picked at a piece of capon. "I warned you."

Robert leaned his elbow on the table. "Warned me?"

"That I was unsuitable."

"Ah." He leaned back in his chair. So, that's what this was all about. He suppressed a smile.

She looked to the pipers again. To avoid looking at her husband, he was certain.

The celebratory feast was endless. Robert had attended many weddings, several of them arranged marriages such as his, but never had he imagined the difficulties of entering such an intimate union with a stranger. It seemed foolish now that he hadn't. He'd thought they'd talk until they found some common interest and rapport would quickly follow. As time went on and they had children, their friendship would deepen. This was generally how it progressed with his mistresses—minus the children. But those relationships had been based on mutual attraction.

Robert's neck grew warm as he slid another glance at his wife. So regal, so perfect. Like the Virgin herself. Larger than life—commanding attention, then shunning it. Shunning him.

Attraction. That was the missing ingredient—the one that was causing him so much discomfort. *Hell, let's be honest. It was more than a lack of attraction. She had no interest in him.* Could it be possible she was interested in no man? That she really was destined to a cloistered life? He shifted restlessly in his chair—wishing to be through with this interminable meal. Others had stopped coming to the head table to deliver good wishes—the heavy silence of groom and bride discouraged it.

His gaze traveled down the table until it found Celia, sulking over the food she shared with her daughter, Larie. How unlike Caroline she was. She had been his most recent mistress, though he had ended it over a month ago upon finding a suitable husband for her. Willing, passionate—showing at times an excess of emotion. Robert frowned, his hand dropping to scratch the shaggy head of the wolfhound beside his chair. Perhaps he was the one at fault here. He had tired quickly of Celia—annoyed by her outbursts, smothered by her clinging and possessiveness. And now, faced with her opposite—a woman who just yesterday he would have believed himself thankful to wed—he was equally dissatisfied.

He felt someone's gaze on him and looked quickly at Caroline. But no, she was still absorbed in the music. He stared at her profile. She was no beauty, but there was something about her, something intriguing. A woman laughed down the table, high pitched and flirtatious. Robert tapped his fingers impatiently on the chair arm. He hoped time would cure this preoccupation with her. He had many other things to contemplate—it irritated him that he could think of nothing but Caroline's behavior.

The sensation of being watched continued and Robert looked down the table. It was Celia, though her angry blue gaze moved away when he caught her staring and narrowed on Caroline. He felt a pang of unease. Perhaps he should not have assigned her to Caroline as a maid. He'd thought it appropriate, as she was from a good family and a widow. He honored them both by employing her so. But now he was concerned she might cause Caroline trouble.

One glance at his wife assured him she could handle any unpleasantness directed her way. And if she couldn't—well . . . who could say what would happen? Her composure just might crack.

The strain was almost too much for Caroline. Nothing about this parody of a marriage was transpiring as she'd expected. She was beginning to expect the unexpected from Lord Annan—anticipate that he would do strange and senseless things—such as insist on watching her eat a strawberry. Or stare at her. *Why must he stare at her?*

When she was certain he'd finally stopped glowering at her, she situated herself so she could see him from the corner of her eye. He brooded now, leaning on the table, chin in hand. The rest of the wedding party was sotted. Wesley argued with a man Lord Annan had earlier introduced as his cousin, betrothed to Caroline's maid, Celia. The subject in debate was the worth of Scottish-bred ponies—Wesley claimed they were bad tempered and difficult, just like their breeders. Father Jasper tried to calm them so the heated discussion didn't break out into violence. Wesley was surprisingly well behaved, considering his loathing for all Maxwells. Fayth's betrothed, Jack, had been like a brother to Wesley. He'd been kidnapped in a skirmish with a group of Annan Maxwells—and eventually murdered. That Wesley had kept his sword sheathed this long was a miracle.

Caroline's husband had two brothers; she wondered where his youngest brother, Alexander, was. Perhaps he, like Wesley and Fayth, deeply opposed this marriage and had chosen to demonstrate his feelings through his absence. Was his brother's hair the same golden brown shade? Were his eyes icy gray, or blue like many of the other Maxwells she'd met this evening? Lord Annan was clean shaven, his jaw strong and square. Most of the men present wore beards—including Wesley, though his was thin and downy.

The pale gray eyes fixed on her again. What now? Would he try to force her to pet his dog? Smiling, she inquired, "My lord?"

Instead of answering her, he stood abruptly, holding out his hand. She stared at it.

"Let us go now, before they force a humiliating bedding on us."

She couldn't argue that point. She stood and when she

didn't give him her hand, he dropped his. Following him, Caroline glanced over her shoulder. Their sobriety during the festivities had ensured that they would remain unnoticed. Few people even looked in their direction and those who did apparently didn't register the significance of their hasty departure.

He ushered her into his chambers and closed the door behind them. After a moment's hesitation, he secured the lock.

Alone with him again. Caroline wanted to retire to her own bed, to think about all that had happened, to plan for what was still to come. But there was only one bed.

"About the sleeping arrangements," she began.

Lord Annan had been staring at the door, but now he turned, arms folded across his chest.

"It is, of course, expected that we share a bed tonight, but in the future will I be provided with my own bed-chamber?"

He circled her. She turned to follow his progress.

"I have no other suitable chambers for my wife. Mine are the finest."

"Do you not think it would be . . . improper—"

"For me to sleep with my wife?"

"I thought we agreed—"

"We agreed that I will not force you—but you will sleep in my bed, Caroline."

His use of her first name unsettled her, along with his proximity. He had stopped in front of her, was staring down at her. He was so tall; she disliked looking up at him.

"It's our wedding night. I should like to see your hair down."

"My lord—"

"Robert, or, if you prefer, Rob."

Inexplicably, she found herself unable to say his

name. She tried to form the words on her tongue, but could not give them voice. The only men she'd ever addressed familiarly were her brothers, and Ridley only on rare occasions—she usually called him "Brother." It implied a level of intimacy she neither felt nor wanted to initiate with her husband.

He watched her curiously, taking a step closer and turning his head to the side. "Rob. Say it, it's easy."

"As your wife, I wish to show you the respect you deserve."

"Aye?" He scratched his chin, eyebrows raised quizzically. "What does that mean?"

"My lord?"

"Or mean it nothing at all—just mindless flattery to divert me from the point."

"Which is?"

"My name—say it."

A shiver of apprehension trembled through Caroline. She wasn't afraid of him exactly . . . but he made her uneasy. When he was near, she couldn't think straight; her mind became sluggish, focusing on other things . . . such as the way his eyelashes curled. They were a darker brown than his hair, but blond tipped, and they *curled*.

Quickly formulating another plan, she moved away from him, crossing to the fireplace, and began removing the pins from her hood. "Very well—if it pleases you I will address you as you wish. In front of the servants, as well?"

He paced again. "I think I understand your definition of unsuitable."

Caroline placed the hood on the table. "My lord?"

He stopped abruptly, turning to face her. She wanted to clap her hand over her mouth, but she didn't. Would he be angry? Well, let him be—the sooner he realized this marriage was doomed, the better.

He was not angry. He was grinning. "You're still doing it."

"Doing what?"

He shook his head, chuckling softly.

Unnerved, Caroline removed more pins from her hair, slowly uncoiling the thick braid, glad for something to do with her hands. When it hung heavily down her back, she folded her hands at her waist and waited. He leaned against the far wall. His face was in shadows, so she didn't know if he looked at her or not. Apparently he did, because he said, "It's still plaited."

"Yes."

He sighed loudly. "Unplait it, please."

Reaching behind her, she grabbed the end of the braid— it brushed against her bottom—and removed the strands of hair securing it. As she ran her fingers through the weaves of her braid, shaking it so the hair fell over her shoulders, she began to feel ridiculous. *A mane, just like a horse. Why don't I neigh for him? Let him check my teeth?* Heat infused her neck. She turned, moving closer to the fire—her savior. It would mask the infernal blush that he seemed to create.

Why was he doing this to her? Was it a jest? She hated jests. She'd once received a love letter claiming to be from a knight in her father's employ. In the letter, the knight declared his love for her and his intention to ask her father for her hand. He'd called her beautiful, likened her to the Amazons of Greek lore. How foolish she'd become. She'd waited and waited, surreptitiously watching every sycophant in her father's service, wondering, *Is it him? Does he pine for me and dare not show it?*

Fool! Fool!

Unable to bear the suspense, she'd confided in Mona,

asking her to discover the man's identity. Mona had been puzzled by the letter, but later told her the knight had been sent away to the Continent. Caroline was heartbroken, knowing her one and only chance for love had left with him. But she had cherished the letter—praying he would return for her.

A few days later she came upon Ridley and one of the young knights their father fostered, discussing the letter. Surprised they knew of it, she'd remained unseen, listening. At first, she'd thought the young man was *the one* (her heart had nearly burst, he was so handsome)—only to overhear Ridley complaining about their stepmother. Mona had discovered they'd written the letter as a jest and had threatened to shrivel up their privates if they did it again. Since it was well known Mona was a witch, they didn't dare defy her. Ridley whined that he'd come so close to making Caroline crack—he was sure another letter would have accomplished it.

He'd always taken pleasure in making his siblings cry, saying mean things, telling them Father hated them, or Mother poisoned herself because they were such naughty children. Before long, they'd all stopped crying, stopped listening to him—and it had frustrated him terribly.

That was seven years ago. He'd attempted other japes, but eventually gave up when he was no longer able to provoke a reaction from her. Caroline frowned into the fire. If this was Lord Annan's idea of a jest, it was unlike any Ridley had ever played. Her heart skipped when she realized he stood behind her. She didn't move, focused on her breathing.

He touched her hair. She stared at the blackened stone of the mantel, eyes wide. It was a gentle touch, his fingers gliding over the hair draped behind her shoulder, wrenching an involuntary shiver from her.

"Cold?" he asked. His voice was low and deep and so close it seemed to reverberate along her spine, prolonging the shiver.

She wanted to blame it on the cold—but a fire blazed before her.

"You have beautiful hair," he said, stroking it again, harder this time. He lifted a lock and . . . smelled it.

Panicked, she moved away. Her breathing was erratic. Fear. She was definitely afraid now. No one had ever touched her so. She had no practice spurning suitors. She didn't like this sensation of drowning, the uncertainty and confusion.

"Have you a knife?" she asked.

He remained by the fireplace, watching her. "A knife? Mean you to stab me?"

"No. As we discussed earlier, consummation must be faked for Wesley to be satisfied. I will cut myself and bleed on the sheets. I should do it now, so it will be dry by morning."

He folded his arms across his chest. "Ah, yes. Consummation."

"A knife, my lord?"

His eyes narrowed when she said "my lord," and she nearly bit her tongue off. She must strive to use neither a courtesy title nor his name—perhaps "Husband" would please him, yet allow her to maintain her distance.

"The knife, Husband," she repeated.

He approached her slowly. When he stood before her, he removed a long dagger from his boot. She reached for it, but he pulled it back.

"Come," he said.

She followed him into the bedchamber. At the bed, he drew back the fur blanket and wool coverlets, revealing pristine white sheets beneath. Before she could protest, he nicked his thumb, wiping the bloody blade on the sheets.

"Enough?" he asked. "Or think you it would have been violent—perhaps you're afraid I will hurt you."

"I'm sure that is sufficient."

"Really? How can you tell?" He resheathed his knife and squeezed his thumb until blood welled up. "There's more here—perhaps you should come look."

Caroline circled to the other side of the bed and observed the small smear of blood. "I'm sure I wouldn't know the amount of blood that would be adequate. You're a better judge than I."

"No—I'm afraid I'm not."

She met his gaze. Was he teasing her? He smiled slightly, but she could read nothing from his expression. "Stop squeezing it. I suppose you could dribble the rest of the blood onto the sheets, that should be fine."

He did as she instructed, then popped his thumb in his mouth. Inspecting the pad of his thumb critically, he asked, "What now?"

"We could discuss the sleeping arrangements."

He sat on the bed. "There's nothing to discuss. We'll share this bed—if you wish me not to touch you then merely say so."

"I wish you not to touch me."

He smiled patiently. "Not now. I mean . . . later."

Why must she tell him again? It wasn't as if she would change her mind! He was a most difficult man.

Not wanting to join him on the bed, she wandered about the room, stopping beside a cabinet. A book was atop it. *Myths of the Greeks*. Unable to resist, she flipped the cover to find a ribbon marking his place. The top of the page was titled *Orpheus and Eurydice*.

"What think you of the tale thus far?"

He shrugged. "It's not one tale, but many. I read—but it's a struggle. It's taken me weeks to get that far." When she didn't respond, he said, "My mother used to read to us. I enjoyed it a great deal and missed it when she passed away. I thought to take up the habit myself, but as I said . . ."

"It does take practice. If you continue to work at it, I'm sure it will soon come easier."

"It comes easily to you?"

"Yes."

"Read to me, then."

What else was there to do? They had an entire night to pass. She took up the book and headed for the chair.

"Here, sit beside me." When she just stared at him he said, "I don't bite. Besides, if someone comes in, it would be best if we were in bed together."

"Very well." She went to the foot of the bed and climbed up.

He reclined, leaning on his elbow. His incredible length astounded her. She edged away from his booted feet, leaning her back against the bedpost.

"Shall I start where you left off, or at the beginning?"

"Start where I left off—I've read the ones before it."

His pale gray eyes never left her face. She cleared her throat and began to read.

Robert was enchanted. Who would believe he was being read to on his wedding night—and enjoying it? She had a lyrical voice, made for reciting or singing, perfectly modulated. It held little inflection when she spoke to him; when she read . . . well—it changed. Her face became animated. He watched her mouth as she formed the words, as she took sips from the goblet he had brought her, as she licked the wine from her lips—and imagined her doing other things with her mouth. Stifling a groan, he rolled onto his stomach—to hide the evidence of his arousal—but kept his head turned in her direction. She didn't notice, never looked up. Lashes, like silvery curtains, veiled her eyes from him.

She thought herself ugly, that much was clear. Why? Robert relaxed against the bolster, his gaze never leaving his bride. Most men being significantly shorter than she was, length had probably repulsed some of them. But certainly not the larger ones—and they were out there, Robert knew—though there were few. He'd once met a man taller even than himself. Some shorter men would surely take a fancy to her—the prospect of having those long legs wrapped about them . . .

It was her manner, he decided, that discouraged advances. She could freeze a man with a single glance. Why was she like this—did she truly believe she was fated to enter a convent? Well, he vowed to himself, he would put fate to the test before he let her go. His eyelids drifted shut as he listened to the story. He'd never heard this one before. Orpheus was leading his love, Eurydice, out of the underworld after making a bargain with Hades.

She stopped reading. He opened his eyes, expecting to see her trying to close the book quietly, thinking he was asleep, but she frowned down at the pages. It was a pleasing picture: golden hair flowing over her shoulders to pool in her lap and on the fur blanket, her smooth forehead lined with agitation. She flipped several pages, scanning them, pushing her hair out of her face impatiently.

"What is it?" he asked. "The story pleased you not?"

Her forehead cleared slightly, but she didn't look up. "It was a very nice story . . . I suppose . . . I like not the ending."

"How did it end? You stopped reading it aloud before Orpheus and his wife escaped the underworld."

She closed the book with a sense of finality. "That's just it. They don't make it."

Robert reached for the book. "But he made the bargain. Did Hades renege?"

"No," she handed him the book, "Orpheus looked back and she disappeared. He was miserable for the rest of his life and was eventually ripped to pieces."

Robert turned the book in his hands, not opening it. "Huh."

Caroline leaned against the bedpost, plaiting a lock of hair, staring up at the canopy.

Very cautiously, he asked, "How would you have ended it?"

"He wouldn't look back."

"He couldn't help himself—he loved her so much."

"If he loved her so much, why did he look back? He lost her forever."

Robert shrugged. "He needed to know she was still behind him."

Caroline smiled slightly and shook her head.

"So? How would you do it differently?"

She was thoughtful. Robert held his breath, wondering how much longer she would be this way. Perhaps she'd only needed to get used to him and she would be this way with him from now on. He wanted to move closer to her—instinct pulled at him to join her, touch her, but unlike Orpheus, he didn't intend to push his luck.

"Perhaps he must defeat deadly creatures at the exit to the underworld—but there are too many . . . one gets past him, moves to attack Eurydice . . . but he slays it without looking at her." She paused, eyes hazy, still fixed upward, fingers plaiting strands of gold. "And though it would be a trial, he would succeed—because that would be proof of his love for her."

A silence grew between them but a comfortable one. Robert contemplated his bride as she drifted to sleep. She had some rather unrealistic expectations of how a man proved his love—but he liked her ending better. Her head slipped against the bedpost several times before she finally gave in to sleep. He slid off the bed and caught her wine goblet before its contents soaked the quilt. Staring down at her, he wondered how to lay her down without alarming her. He pressed her shoulder gently. With no further prompting, she curled up on her side. Her hair spread over her body like a mantle.

After covering her with a fur, he returned to the head of the bed and stretched out, hands folded behind his head. As sleep overtook him the thought drifted through his mind that they weren't out of Hades yet.

6

Wesley strode into the bedchamber, dressed for travel. Caroline masked her sour mood, caused by her aching ribs. Last night, she'd not undressed, and so slept with her stays still binding her upper body. She was paying for it now. Father Jasper stood beside her, next to the bed, waiting. Caroline had not seen Lord Annan since last night—she'd woken to the clatter of Celia slamming things about the room. Stretched out at the end of the bed, a fur spread over her, she'd been quite alone. Celia now stood on the opposite side of the bed, staring at the bloodstained sheets.

Wesley looked down at the bed, pensive. After a moment, he inclined his head at Caroline. She followed him into her withdrawing room, walking slowly, for each step, each breath, constricted her chest painfully. He closed the door behind them and paced the floor, his gloved hand gripping his sword hilt. Stopping in front of her, he looked her up and down—looking up to meet her gaze.

"You are still a virgin?"

Uncertain if Wesley was her ally, she didn't answer immediately. He was one of the few people she could always count on and something grew small inside her that she was forced to doubt his loyalty, his intentions. She was no longer a Graham, but neither was she a true Maxwell. She was no one.

"Please tell me you are," he whispered, averting his eyes.

Caroline sighed, relieved. "Yes."

"Will he let you go, if this marriage brings no peace?"

"I know not."

He gave her a curt nod. "If he refuses, I'll come for you." He turned to leave.

She stopped him, a hand on his sleeve. "About Ridley—what will you tell him?"

"I'll tell him I saw the blood. He'll not question me further."

"He'll release Lord Annan's brother?"

Wesley looked away from her, his mouth thinning. "Keep your counsel on this, Sister—but I don't know if he ever intends to release Sir Patrick—marriage or no."

Caroline frowned. "What? I don't understand—"

Wesley gripped her hand. "Neither do I—but as I said, keep your counsel. I know not that my suspicions are true—he doesn't share his mind with me. It doesn't behoove you to share this information with your husband—or any other Maxwell."

Caroline nodded.

Wesley's grip tightened. "I vow to you, Carrie, if this goes sour, I'll not abandon you."

An unexpected lump rose in Caroline's throat. Wesley was not one to express his softer emotions freely. This show of concern was a gift she would cherish.

"God be with you," she whispered.

"And you." He strode through the door.

Caroline stared at the empty doorway, her chest hollow and aching. Father Jasper was all she had left. When she returned to the bedchamber, Celia was stripping the bloody sheets from the bed. Her black hair hung thick and glossy down her back. Her bodice was cut low, the round globes of her breasts rising above it. Celia was not a mere servant, as Caroline had learned last night, and as such, should not concern herself with laundering.

"Leave those for the laundress, Celia. You have other duties to attend."

"Not these, my lady. I must set these aside—to prove the marriage is binding." She smirked when she said the last. Caroline held Celia's insolent stare until the little woman looked away. Cheeks flushed, she stripped the bed with new vigor.

"Well then, when you're finished there, perhaps you could fetch the house steward for me. I'd like to discuss the running of the castle with him." The ache in her ribs was becoming bearable, so she went to the tall cabinet near the bed and removed her cloak. "The first thing I should like is a tour of the grounds."

Caroline swung her cloak on, clasping it at the neck, and turned to her maid. Celia stood beside the bedpost, fingering the carved wood. She smiled slightly, her blue eyes narrowed with malicious humor. Caroline braced herself. The little elf obviously knew something Caroline didn't and was about to delight in telling her. Well, Caroline would give her no satisfaction.

"I see no point in a tour, when you cannot leave the grounds without an armed escort. Should you be set on it though, I'm sure your guards will oblige you." She gathered the sheets in her arms and went to the door. "Dinna fash about the running of Annancreag, my lady. You're not to be trusted with any responsibilities until Rob—er, Lord Annan says so."

She was gone with a flick of dark hair. Caroline looked about the room, deeply distressed. She was no wife—not even a pretend one. She was a prisoner. Was that his plan? If she refused to rut with him she would be deprived of all other duties? And what of Celia? She'd nearly addressed Lord Annan with unseemly familiarity! Did he saddle Caroline with his mistress? To keep an eye on her? And why did the wench not wear her hair covered as was proper? Clearly, she meant to entice men—such as Caroline's husband! Caroline thought of Celia's sleek hair, her large, round bosom, and was assaulted by an unexpected pang of envy.

Anger and humiliation quickly followed, squeezing her chest, burning her cheeks. She was so unaccustomed to the horrible rush of emotion that she couldn't move— was frozen in the middle of the room. That . . . *woman* dared speak to her in such a manner because she knew her lover—Lord Annan—would do nothing! And Caroline had been wondering why she'd been granted a reprieve from his attentions last night when he'd made it clear he would try to bed her. He'd apparently found more willing bedsport! So, that's how it was to be. She was *required* to sleep in their bed, but he could sleep wherever—and with whomever—he pleased.

Her rapid breathing pained her sore ribs, bound up as they were in her stays. Footsteps approached. Caroline turned her back to the door, pressing her hands against her cheeks, willing the heat to recede. The fire had died to embers—it could not save her. She pulled her hands away from her face, horrified to see they trembled.

The footsteps paused in the doorway. "I just saw your brother off." *Lord Annan.* "I trust you're rested?"

Caroline pulled her hood over her head, then buried her traitorous hands in the velvet folds of her cloak before she turned to face him. "Yes, thank you. Wesley and I said farewell earlier."

Lord Annan approached her slowly, warily. "He seemed convinced consummation had taken place."

"There is a matter I should like to discuss with you."

He stopped in front of her and sighed heavily. "Last night . . . you were different."

"My lord . . . Husband?" *Different?* He seemed genuinely disappointed she was no longer *different.* "I know not what you mean."

"When you were reading . . . and after."

She'd been thinking about the story and imagining the new ending—her ending and how much better it would be. In fact, she was now quite fond of the tale. She would tell it to herself often. She had many such tales that she'd heard, altered, and filed away to ponder on long journeys or when sleep eluded her.

"I'm afraid I don't understand."

He contemplated her silently. "I thought much about what you said about Orpheus and Eurydice."

He did? She masked her surprise, trying to show only mild interest.

"Why not write it down? So when you read it again, you could end it well."

"I don't need to write it down for that."

"Well—" He laughed shortly, a cross between amusement and exasperation. Dimples dented his cheeks, surprising her again. He was quite handsome when he smiled. "Write it down for *me.*"

Surely he jested? "It is not meet for me to write such things."

"Why not?"

"Because it's not done."

He waved that away. "Then you shall be the first, aye? What matter, anyway? Who's to know but you and I?"

She opened her mouth but nothing came out. As she searched for some response to his bizarre request, she noticed he was grinning, obviously pleased with himself. Then she knew. He was trying to shock her. He derived great amusement by witnessing her lose composure. What an odd man! And how like Ridley. That thought hardened her heart against him—though until that moment she hadn't realized she'd been softening. She would not continue to be an outlet for his amusement.

"Very well, Husband. As you wish."

His smiled faded. "I'll have Henry bring you paper and ink."

"That is the matter I wish to discuss—your steward."

He wandered about the chamber, stopping to pick at a basket of flowers. "Aye?"

"The maid you assigned me, Celia, informed me I'm not to take on any duties."

He quirked an eyebrow. "You want to perform wifely duties?"

"I want to run the household, yes. It's what I know, all I have to offer. I will do it well—you shall see."

He pulled something out of the flowers—it looked like a bundle of dried herbs tied with string from where she stood. He frowned at it and moved to the next basket. "That's all you have to offer? Household management?"

Why did he ask such peculiar questions? Did he really care about the answers, or was he merely being difficult? "Celia informed me I'm not even allowed out of the castle walls."

"That's only for your protection." He removed another bundle of herbs from the flowers. He moved to the third vase with more purpose.

"From whom do I need protection?"

He fished a third bundle of herbs out of the flowers before turning to her. "There are some who do not support peace between our families."

He scanned the room, apparently looking for more flowers. She wanted to ask him what the bundles were but didn't want to change the subject.

"I would hate for them to act on their feelings, causing you harm."

"It's odd that they would hate someone they know not, merely because of my surname."

"I agree, it makes no sense at all. Those who still have reason to nurse the hate are long dead. I've lost a father to the feud—I'll not lose anyone else. That's why you and I are married." He approached her, holding all three of the bundles in one palm. "They need time to see you're different, that these aren't the same Grahams who tricked and massacred us three score years ago."

"Tell me of this trickery, I know little."

To her surprise, he looked reluctantly toward the door, then frowned back down at her.

"My lord? Is something amiss?"

Judging from his grim, tight-lipped expression, he considered something very weighty. He looked her over. "You're dressed to go out?"

"I thought I might have a tour of the castle and the surrounding area."

"Excellent." He placed a hand on her shoulder, steering her toward the door. "I have much to do today and little daylight. You may accompany me."

This wasn't what Caroline had in mind, but it appeared there was nothing else for her to do. The prospect of riding a horse with aching ribs was highly unappealing, but she was never one to complain. Perhaps she could persuade Lord Annan to give her control of the household. She would very much like to examine how things were done here.

Celia loitered outside the bedchamber, in Lord Annan's withdrawing room. Lord Annan seemed to think nothing of it. He handed Celia the herb bundles. She caressed his fingers, thrusting her chest out. He pulled his hand away abruptly, giving her a hard look.

Caroline glanced down at her own cloak-draped chest surreptitiously. Beneath the cloak her chest was covered with a partlet and flattened by her stays and bodice.

"Get rid of these," Lord Annan said to Celia. "See to it I find no more hidden about our chambers."

"Aye, my lord." Celia turned to leave.

"One moment, Celia."

Celia turned, her cheeks crimson, eyes snapping. "Aye, my lord?"

"Lady Annan needs a mount. Take her to the stables and inform Sandy to saddle Heather." He smiled at Caroline and for some strange reason her stomach dipped. "I'll join you directly."

When he was gone, Celia stalked to the fireplace and tossed the herbs into it. Were they lovers still? He'd not treated her as such. The heaviness that had been pressing down on Caroline's chest lifted slightly. He wouldn't humiliate her by favoring his mistress over her. That was a good quality in a husband.

Celia stood at the fireplace, watching the herbs burn. A sickly-sweet odor rose from the flames. She turned to Caroline, her face pale and tight. "Follow me, my lady."

* * *

They rode west, where Robert's lands consisted of moor and forest. It wasn't the easiest riding, but Caroline never complained. In some places the ground was so soggy they were forced to dismount and walk their horses. They picked their way, side-by-side, across the sodden and rock-strewn ground, men-at-arms before and behind them. The men in front guarded a prisoner—the purpose of the journey. Robert transported him to the warden of the West March.

"Why, you're as good as any lad," Robert commented, after she skillfully unstuck her mare's hoof from the sucking bog without exciting it. When she didn't reply, he regretted his words. "I don't mean you're like a lad— only as good as one."

"That is what you said. I understand and thank you, my lord."

He gritted his teeth and prayed for patience.

"You were to tell me of the Grahams' trickery all those years ago?" she said, stepping over a jagged stone.

"Aye." He moved to the other side of his horse, so he walked beside her. "I'm surprised you never heard the stories."

"In my home, no one told stories."

Robert glanced at her, noticing lines of strain beside her mouth. "Are you well? Would you like to ride? I'll lead the horses."

She shook her head and the lines smoothed. It was a conscious effort for her, though, and he wondered why it was so important for her to conceal all weakness. "I'm fine. You were saying?"

"Well . . . it all started three score years ago. The bad blood between the Maxwells and the Grahams went back further than 1482, much further, but in that year it became more than a mere feud—it became deadly. Lord

Annan, Malcolm Maxwell, my great-uncle, had decided to put an end to the feud. I'm not sure why, for it's said he was as irascible as my father. There was much talk of truce, but neither clan would stop their reiving and killing without pledges. As you know, hostages escape, often ruining everything. So, a marriage was negotiated, wedding the Graham laird's daughter to Malcolm.

"Only a small party of Grahams were allowed to accompany the lass, to guard against treachery, but all seemed well, and the night of the wedding the Maxwells let down their guard, celebrating with the Grahams like brothers. Malcolm was apparently completely besotted with his bride; it is said she was so beautiful it hurt the eyes to look upon her." Robert noted Caroline, who had been looking at him while he spoke, averted her eyes at the mention of the other Graham lass's beauty. It occurred to him to flatter her, to compare their marriage to the one long ago, to expound on her beauty, but he knew she would not believe him. She would think him a fool and a liar. He'd never been good at flowery speeches anyway. He held his tongue.

"Because of their drunken state and their lowered guard, she was able to let in a Graham raiding party that had been waiting in the forest. They murdered Malcolm and his youngest brother. William, my great-grandsire, was a mercenary and away, fighting on the Continent, so his life was thankfully spared. He returned as soon as he got word to take up the mantle of Lord Annan and wage bloody and unending retribution. And all for some stone that doesn't exist."

"What became of the Graham lass? She must have been a cousin to me and yet I don't remember ever hearing anything about her."

Robert shrugged. "I know not."

Their way became more treacherous as the bog sucked at their horses' hooves. Caroline fell silent, focusing on the ground before her. The sky darkened, a storm moving in. It would be impossible to complete his business with the warden and make it back to Annancreag tonight. Normally, since the warden was also a Maxwell, he would gladly shelter a kinsman for the night. But Robert couldn't be sure of their reception, especially since he'd brought his Graham bride.

As well as being Robert's overlord, Lord Maxwell was a distant cousin. Robert's father, Red Rowan, had been one of Lord Maxwell's deputy wardens for many years. Often, the office, though not hereditary, passed to the heir anyway. In Robert's case, Lord Maxwell had yet to invest him with the duty—but he'd not given it to anyone else, either.

Not as full of bluster as Red Rowan, Lord Maxwell was nevertheless a border reiver of the same caliber. Being warden didn't hinder his pursuit of blood feuds or collection of black rents, which was typical on both sides of the border. Most wardens didn't let their duty as enforcers of the law interfere with their livelihood of raiding and reiving. All of which contributed to Lord Maxwell's current wariness of Robert taking over the helm of the Annan Maxwell family. For Robert had now made peace with two of the Maxwells' staunchest enemies—the English Grahams and the Scottish Johnstones. Robert's peace with the Johnstones was not nearly as solid. Prisoners had been exchanged as pledges, but the Maxwell prisoners had already escaped from the Johnstones and returned home—a situation not likely to please the Johnstone laird.

Neither had Robert asked permission to wed a Graham, as he should have. But, as warden, Lord Maxwell could have blocked the union had he a mind to. Intermarriage between the Scots and the English was illegal on the border—not that anyone heeded this law. Bonds of kinship reached across the border, regardless of nationality, and were stronger and more enduring than any borderer's fealty to their sovereign. A fact neither king seemed to comprehend.

Once they were clear of the moor and riding again, Caroline asked, "The stone you referred to, is it the Clachan Fala? Was it the cause of the feud?"

Robert scanned the sky as the first drops of rain sprinkled his face. They wouldn't make it to Lochmaben in time.

"No one knows with any certainty. Some believe the marriage was nothing but a sham. There's a tale that claims a union between our families will bring peace and prosperity to our people. The first male issue will grow to be a great man—powerful and undefeated in battle—owing to the stone. It's said to protect all who possess it. I've even heard that the owner will be king. In other tales, he will defeat the English king. And yet another says he will merely bring peace to the borders of Scotland. What rubbish! You'd think he was King Arthur returned. The fable claims that in order for him to accomplish all these miracles he must be in possession of the Clachan Fala. It makes him invincible or some such nonsense."

She seemed distracted—not quite troubled, but as though something he said touched a chord within her. "And how is he to come by the stone?"

"I know not where it is—but it will find its way to his parents. It will keep them safe until his birth, and then it will be bestowed upon him." He shrugged. "A sort of Excalibur. And just as real."

"So . . . someone orchestrated the marriage because they believed it would bring the stone out of hiding?"

"That has been said, though it seems doubtful. You know how legends grow up around these things."

"But what if it's true?"

He snorted.

"Do you not believe King Arthur lived?" She stared into the distance, unseeing. Was she recrafting the Maxwell-Graham blood feud in her mind? Turning some massacre with no other root but mindless retribution and hate into a tale of chivalry and romance, a quest for a magical stone. Robert smiled to himself, wondering if he should ask her to record it for him.

His smile faded when he remembered the bundles of dead weeds he found this morning, planted in all the flowers. He recognized them as evil wishes, planted by someone in his household. Celia? Assigning her to Caroline had been a mistake—one Robert intended to rectify as soon as they returned to Annancreag.

It vexed him that someone hoped to cause discord in his marriage through witchcraft. He didn't like to think Celia had been the one who planted the evil wish, but he could take no chances. He glanced at his wife again. She was deep in thought, a small frown creasing her brow.

The similarities between this marriage and the fateful one of long ago suddenly seemed ominous. He watched his wife more sharply, but her attention did not return to him—instead she appeared contemplative, taking in the scenery around them. *A nun. A life of contemplation.* Contemplating what? Happy endings? Tales of love and chivalry? He had initially thought she was a contradiction—a wonderful one that would keep him fascinated for a long time. But now he wasn't so certain he wasn't being toyed with.

Could this all be a ruse? Could Ridley have forced her into this? So she concocted the convent story? Knowing how this must end, she intended to keep herself pure, unsullied by enemy Maxwells. Had they planned to attack at the feast, but were forced to wait because of Robert's diligence in guarding the castle? Were they biding their time, waiting for Caroline to win him over, for him to become complacent in his new marriage, drop his guard, allow Grahams to visit?

He hated this suspicion and tried to banish it, but the tale haunted him. It had been such an elaborate trick—and Malcolm, smitten with his bride, had been caught completely unaware.

Robert felt Caroline's gaze on him and turned, surprised she would look at him when it wasn't required of her. But he was wrong, she surveyed the woods behind him and to his right . . . or was she? He'd thought, for just a moment, that he caught her rapidly averting her eyes. Perhaps she was not so disinterested in him as she pretended. He continued staring at her until she could no longer ignore it.

"My lord?" Her pale green eyes rested on him, cool, assessing. He searched her face, her beautiful eyes, so large and solemn, for . . . something, he knew not what. Some clue to confirm or disprove his suspicion.

"My lady?"

A golden eyebrow arched the tiniest bit in question, before she looked away. She would reveal nothing to him willingly.

Robert slouched in his saddle as the sky opened and rain pounded down. He pulled the hood of his cloak over his head, glancing at Caroline as she did the same. She looked upward, at the boiling clouds. Lightning split the sky and thunder crashed. Her shoulders jerked, her gaze fixed on nature's fury. Rain slicked her face, her mouth. Her lips parted and her tongue darted out.

Robert tore his gaze away, thoughts of the coming night—a warm bed and his wife in it—stirring his imagination. She had forgotten about the statement she was to compose for him to sign. He smiled to himself. By his calculation, it would soon be rendered unnecessary.

7

Teeth chattering and sopping wet, Caroline stood in the entryway of Lochmaben's great hall with her husband. Their cloaks dripped in puddles on the stone floor around them, echoing in the cavernous and empty room. Caroline was exhausted. Her ribs weren't the only thing aching, and despite a good drenching, she still felt gritty with road dust.

She glanced up at Lord Annan. He seemed distracted, troubled.

"What business have you with the warden?" she asked.

He looked down at her, as if her words startled him. A violent, involuntary shudder racked her body.

"You're freezing," he murmured. He slid his arm around her shoulders and pulled her against his side. She stumbled into him, her body stiffening. His arm encircled her, his hand gripping her forearm to hold her close. His cloak was as wet as hers was but where their bodies touched, the fabric became warm. Or was it her skin, feverish inside her clothes? Her thoughts were muddled, but she held herself rigid, gaze fixed blankly before her.

This was a pose she'd seen many times, a man with his

arm about his sweetheart. Her heart stuttered. She closed her eyes, searching, fighting for control. She had anticipated this—that he would touch her. Why, then, was it such a shock? She fought not to reveal her discomfort, but was losing the battle. Her chest seemed to be heaving. Perhaps he didn't notice? He did seem preoccupied. Why was she panicking? She was nearly hysterical! It wasn't as though he would rape her right here, in the entryway of his lord's castle, while sopping wet.

At that thought, her erratic heart began to slow. He had been speaking to her, answering her question about the purpose of this visit. So overcome with anxiety, she hadn't absorbed a word. He paused. Did he wait for a response? *Concentrate,* she ordered herself. With great effort she wiped her mind clear.

The heat receded from her face and the infernal trembling abated. The heavy weight of his arm was warm and pleasant. He smelled of horse and damp wool. She was almost accustomed to his embrace when he began rubbing her arm with his hand. Panic welled in her chest again, choking her, her mind filling with images of him— doing things much more intimate to her. Her stomach churned from such wickedness, yet she was powerless to control the direction of her thoughts.

"You've stopped shivering," he said, his voice soft near her ear. His breath stirred the loose hair and she made him a liar with her sudden shudders. He rubbed her arm more vigorously. "Don't want you catching a chill. I'll have a bath sent up for us."

A bath? Sent up? For *us?* Her mind cast about, trying to make sense of his words. She would have to disrobe in front of him? Why did she agree to join him on this ride?

At the sound of footsteps, she nearly sighed with relief. He would speak with their host and forget about her.

Lord Annan didn't remove his arm. She felt him straighten, drawing himself up taller, his body tightening. Never had she been so in tune with someone physically and couldn't stop herself from looking up at him. He gazed to his right, eyes guarded, his mouth grim, his chin a hard line. The footsteps halted abruptly. Caroline leaned forward to see past her husband.

A man, middle-aged and stocky as a bulldog, glared at Lord Annan. His gaze moved to Caroline, boring into her. Lord Annan didn't speak, but Caroline said, "Good day." Lord Annan's body relaxed and his arm tightened about her briefly—as if in a hug.

"So this is the Graham Mare," the man said, strolling over to stand in front of them.

Lord Annan tensed. "I'll thank you to hold your tongue in our presence. I only give one warning—you speak ill of my wife again and I shall call you out."

Caroline was glad Lord Annan could not see her face. She was unable to mask her astonishment at his words. Call him out? *Was he serious?* What an absurd thing to say—to do! She was numb to such childish name calling—no sense in hurting himself or anyone else over it. And yet, something akin to pleasure spread warmly from the pit of her stomach outward.

The man's shrewd gaze measured her. "I didn't realize you'd already married her. My apologies, Lady Annan. I see that the name is obviously a gross misunderstanding."

Caroline inclined her head. "Thank you."

His gaze lingered on her longer than she thought appropriate, but she did not lower hers. He looked away when Lord Annan introduced him as Lord Maxwell, warden of the Scottish West March.

The warden, hands fisted on his hips, stared hard at Lord Annan. "So, come ye here wi' a prisoner."

For a moment Caroline thought he referred to her, then remembered the man Lord Annan's men-at-arms had been guarding.

"Aye, as your man, I'm sworn to deliver outlaws to you."

"You're my man, eh?" The warden's gaze darted to Caroline.

"I am."

The warden's calculating stare turned into a frown. He waved a hand at Caroline. "What would your father think of this, eh?"

Again, Lord Annan's embrace tightened, but Caroline was no longer alarmed. He would carry it no further in the warden's presence, and oddly, she felt as though he . . . *needed* to touch her, as if it somehow bolstered him. Though she immediately rejected the fancy, the nuances of his body made the impression return repeatedly. Why would a man such as Lord Annan derive any comfort or courage from the touch of a mere woman—and one he hardly knew?

Lord Annan said, "We both know what he would think—which is why I'm so old and only just now marrying."

"If you're so set on peace, why would you risk a feud with me over this?"

"I thought it best not to defy you. You might say no— better to beg forgiveness than risk refusal, methinks."

The warden laughed, a loud gravelly sound, and motioned them to follow. "I wondered why I wasn't invited. Mayhap you're more like your father than I thought."

Lord Annan's arm dropped from Caroline's shoulder and she was able to breathe easier. At the enormous fireplace, two chairs and a bench were quickly assembled. The warden lowered himself in the chair closest to the fire. Caroline sat on the bench, while Lord Annan took the chair opposite their host.

"When was the wedding?" the warden asked as a servant brought them pewter tankards brimming with hot, spiced ale.

"Yesterday," Lord Annan said, darting a secret look at Caroline.

"Yesterday!" the warden bellowed, sitting forward and looking from Caroline to Lord Annan incredulously. "What the hell are you doing here?"

Lord Annan shrugged, ignoring the insinuation. "Caroline is a most practical woman and cannot see wasting a day in sloth, simply because she is a new bride."

The warden laughed. "Then it's a good match, eh? Never have I met a man less inclined to sloth than you." He fell silent, regarding Lord Annan for a long time. " 'Tis glad I am you've not a mind for feuding."

Caroline sipped her ale. Its warmth, and the blazing fire, began to drive the chill from her bones. She felt comfortably sleepy, lethargic.

The warden turned to ponder the fire, rubbing the black and gray whiskers on his jaw. The craggy lines of his face deepened. "This is not the time to be making enemies. With the English king fortifying the borders and Lord Wharton running raids into my march at Henry's behest, I've enemies enough. The East and Middle Marches are in chaos and King James cannot be bothered, what with his wee sons passing on. He is ill of body as well as mind. We must needs stick together in this time of strife. King Henry has lost reason since killing his last wife . . . he takes his rage out on others. James sore insulted him by agreeing to meet him at York and then never showing."

"It was probably a trap," Lord Annan said. "I think it best he stayed home."

"Oh, aye—he should never have agreed to meet Henry, though. He's incurred the Great Harry's wrath, and that is an ugly thing."

Caroline silently agreed. Even her father, though he remained true to his faith, had not openly defied the king for fear of losing all.

"There are many Scots in his pay," the warden continued, "causing mischief on my march. The Grahams in the debatable land . . . they are most difficult to control. These are your lady's kinsmen, eh?"

Lord Annan shot a look at Caroline. "Aye, Lord Graham has estates there. I'm sure he has vexed Wharton by wedding his sister to a Maxwell. But the Grahams have always followed their own path—as much Scots blood courses through their veins as English blood. They cannot quite decide whom to give their allegiance to. For now, however, Maxwell lands are safe from Graham raiders."

Wesley also had been concerned about Wharton's anger and possible retribution, but Ridley had assured them he could handle the warden and that in the end, all would fall into place. Caroline wondered now what he meant by that. It was as though he imagined great things would come of this rather insignificant union—things out of proportion with reality. It was true the Grahams were a powerful force on the West March, but Ridley himself was only a minor lord.

The warden turned his contemplative stare on Lord Annan. "I find it odd that a worm like Lord Graham would risk his king's displeasure."

"Since his father's death Ridley has converted to King Henry's reformed religion, making him a much needed ally in the Catholic north. After the Pilgrimage of Grace,

Henry will not alienate any lord willing to uphold his church. Ridley claims his king will overlook this marriage. He's likely right; Henry has more pressing matters claiming his attention."

The warden's mouth twisted as if he'd tasted something nasty. He turned to Caroline. "What of you? Be you a heretic? A follower of Luther?"

"No, my lord. I'm pleased to again be in the bosom of the true religion."

He nodded approvingly.

"That's why Lord Graham offered her to me," Lord Annan said, a bit smugly. "Because he could not force her to convert." Was that pride touching his features?

Maxwell patted Caroline's hand. "Good lass."

Caroline merely smiled and glanced at her husband. Elbow rested on the arm of his chair, leaning slightly to one side—in her direction—he watched her. His eyes were cool gray pools of water on a hazy day, unfathomable yet compellingly beautiful. And suddenly she felt it again—his touch. As if by merely looking at her, he caressed her.

Her heart thumped wildly against her ribs. Before, she'd thought it signaled anxiety—that his intense determination frightened her, but now she feared it was something more. Excitement. She was glad for her cloak—surely he'd see her pulse throbbing in the hollow of her throat if not for the cloak's cover. Frustration—at herself—drove her to grip her hands together tightly in her lap. He held her gaze for what seemed an eternity to Caroline. She forced herself not to look away, not to show timidity. Men used weakness, so she must give him none. He finally looked away and the tension slowly seeped out of her limbs. Glancing down she saw four half moon indentations on the back of one hand where she had gouged herself. How was she to survive another week with this man, let alone a year?

"Aye," the warden was saying. "Henry won't be happy until he forces King James to turn heretic as well."

"That'll never happen," Lord Annan murmured.

The warden waved a servant over. "Lady Annan looks fair soaked and stiff with cold. Show her to her quarters and fetch her something warm to wear."

Caroline stood to follow the servant.

Lord Annan said, "A bath, too, if it's not too much trouble. Hot."

Lord Annan's request seemed to surprise the warden, but he shrugged and instructed the servant to "see to it."

The chamber Caroline was deposited in was small and drafty. The rushes were dark with age and filth, and Caroline was quite certain a rat rustled about behind the screen hiding the closestool. The bed, though, appeared free of vermin. She glanced around the room nervously. There was nowhere else to sleep—certainly not the floor.

She removed her cloak and draped it over a chair in front of the fire. She shivered again, but since she was alone, she made no effort to control it. She stood in front of the fire, rubbing her hands over her arms. She longed to remove her bodice and stays, to ease the pressure on her ribs, to wrap herself in a quilt and sit in front of the fire with a book.

Two maids entered, one dragging a wooden tub, the other bath linens, a soap ball, and garments. When they were gone, Caroline inspected the items, impressed with the quality. The soap smelled of lavender. The shift was fine lawn with ribbons and scalloped lace at the neck and sleeves, and the pale blue dressing gown was exquisitely embroidered velvet. *Probably pilfered from an English manor during a raid.* That was simply the border way. Some of the gowns Caroline's father had gifted her with had still smelled of the previous owner's perfume and sweat.

Such was life on the borders. Her father had tried to insulate his youngest children from its harshness, but that was impossible. She and Fayth had been kidnapped once, when they were very young, and held for ransom. Caroline remembered little of the incident, except it was an Englishman who showered them with gowns and trinkets—at her father's expense, of course—and eventually sent them home unharmed. When she'd told her father that the man had been very nice, he informed her that the "nice man" murdered their uncle and would pay for the deed with his life. Such doings had shocked Caroline then, but had since become commonplace.

The maids returned with buckets of steaming water. Should she wait for Lord Annan to return? He should use the water first. She stood before the fire, pondering all the ways in which her life had changed in only two days. Her perfectly ordered world had been turned on its head. With a jolt of shame she realized she'd not prayed since she stepped foot in Lord Annan's home. And she wished to devote her life to God? She gripped her arms tighter. Worship had always been a trial—impossible to keep her mind focused on prayer when her thoughts wandered about, spinning tales in her head.

Oh, she knew what was happening. She was a woman and not devoid of feelings. It happened sometimes, a knight of her father's, fine of form and face, caught her fancy. Such feelings were unfitting, she knew—especially for her. Men would not welcome the knowledge that the Pious Graham Mare lusted after them. She forced herself to never look at these men again, to bury her licentious thoughts in books and stories—easier to attribute such feelings to the characters that populated them.

Now, she felt those things for her husband; and somehow he . . . desired her—for no other reason than that she'd challenged him. But still, having a man want her was beyond her realm of experience. How she wished Father Jasper were here, to advise her, to direct her in prayer. She would pray to the Virgin as soon as she bathed—bare her soul, beg for aid. She would not allow her thoughts to turn to fanciful things such as Orpheus and Eurydice. Caroline knew lust was fleeting, especially for men. Men promised many things in the grips of desire, but when lust was gone, words were forgotten, leaving nothing in their place.

The splash of pouring water soothed her and she decided that if her husband didn't appear by the time the maids finished she would not let the hot water go to waste. Besides, she thought, glancing uneasily at the screen across the room as it trembled with the force of whatever scurried about behind it, if she waited to bathe after him, she would be forced to either dress in front of him, or retreat behind the screen. Neither option held much appeal. Yes, it was best to be finished and in bed, fast asleep (or pretending to be) when he returned.

By the time Robert finally escaped Lord Maxwell's wagging tongue, he was numb with cold. The warm ale had helped a bit, but the metal plates sewn into the heavy leather jack he wore were cold as ice, chilling him to the bone. He was pleased with the fruits of his visit though. Maxwell was not angry about the wedding and implied he would give Robert the office of deputy warden. Robert's prisoner was an Armstrong in the pay of Wharton. After Robert was dry and fed they would question the prisoner, see if he was willing to exchange intelligence for freedom. Maxwell was King James's man, despite his border ways, and Scotland needed all the help it could muster if it were to win a war against England. And indeed, if things continued to deteriorate, war was inevitable.

Robert was already unhooking his jack when he pushed open the door to his chambers. The sight that greeted him stopped him in his tracks, frozen in the doorway, hand gripping the latch.

Visible through wisps of rising steam, Caroline stood in the wooden tub, wearing nothing but the mantle of her hair. She came to a standstill, too, caught in profile, her head turned to stare at him. His curiosity about her breasts was finally satisfied. Neither small nor large, they were nonetheless round and ripe, pink nipples puckered from the cold. Legs, long and slim, extended downward until they disappeared into the wooden tub. Thick golden hair, darker from the water, hung to her knees, clung to her skin like a web.

He was no longer cold. Warmth pumped through him and his loins tightened with arousal. He was aware he stared, mouth slightly ajar, but was powerless to stop. She turned away, trying to hide her body from him, but it only gave him a view of her bottom, round and lovely, curving upward into a narrow waist and back. Her skin was fine and unblemished, flushed from the hot water.

They were not alone. She whispered to a maid who came forward with a bath linen held out as she stepped from the tub. He shook off the strange stupor and moved into the room, closing the door behind him.

Swaddled in the linen sheet, Caroline turned to him. "The water is still hot, my lord."

Robert gestured at the maid to leave. She hurried from the room. He shrugged out of his jack, dropping it on the floor. Caroline approached him and he held himself very still, barely daring to breathe. Movement might frighten her. When she reached him, she bent down, one hand poking out of the shrouding linen, and grabbed his jack.

"Don't want to leave it there. I suspect the rushes are infested with fleas."

The breath he'd been holding whooshed out of him. What had he expected? To be seduced by a nun? He watched her, disappointed, as she hung the jack over the back of a chair, gathered some clothes, and headed for the screen at the other end of the room. She paused, peering cautiously behind the screen before disappearing from sight.

Robert sat on the bed and pulled his boots off. Interrogating the prisoner had suddenly lost appeal. He'd much rather stay here. He was untying his shirt when Caroline yelped. She backed rapidly out from behind the screen, wearing nothing but a thin shift of lawn. She held her ribs as though they pained her.

"What is it?" he asked, coming to stand beside her.

"Just a rat—but it surprised me."

Robert's lip curled. Annancreag was not without its share of vermin, but he made certain they didn't reside in his chambers. "We need a cat," he said, turning his attention to her hands. He placed his hand over hers, where she clutched herself. "Are you hurt?"

She jerked away. "I'm fine, my lord."

"You've no need to fear me, Caroline, I'll not hurt you."

"I'm not afraid," she said and this time her calm was forced. "Might I see your sword?"

Her request conjured all manner of bawdy images in his head that she had obviously not intended. He held up his hands. "There's no need to hold me off at sword point."

She smiled—that empty yet polite curve of her lips he was coming to hate. "I need it to kill the rat."

Determination to coax a true smile from her compelled him to say, "Step aside!" He drew his sword and advanced on the screen. "Let it not be said my wife is forced to slay her own beasts."

Behind the screen a single candle burned. A closestool was in the corner along with a jar of clean water and a towel. Her velvet dressing gown was mounded on the floor. He poked at it with the tip of his sword. It squeaked.

"Orpheus advances on the ferocious beast," he said. "Careful, though, not to look back—for if he catches sight of his beloved Eurydice, all will be lost." He was encouraged by the lovely sound of soft laughter behind him. "Would that I had Perseus's shield, so I might look upon my love in its reflection." He reached down and yanked the gown, tossing it haphazardly behind him. "No—I mustn't look—must slay the beast!"

A rather pathetic foe, the rat was little more than skin and bones, covered in bald spots. Robert dispatched it swiftly, but dramatically, and tossed it from the room. When he turned back to Caroline, he wondered if he'd imagined her laughter. "The beast is slain and my lady is not disappeared. All is well in Camelot."

She smiled again, her eyes crinkling and bright. "You have your stories confused, my lord." He thought he caught a glimpse of a dimple denting one cheek, but it was gone before he could be certain.

He sheathed his sword. "And you are a most defiant woman."

"My lord?"

"Did I not ask you to address me as Robert?"

She bent to pick up the dressing gown. A curtain of wet hair slid down to conceal her expression. He longed to kiss her, to make her his wife in deed. She straightened, holding the gown to her breast. "Robert. Does that please you?"

"Aye."

Her eyes were luminous in the dim candlelight. She looked like a girl, a young and innocent lass, sweet, untouched. He took several steps toward her. She did not retreat.

"Are you afraid of me?" he asked when less than an arm's length separated them.

"No."

He searched her face for signs of emotion. Nothing. She was a statue, cold as marble and just as flawless. Frustration drove him to touch her, as he had yesterday. A fingertip, trailing a path down her jaw. Soft as a flower petal, warm with life. She didn't blink, didn't lower her eyes, her skin didn't flush.

His finger traveled to her chin where he gripped it lightly, sliding his thumb over her bottom lip. Her mouth thinned, sealing her lips against him. She breathed deeply, inhaling through her nose, but that was the only sign she was at all unsettled. He took another step, closing the distance between them, forcing her to tip her head back to keep eye contact. The scent of lavender teased him.

He opened his hand, spreading his fingers against her cheek. "I've not kissed my bride."

Her gaze dropped from his, to his mouth and back again, her eyes wide, wary. Her lips parted as if to speak, then closed again.

"Tell me when to stop," he whispered, lowering his head to kiss her.

She never took her eyes off him. Thick golden lashes lowered as if entranced, following the progress of his mouth. It inflamed him, this innocent curiosity, though he could not fathom why. His hand slid to her neck where her pulse beat wildly against his thumb.

His mouth hovered over hers, drawing in her warm breath, until he saw her lashes flutter shut. Then he kissed her. Her lips clamped together and she went rigid. Not very encouraging, but he wasn't giving up just yet. He pressed feathery kisses to the corners of her mouth.

"Caroline," he whispered against her mouth. "Has . . . anyone ever kissed you?"

Her eyes opened slowly and she shook her head. She strained away, turning her head. Her hands came up as though to ward him off. He slipped an arm around her waist, holding her fast.

"Don't run. What are you afraid of? It's just a kiss."

She met his gaze and he saw the obstinacy had returned. He smothered the smile threatening to break through and ruin the moment—she would not appreciate being laughed at, of that he was certain.

"I told you, I'm not afraid." She closed her eyes purposefully and lifted her head, giving him full access to her mouth.

He did smile then and ran a thumb over her bottom lip. "Part your lips." She did as he bid. Using his thumb, he tilted her chin up. So lovely, so brave. He brushed his lips against hers. She inhaled sharply, but didn't seal her lips against him. He kissed her softly, fully on the mouth. Her lips remained pliant and he kissed her again. This time she responded. Her kiss was innocent, unschooled, eager. And infinitely sweeter than anything he'd ever experienced.

He brought her body more fully against his, slid his hands over her hips. Her head turned without his instruction, to deepen the kiss. He heard himself groan—was afraid he'd frighten her—though he couldn't help himself. Her body grew yielding, melting against him. Her mouth was lush, soft, her kisses filled with naked desire. She operated on instinct now, as he did. Lust fogged his brain. He wanted to have her now, here—on the floor, in the bed, it didn't matter. He ground her hips against his and ran his tongue along her lips.

She turned her head away, her body stiffening. "Stop."

He drew back. He was breathing hard, clasping her to him. She twisted, trying to escape, but he was intent on finishing what he'd started. "Why? What are you afraid of?"

"You said I had only to tell you to stop—that's what you said."

His body clenched in frustration. Bloody hell, he wanted her! He exhaled loudly and took a step backward.

She was definitely in a panic, though trying to hide it. Her hand touched her swollen lips, eyeing him warily. She retrieved the dressing gown she had dropped, holding it in front of her, as if she could hide from him. He'd seen her and felt her—would remember every time he looked upon her. He couldn't speak, even to apologize for pawing her—but damn it—he wasn't sorry.

She walked to the fire where she slipped into the dressing gown. "You should use the water, while it's still hot." The cool tone was like a slap in the face. He frowned, trailing after her. He'd not been mistaken—she'd been aroused . . . or was she frightened?

He followed her, unbuckling his belt, confused and not liking it. He untied his shirt, pulling it from his breeches. "What if henceforth Maxwells and Grahams live together in harmony?"

She turned, a blond eyebrow, silvered from the firelight, arched slightly in question. "What if they don't, my lord? You promised to let me go."

Robert stared at her, hands on hips, irritation and need

surging through him. "And I will keep my promise." It infuriated him that she was so determined not to be married, to enter her convent, that she would not even give this a chance, give him a chance.

She put her back to him. "If this peace is successful, I will do all you require of me."

Require. The word reeked of resignation, force, empty duty. Not what he wanted. Agitated, Robert decided he no longer desired a bath. He retied his shirt, which was beginning to dry. At the bed, he shoved his feet into his boots.

"You wish not to bathe?" she asked, never leaving her station at the fireplace.

He gave her one of her own empty smiles, modeled after hers, though he suspected his contained more sarcasm than aught else. "I suspect another cold dousing is exactly what I need at the moment, Wife."

He slammed out of the room, taking dark pleasure in the sound. Maxwell had said he would be in the stables, so Robert left the keep and headed for the outbuildings.

Just outside the stable doors he paused, staring at the black sky as the rain braced him. He almost went back to her. Finally, he ducked into the warm stable. His anger had faded and reason returned. He'd been too eager, too forceful. It was obvious she'd never been kissed—perhaps never even been held. And she'd prepared all her life to enter a convent. She needed time to adjust. He must exercise patience.

Maxwell's voice could be heard farther down, talking to a servant. Closing his eyes, Robert breathed deeply, wishing for a Caroline-like calm, for nothing to affect him. But he could not detach himself from life—and she was his partner in life now. It was not her fault, he reminded himself. She made it clear she was not a willing participant in the union, that she was *unsuitable.* He opened his eyes, glared into the dim stable. A strong-willed and intelligent woman such as Caroline would never abandon her position easily. She must be brought around skillfully, carefully.

He laughed at himself; amazed he was expending so much thought on this. How could one woman agitate him so? Well, no more. He shook the rain from his hair and rejoined Maxwell.

Caroline pretended to be asleep when he returned. She'd lain awake for hours trying to pray, but unable; instead, thinking about what had happened. He'd been angry when he left—but he'd stopped kissing her when she asked him to. That was something. She was not completely powerless.

He moved about the room, undressing. Her first plan had been to take up the entire bed, lying in the middle, so when he returned he'd think there was no room and find a bed elsewhere. But when she thought about it, she realized that was too dangerous a game to play—just like her bravado earlier—practically daring him to kiss her. Fool!

She'd seen the heat in his eyes, felt its answer deep in her belly. Why had she let it go on so long? What if she'd let it go on longer? Would he have stopped then?

She huddled at the edge of the bed, hoping he would just go to sleep. This was no different from sleeping with Fayth. She'd been sharing a bed with her sister since they were little girls. After Father died, Mona had slept with them and it had been quite cramped, arms and legs everywhere. Nothing to it. Just like sleeping with family.

The bed shifted under Robert's weight. She cracked one eye. He'd blown out the candles and the room was black. She stared into the dark, listening to him move about beside her. What if he tried to kiss her again? Her belly knotted, warmth spreading through her. *Stop it!*

She put the memory from her mind. Mustn't think of it anymore. *That's* what had kept her awake—reliving his mouth on hers, marveling that he had a *taste*—something she would have never imagined—and wondering what would have happened if she'd allowed his tongue inside.

Finally, he became still.

Caroline closed her eyes, determined to sleep, and to her surprise, she did. She woke sometime later—the room was still dark. The shutters had been closed against the rain, so not even moonlight softened the blackness.

Something wasn't right. Sleeping with her sister, she'd often woke pressed up against a warm little body, especially on cold nights—or smashed between Fayth and Mona. But this was not like that. The body she pressed up against was not small or harmless. It was long and warm and solid. Robert.

He was asleep, she realized with relief. He breathed slow and deep, his heartbeat steady beneath her hand. Good Lord! He had no part of this—her head rested on his shoulder, her arm draped across his chest, her thigh bent on his. In fact, she felt his hand near hers, her breasts against his arm.

He was shirtless. His skin burned under her cheek. Her fingers itched to stroke the crisp hair beneath them. She didn't move, contemplating what to do. She was comfortable and what if she woke him by moving?

More foolish thoughts. What if he woke and assumed too much? Her imagination conjured images of being wrapped in his strong arms, tasting his lips again.

In one move, she rolled away, back to her edge of the bed. Her cheeks flamed, and she burned again, deep in her belly. She wanted to be away from this turmoil. To live in a convent where she could read and write and be with like minds. It wasn't fair he did this to her, made her feel this way. This . . . wanting—it fed on itself and grew. To him it was a game and once he won, he would move on to the next challenge, while she lost everything.

And still there would be the wanting. She vowed to herself that she would not lose.

8

Caroline's knees hurt, her shoulders ached and her mind was woolly, but she remained immobile, hands clasped in prayer, eyes fixed on the wooden statue of the Virgin. Lochmaben's small chapel, more of an alcove, really, equipped with candles and statue, was cold and quiet. Water dripped somewhere. A flame sputtered. Caroline knelt on the stone floor—as a nun she would be expected to mortify herself in worse ways than this, or so Father Jasper had told her. Pain and deprivation would bring her closer to God. And that was what she wanted . . . wasn't it? To devote her life to God and learning?

Yes, yes! She squeezed her eyes shut, trying to will away the other thoughts that churned through her mind. *Must clear mind for prayer.* But it was so difficult. She'd never been good at worship. She did try, but always her mind would drift on to other things, and before she knew it, she would be contemplating Lancelot and Guinevere, rather than the Lord.

She'd lain in bed, unable to sleep for fear of waking again, draped across him. She'd finally risen early, while he still slept. After looking upon his sleeping face—so peaceful and achingly beautiful—for an unseemly amount of time, she'd sought out a sanctuary where she could pray for answers. And here she knelt, on a freezing stone floor and still all she could think of was Robert. *Lord Annan!* Not Robert! She must stop thinking of him in such familiar terms. *Must pray.*

Her body was cramped with exhaustion and hunger. Instead of feeling closer to God, she was cranky and annoyed, unable to stop the errant thoughts from possessing her mind. Her stomach growled sullenly, her knees were numb, the muscles in her arms trembled with fatigue from holding them clasped in prayer. How much longer must she kneel? The discomfort was unbearable. She wanted to cry with frustration. Was this really the life of a nun?

She was no longer certain she wanted this—but the alternative was unbearable. If she gave in to lust it would be over so quickly; he would tire of her and she would be forced to endure his dalliances with other women, watch his bastards spring up all over the castle and be powerless to say or do a thing about it. He would visit her only to get heirs on her. She would weep endlessly until the tears were gone, then sit in the solar, making tapestries, the words and tears dried up . . . until she died, releasing everyone from the misery of her presence. Oh, she understood her mother now.

Never would she become her mother! There were no real happy endings. Giving in to Robert would kill the beauty she saw in everything, deaden her mind, shrivel her heart. Would children even be a comfort, as she'd once thought? They'd never comforted her mother. Had Mother ever loved Father? According to Father Jasper, she'd tried to. Was it loving, or trying to love that killed her heart, her mind? Caroline regretted never trying to talk to her mother about it, never asking her—but Mother had been a shell, the spirit and life fled long before the body gave out.

Caroline lowered her arms with a sigh of relief and slouched. "Ahh . . ." That was enough for today. *Must work on self-discipline.* She would speak with Father Jasper as soon as they returned to Annancreag. He would advise her how to live as a proper nun, how to fight lust— for though Father Jasper was a priest, he was a man, too, and must have learned how to deny himself the pleasures of the flesh. Or did those who gave themselves to God simply not experience lust? But no, that wasn't true— everyone knew of the wicked priests and the corrupt monasteries. That was why King Henry closed them. But surely they couldn't all be bad?

More questions for Father Jasper. *Must try to read the lives of the saints again.* She'd tried to read them on numerous occasions but always fell asleep, or found her mind wandering. Sir Thomas Malory's tales of King Arthur were much more interesting . . .

She started to stand, her legs protesting painfully, when she heard footsteps. She hesitated, then recognized the prowling gait of her husband. She resumed her position of prayer. Perhaps if he saw her this way he would stop seeing her as a potential bed partner and begin regarding her as a nun.

The footsteps stopped at the door of the alcove. Her eyes remained fixed on the Virgin, trying to pray, but instead listening to the silence with growing dread. What was he doing? Was he just standing there, staring at her? She was startled to hear movement to her right. She hadn't heard him leave the doorway. He knelt beside her. She didn't look at him. She prayed with renewed effort, trying to block out his scent, her acute awareness of his proximity. He didn't touch her, and yet, his very nearness was a subtle caress to her senses.

After several minutes of silence, he whispered, "What do you pray for?"

She blinked, her mind blank. What *was* she praying for? "For . . . the Lord to show me the way."

"Hmmm . . ." Silence again. He shifted restlessly. "Has He? Shown you the way?"

"No."

"Where do you want to go?"

"What?" She lowered her hands to frown at him. He looked much more rested than she was. Dark whiskers shadowed his jaw. His clothes, though dry now, were wrinkled, but his gray eyes were bright and unfatigued. Unlike Caroline. The thought brought forth a wave of resentment that she was the only one losing sleep over this. It was naught but sport to him.

"Where do you want to go?" he asked again.

She shook her head, turning her attention back to the statue, trying to focus on it, to see the Virgin in it. Instead, she saw garish paint and wood, warped and cracking from the damp air. It was an ugly piece, really, shameful that she prayed to it. Perhaps a more beautiful Virgin would facilitate prayer. "I don't understand."

"You said you want the Lord to show you the way. The way to where?"

He was being difficult. He knew what she meant.

"I wish Him to reveal His . . . plan to me. What He wants me to do."

He made a thoughtful noise and shifted about some more. "Has He told you yet?"

Caroline closed her eyes. "I just said no."

"No—I mean, since then, because I don't hear anything."

Caroline fought the smile that threatened to curve her lips. This was not amusing! He was being blasphemous! She should not see humor in his words. The effort not to laugh, however, was great. He had forced laughter from her last night, with his silly parody of Orpheus. It had been a fine moment—she truly liked Robert and did wish they could be friends, but her laughter obviously encouraged him to touch her, to try to kiss her. She feared if he kissed her again, she would be lost. Her belly fluttered at the memory that a *man* could have such a fine taste . . .

Mortified at the direction of her thoughts, she said, "No, my lord, it is difficult to listen with my inner ear when you're yammering in the outer one."

"Oh, forgive me." He wasn't apologetic. This was a jest to him. She felt cross again and focused harder. She must prove to him how important worship was to her. After a moment he asked, "Where exactly is an inner ear?"

Caroline dropped her arms in defeat. She started to stand, but he was on his feet first, taking her arm and helping her.

"I've distracted you from your prayer."

She pulled her arm away. "Methinks that was your plan."

He shrugged, giving her a sheepish grin that made him wince. The side of his face that had been turned away from her was injured. Dried blood caked a cut at the corner of his mouth and his right eye was discolored.

"Have you been fighting?"

"Well . . . aye." He touched his bruised eye, grimacing.

"Did you start it? Or did he hit you in an attempt to silence you?" She clamped her lips shut, struggling to control her sharp tongue. It had been a problem in her youth, but she'd long since stopped saying the first thought that popped into her mind. Now, however, agitated beyond anything she had experienced before, her iron control slipped.

Robert took no offense—he seemed delighted with her sarcasm. She was showing weakness and, as a man, it gave him power. He already had too much power; she must not let him know it. She swept past him before he could answer, then chastised herself. That wasn't it, either. She should have listened to him as though she really didn't care! *Too late now.* This was what came from lack of planning. From this moment forward there would be no eventuality she wouldn't prepare for.

He fell into step beside her as she made her way to the great hall. He offered no explanation of the beating he had sustained, which increased her self-annoyance—she desperately wanted to know why he'd been fighting.

A sideboard was set up in the hall. Caroline went to it but stood back, allowing Robert to fill a plate for them both. His hand hovered over a bowl of fruit.

"No strawberries," he said, and chose a pear.

They joined Lord Maxwell at the table on the dais. Caroline masked her impatience as Robert sliced the pear. Her stomach ached with hunger. He took his time, chatting with the warden. She was reaching surreptitiously for a piece of cheese when the warden said, "Prithee, accept my apologies about last night. I would have flogged him myself had you not administered such a sound thrashing."

"Who, my lord?" Caroline asked.

Robert shook his head, pushing the pewter plate between them. " 'Tis naught, a minor altercation. Don't trouble yourself."

The warden made a scoffing noise. "Och—such modesty! It's unbecoming! This is the way to woo your bride, tell how you leaped to her defense, defending her honor."

Robert had stopped slicing the pear. His hands were

fisted on the table, his eyes locked on the warden. "It's of no interest to her, my lord."

The warden seemed to finally understand that Robert was not being modest. "Verra well," he said briskly. "I'll draft that letter today and send it to the king—"

"I do wish to hear how my lord leaped to my defense," Caroline said.

Maxwell opened his mouth hesitantly, his gaze darting to Robert, who had gone rigid beside her. She glanced at her husband. The shake of his head was nearly imperceptible, but Caroline caught it. She placed a staying hand on his sleeve. His attention immediately focused on her.

"Please, Lord Warden, I want to know."

The warden sighed. "Sorry, Annan, I've never been one to say no to a lass—especially one as comely as yours."

Caroline barely managed not to roll her eyes at the ridiculous lie.

The warden leaned back in his chair, rubbing a hand over his large belly, letting it come to rest wedged under his belt. "Well . . . last night we questioned the prisoner till late. My master of the guard, Duff, though a good enough lad, thinks himself something of a wit. We'd just come up from the cellars, where the Armstrong scut is currently rotting until I decide what to do with him. I offered your husband a dram afore he retired, then immediately thought better of it and told him to go to his bride, as you were keeping the bed warm for him." He raised censorious eyebrows. "Annan opted for the whiskey. As we were walking to my chambers, Duff said—"

"What Duff said is of no import," Robert said.

Caroline realized her hand was still on his arm. The muscles were hard and tense beneath her palm. She quickly removed her hand, folding both hands together in her lap. "I should like to know what Duff said."

"No," Robert said firmly.

The warden nodded. "Aye, lassie, your husband is right, it's not worth repeating. Let's just say he . . . slandered your surname. And that was it—Annan here lit into him." He shrugged. "There you have it."

Caroline lowered her gaze to the slices of pear on the plate before her. Her piercing hunger had disappeared, replaced with a strange queasiness. *Slandered your surname.* She was not stupid. Duff had done more than insult the Grahams—he had probably insulted *her.* And Robert trounced him for it.

Her heart throbbed too hard, too fast—in her ears and throat, and she feared she would be ill. She wanted to speak, to assure them somehow she was not troubled by name calling, but if she spoke, it would open a floodgate. Instead, she forced her hand upward, lifting a slice of pear to her lips. What must he think, having to defend his wife constantly? Surely he would soon tire of it, perhaps even begin agreeing that she was a dray horse, manly, a hag.

"You should not brawl on my account, my lord," she heard herself saying. "I've told you before such things trouble me not."

After a moment of uncomfortable silence, Robert said, "What do you plan to do with the Armstrong?"

"I'm certain Wharton is paying them to raid our lands, to weaken us in preparation for an English invasion. I'll dunk him a few times—if he still doesn't confess, I'll drown him."

Caroline's thoughts turned inward and Robert didn't speak to her again. Why had he defended her? She'd been thinking of herself all along—how difficult this union was for her. But this could not be easy for him either. Resisting him was surely the best thing for them both, she told herself, even as her chest ached. The sooner he realized what an unsuitable wife she was, the better.

It was late when they arrived at Annancreag. Robert disappeared immediately. Celia waited for Caroline in the bedchamber.

"Shall I help you undress, my lady?" Celia's manner was subdued, her tone respectful, but her blue eyes simmered.

"Yes." Caroline unhooked her bodice as Celia removed a night rail from the trunk. "Is it just me you hate, or all Grahams?"

Celia started, whirling around to stare at Caroline, wide-eyed. "My lady?"

"It will be easier for us if I understand where our difficulties lie—if it's something I can remedy, or if it's part of this ridiculous feud."

Celia clutched the night rail tightly. "Your father murdered my husband."

"I did not know."

Celia approached her. "And now you're here, his spawn, ingratiating yourself to Lord Annan. It will be just like before—you'll open us wide for massacre!"

"I will do no such thing," Caroline said, handing her bodice to Celia. She tried for patience. Celia had been raised on this blood feud, just as she had. She'd lost a man to the hate—just as Fayth had. Caroline couldn't expect her to just forget. She turned so Celia could unlace her stays.

"As if a Graham's word means aught." Celia yanked violently at the ties.

"Your husband's death is the result of this feud. Maxwells have killed as many Grahams as Grahams have Maxwells. And who is truly to blame?" Caroline slipped out of her stays. "This blood feud goes back generations.

That is where the blame lies, not with me—or even my brother. He endeavors to end the bloodshed. That *is* why I'm here."

"Aye, and Grahams haven't changed a bit since then!"

Caroline held her kirtle out to Celia. Celia grabbed it and tried to rip it from Caroline's hands, but she held tight, sick of her maid's surliness. Caroline gave the kirtle a yank and Celia stumbled toward her.

"There are worse duties to perform than being a lady's maid. Continue this insubordination and you will discover some of them."

Celia's mouth opened in indignation, but then her eyes traveled over Caroline's greater size. "Lord Annan would never allow it," she said, but there was a quaver in her voice.

She was probably right and this infuriated Caroline. Let Robert try and forbid it—if there was one thing Caroline did well it was manage households and people. And she intended to manage Celia. Celia seemed to read the determination in her face because she stepped back, swallowing hard. Caroline released the kirtle and turned away.

She pulled her shift over her head and replaced it with the heavy night rail. "How do you know the Grahams haven't changed? I would think everyone involved is dead."

Celia sniffed, tamed for now, her arms loaded with Caroline's discarded garments. "Agnes—from in the kitchen—still lives." Celia dumped Caroline's clothes on the bed and began to fold them. "Then there's Sandy in the stables—both were bairns when it occurred. They were spared, though their parents were murdered."

Caroline unpinned her hair thoughtfully. The heavy braid fell against her back. Perhaps she could interview these survivors of the massacre and discover the truth. There must be some other way to end the feud than marriage because judging by Celia and the other Maxwells' behavior this union was worthless. Even if she won over the household servants, how could she possibly gain the trust of every other Maxwell? But perhaps truth could succeed where diplomacy failed.

Celia finished putting away Caroline's clothes. "Is there aught else I can do for you, my lady?"

"Yes. Please send Father Jasper to the solar."

Celia left, eyes downcast, probably to hide the boiling resentment. Caroline retreated to her withdrawing room. Her few personal items rested atop a cabinet. She was crossing the room to retrieve her sewing when she noticed a piece of furniture that hadn't been there yesterday.

A desk, situated beneath the slit window. Tall iron candleholders flanked it and more candlesticks burned on the desktop. She circled it, trailing her finger along the sturdy oak. A carved bench was behind it with an embroidered and tasseled pillow on its flat surface. Though the desk and bench were well made and attractive in the fine, utilitarian fashion of Annancreag's other furniture, this was not what drew her attention, arrested her breath.

A book, bound in leather, rested in the center of the desktop. Beside it were quill, inkpot, and sand. Tentatively, she touched the book, first with her fingertips, then smoothing her palm over it. An odd lump in her throat made swallowing difficult. She sat on the padded bench, staring down at the book. She opened it.

Dearest Caroline, Record here all your happy endings. Robert

She couldn't blink—afraid if she did, the words would vanish. But then they began to blur and she pursed her lips, then bit them, to force the foolish dampness to recede. She had no idea how long she stared at her husband's brief message, but when the urge came over her to touch his words, she looked up, to be sure no one witnessed it.

Father Jasper stood in the doorway, watching her.

Caroline closed the book abruptly and stood. "Father?"

He entered the room. "You sent for me?"

She stared at him dumbly until it came flooding back—advice on being a proper nun . . . "Yes, I did." She came around the desk, but he swept past her and picked up the book.

"What is this?"

"Nothing—a gift."

He turned the book over in his hands, opened it to the middle where smooth blank pages begged for words. "A very fine gift. From your husband?"

"Yes."

He opened it to the first page and read the inscription. To her surprise, the priest's mouth turned up in a wistful smile. He closed the book, his palm resting upon it thoughtfully.

"It is unseemly," Caroline said, wanting to break the uncomfortable silence. "I shouldn't write such frivolous things."

Father Jasper returned the book to the desktop and turned to contemplate her, hands clasped in front of him. "Why?"

"Because . . . if I write, it should be things worthy of reading . . . perhaps devotions for women . . . something useful . . ." Father Jasper regarded her in such an odd manner, as if he knew some secret she didn't. "That is why I summoned you. I should be writing the things nuns write—to prepare myself. Tell me what I must do."

Father Jasper let out a long breath. "Caroline, my dear . . . you have been blessed with an indulgent husband. Do not persist in this folly, you've never been suitable for the cloister."

Stunned, Caroline said, "But you are the one who suggested—"

"I know, I know—forget all that."

Caroline let out another astounded breath. "How can I? You've been preparing me for years . . . I've had my heart set on it!"

Father Jasper gave her a skeptical smile. "Have you really? I find that difficult to believe. Please, recite for me the principal virtues."

"Er . . . Faith . . . that is be—have! very belief in God . . ." She couldn't remember the rest of Faith. "Oh! Hope—steadfast hope in God's mercy . . . and uh . . . charity. . . ." She kept her eyes downcast, searching for the correct words. There were seven virtues, she should know them, but her mind was blank.

"Oh, stop," Father Jasper said. "You see? All the while I've been preparing you, you've been spinning tales of knights and maidens in your head."

"Forgive me, Father . . . I know I've been lax in my studies, but I *will* work harder—"

Father Jasper placed gentle hands on her shoulders. "No, child, you are not at fault."

Caroline looked up into his kind face. Until Lord Annan, his was the only face she'd ever looked up to since becoming a giant at the age of fourteen.

"Monasticism is not for everyone. Certainly many of us turn to God for reasons other than great faith, but Lord Annan will be good to you. See what marriage has to offer."

Caroline shook her head, desperate now. "No, Father—you don't understand! I cannot bear it—Mother, she—"

Father Jasper's gaze sharpened. He dropped his hands from her shoulders. "What has your mother to do with this?"

"I don't want to end up that way, like Mother."

The priest looked old suddenly, his face lined with years of grief and suffering.

"You knew her . . . before—tell me, what made her turn from life?"

He moved away, put his back on her. "Yes, I knew your mother . . . before."

"Was it love that killed her heart?" Father Jasper's shoulders hunched, but he didn't answer. Caroline went to him. "Father?" She laid a hand on his arm. "What is it?"

His long thin fingers covered hers. He looked into her face, searching. "You're like her, you know."

"That's what frightens me . . . that I'll be like her. Tell me about her. Please."

Father Jasper sighed deeply. Hands folded behind his back, he crossed the room, circling the desk, to stare out the darkened window. "I was assigned to the scriptorium at the abbey when Hugh Graham sent word that he needed a priest . . . his wife was dying. I was the logical choice to send, being a relation of Lord Graham. However, there was a friar residing temporarily at the abbey, Father Ambrose—from Florence. I was much in awe of him. Though my life was devoted to the Lord, I longed to travel and see the world as he did. Since he was preparing to leave, with no destination in mind, he volunteered to attend Lady Graham in her final hours. Father Ambrose was a . . . perceptive man"—Father Jasper turned slightly away from the window, a faraway smile curving his thin lips—"and knew I longed for something more. He thought the life of a friar would suit me and so invited me to join him—which is how I found myself at Graham Keep."

He fell silent, eyes downcast.

"But you didn't stay," Caroline prompted. "You and

Father Ambrose. You were only there a few months, then left . . . it was years before you returned—why?"

He nodded, still not looking at her. "Your mother was dying in childbirth . . . she had sustained many miscarriages. Ridley was a strong and healthy lad—he was nine years at the time, but Lord Graham was displeased with him, always finding fault in the boy." He shook his head sadly. "Your mother wanted to give him another son . . ."

Father Jasper put his back to her. "What is it?" Caroline went to his side. "Did she love Father? He was cruel to her?"

His mouth was flat, as if holding in some great emotion. "She wanted to love Lord Graham . . . and in a way, she did . . . but it was borne of awe more than tender feelings. Hugh Graham was powerful and handsome and fearsome. She always saw him as her knight, tried for many years to ignore his blatant mistresses . . . but it became difficult when he would accost serving wenches in her presence."

Caroline nodded with distaste. She knew exactly what Father Jasper spoke of, had witnessed her father acting in such a boorish manner. Even the presence of his young daughters did nothing to improve his behavior. He'd once slapped a servant who protested at him slipping his hand in her bodice in front of the children.

"Father Ambrose was not only a fine priest, but a skilled healer. He saved your mother's life. We stayed for a time—Lord Graham liked Father Ambrose, he had many tales to tell, and in fact, attempted to secure him as the castle's chaplain. In those months, your mother and I became friends."

"Yes," Caroline said eagerly. "What did she tell you, about marriage, about love?" He only shook his head. He started to retreat, but Caroline caught his arm. "Father Jasper, what is it?"

His face, so very dear to her, was strained and gray, his green eyes bright. "You are so very much like her, Caroline. She was a clever woman, full of wit . . . but downtrodden from Lord Graham's treatment . . . the beauty and life that filled her were slipping away, even then . . ."

"If you were her friend . . . why did you leave? Surely she needed friends desperately."

"It was a mistake." The sadness left his face, replaced with a grim determination she had rarely seen. "I will not make another such mistake. You have given me much to think on."

He started to leave, but Caroline caught his arm again. "What do you mean?"

"Lord Annan appears to be nothing like Lord Graham, but perhaps there's more to this than I comprehend." He regarded Caroline for a long time, as if he weren't seeing her, but someone else. "It is too soon for love to have grown between you and Lord Annan . . . but do you think you could love him?"

Caroline crossed her arms at her waist. "I don't want to love any man." When Father Jasper just frowned reproachfully, she added, "He has a mistress—Celia, my maid." And with an uncharacteristic burst of emotion, cried, "Can you believe he made his mistress my maid!"

Father Jasper's face grew grimmer still. "I did not know this." He sighed, looking heavenward. "Continue on as you have been. We will speak again soon. I will pray for an answer."

Seconds after he swept from the room a woman scratched at the door frame. "My lady?"

Caroline took a deep breath, composing herself. Her conversation with Father Jasper had left her confused and unhappy. "Yes?"

"I've brought ye some water to wash wi' and turned down the bed."

Caroline started to dismiss the woman, then asked, "Where is Celia?"

"Och, I'm yer maid now—Lord Annan just informed me."

Caroline dismissed her. This could have nothing do with what she just told Father Jasper. Even if the priest had approached Robert, there hadn't been time enough to make new arrangements. Besides—that was not what she wanted and Father Jasper would know that. Celia must learn her place. Caroline paced the empty room. Why had Robert replaced Celia? Did Celia ask to be removed? Because she hated Caroline? Why had he not consulted with Caroline, at least? She would never gain the servants' respect or obedience if they could change duties at will! Or did he do it because Celia was his mistress? Perhaps he had need of her this evening and her duties interfered with his pleasure!

The idea of that woman having such power enraged Caroline. Palms pressed against her hot cheeks, she tried to will the strong emotions away. She'd spent so many years working for calm, for serenity. Even if she couldn't achieve it inwardly, she'd managed the outward appearance and often, the knowledge she controlled how others perceived her was a soothing balm in itself, giving her rare power. That power was whittled away every moment she spent with Robert. She must regain control—must keep control until Father Jasper could advise her.

Plan. She would speak calmly to her husband, explain the importance of Celia remaining her maid—at least until she could get the woman's behavior in hand; for Celia to get her way now would only reinforce future insubordination. Caroline would offer to allow Celia to retire early, so it didn't interfere with his *plans*. A picture of Robert formed in her head—his incredible length bent over Celia, kissing her. An ugly stab of jealousy seared her. What did she care? She would not lie with him—let him take his pleasure elsewhere!

When she realized she stalked angrily about the room, she came to a standstill. *Deep breaths.* She closed her eyes, clearing her mind of all thoughts. Her heart slowed. The heat receded from her face. *There.* Under control again, she entered the bedchamber. The door to Robert's chamber was open a crack and she heard movement within. Purposefully, she strode to the door, meaning only to shut it, when she heard Celia's voice. Her hand froze on the latch. She didn't want to hear this, to know this, but was unable to resist.

"My lord," Celia was saying, "you must rest, you're weary and hurt."

He didn't answer. Rest from what? How was he exerting himself? All manner of sordid images flashed through Caroline's mind until she became aware of an insistent scratching sound. She identified it as a quill scratching against parchment.

"Robert," Celia purred. "If your marriage bed is cold—"

"That will be all," he said curtly.

"But—"

"That will be all." Louder this time.

"Verra well," Celia murmured and seconds later the door clicked open and shut.

Caroline didn't move, frowning to herself. The scratching continued, but it was different from when she wrote. This wasn't the rapid scrape of pen across paper, but slow and laborious. The statement! She hadn't thought of it since their wedding night. She must not forget!

Caroline hesitated and finally knocked. The writing stopped. She almost waited for admittance to be granted until she remembered she was his wife and should simply enter.

He stood behind the desk. He hadn't changed or washed. "Caroline?"

"There is a matter I should like to discuss with you."

"Aye?"

"You've replaced my maid."

His gaze was steady. "Aye."

She moved closer, wanting a glimpse of what he wrote. "Unless a servant has personally offended you, I feel it's inappropriate for you to dismiss her without consulting me."

He looked at the desktop, tapping the quill pensively.

"Has she offended you?"

"Not exactly. I think she is ill suited. And she is to be wed soon."

"I don't agree. I think, with a bit of discipline, she will work out splendidly. And her daughter can take over when she leaves."

He nodded reluctantly.

"Please ask her to resume her duties in the morn."

"As you wish."

With that out of the way, she would broach the subject of the statement. Since she still hadn't written it, she wasn't certain how to bring it up. Perhaps she could ask for a piece of parchment and compose it immediately.

"Is that all?" he asked, when she didn't leave.

The book she'd read to him on their wedding night rested on the corner of his desk. "Have you been reading?"

He shook his head, sighing. "I meant to—but I don't think I'll be getting to it tonight." He sat back in the chair, dipped the quill in the inkpot, and brought it to the parchment, where it hovered. When he finally began to write again it was slow and awkward, though the letters produced were passable. It would take him all night to write one letter!

"Have you not a secretary?"

He shook his head, never looking up from his work. "A good scribe is hard to come by. Few are learned, and those who are, read better than they write." He shrugged. " 'Tis easier this way—at least until I find someone I can trust, no simple task—a lettered *and* trustworthy servant."

It didn't look easier. He was working very hard and very diligently. Her mind at war, she toyed with the book until he looked up.

She gave him a small smile. "I write very well. I would be happy to draft letters for you."

As he stared at her, she tried to fathom his expression, but it was impossible. Her pulse raced as she waited for his response. Her palms grew damp. Finally, he shook his head. "My thanks, but it isn't necessary." And he bent back to his letter—an obvious dismissal.

She might be lettered, but apparently, she didn't qualify as trustworthy. She backed away from his desk. "Good evening, then," she said, and hurried from the room, statement forgotten.

9

As the days passed, Robert found marriage to Caroline, even without the intimacy, agreeable. He would even hazard to say he was content as he'd never been. He had much to do and so saw little of her during the day, but in the evenings she shared a meal with him, either in the hall or in their chambers, and afterward, she read to him. And sometimes, if not too tired, they would play chess or cards. They talked of many things—politics, theology (she was not as well versed as he would have thought)—but mostly they discussed the book they read. She put far more thought into the stories than he did and had opinions on every aspect. Opinions he often disagreed with, just to be difficult.

And then there were the nights. . . . He didn't know if he could bear another night of lying awake while she pressed against him like a kitten. She didn't know she did it, of course, which was why he restrained himself. When he came to bed, she was invariably huddled at the edge, asleep—or pretending to be. But before long, she was all over the bed. He wasn't used to sleeping with another person and so it he kept him awake. And mad with want and indecision. He'd fought with himself—wanting to take her in the realm between sleep and wakefulness—make her statement worthless. But he wanted her willing and aware—a partner, not a victim.

Robert put down the quill and flexed his hand. Never adept at writing, it had become worse after hitting Duff at Lochmaben—his hand was still sore. He'd thought perhaps he'd broken it, but as he could move all the fingers, it seemed not. Nevertheless, tasks requiring his right hand had become difficult. Writing most of all. And so it was that he spent far too much time in his chambers, bent over his desk, squinting in the candlelight.

"I feel like a toadstool," he muttered to himself, running a weary hand over his face. He leaned back in his chair, stretching. His master of guard was seeing to the men's training, and Caroline had control—grudgingly given—over the household. He had rents to collect and patrols of his land to conduct, but none of that could be done until he'd written these damn letters. The one he currently drafted concerned his brother, Patrick, as well as the tocher Caroline brought to the marriage. It included an estate in the debatable land, a sizable head of kine, and several hundred pounds sterling.

There had been no word from Patrick, nor had Robert received the deed to the property, or anything else from Ridley. It had been over a week, time enough for Wesley to return home and for Patrick to be released. Robert currently composed a letter to Lord Graham, inquiring as to the disposition of these items. He wanted to be reasonable—mishaps occurred frequently on the March. Perhaps Wesley had been waylaid? Or Patrick, for that matter. Maybe Ridley was displeased with the handfasting? Diplomacy was still in order.

Staring at the candle's flame, he thought again of Caroline's offer to write for him. He looked down at his hand, slightly swollen and cramped from the strain. God, he wanted her help. Needed it. It would make his life much easier, as well as finish his current task swiftly so he could finally leave the stifling air of this room. But if she were not all she claimed he could not allow her access to his correspondence.

It had been a week since she'd brought him the carefully worded statement. He'd signed his name to the effect that consummation had not taken place, that it had been faked on their wedding night for the purposes of securing Sir Patrick Maxwell's release. He didn't like it, but he'd promised. And now, it loomed between them, this statement. It made her motives even more suspect. Whatever happened, so long as she remained a virgin (even if she didn't, she could lie) she could wiggle out of this marriage as if it had never been.

No, he didn't like it at all—regretted agreeing to it.

Robert returned to his work, scowling down at the parchment. She distracted him even when she wasn't present. He wanted out—needed out—and yet these letters must be written, correspondence must be answered, accounts must be kept. Lord Maxwell had made him deputy warden, yet more correspondence was coming his way. He would soon be submerged in parchment and ink, for he could not keep up with it all.

There was a knock on the door. He threw down the quill, welcoming the distraction. Before he could grant admittance, the door opened. *Caroline.* He smiled. She brought him no complaints, handled every problem that arose on her own—much to the household's dismay. According to Celia, she'd started in the kitchens, interrogating Cook on how things were currently done. Lists of supplies had been drawn up and menus designed. New instructions for cooking, cleaning, and storage were given—when they weren't carried out immediately, she did them herself. This spurred the kitchen staff into action—Robert would have been displeased to know his wife was forced to perform such menial tasks, and well they knew it. She organized all the children currently living in the keep and the surrounding village to attend morning lessons three times a week, conducted by her priest. She also put her priest to saying Mass every morning and forcing the castle's inhabitants to attend. The food left over from meals was distributed to the poor, along with various other alms she felt it her duty to provide. Everything, down to the exercise of Robert's sleuth dogs, was now scheduled and carried out under her direction.

"My lord husband?"

"Aye?"

Caroline swept across the room, a leather packet in her hands. Cool and composed as always, she stopped in front of his desk. "A messenger from my brother has arrived. He's taking refreshment in the hall. Have you any correspondence you wish to send back with him?"

Robert straightened, holding out his hand for the packet. "Aye, I do—but let me read these first." Perhaps there was news of Patrick within. The packet was light, which told him the coin portion of her tocher had not arrived either. He untied the packet and opened it, but paused when she didn't leave. After accomplishing her goal, she never tarried—she was far too busy reorganizing his household. "Is there anything else?"

She smiled: empty, placid. "My things—books, gowns, some furniture, bedding, other such possessions—were to be sent along after me. I would have expected them to arrive by now. I wonder if there is a letter for me or if Ridley makes any mention of when they might arrive."

Robert removed several letters, sealed with wax. No deed to Caroline's estates. He knew his displeasure was apparent when Caroline asked, "What is it?"

"Aye, there are three letters for you." He handed them to her and she shuffled through them, her smile softening.

There was only one letter for Robert. He broke the seal and stared incredulously at the familiar scrawl. He had seen it far too many times in the past months and thought it was at an end. "I cannot believe this."

Caroline lowered her letters. "What is it?"

"This!" He stood, shaking the parchment at her.

She came around the desk and took it from him, scanning the contents briefly. When she looked back at him, she frowned as deeply as he did. "Why, it's a bill for Sir Patrick's upkeep."

"Aye—why has he not been released? Why am I still paying for his imprisonment—and look at this rubbish! New doublet and hose? Twenty pounds! This is most unlike Patrick—something smells foul."

Caroline stared at the letter for a long time before setting it gingerly on the desk.

"Can you explain this to me?" he asked.

Her face cleared, becoming tranquil once more. "No, my lord, I cannot."

Robert snatched her letters off the desk. "I will read these first."

She said nothing, but her eyes narrowed as she averted them. Had he angered her? Good—he was incensed. The sum requested for Patrick's maintenance was larceny! What games did Ridley play? If she knew anything, he vowed he would discover it.

He broke the seals of the letters and slowly read

them, one by one, with increasing discomfort. There was a letter from Caroline's sister Fayth (she prayed daily for Caroline's deliverance from hell), one from Wesley (reminding her that if the Maxwell pig mistreated her he would return to gut him), and the last from her stepmother. Nothing incriminating, just well wishes and idle chatter, offers to send the comforts of home. Robert carefully refolded the letters.

It had taken him half an hour to read all three. She stood motionless by the fireplace, watching him, like a sentinel. He had been feeling abashed, but her stoicism irritated him. He had acted thoughtlessly—she should be angry, berate him.

"Have you discovered our plans for invasion?" The quip was delivered in her perfectly modulated, emotionless voice. It pleased him nonetheless.

He joined her at the fireplace, proffering the letters. "I'm sorry."

She took them. "Are my possessions to arrive shortly?"

"No mention was made of them." She turned to leave, but he caught her arm. His hand wrapped completely about her delicate elbow. A tremor shook her arm.

"You saw my brother, Sir Patrick, when he was a prisoner?"

"I saw him once . . . before Father died. He was kept apart. Father said he was wicked and would seduce and impregnate all the women in the keep." She quickly added, "He wasn't so much worried about me, as Fayth and Mona . . . and the servants."

Robert couldn't take his eyes off her. A faint blush had risen in her cheeks, but she held his gaze, steady, regal, proud. Who had done this to her? Anger and a strange, twisting pain crept into his heart. It was true she was no great beauty, but she was certainly not ugly. Who had given her this monstrous vision of herself? Her features and form were pleasing, but more than that she had a charm all her own; grace, wit, strength, and a soft vulnerability she guarded viciously. She was awe inspiring, dignified—these things made her beautiful.

"If I were him, I would have worried about you most of all."

The placid smile curved her lips. "You are kind."

"Jesus God, I am not!" He grasped her other arm, pulling her close. She held herself stiff, but didn't resist. "I am wicked—more wicked than Patrick when it comes to you, Wife."

Her features tightened, her throat worked. His gaze raked over her face, down the length of her white throat. His desire for her grew daily. Why it should, when she offered no encouragement, was a mystery. Perhaps it was the need to conquer her. *Perhaps.* He thought not.

Her bosom rose and fell rapidly and she tried to detach herself. He held fast. She smelled fresh and clean, bringing forth visions of her pressed against him at night, tempting him with the smell of her, the feel of her. Well, she was awake now.

Her hair was covered, as usual, but he could see it in his mind, falling down her back, over white shoulders. A golden cape. She watched him warily, pale green eyes wide, and those long, blond lashes belying her show of impregnable strength, fluttering as she blinked.

So still, she held herself. He knew what she was doing, planning her way out of this, crafting something sufficiently freezing to kill his lust.

So he spoke first. "At night, in bed, you're not so cold and stiff."

She inhaled—and didn't exhale. A flush crept up her neck, stained her cheeks. She knew! He'd wondered—but as he woke before her, he thought perhaps she slept through it all.

"It's cold at night . . . and you're . . ."

He pulled her closer. "Aye?"

"You're very warm," Caroline said, her voice strange and breathy even to her own ears. She couldn't look away from him. He was going to kiss her again. She should struggle, try to wrench herself free. But his pale eyes transfixed her, the way they roamed over her face. No one had ever looked at her the way he did. And sometimes . . . well, sometimes, she liked it.

And besides, it was just a kiss. He was not taking her maidenhead—he'd promised to stop if she asked him to. Thus far, he'd been true to his word—forcing nothing upon her.

And so she didn't pull away, as she knew she should have.

When his mouth covered hers, she let her head fall back, didn't protest when he yanked away her head covering. She did as he'd instructed before, parting her lips slightly. There was something intoxicating about kissing— like drinking too much wine. It made her head swim, her body overwarm. Indistinct urges replaced thought. The fluttering of her heart, the way his mouth made hers tingle and thirst for more, the way her limbs became liquid.

Then he stopped. She blinked, his face swimming into focus. He frowned. She'd done it wrong. Her temperature increased—with embarrassment now. She strained away from him, but his arms were hard, imprisoning her.

"Has *anyone* ever kissed you before?" Before she could answer he added, "Or held you? Mother, sister, father, even?" He gathered her closer, as if to illustrate.

She lowered her eyes and saw her hands in rigid fists against his chest, the knuckles white. She searched her memory for instances, and only two came to her—vivid because of their strangeness. Both of her stepmother, Mona, trying to embrace her and both times Caroline, enduring it uncomfortably, patting her stepmother's back.

"My stepmother hugged me . . . sometimes."

His hands stroked over her back, calming. "There's nothing wrong with showing affection—sometimes, a kiss, or a hug, says things words cannot."

She refused to look at him. She felt unnatural—an oddity. As if it were somehow her fault she was unused to physical demonstrations. When she pulled away he released her, but his gaze remained on her, keen. He'd seen too much and she didn't like it.

"I'll wager even nuns hug each other—when they're happy."

She smiled stiffly. "I'm sure."

He walked around the room, putting his back to her. "If you're so set on living out your life in a nunnery, why, at four-and-twenty, are you still not there?"

"My lord . . .?"

"Your tocher is substantial, your father was generous—a fine endowment for any convent—what has kept you from the cloister?"

He was moving toward some point, she knew. He delighted in undermining her faith, trying to prove she was unfit to be a nun. "As you know, King Henry dissolved the monasteries and convents in England."

Robert shrugged. "The Grahams have many allies in Scotland—some would argue that a Graham is as much Scots as English—there's certainly evidence to support the argument. So why not a nunnery in Scotland? Convents abound on the Continent—you speak Latin and French, so language is no impediment. Why have you delayed assuming the veil?"

"I did not wish to leave my father . . . my family, Father Jasper—"

"Did you think your father would live forever?" he asked skeptically, circling her. "That your brother would be as indulgent as your father? You do not seem the vacillating type to me. What has held you back?"

She turned, following his progress. "It was a very complicated—"

"Oh, I think it's quite simple."

Her eyebrows rose. "How so?"

"You were waiting."

He was being foolish again, but she couldn't stop the tug at the corners of her mouth. He often argued with her—his logic purposely skewed—just to exasperate her, to make her laugh.

"This should be interesting," she said. "What was I waiting for?"

He stared at her thoughtfully. "For some hero from your stories. And you got me." He grinned.

She cleared her throat, fighting the answering smile. "Methinks we should change our reading material, my lord. You're becoming confused—."

He halted, hands clasped behind his back, and peered at her. She raised her brows in question, but he only came closer. "You have a dimple," he said, and touched her cheek with one finger.

Suddenly short of breath, Caroline stepped away, unsettled by the pleasure on his face, all because she had a dimple! "We've discussed this before," she said, returning to a safer subject. "I wish to wed myself to God because it is the practical thing to do. The Lord is more forgiving of a woman's flaws, desires only her loyalty and love. I wish to be somewhere that my talents will be put to good use and appreciated." *And the Lord will not tire of me, as a man will, once he gets what he wants.* She knew now, what she had always suspected before. She would not be a godly nun—but she would be a hardworking one. According to Father Jasper, many monastics were not very godly. So, it was not wrong to want this. He also told her (to her great relief) that even the chaste felt lust—and that he himself had not always been chaste.

Robert held her gaze for a long time, his expression grim and slightly troubled. "You know so little of men and the world, Caroline."

She blinked and turned to the fire. "I never claimed to know men." He still stared at her, she could feel it—boring into her, as if he could read her. She didn't like it. After a moment she tossed another log on and prodded at it with an iron.

He returned to his desk. She did not leave—there was something else—something about Ridley that she wanted to tell him, but didn't know how. He obviously did not trust her, and she couldn't blame him for that—but she didn't want to do anything to aggravate it either. She tried to tell herself it didn't matter whether he trusted her or not. She had no intention of staying and making this work, so why bother building trust? And Wesley's warning not to discuss Sir Patrick with any Maxwell returned to her.

She was still loitering around the hearth when Robert asked, "Caroline? Is there something else?"

"Yes." She paused. Gathering her resolve, she approached his desk with her usual composure in place. "It's about your brother."

Robert sat forward. "Aye?"

"The sum Ridley asks for his upkeep is outrageous and not just for the obvious reasons." She hesitated, carefully considering her words. "Sir Patrick was being held in the dungeon . . . he ate no better than the servants and certainly did not receive candles and clothes as the bill suggests. I cannot explain why Ridley seeks to cozen you, but cozen you he does."

When Robert did not respond she said, "I just thought you should know." She crossed the room, to leave.

"Caroline, wait."

She turned, her hand on the latch.

He stood. "I need you . . . to write a letter for me. Please."

She could not speak at first, overcome by what his request implied: he trusted her.

"Of course," she said, and returned to him with a smile that she knew revealed her dimple—yet couldn't help herself.

Robert shrugged into his leather jack—eager to leave his chambers at long last. Thanks to Caroline, his letters were written and the messenger would soon be on his way back to Graham Keep—and hopefully return with a reply in less than a sennight. Perhaps it was nothing more than a misunderstanding. An ugly thought had begun to plague Robert since Caroline's revelation of Patrick's treatment. What if Patrick were ill—or dying? Ridley would not want Robert to know. He would nurse Patrick back to health before returning him. Or worse—what if Patrick were dead? Killed in an escape attempt, or murdered? Before, Robert hadn't worried overmuch, as it was considered poor form to treat a noble prisoner as less than a guest—but it seemed Ridley didn't hold himself to any standards but his own if he kept a knight of a good family in his dungeon.

There was a scratch at the door. Robert flung it open impatiently. "Aye?"

Father Jasper stood just outside, looking solemn and

pious, as always, but robed finer than any churchman Robert had ever seen. "Father?"

"A moment of your time?" Misty green eyes gazed at him, cool and detached.

Robert nodded, stepping back and waving the priest in. Though Caroline's priest had taken to watching him closely and with thinly veiled disapproval, he'd never ventured to speak with Robert alone.

"I'll be quick, as I know you've other business to attend." He crossed the room, his steps purposeful. "Why did you make your whore Caroline's maid?"

Robert blinked, the priest's forward manner rendering him speechless.

"Did you see some humor in it? For it is a cruelty to both women, though my concern is for Caroline."

"No," Robert said, slowly. "It was not my intention to insult either woman."

"Your mistress—Celia. Will you keep her? Or perhaps bring other lemans into the castle?"

Robert laughed humorlessly. "Celia has not been my . . . *leman* for a very long time. And if she had been, I would have ended it with my marriage to Caroline. I'm not such a bad husband, really." He shook his head, smiling bitterly, wondering why he hadn't expected such a confrontation. The priest had been protective of her from the beginning. "It was poor judgment to assign Celia as her maid . . . but at the time, well—it seemed a perfect idea. Celia is the highest ranking woman in my household. I thought it appropriate."

The priest said nothing, but stood, hands hidden in his sleeves, watching Robert. As Robert stared back at the other man, he recognized the stance and expression on Father Jasper's face as Caroline's. She'd modeled herself after the priest. The notion gave him pause—and an idea.

If he could gain Father Jasper's trust, the priest would be a valuable ally in winning Caroline.

"Father," Robert said, moving to the fireplace and sitting down heavily. "I need advice."

The priest approached him and stared down his nose. "Is this a confession?"

"No, I don't want to be shriven. Only to talk. You've known Caroline all her life?"

Father Jasper nodded. "Most of it."

"And you are friend to her?"

"Yes."

Robert sighed and gestured to a nearby chair. "How did she become this way?"

Father Jasper's face closed up. "I know not what you mean. She is a fine lady."

Robert sighed, annoyed at himself. "That's not what I meant—"

"Then what did you mean?" The priest still stood, refusing the offer to sit. "Does she displease you? Do you find her unsuitable?"

"No! I don't know what unsuitable means. She still hasn't told me."

The priest raised his chin slightly, frowning, and asked cautiously, "How did she become . . . what way?"

Robert leaned forward, elbows on his knees. "No one has ever kissed her, or embraced her, and I just can't see how this could be. My own father showed me no affection, but my mother did . . . and my nurse—and others."

Father Jasper regarded him for a long time, his expression assessing. "You care for her?"

Robert nodded. "Aye—I wish to make this union work. But I can't see my way with her . . ."

Father Jasper's mouth flattened. "I can only tell you about her life before she came here. Perhaps it will help you see why she has chosen to be a nun." He took the chair opposite Robert. He breathed deeply and looked upward, as if gathering his thoughts. "She has always been overlong—though we never guessed she would be a giant until she surpassed everyone in stature when she was fourteen. She was very thin and spindly . . ." He shrugged. "She was never like the other girls. She sought me out for company rather than other women." The priest looked down at his hands. "I am as much to blame as her family for her faults. I taught her to read and write . . . I also advised her to enter a nunnery."

Father Jasper looked up, as if asking for understanding. "I truly thought it was best for her. Being left out—or treated as a man—hurt her deeply—though she always insisted she accepted what she couldn't change. I couldn't bear to watch it, to imagine her whole life a series of degradations. In a convent, she would be valued, loved. Other monastics would see past the giant, to the beauty inside. She would contribute to something greater than herself and perhaps even be remembered for it. She has so much to offer—so much that would never be realized if she were merely a wife."

Robert opened his mouth to protest but the priest held up a staying hand, his brows raised guiltily, lifting one shoulder. "This is what I told her—the words she likely mouths at you, I have given her."

The priest slouched, his eyes narrowing. "And then there was Lord Graham and his son." His mouth drew into a thin line. "Ridley was never good enough for Hugh Graham . . . I'll never understand why he so hard on the boy, why Ridley never measured up—for the boy did try. Hugh wished for another son desperately . . . I often feared were he granted his wish, something ill might befall Ridley. But Wesley is proof Hugh wasn't so depraved.

"When Caroline was finally born . . . well, he must have decided he would make do with her . . . and so raised her as if she were a boy. I . . . wasn't present for her early years." The priest swallowed, averting his eyes. "I returned to Graham Keep when she was six. Her father's great pride, she was. But, like Ridley, she would never quite measure up—for she was a woman." He shook his head. "Her father expected her to be like a man and then when she acted like one, he would ridicule her for being unladylike. At the very least, he confused her . . ." Father Jasper shrugged sadly. "In his heart, I don't believe he meant to hurt her, since he often said it with affection . . . but wound her he did. Had she not been so . . . large, had she been blessed with great beauty . . . well, things might have been different.

"And what about Ridley?" Robert asked.

The priest paused, the lines in his skeletal features deepening. "He hates her . . . he hates them all—but mostly her. She is everything he isn't—and yet a *woman* . . . and she'd had what he wanted: Hugh Graham's pride, his regard. He was a sly lad . . . prone to jests and trickery.

"He used to play cruel jokes on her, to humiliate her in front of others—especially Hugh. Ridley nicknamed her 'Pious Graham Mare.' He likes to pretend he did not, but I know."

Robert rubbed his temple, heartsick from the priest's story—and yet an unpleasant thought occurred to him. If this wedding *were* a ruse, would Ridley not need him to believe Caroline had no love for her brother? Would a priest truly be party to such conniving? Robert glanced at Father Jasper's head, noting as he had before the lack of tonsure. He'd thought nothing of it—indeed, he'd come to expect such laxity from the Scottish churchmen he'd encountered. And yet in every other way, Father Jasper seemed the perfect man of God.

Robert stood, sickened at such torturous thoughts. He couldn't carry this twisted suspicion around in his heart forever—for then the failure of this union would be as much his fault as hers.

Father Jasper stood also, taking a hesitant step toward Robert. "Be patient with her. She knows nothing of men or their ways." Robert nodded and the priest's somber expression broke. He smiled as if a great weight had been lifted from his soul. "Let me bless you before you ride."

Robert backed away. "I'm not going on a raid—just to collect rents."

Father Jasper raised his eyebrows. "You never know what might happen out riding on the borders—particularly in this area. Please. I will rest easier."

Robert grudgingly allowed the priest to pray over him and make the sign of the cross. He seemed to linger over the task, but finally, when Robert began to shift uncomfortably, Father Jasper patted his shoulder and started for the door, his pace purposeful, measured.

Curiosity compelled Robert to call after the priest. "Caroline's mother—what color were her eyes?"

Father Jasper frowned, head cocked to the side, but answered readily enough. "Brown."

"Her father?"

"Blue—I think."

Robert nodded. The priest turned away, but Robert halted him again. "Father? One more question."

Father Jasper turned back, one eyebrow raised slightly, an expression so familiar Robert was startled he hadn't noticed the resemblance before. "Were either of her parents overlong?"

Father Jasper's gaze sharpened and he took several steps toward Robert. "Why is it important?"

Robert shrugged. "It's not—I'm merely curious."

"Hugh Graham was not a little man, but no, he was not uncommonly tall. Her mother was . . ." His voice caught and he cleared his throat. "Lady Graham was small— even for a lass."

Robert nodded meditatively, but said no more. Whether his suspicions were right or wrong, he helped no one by giving them voice. Robert allowed the priest to leave and called Henry to help him find his spurs.

10

Caroline went through the rest of the day with an unnaturally light heart. She had the most foolish urge to skip—as though the blood thrummed too quickly through her veins and she must hurry along with it. Passing through the hall, Caroline noticed the messenger from Ridley had finished eating and now chatted with Celia before the fire. Some of Caroline's happiness dissipated at the sight of her lazy maid flirting with the young man. He stood very close to her. Celia's head was tilted down, as if demurring, but she gazed up at him through a sweep of sooty lashes.

They didn't notice Caroline's presence and she did not make herself known. She was somehow compelled to watch this love play that she'd spent the last decade ignoring. It had been easy, as she had never been part of it. She had accepted such behavior as an inevitable and immutable part of human nature—one she would forever be outside of. *Until now.*

Ebony locks escaped Celia's plait to twirl enticingly across the bare tops of her breasts. The young man raised his hand, twining a curl about his finger, his knuckle brushing against the swell of Celia's breast. Heat rushed to Caroline's chest and neck, as if in response to a touch. Her cheeks burned. She was not offended, or disgusted, as she would have thought. She was riveted. There was a warmth, a restlessness in her. She'd felt it before and had always been successful at ignoring it and returning her body to the emotional void that was so much more satisfactory—so much more predictable. Now, however, she burned. It grew each day she spent with Robert. And it refused to be ignored.

Oh Lord. She closed her eyes. She couldn't think it, even in her mind, this place where she ached. And yet she opened her eyes immediately, unable to resist. The young man still toyed with Celia's hair and she did not protest—in fact, she'd shifted her stance, moving her body closer. His knuckle now gently rubbed the swell of Celia's breast as he spoke to her, leaning close, his foot resting on the hearth—boxing her in. Caroline could almost feel his warm breath against her own ear, his roughened hand against her skin—but it wasn't the messenger she imagined, it was her husband.

Liquid heat shuddered through her. She fought to clear her mind. It would not do for Robert to discover her here, body aquiver with wicked thoughts. She cleared her throat loudly and advanced upon the couple. They sprang apart, Celia looking wildly about for her sewing.

Caroline gave the messenger the leather packet and advised him to stop by the kitchen before he left to provision himself for his journey. When he was gone she said, "He was a Graham. I thought you hated Grahams."

"I would never allow a Graham to touch me." Celia sniffed. "Nay—he was an Armstrong, he only works for your brother."

"He was beneath your station. Have a care Celia."

"Such things are easy for you to say. Men aren't drawn to you, as they are to me." She smiled coyly. "He was handsome—can I help it if he desired me?"

Caroline didn't rise to the bait, having heard it often enough. "Yes, you could, by covering your bosom and not shoving it in his face." She smiled now, done with her dutiful reprimand—today she didn't feel like wrangling with Celia. She wanted to be outside in the late summer sun. Unfortunately, there was no summer sun—the day was overcast and foggy—but fresh air would suffice. "Fetch my cloak. I wish to visit Agnes."

Caroline inspected Celia's needlework as she waited, admiring the neat stitches and attractive pattern. Perhaps there was hope yet for Celia. Robert exited his chambers. Caroline pretended she didn't notice, though every hair on her body tingled, wondering if he saw her—did he look at her? Would he speak to her? Where was he going? He'd been holed up in his chambers for days now, hunched over his desk.

Hearing his footsteps approach, she set the needlework aside. "You're riding?"

"Aye—thanks to you." He smiled at her, his gray eyes warm. "I thought I'd never finish those letters."

"I'm always happy to help. Prithee, call on me in the future need you a secretary—there is no cause to employ one."

He didn't respond, only stared at her in that intense, probing way of his that simultaneously unnerved and pleased her. She refused to look away, however, and returned his bold stare. His cut lip had healed nicely, no more than a thin pink scar now, and the bruise around his eye had faded completely. He looked a bit pale of late, but that was because he'd spent so much time indoors. It hadn't waned him in any other way. Still broad and imposing as ever, he towered over her. He moved closer, propping a booted and spurred foot on the hearth, closing her in. He ran a hand over his hair, thick and springy. The chestnut waves reflected the firelight with a warm glow.

And that's when she noticed that the frown—a permanent feature of his countenance since she'd first met him over a week ago—was gone. His forehead was smooth and untroubled as he gazed at her. Could it have aught to do with her? The very thought brought a rush of pleasure so intense she was forced to turn toward the fire.

"You are blushing," he said.

"I'm not," she responded too quickly. " 'Tis merely the fire."

He made a low, thoughtful noise that shouldn't have sent shivers chasing each other down her spine—but it did. As he continued to smile down at her, the scene she'd just witnessed between Celia and the Armstrong messenger invaded her thoughts. Robert stood just as he had—so close, looking down on her in a similar fashion.

"Are you chilled?" he asked.

"No."

"I wonder then why you spend so much time hovering about fireplaces." He grinned.

Exceedingly uncomfortable, she cast about her mind for something to say—to change the subject—but she couldn't stop thinking of him kissing her again and that he knew she pressed up against him at night, in her sleep—had even woken up in his arms. And not moved away.

She was relieved when Celia returned with her cloak.

Robert stepped away, his smile fading. "Where are you off to?"

"To visit Agnes."

"Agnes?"

Caroline secured the cloak at her neck. "Yes. She

works in the kitchen, but has been with her daughter this past week, delivering her of a child. She oft acts as midwife. I want to wish them well, bring blankets for the babe."

"Good. Well then . . . good day, ladies." He hesitated a moment before striding away.

Celia followed her out of the hall, up the stairs and down several passageways and another flight of stairs, to a remote tower room. Caroline liked this room very much. Though smaller than the chambers she shared with Robert, this room was circular. It had three narrow windows and on a bright day, it was awash in light. Today was no such day. Foggy and gray, the mist crept in through the open windows, veiling the ancient bed in a haze. The bed was sturdy, like all the other furniture in the keep, but the bedding and curtains were moldering and moth-eaten. Caroline considered the room as she had done many times over the past week. The bed needed work—but this would be a suitable chamber for her. If only she could convince Robert of the same.

Two chests full of linens and blankets were stored in this room. Caroline chose two warm woolen blankets and turned to leave. Celia's daughter, Larie, entered the room, carrying a sack, followed by the laundress. Larie resembled her mother, with ebony hair and blue eyes. Too young to have acquired her mother's well-rounded figure, she was still a striking girl. Her gaze darted to her mother before returning to Caroline.

"We're here to launder the bedding, as you requested," Larie said.

"I also asked you to examine the mattress—see if it can be repaired, or if it must be replaced."

Larie blinked stupidly at her, as if she did not recall Caroline giving such instructions. Caroline sighed and set the blankets aside. "Come," she instructed, motioning Larie and the laundress to the bed. Larie handed her mother the sack and followed. Caroline removed the bedding herself and instructed the young girl on how to inspect a mattress thoroughly. Through it all, Celia loitered around behind them, not offering a bit of help. Once Caroline turned to look at her maid and Larie coughed loudly. Celia whirled around, hands behind her back, a stiff smile on her face. Finished at last, Caroline fetched the blankets, ready to leave.

Celia no longer had Larie's sack. It was crumpled on the floor. Caroline's gaze swept the room, examining the face of each occupant. They all watched her expectantly. The laundress looked away when Caroline caught her eye, busying herself with the mattress. Larie stared at her mother with barely suppressed panic.

"What—" Caroline began, but the blankets squirmed in her arms. She nearly shrieked and dropped them in horror, but managed to restrain herself. Celia looked as if she might explode.

Caroline pulled off the top blanket and a toad sprang at her. She jerked as the toad bounced off the stiff material of her bodice, landing back on the blanket with its three companions. Celia burst out laughing and Larie giggled into her hand. The laundress, however, kept her eyes on the bed, her hands busy.

"How amusing," Caroline said through gritted teeth. "Larie, prithee remove the beasts to the moat."

Their laughter died immediately. Larie came forward hesitantly, as if she were afraid of being struck. "Forgive, my lady . . . it was stupid of me."

One of the toads hopped off the blanket, landing on its back on the floor. It struggled to right itself. Larie gathered the toads in her kirtle and scurried from the room.

Celia stared after her sourly before turning to Caroline with a shrug. "Bairns! The jests they'll pull."

Caroline gave her maid a long look. "You put the toads in the blankets."

Celia had the audacity to look amazed. "Me?"

It was well within Caroline's rights to flog her maid for such behavior—and she was sore tempted. But to give in to violence, like any emotion, was to show weakness. "Alice?" Caroline called, never taking her gaze from Celia.

The laundress shuffled forward as if she'd rather be any place else. "Aye, my lady?"

"Please inform the chambermaid that she has the night off. Celia will assume her duties tonight." Which included scrubbing the closestools and chamber pots.

Celia gasped.

"Aye, my lady," Alice said.

Celia's eyes blazed with defiance. "My lady! I shall take this up with Lord Annan!"

"Please do," Caroline said, and felt a strange surge of triumph in the knowledge that Robert would back her up.

Celia held her cool stare for a few seconds before lowering her eyes and fixing them on Caroline's chest. Flags of red painted her cheeks.

Caroline dropped the blankets in her maid's arms. "Shall we?"

As they left the keep, several men-at-arms came to attention. When it was noted she headed for the open portcullis, one of them yelled out orders and within seconds two heavily armed guards flanked her.

"Will you be riding, my lady?" one asked.

"Nay, I should like to walk to the village."

Celia groaned behind her.

The day was damp and the cold chill seeped its way through layers of clothing to settle in Caroline's bones. She followed the beaten dirt road down the hill and away from the castle. A bell tolled somewhere in the distance, but the hamlet down the road did not possess a church. Caroline glanced back, but the castle was barely visible, obscured by fog. Annancreag sat on a hill that was on one side steep with jagged rocks, and on the other a gentle swell, blanketed in heather. The latter was the way to the village and even through the misty haze Caroline enjoyed the beauty.

The village was no more than a dozen cottages clustered together and another ten scattered farther out. Caroline could just make out men and women at work in the fields that fanned out from the village, shadowy figures like ghosts. Celia took the lead once they arrived at the village's single lane and stopped at the third cottage. She rapped soundly on the door.

An old woman poked her head out of the open shutters. Wild gray hair stood out around her face. She gave them a nearly toothless smile. "Why, if it ain't Lady Annan!" She disappeared inside the cottage only to open the door seconds later. "Come in, come in! Welcome—I canna believe ye're here!"

Caroline had to duck her head to enter—the door had been cut for people of normal stature. Agnes tidied the little one-room cottage, brushing off benches and shooing the dogs and chickens out the door.

Her daughter slept on a straw mat in the corner, a baby swaddled in her arms, also asleep.

"Here, my lady, sit here," Agnes crooned, her leathery face flushed with pleasure. She gestured to a bench she'd wiped off and covered with a clean cloth. She stopped in front of Caroline and looked her up and down, craning her neck to look at Caroline's face. "I'd heard ye were long—but my, ye are a big lass!"

Caroline smiled, charmed by the woman's fuss.

"Thank you for making me so welcome." Before sitting, she took the blankets from Celia and gave them to Agnes. "These are for your daughter and the babe, to keep the fever at bay. Tell me, how does she?"

Caroline's guards waited outside the door and Celia stood just inside the door, unacknowledged by Agnes.

"Oh, thank ye, my lady—these be fine warm blankets—ye're as generous as ye are long!" Agnes took the bench across from Caroline. "Oh, she does well—'tis a strong lusty lad she had." Agnes's face creased with worry. "But her milk's dried up."

"Is there not a wet nurse to be had?"

"Bonnie—our wet nurse—was raped two months past—almost died, and her milk dried up."

"That's terrible! Who did this? Was he brought to justice?"

Agnes glanced at Celia for the first time since they arrived. The maid raised her eyebrows with a smirk and looked away. Agnes turned back to Caroline, obviously discomfited. "Weel, my lady—it be a Graham who did it . . . the raid was led by yer brother—the younger."

Wesley? Caroline's mouth tightened. His hatred for the Maxwells ran deep. She only prayed he was not the one who committed the atrocity, though condoning it was nearly as evil. "Please accept my apologies . . . I hope my marriage to Lord Annan ends the feuding. What have you been feeding the babe?"

Agnes told her the different remedies she'd tried—some cow's milk, some barley broth—the babe liked none of them. Caroline promised to send her a goat, for she'd heard goat's milk was a good substitute. Agnes was well pleased and thanked her profusely again.

"I've been told you lived through the massacre that occurred, sixty years ago."

Agnes nodded sagely. "That I did. I were six when the seventh Lord Annan—that be Malcolm—took a Graham to wife."

Caroline leaned forward, hands clasped. "What do you remember?"

Agnes's mouth flattened and she leaned back, inhaling deeply through her nose. "Weel . . . I remember hearing Malcolm had lost his heart to a Graham lass—I was but a bairn at the time and at first I thought the lass killed him and cut his heart oot!" She hooted with laughter, then became serious. "I suppose that's just what she did in the end."

"So, the Grahams were at fault?"

Agnes nodded, patting Caroline's hand. "Aye, it was. I remember, it were a huge feast. A rope was thrown over the wooden candleholder that still hangs in the hall. Me da swung me round and round—I'm surprised the chains didn't snap—grown men were swinging aboot on it. I bocked under the table. There I lay, dead to the world— but Grahams be sitting at the table above me. They called us drunken fools . . . they hadna touched a drop of ale or whiskey—seemed to be biding their time. I didna realize why then—I was so young, and no feeling too fine, at that." Agnes shook her head. "If only I'd understood . . ."

Her mouth turned down, the vertical lines beside it deepening. "They whispered aboot the Clachan Fala. An old witch appeared right after the vows been said—she had an enormous red stone—the Blood Stone. I've never seen aught like it before or since. It was a grand moment—everyone quiet, awed. Me da said something aboot only thinking it be a legend, that it werena real. The witch gave it to Malcolm and his bride."

The Clachan Fala. A chill raced up Caroline's back. "Did the Grahams take it?"

Jen Holling

"Nay. They killed near everyone but some women and bairns—then came back, even afore word could be sent to Malcolm's brother, the new laird—and burned everything, raped, killed . . ." Agnes's voice wavered and her eyes grew bright. "Tortured . . . looking for the stone. But it disappeared."

Caroline let out the breath she'd been holding. "Good Lord."

"When Malcolm's brother arrived, he raised the Maxwells and the blood feud took an ugly turn. He looked for the witch, but couldna find her. He became obsessed wi' finding the stone. But no one ever did."

They were silent for a long moment, both deep in thought.

Agnes said, "There's an old woman—a Maxwell widow—she be older even than me and Ole Sandy—four score, methinks. Old Bess, they call her. She could tell ye aboot it—even if she wasna there for the feast. She lives at the edge of Lord Annan's lands. She likely knows something more—if ye be wantin' to find that stone yerself, that is."

Caroline shook her head. "Oh, I don't care about the stone. I guess I'm just hoping there's some way to discover the truth of what happened. Maybe the hate can be set aside."

Agnes gave her a gap-toothed grin. "Ye're a fine lady! I wish ye well!"

Caroline was about to respond when panicked shouting from the fields distracted her. She stood as Celia stepped outside. The shouting grew louder, followed by the thunder of galloping horses. Fear coiled tight in Caroline's belly. Living on the borders, she was no stranger to the sound of a raid—and this was no small raiding party, judging by the pounding of hooves through the village.

Caroline's guards pushed their way in the door, their faces stark with fear—not for themselves, but for her. "My lady," one of them gasped, grabbing her arm. "We must make haste back to the keep—'tis the Johnstones!"

She knew they were right—she was a valuable commodity—if the raiders got their hands on her, the ransom Robert would be forced to pay for her safe return would be exorbitant. Her safety was in their hands and by the greasy sweat that sheened their faces, they well knew it.

Before she could exit, however, the guards quickly bustled both her and Celia back inside, a finger to their lips. Agnes moved to the corner, with her granddaughter and daughter, now awake and wide-eyed, but quiet. Caroline's heart pounded in her ears, her palms were sweating—she clasped them together tightly. Celia clung to Caroline's arm. No one spoke in the cottage. Their breathing, heavy, strained, was the only sound. Celia trembled, pressing closer to Caroline.

The horses halted in front of Agnes's cottage. There was much stamping and snorting and jangling of bridles. Could someone have told them she was here, in this cottage? Or perhaps it was chance they stopped here to begin their ravage on the village? Had they seen the guards outside the door, and knew someone important was within?

Her questions were answered when a surly voice called out, "No use hiding, Lady Annan—we know you're in there."

11

"Out the back," Agnes whispered, hurrying to a window at the back of the cottage and pushing the shutters open. The haze of an indistinct landscape swam in and out of focus with the swirl of fog.

"Surely they've surrounded us," one of the guards said, following the old woman. The other guard remained near the front door, sword drawn.

Caroline's mind sped forward, trying to decide the best course of action. Sometimes these things weren't violent, but often enough, they were very bloody. Next to the livestock, she was the most valuable item they would get their hands on today, for the castle itself was heavily guarded. If she submitted to them, that might prevent any further destruction. But then she might find herself rotting in a dungeon just like Robert's brother, Sir Patrick, until the ransom could be raised.

"If ye come out peaceably, my lady," the voice yelled, "no one gets hurt."

"I don't see anyone," said the guard at the back window. "Come, my lady."

Caroline didn't move. "I cannot—they will hurt someone—maybe Agnes or the child. I should go with them."

"Go, my lady!" Agnes urged. "That's Bean Johnstone—he's but full of bluster. He'll no harm old women and weans. Make haste!"

The guard at the window said, "Lord Annan promised to flog any man that allowed harm to befall you. I dinna intend to lose any skin on me back, my lady—so get you to the window."

Caroline continued to hesitate until the guard at the door shouted for her to go. The Johnstones were attacking. He swung his sword. Metal clashed. Heavily outnumbered, he would not hold them back for long. Celia pushed her toward the window, whimpering. Caroline lifted her skirts and let the second guard lift her through. Outside, Celia continued to shove urgently at her. But Caroline was too disoriented to rush blindly forward. Thick mist swirled around her like a dream. Shouting and sounds of battle were audible, but she couldn't determine from which direction they originated.

"The Maxwells," the guard said, his voice rife with relief. He grasped her arm and pulled. "They've arrived."

Caroline felt no such relief. Though she could now make out the cry, "A Maxwell!" in the distance and she was not alone, one guard would be little protection against a horde of Johnstones. Robert had gone riding. Would the men-at-arms from the castle be able to locate him in time? How would he know whom he fought or where to find Caroline in this soupy mist?

"This way to the castle, my lady," the guard said, still urging her along. "They'll not find us in here."

The ground gave way beneath her feet as they entered

the fields. She stumbled across the soft ground, pushing her way through tall stalks of oats. She gasped for air, lungs burning. They reached a break in the field. A figure on horseback loomed out of the haze, galloping down on them, as surprised by their appearance as they were at his. His horse reared and he pulled on the reins as the horse jibbed about them.

"Red Alex!" the guard cried.

Caroline's heart seized—she'd heard of this man. A notorious Maxwell reiver—he'd raided Graham lands many times—Fayth insisted he'd murdered her betrothed. But he was also a Maxwell, so perhaps she was not in danger.

The man dismounted. He was as tall as she, his long russet hair tied back. His gaze flicked over her dismissively. "Lady Annan?" he said, addressing her guard.

"Aye—the raiders tried to kidnap her."

Red Alex looked behind them, his face grim. "Looks like they tried to burn you out."

Caroline whirled. A faint orange glow illuminated the fog behind them. "Agnes!" she breathed and started toward it.

Red Alex moved in front of her, blocking her way. Icy blue eyes regarded her with disdain. "I'm afraid I cannot let you do that—my brother'd have my hide. Come." He gestured to his horse.

Several more men on horseback materialized from the mist to surround them. "Will," Red Alex said, jerking his chin in the direction of Agnes's cottage. "See to Agnes." A man separated from the group and spurred his horse into the mist.

Caroline eyed them warily; this could be another kidnapping attempt—just because he was a Maxwell and knew Agnes didn't mean he was loyal to the Annans.

"I don't know you. I refuse to go with you."

"He's your brother-in-law!" Celia hissed beside her. "He's rescuing you!"

Caroline stepped back in surprise, bumping into Celia. Red Alex, her *brother-in-law?*

Smiling sarcastically, the man bowed low. "Alexander Maxwell, at your service."

The guard took several steps forward, head lifted as if smelling the air. "I hear them—they're coming."

Alexander snapped to attention, his mouth firm with purpose. "Up, Sister—onto my horse."

Caroline didn't like her new brother-in-law and he obviously didn't like her. "No." She looked around, deciding on the likely direction of Annancreag. "Come, Celia."

Alexander was in front of her again, scowling fiercely. "Do not be difficult—get on my horse."

Seeing he would not relent, she inclined her head. "Very well. But your manner offends me."

Alexander opened his mouth to reply, then shut it abruptly. He drew his sword and shoved her behind him. His head was cocked, his stance ready. Caroline heard it now, the thunder of approaching horses.

"You and Celia—get on my horse and ride!"

Caroline wasted no time, slipping her foot into the stirrup and swinging into the saddle. "Which way?" she asked, offering Celia her hand. Her maid scrabbled up behind her.

Alexander pointed to his right. "Go!"

Caroline dug her heels into his horse's flanks just as a dozen men burst through the fog and rows of oats, torches blazing and lances leveled. Alexander and his men attacked. The horse flew through the field at a run. Celia shrieked behind her, clinging to her waist. Caroline's head covering, soggy from the damp air, slipped forward, into her eyes. She tore at it, throwing it to the ground.

The terrain changed, from field to grass to the packed dirt of the road. Caroline sawed on the reins, dancing the horse in a circle, trying to decide which way to go. Celia sobbed hysterically.

"Silence!" Caroline said in a harsh whisper. Cursing her horrible sense of direction, made worse by the thick fog, she chose the right and spurred the horse forward. Alexander's horse shrieked and reared as they rode straight into a pack of men on horseback. Celia slipped backward, her nails digging into Caroline's arms. Caroline fought to control the horse, her thighs and arms trembling from the effort.

Men surrounded them, grabbing the horse's bridle, pulling Celia down. Caroline recognized none of them. *Johnstones*. Celia screamed as several men dragged her into the fog. Caroline was lifted off the horse and set on her feet. She knew they wouldn't harm her. But Celia! Caroline struggled against her captors.

"Easy now, Lady Annan, they just want a bit of fun," a man breathed in her ear.

Caroline drove her elbow into his midsection and he released her with a muffled curse. With the element of surprise on her side, she sprinted after Celia. Indistinct forms solidified ahead. Celia fought wildly as two men forced her to the ground.

Caroline had no weapon, but the ground was littered with jagged rocks. She grabbed one with a sharp edge and ran at one of the men. "Release her!" she cried, striking him in the back of the head. He fell over, howling, clutching his head. The other man sprang off Celia. Her maid immediately curled into a ball, hands covering her face. Caroline dropped down beside her.

The men were at her again. Panic took over as Caroline fought against them, clinging to Celia's waist—for she was the only thing standing between Celia and rape—but to no avail. More men arrived. They pried her hands free, held her back. Celia's screaming stopped—a rag was stuffed in her mouth as she was forced to the ground again.

"Caroline!"

Robert! Caroline's breath caught at the sound of his voice, her heart tripped over itself to race faster.

"Robert! I'm here!" she called before a filthy hand clamped over her mouth, silencing her. But it was enough—the sound of approaching riders filled the air around them.

The man released her and sprang to his feet with the others, circling the women, swords and lances drawn. Celia clutched at Caroline's skirts. Caroline pulled the rag from her maid's mouth. "Larie," Celia whispered hoarsely. "She was at the loch—what if she didn't get back in?"

Caroline couldn't think of that now. The stamping of hooves, the snorting of horses, the creak of leather surrounded them, but it was nothing more than phantoms, hidden by the mist. She strained for some sign of Robert and his men. Everyone held their breath, scrutinizing the wall of swirling white. Maxwells burst forward and Caroline's heart nearly stopped. The raiders panicked at the sight of a score of roaring Maxwells bearing down on them and scattered. Caroline dragged Celia out of the way. She spotted Robert, tall and straight on horseback, sword drawn, then he disappeared in pursuit of the raiders.

Caroline sank to the ground, her arms around Celia. "Let's wait here," she said and was surprised at how level and calm her voice sounded.

"You stopped them from—from ... you came after me," Celia said, hiccuping. She clung to Caroline like a child, her hands fisted in Caroline's skirt, face streaked with dirt and tears.

Caroline didn't answer, her mind sharp with fear, eyes ceaselessly scanning the white wall of fog. Men shouted and fought around them, but it was all hidden. A horse cantered toward them and Caroline sat up straighter, grabbing a nearby rock.

"Caroline?"

"I'm here!" She dropped the rock and rose, pulling Celia up with her.

He materialized out of the mist. When he saw her, he dismounted. An urge to run to him, to touch him, to assure herself he was real, sprang to life inside her, but she remained immobile—confused not only by the urge, but also by her inability to act on it. As he drew closer, she visually inspected him, noting he was unhurt. She sent up a silent prayer of thanks.

The frown was back between his brows; his mouth was hard and grim. He stopped in front of her and looked her over. His gloved hand went to the top of her bare head, drawing her close.

"Are you hurt?" he asked, his hand sliding down to the back of her neck.

Caroline shook her head, her throat too tight to speak. She could not look in his face, meet his eyes—he would see *everything* if she did. And she did not yet know what *everything* was. She longed to embrace him, to thank him, to ... she didn't know what else she longed for, but it welled up inside her, like a dam near to bursting. And still, her limbs were seized with a strange paralysis, unable to move toward him, or speak her thoughts. She did not know how to express such feelings—did not know if she should. Despair washed over her, displacing the myriad of other inexplicable emotions, and she turned her face away.

Robert dragged her against him, his arms circling her, crushing her against his chest. The leather of his jack bit into her face. His cheek pressed against the top of her head. Her hands curled into the tough leather sleeves, anchoring herself as her world tilted, giving her a glimpse of something forbidden.

"I was so afraid," he whispered against her hair.

Her eyes, wide with surprise and confusion, squeezed shut against the burning moisture. Nothing would ever be the same. The cloistered future she'd prepared for her whole life was a shattered dream. She couldn't see how to fit the pieces back together.

Infatuation. Lust. *Love?* She didn't know what it was, but it twisted her heart and mind in a knot—it was joy, agony, desire, despair—desperate yearning. She couldn't bear it and yet reveled in it. Wanted it to end and yet wanted more. She thought of him endlessly, every task she carried out was done with him in mind. It had been this way since their first meeting. Never had her emotions consumed her, been so sharp and vivid.

Other men appeared and he stepped away from her, his hands framing her face, searching. She stared back, eyes wide, heart pounding with some new, secret knowledge. She quickly shut her eyes, shaken—unable to hold that beautiful gray gaze that had made a shipwreck of her life.

After a moment, he turned and with his arm about her shoulders, led her home.

Robert's men waited for him in the bailey. The Johnstone raiders had set the village on fire and burned his

crops. Alex and his band of broken men took after the
raiders immediately while Robert and the Maxwells from
the castle and the village fought the fire. It was out now,
his fields black and smoldering, half the village destroyed. Caroline had organized the women and children
to tend the wounded. His hall overflowed, but thanks to
Caroline's efficiency, it was not chaos.

The youngest children were in a far corner, out of the
way, playing with his hounds, watched over by two
young women. The older children were near the fire,
shredding sheets into bandages under Larie's supervi-
sion. The women worked together, either boiling water,
tending wounds, or preparing food. Robert spotted Caroline, her blond head above all others, striding through his
people, overseeing it all with calm dignity. She was not
cold to them, not haughty or unapproachable. She
stopped to help the children, to speak to a wounded man,
to hold a baby. She inspired confidence in the people. She
inspired far more than confidence in him.

He could not stay. His men were organized to pursue
the raiders. He could not leave them to Alex, who would
make a bloody mess of everything. He watched as Caroline knelt to speak with a man. He was badly burned. Another woman tended him, but Caroline placed a
comforting hand over his. Golden hair escaped her braid
to obscure her face and she slid the locks behind her ear.
She rose, fetching the man water, and knelt again, holding his head while he drank.

When she stood, she spotted Robert watching her
from his doorway, and hesitated. He gestured for her to
join him. He wanted her alone, to say good-bye. She
looked weary when she entered, but took up her usual
station at the fireplace, hands clasped at her waist. The
picture of serenity. Her bearing dared anyone to get close

to her and promised to shred with disinterest all who tried. He'd been sick with fear for her. He hadn't been far when he'd heard the shouting—knew something was wrong. All he could think of as he'd ridden for the village with his men was *Caroline*. In little over a week, she'd filled his life. He would not go back to how empty it had been before her.

"I'm leaving now," he said. "You have everything in order—so I must go after the raiders."

"I understand. God be with you."

He continued to stare at her—hoping to unsettle her. He did it often and it rarely worked. A smudge of black marred her cheek and the ribbon on her partlet was undone. He could see the hollow of her throat, soft, delicate, unprotected. He wanted to kiss it.

He approached her. "Is that how to send a husband off to battle? To possible death?"

Her eyes took on that wary cast, one golden eyebrow slightly arched in question. "How should one . . . send a husband off?"

He stopped in front of her. "With a kiss."

Her throat worked, but her hands remained clasped. Her skin seemed tight, her jaw clenched. He traced a finger over her cheek. Like silk. Like the finest fabrics from the Orient, exotic, an indulgence. He let his finger follow the line of her throat, to the hollow where her heartbeat thrummed against his finger. He longed to feel the pulsing against his mouth, to taste her skin. He was tired of holding back, of waiting.

His hand circled her neck, his thumb rubbing the sweet hollow of her throat.

She continued to hold his gaze. Her eyes were green pools, guileless, innocent, apprehensive. He could stand this way forever, lost in her eyes, if it weren't for other, baser urges making themselves known. He wanted to do far more than look at her. Her color was high—and this time she couldn't blame it on the fire. The muscles in her neck tightened.

"I can't," she whispered, looking away.

He paused, his hand gentling her throat, his other coming up to turn her face back toward him. She didn't resist, but kept her eyes downcast, the long sweep of her lashes hiding cool green.

"You can't?"

A sigh shuddered through her. "I try . . . and I cannot."

I try . . . and I cannot. What did she mean? She tried to want him, but couldn't? She tried to bear his touch, his attention, but could not?

"I don't understand."

She squeezed her eyes shut. "I . . . before—I wanted to. . . ." She shook her head. Her cheeks flushed crimson, her skin hot against his hand. His heart pounded as hard and fast as hers did beneath his fingers. He'd never seen her in such a state before. He thought he knew what she meant—what she wanted—but after speaking with the priest, he was besieged by a strange hesitancy, as if she were a fragile thing he must treat with care.

She strained backward, away from him, and he knew he'd hesitated too long. However, he didn't relinquish her. He slid his arm about her waist and caught her to him. Her eyes flew open and her hands came up, pressing against his chest. She didn't push him away.

"What do you want?"

Her breathing had become labored, as she struggled—with words. Her mouth opened and closed, her tongue darted out, wetting her lips and sending shards of desire through him. But still he waited, holding her, rubbing hands gently over her back.

Her hands slid slowly up his chest and clasped together behind his neck. He held his breath as she moved closer, bringing her body fully against his. Then laid her head against his shoulder and sighed.

His arms tightened and he buried his face in her neck. Something warm and strange welled up inside him, as unfamiliar as it was unsettling. He was possessed by the notion that he could right all the wrongs done to her.

He kissed her neck. She trembled. He lifted his head, looked into her face. Her head still rested against his shoulder, her eyes closed.

"I must go. I've taken too long."

She nodded and lifted her head.

"I'll have my kiss before I go."

And she met him halfway, her lips soft and responsive. It felt so right to kiss her, to hold her, that he couldn't stop. She opened her mouth wider. When his tongue touched hers, she inhaled. He pulled back, to reassure her, but her hands were still clasped behind his neck and she brought his head back down. Her mouth opened readily beneath his, her tongue meeting his to stroke and twine. Her fingers brushed through the hair at his neck. He shuddered, his control tenuous. He wanted to ravage her, to have her against the wall—he thought he would die if he did not.

His hands slid down her hips, bringing her up hard against him. She did not stiffen, but pressed against him, urgent. His heart hammered in his ears—then he realized it was not merely his heart, but someone hammered on the door to his chambers. He tore his mouth away as the door burst open.

Caroline's eyes remained closed, her lips rosy and swollen. She was limp in his arms.

He didn't even glance over his shoulder, could not

stop looking at her. "What?" His voice surprised him—
raw and angry.

Caroline's eyes opened slowly. She had the look of a
woman in the throes of passion and it fueled him. He was
rigid, aching.

The man at the door said, "One of Red Alex's men just
arrived—he says the Johnstones murdered your brother!"

12

By the time Robert arrived at his brother's encampment, he felt like bloody hell—his body aching from the skirmish with the raiders and the hard ride, his mind a whirl of sick confusion. *Alex, dead?* It simply couldn't be. It was like losing his father all over again—the anger, the regrets. Robert froze when he spotted Alex laid out beneath a tree, so still. His throat thickened, his eyes burned.

He approached his brother's body slowly. One of the criminals Alex rode with tried to stop him. "My lord—"

Robert pushed the man away. "Leave off."

Alex's face was turned away. Robert didn't think he could look upon it. Would he look as Father did? As fierce as in life—as if he'd battled death. Regret knifed through Robert anew. Their last words had been so harsh and now he could never tell his brother that in spite of it all he did admire his fire, his courage, his conviction. Robert's vision blurred. He looked upward, blinking rapidly. Thick fog obscured the sky, but he could see nothing through the haze of moisture.

"Christ. Are you crying?"

Robert's gaze jerked back to his brother, who struggled to sit up. Alex groaned, gripping his side.

"I thought you were dead."

"I'm not?" Alex fell back. "I thought this was hell . . . but it appears not."

Weak with relief, Robert knelt beside Alex. He called for ale and helped his brother to lean against the tree.

"Why didn't someone tell me? They told me you were dead—I was grieving, damn it," Robert muttered, unhooking Alex's leather jack while his brother hissed and jerked.

"The bugger clouted me, too—they saw all the blood and me snuffed out—and well, thought I was gone."

The man who brought them a skin of ale was the same who'd tried to stop Robert when he arrived. "I tried to tell ye, my lord—but ye told me to leave off."

"So I did." Robert held the skin to Alex's lips. "I'll send you back to Annancreag. Caroline will tend your wounds while I see to the reivers."

"Nay," Alex gasped between gulps of ale. "I'll not ride back in a litter like some woman—I go with you."

"Don't be a fool. You're worthless wounded. You will end up dead if you refuse to heal."

Alex muttered something under his breath as Robert pulled the jack off an arm and ripped his bloody shirt open. Robert poked at the wound, causing Alex to yelp in pain. "Thank you for trying to help Caroline back there."

Grimacing and breathing harshly, Alex squinted at his brother. "She has much to recommend her . . . I'll admit."

Robert sat back on his heels. "Well . . . I know that hurt."

"That doesn't mean I trust her, mind you—just that she's brave and strong—and certainly no mare."

Suffused with warm pride, Robert forgot to help his brother. Alex struggled to free his other arm of the jack. "Could you help me?"

"Oh." Robert gently pulled the jack off and tossed it aside. Water and rags had been brought. "I'm pleased you find her acceptable. Patrick will love her." *If Patrick is alive to meet her.* But Robert couldn't voice his fears to Alex—his brother might take matters into his own hands.

"Is there a lass Patrick doesn't love?" Alex placed a bloody hand on Robert's wrist. "I'm serious, Brother. You mustn't trust her."

Robert didn't reply. The white of his brother's ribs gleamed at him. The wound was deep but not life threatening. It needed a woman's care and stitching, however, if it weren't to fester. "I trust her with my own brother's life."

Alex's jaw clenched and he looked away, shaking his head slightly.

They were silent while Robert dressed the wound and wrapped a cloth about Alex's chest, securing it tightly. Already blood seeped through to stain it. "We must get you to Caroline." He ordered a litter to be constructed.

Kneeling beside Alex again, he asked, "How feel you?"

Alex's normally ruddy tan complexion was pale and sheened with sweat. White surrounded the tight line of his mouth. "Fine."

"It looks worse than it is, methinks. Caroline will sew you up. Then you are to do as she says. Understand?"

Alex's gaze fixed on a far tree. He didn't respond.

Let him sulk. Alex didn't want to like her because she was a Graham. Such obstinacy could cost Robert his peace—he would not tolerate it.

After a moment Alex said, "I've never seen a lass so tall."

"Aye. She is also very well lettered, far more so than I—or even you."

Alex raised his brows. "So she has the mind of a man—unusual."

"She wants to enter a convent—never wanted to wed."

Alex's eyebrows rose. "You're wiving a nun?"

Robert closed his eyes wearily and shook his head. "She's not a nun."

"Perhaps not in deed—but in her heart, surely."

Robert didn't open his eyes. "Not in her heart either!"

Alex groaned, holding his side and motioning for the wine skin. Robert held it for him. He lay back, breathing hard, and said, "About the horse's ass misadventure . . . had I known she was standing there, I never would have said those things."

"Really? And here I thought you did it on purpose, so she wouldn't marry me."

"I shouldn't have left. I would've liked to see you talk your way out of that one!"

"She is a reasonable woman. She doesn't take offense at every imagined slight, like you."

"How verra nun-like!"

"Trust me—there is nothing nun-like about my wife."

Alex grinned wickedly—throwing himself into the teasing. Having been destined for the church himself once, he relished poking fun at it. "You tell yourself that so rutting on God's chosen doesn't seem so much like sacrilege."

"I have not lain with her—yet."

Alex's eyes widened hopefully. He tried to push himself back up on one arm. "This is good! Since the peace is a failure, the marriage can be annulled!"

"The peace is not a failure."

"Where is Patrick?" Alex asked stubbornly. "And what of that raid?"

"That was the Johnstones."

"Was it? I did see Bean, and a few others, but I also saw Armstrongs and Grahams."

Robert dismissed this with a wave. "Broken men—like your lot. They owe allegiance to no one."

Alex grunted. "Perhaps . . ." He eyed Robert thoughtfully. "Why have you not lain with her?"

"I don't want to talk about it."

"You can't—because she's so pious—or she won't let you!"

Robert glowered threateningly at his brother.

Alex grabbed his brother's arm. "I jest, Brother! This really troubles you."

Robert shook his head. "I'm not troubled."

Alex took the hint and changed the subject. Robert barely attended to the conversation. All this talk of Caroline being nun-like troubled him greatly, though he'd never admit it to Alex. Could he be deluding himself? Could he be forcing her to sin, to turn away from God?

Sacrilege. He'd never thought of it that way.

They discussed Robert's impending pursuit of the raiders. Alex was an experienced reiver and so Robert noted his brother's advice with interest. When the litter was finished, Robert helped them situate Alex and cover him with blankets. The litter was attached between two horses. Alex scowled petulantly the whole time.

"What will you do when you catch them?" Alex asked as Robert checked to be sure the litter was secure. Alex was far more vengeful than Robert and they often clashed on the subject of punishment. Robert knew punishment must be meted out—if for no other reason than as a deterrent to future raids—but he also felt it shouldn't be so harsh as to close the door on peace.

"I've sent a rider to Lord Maxwell, informing him I've undertaken a hot trod. The kine will slow the reivers down. I've sent two trackers ahead with sleuth dogs. I expect we'll recover our goods."

"That's not what I asked!"

Robert signaled for Alex's men to head out. They were to escort Alex to Annancreag and wait there for further instructions.

Alex tried to sit up, his gaze riveted to his brother. "You will interrogate them! You will find out who the Grahams and Armstrongs are working for! And then—take retribution!"

Robert just waved his brother off. "What was that? Oh, aye! Caroline will take good care of you!"

Alex's face reddened and he snarled like an angry mastiff.

When Alex was gone, Robert followed the trail left for him by his trackers. Twenty armed and mounted Maxwells accompanied him. Because of the thick fog, he'd been unable to determine how many raiders they were up against, but he thought it was no more than two dozen. Their way was slow, owing to the bog. Much of Robert's lands consisted of fen and forest, very little was arable. But the hunting was good and his neighbors rarely complained when he grazed his sheep and kine in their pastures—and he turned a blind eye when they hunted in his forest or fished in his lochs.

Everything had been going as planned until this damnable raid. He couldn't understand it. Bean was close to the Johnstone laird and would not undertake such a venture without his lord's blessing. What if Alex was right? What if this had something to do with the Grahams? What did that mean for Patrick? Robert didn't want to think of that. He was so close to making his marriage real and binding ... Alex's words haunted him. How could he lie with her in good faith knowing this morning's attack might have something to do with the Grahams? But damn it—she was not a nun at heart.

He must bed her. The decision appeared so simple that he should be able to put it from his mind. Bed the lass—but for now, mind to the matter. Hot trod.

He was so deep in thought that when the raiders burst from the trees he did not immediately comprehend what was happening. An ambush! He yanked his sword from the scabbard and swung as a raider bore down on him. Metal clashed and caught, blades locked. Robert's horse reared. His opponent slashed at Robert's mount. The horse screamed and lost its balance. Robert fought to remove his boots from the stirrups, but his spur caught. The horse crashed onto its side just as Robert yanked his foot clear and threw himself backward. He landed on his back. The air whooshed out of his lungs. Pinpoints of light obscured his vision.

He still gripped his sword. He rolled instinctively, hearing the thud as the ground was struck where he had just lain. On his feet, his vision cleared. The fog had lifted some but his attacker had disappeared. Battle was visible through the trees. Robert scanned the area and started for his men. Someone dropped from a tree, onto his head and shoulders, knocking him to his knees. Grabbing his assailant's hair, he yanked him off and backhanded him, sending him sprawling into a tree.

The man scrambled to his feet. Robert recognized him—an Armstrong. Robert had lost his sword, but nonetheless, he attacked, barehanded, well aware his size cowed greater opponents than this wiry man. The Armstrong's eyes widened and he ran, kicking up pine needles. Robert tackled him and flipped him onto his back.

"Who sent you?" he demanded, slamming the man's back into the ground. The Armstrong swung at him, tried to buck him off. Robert shoved his forearm into the man's throat, pinning him. "Answer me! Who sent you?"

The man's eyes shifted, to something behind and above Robert, then moved quickly back to Robert's face. His body went slack. Robert grabbed the man's shoulder and rolled, pulling the Armstrong atop him as a shield. The body slammed into him. A sword drove through the Armstrong's back—the point ramming into Robert's leather jack. Robert threw the body aside and leaped to his feet, but the other assailant fled into the trees.

Robert yanked the sword from the body and rolled the Armstrong over. Blood spilled from his mouth but he was still alive.

"Who sent you?" Robert asked again.

The man gasped something.

Robert leaned closer. "Tell me."

"Blood Stone . . ."

Robert reared back, staring at the man in astonishment. "What?"

The Armstrong's eyes glazed and his last breath sighed between bloodied lips. Robert stood, perplexed. The Blood Stone? What had that legend to do with aught? He went to his horse. Its sides heaved as it strained for air. He knelt, running his hands along its chest until he encountered gore. He bit his lip as he examined the gaping wound. He didn't understand it. Never would a borderer purposely injure a horse. They were too valuable—they were plunder.

Robert stroked the horse's black nose as his men surrounded him. They were bloodied and not a horse among them. "Did they do this to all the horses?"

"Aye," Geordie answered—his chief man-at-arms. "They tried, at least."

When the horses were put down, Robert and his men gathered in a clearing. Two Maxwells and one of the raiders were dead. The Armstrong. Robert leaned against a tree, trying to decide what to do next. Two of his men stripped the Armstrong's weapons and clothing. Geordie approached, bearing a distressingly familiar leather packet.

Robert snatched it from his guard's hands, appalled. "This was on the Armstrong? You found it on his person?"

"Aye."

"Were there Grahams among the raiders?"

Geordie nodded, the thick lips poking out of his wiry beard pursed. "I'm sure I saw at least three. And one of them was Wesley Graham."

A rider arrived ahead of Caroline's brother-in-law with a verbal message from Robert. He said his brother was much in need of her ministrations and that he did not know when he would return. Caroline quickly readied her own bed for her brother-in-law's arrival. By the time he was carried, moaning and swearing, into the bedchamber, Caroline stood beside the bed—needle, thread, and hot water waiting. She untied the dressing from his ribs and peeled away the blood-soaked cloth. He had been sliced like a side of beef, but no skin was missing, the flap could be sewed closed leaving only a scar.

"This will hurt. Perhaps you should get drunk." She paused thoughtfully. "But only if you're not a violent drunk."

Alexander glared at her. "Give me the whiskey."

She held the bottle just out of his reach. "You're aggressive. Surely it will only increase your agitation."

He muttered some of the vilest words she'd ever heard—even from her father. When his foul mouth coaxed no reaction from her, he stared sullenly at the far wall. Caroline decided to control the whiskey and poured him a cup. He tossed it back and held it out for more.

She wet a cloth with hot water. "That's enough for now."

He made no sound as she worked, though at times, his
eyes were squeezed shut and his breathing shallow. She
set aside the blood-soaked rag and poured him another
cup of whiskey. "This is a large wound, so it will take a
while to suture." She held up the tiny curved silver needle, threaded with her finest cotton thread. "You will certainly feel it, but the needle's size will minimize the pain.
It will also make for a neater scar."

"Just do it," he rasped. His face was bloodless as he
stared at the needle.

"Celia," Caroline called. Celia came forward from
where she hovered near the door. "Fetch me the bench
from my desk."

"Aye, my lady."

Caroline frowned after her maid. No trace of nastiness
or hate remained. Perhaps Celia was just too exhausted to
be disagreeable—she had worked very hard today, tending
the wounded. Caroline decided that if Celia forgot about
her extra duties this evening, she would not remind her.
Celia returned with the bench and situated it beside the
bed before she withdrew, eyes downcast, back to the door.

Alexander didn't speak to her throughout the stitching. The light faded and Celia brought more candles.
Sweat broke out on Caroline's brow and at one point, she
removed her partlet, before it strangled her. Celia was
right there at her elbow. She took the partlet and seconds
later pressed a cool cloth to Caroline's forehead.

As she worked, Caroline's mind wandered back to
Robert—to the kiss. The ones before it now seemed
tame—innocent, even—compared to the last. It had driv-
en every thought from her, robbed her of logic, sense. Her
mouth tingled just from the memory and she had to pause
to gather her wits again. Another kiss like that and he
would win. And then what?

She slowly became aware that Alexander watched her. "Are you in pain?"

He raised his russet brows. "Och, no—it tickles."

"I'm trying not to hurt you." She stopped stitching long enough to give him more whiskey.

He drained the cup more slowly this time. "It's not so bad—anymore. This is nothing. Look here." He gestured to the side of his head. Caroline stared blankly at him. He nodded encouragingly. Apparently, she was to look at his scalp. She stood and ruffled his thick hair aside. A long gash, puckered and knobby, stretched from just behind his ear to the crown of his head. Caroline grimaced in sympathetic pain. Such a wound would kill most men.

" 'Twas a Graham—he nearly killed me."

Caroline returned to her bench and began stitching again. "Your head must be harder than most."

His eyes narrowed and his lips twitched. "Aye, so it seems."

"I'm almost done," she said, discomfited that he still watched her so intently.

Finished finally, she tied the thread off and redressed the wound. He had other wounds, but they were minor and Celia had cleaned them as Caroline stitched. Alexander looked down at the clean linen swathing him, then up at her as she stood. He grabbed her hand and opened his mouth to speak, but Caroline yanked her hand free.

He was still frowning at her when Caroline instructed Celia to bring him food. "Then send a bath to . . . to the tower room." She had to sleep somewhere, after all, since Alexander should not be moved.

Celia cocked her head, puzzled. "The tower room, my lady?"

"Yes—and then send two maids to begin transferring my things to the tower."

Caroline left them and went into her withdrawing room. She stared around the darkened chamber, strangely empty inside. If she didn't give in, if she held fast to her virginity—would she truly win? But Robert wouldn't always be this way with her. Once the challenge disappeared he would become bored.

She put her hands to her head, as if she could squeeze the miserable thoughts away. *Impossible not to think about it, not to remember, to relive it.* The pressure of his mouth, warm and tender. His tongue, stroking hers, building a fire she had yet to extinguish. That perhaps would never be extinguished. She would always burn for more—even after she left and spent her days in silent prayer with other good women, she would relive every moment. And burn.

Time. That's what she needed. Time and distance. It would go away. She would stop burning. Nothing good could come of giving in to him. Her own lust would trap her into a life of bondage.

The door opened behind her and she dropped her hands, turning. Father Jasper stood silhouetted in the doorway. She realized she was standing in the dark—hadn't even lit a candle.

"Caroline," he said. "You asked for advice, before. I have prayed—and I have also spoken with your husband."

Caroline lit the candles on the desk, her fingers trailing over the book Robert had given her. "And?"

"Celia is no longer his mistress."

"I know."

Father Jasper approached, his robes swishing about him. He looked exhausted, his eyes hollowed and haunted. He'd worked as hard as everyone. In some ways, his part was the hardest, trying to explain why God had allowed the village to be destroyed, the crops burned, the kine stolen.

"Give the marriage a chance."

Caroline's chest hurt. She needed better advice—she needed reasons. Why should she give it a chance? What could she gain? What could she lose? "You told me a few days ago that you weren't always chaste."

That pained look came over his thin face again, as if he wanted to bolt.

"I know you were trying to make me feel better, but what did you mean? When were you not chaste? Did you love her? Or was it lust?"

Father Jasper's eyes darted about the room, as if searching for an escape. He looked over his shoulder suddenly. "I think someone called me . . ." He started for the door.

"Father! No one called you."

He turned, rubbing his chin. "Are you certain? I could've sworn—"

"Surely you wouldn't swear?"

He dropped his hand, scowling wearily, and she knew she'd won.

Caroline went to him. "Why won't you speak of it with me? Is the memory painful?"

He sighed, shoulders slumping. "I came into the church much like you want to—without a calling. I'm no warrior, had no lands or titles, and had always a love for books and learning. It seemed the sensible thing to do. I had nothing to offer a lass of my standing . . . I hoped, in a world surrounded by men and learning and godliness, that I would be content."

Caroline stared at Father Jasper in amazement. She had never suspected that he wasn't meant to be a priest, that it hadn't been his calling.

He seemed discomfited by her shock and retreated to the desk. "There was a woman once. . . . We could never have been together. It was doomed from the start. And yes—there was lust and love, they are often inseparable."

"Who was she?"

He only shook his head.

"Was it worth it? If you could do it over again, would you?"

"Sometimes, I think, no." He came to her, his expression drawn and grim. "But mostly, I think, yes." His expression softened. "Give him a chance, lass."

Caroline stood there for a long time after he'd gone, considering his words, filled with uncertainty and misgivings. She was more confused than before she'd spoken to him! He was no help—and since he wouldn't tell Caroline why he couldn't be with the lass, his advice was of little use. If he didn't deem love worth fighting for, why should she? Perhaps when the lust finally burned itself out, there was nothing left. Oh, she'd never understand if he didn't explain it! And she knew he'd say no more—at least for now.

She gathered up her writing book, ink, and quill. After making certain everyone was settled in the hall and Alexander was comfortable, she headed for the tower room. The walk seemed much farther than before. Her feet grew heavier and heavier until she reached it. She stood outside the thick oak door. Her room now—her place, her bed. What would Robert think of this bold move? She didn't care, she told herself, pushing the door open. It was too hard, sleeping with him—too easy to give in. After that kiss, she knew he wouldn't leave her be when she curled against him at night.

She turned in circles, wanting to love this room she'd thought so much about. It seemed empty and lonely now. The mattress had been restuffed with dried heather, and clean sheets and furs draped the bed.

She sat on the bed, situating the inkpot nearby. She

was writing a story. It had begun as a retelling of the Orpheus and Eurydice myth, but had changed somewhere along the way. It was so different she considered changing the names. She tapped the quill against her chin, trying different names on her characters. The tension drained from her limbs as she immersed herself in her thoughts. Perhaps Orpheus would kiss Eurydice . . .

She was scribbling madly when Celia cleared her throat. Caroline's head jerked up and she scanned the room frantically, guiltily, until she spotted her maid. Her cheeks flamed—as if caught in some wicked act—which was perhaps closer to the truth than she'd care to admit.

She wanted to slam her book shut, but realized she'd forgotten the sand. That would not do. "Yes, Celia?"

Celia proffered a small enameled box. "You forgot your sand."

Caroline took the box and poured sand over the pages she'd written. Celia peered at the book curiously. Caroline fought the urge to hide her writing. Even if Celia could read, which was doubtful, she certainly would not be able to read quickly enough to grasp what Caroline wrote.

"I've never seen anyone write so fast," Celia said. "Not even Red Alex—and he is verra learned."

After pouring the sand back into the box, Caroline set the book aside. "Alexander? Robert's brother?"

"Oh, aye—he went to a monastery, was to be a priest."

Caroline could not hide her astonishment. "Really? I suppose it's obvious why he's not one now."

Celia laughed. "Aye—it is! They wouldn't have him—sent him home. Said he lacked humility and discipline."

Caroline regarded her maid oddly. There was no mistaking the difference in Celia's manner. She wondered if she should comment on it, or if that would ruin the spell. Instead, she said, "Do you read or write?"

"Oh, no—not a word!"

"I could teach you . . . if you like."

Celia shrugged. "Why? I have no need of letters and my betrothed would surely be displeased as he thinks women should keep to their place."

Caroline hadn't expected any other answer. Most women didn't see a point in literacy, just as many men didn't. Caroline couldn't imagine life without books and words, but then that was further proof of how different and unsuitable she was. Caroline started to remove the pins from her hair when Celia placed a hesitant hand on her shoulder, turning her slightly.

"I'll do that, my lady."

Caroline turned. She found herself strangely at a loss for words and so sat silently as Celia unbraided her hair and combed it down her back. Throughout, the tub was brought up and filled with hot water. When the servants left them alone again Celia came around to stand in front of Caroline. Celia pulled the hair over Caroline's shoulders and stroked it. "Ye've such bonny hair, my lady. You should wear it down . . . at least for Lord Annan."

"Thank you." *What was this?* With some trepidation, Caroline waited for Celia's next surprise.

"The partlet should go as well . . . ye've a fine bosom—why not show it?" Caroline opened her mouth to tell her why but Celia cut her off. "Now, I'm not saying you should wear it as low as myself—that's simply not befitting a grand lady such as yourself . . . and well—it doesn't suit you anyway. But a glimpse is lovely." Celia touched the lace that trimmed Caroline's shift. With her partlet gone it peeked out the top of her bodice.

Caroline looked down and saw the slight swell of her breasts, edged with lace. Perhaps there was something . . . mildly attractive about it. "Is there something wrong with the way I dress?"

Celia's lips thinned. "To be truthful, aye. It's as if you're trying to look like a nun, or a matron—as if it's a . . . a mask you hide behind." She snapped her fingers. "As if you're ashamed of being a woman."

Caroline was at a loss, but loath to show it. She stood and unhooked her bodice, moving toward the brass tub. "I'm ashamed of nothing." She removed her bodice and tossed it on the hearth. "Bring me the soap."

Celia brought the soap, then disappeared behind the screen. She reappeared with the pot from under the close-stool. This time Caroline could not hide her amazement. Celia, performing her extra duty, with no prompting?

"Celia! What is the matter with you?"

Celia shrugged, one hand on the door latch. "I'm not so bad—really, my lady, and I mean to show you. I know when I'm wrong and I can admit it." When Caroline just gaped at her she grinned. "Good e'en, my lady."

After her bath, Caroline slipped beneath the heavy blankets just as thunder crashed and lightning lit the sky. The air had been heavy with moisture all day, the sky low and dark, brewing a nasty storm. Was Robert out in it? Was he dressed warmly enough? She hoped he found shelter.

She blew out the candles and lay against the pillows. She should get up and close the shutters, but her furniture had not yet been brought up and there was nothing beneath the windows for the rain to ruin. She gazed out at the night as lightning rent the dark. The driving rain looked like silver needles slanting to the earth. She loved the sound of it, pattering against the stone, the whoosh of the wind. Wild and unleashed—just like her emotions. Just like his taste, on her mouth, in her blood now.

No! She would not think of him, she ordered herself. Instead, she would dream of Orpheus and Eurydice and their kiss. So what if in her imagination Orpheus was tall with chestnut hair and penetrating gray eyes? And so what if the shadowy figure of Eurydice she had yet to give a face happened to stand nearly as tall as her lover? It was not the same.

And it was safe.

13

Ridley paced his chambers, waiting, with increasing impatience, for his brother. He'd been alerted of Wesley's arrival nearly an hour ago and had ordered him to report immediately. This was most unlike Wesley and did not bode well. Or perhaps, Ridley thought, turning toward the door uneasily, Wesley meant to cozen him. Could he have gotten his hands on the stone and now meant to keep it for himself? That was the difficulty in having to rely on others. Incompetence. Untrustworthiness. It was so much easier to do it himself. But now that he was baron, he could not jeopardize relations with other families. And so he must rely on hired men—men he could denounce if they were caught and somehow connected with him.

First Mona, then Fayth, and now Wesley—it was almost more than he could bear. He'd been waiting weeks for his stepmother to make some move. If she truly were the keeper of the stone, as Father had insisted, why then did she do nothing? She refused to speak of it, though she'd never denied she was the keeper. Could Father have been wrong? Could the true keeper even now be at An-nancreag?

Frustrated, Ridley started for the door, determined to beat his brother dead if he attempted to deceive him. The door opened and Wesley entered, grim faced. He quietly shut the door behind him before facing Ridley, hands clasped behind his back.

"Where have you been? I sent for you an hour ago."

"I wanted to see how Fayth fared."

Ridley's lips tightened. Wesley was useful but for this tenderness he had for their sisters. It might prove prob-lematic. "And?"

"She mends. She's regained much of the use of her arm. But she is distressed at being kept prisoner." Wesley masked the accusation well, but Ridley perceived it nonetheless.

Ridley approached his brother slowly. "I assume by the long face you did not fetch me the stone. Did you at least learn of its disposition?"

Wesley shook his head. The firelight glistened on the fine golden-brown whiskers shading his jaw. "Nay, my lord. The man who spoke with Caroline's maid is dead, but he did tell me the maid knew nothing."

Rage bloomed in Ridley. "Dead? Pray tell how you managed to lose a man? This was not a mission of bloodletting—a simple foray to gather intelligence. Nothing was to be attempted unless you were certain they were in possession of the stone and you could see a way to take it."

Wesley's jaw clenched but he showed no fear or re-morse for having failed his brother and lord so utterly. "The maid assured the messenger there was no love be-tween Caroline and Lord Annan . . . so I attempted to kidnap her."

Ridley took an exaggerated step backward. "What? Who gave these orders? I gave no orders to kidnap."

Wesley's eyes were averted, staring sightlessly at some point to Ridley's right. "No, my lord, you did not."

Ridley moved into his brother's line of vision, getting right into his face, forcing Wesley to crane his neck. "Caroline is married now—she is her husband's responsibility. I want no more of this foolishness! There is no longer anything you can do—consummation has taken place."

Wesley's lip twitched and he jerked his chin down. Ridley's anger grew.

"Consummation did take place, did it not? You told me you saw the sheets."

"There was blood on the sheets, aye."

Ridley paced away, his mouth tilting sardonically. "I see. Your crime then is omission. What—did she cut herself? Did he?"

"There was blood—that's all I know."

Ridley needed to think. Wesley had never been so defiant. He felt more strongly about this than Ridley had first thought. Since the death of his friend and Fayth's paramour, Jack, Wesley and Fayth had become bitter cohorts in their hatred of all things Maxwell. It annoyed Ridley. So a man had died? Scores of men—Grahams and Maxwells alike—had died in this feud. Why should one more make a difference? But when he said these things to them, they became impossible, so he'd stopped and pretended sympathy. Still, he'd never anticipated it would lead to such disobedience. Not when he'd promised Wesley that when the time came, he would be free to wreak his vengeance on the Maxwells—in addition to the Bells, Irvines, and Carlisles.

Ridley must find a way to make this work for him rather than against him. Time was running out. Lord

Annan would not remain passive much longer—if that stone was not located soon, Ridley would be forced to release Sir Patrick to appease the laird and buy time. He did not want to do that—Sir Patrick was a formidable opponent and had not been easy to capture. Ridley wanted him to stay put until he had a use for him.

Ridley folded his arms over his chest, turning back to his brother. "Tell me the rest."

"When unable to get information, or Caroline, we set the village alight."

Ridley closed his eyes, praying for patience. Wesley simply could not resist despoiling a Maxwell. It was like setting an angry bull loose in a henhouse—everything trampled and destroyed.

"Red Alex pursued. I tried to keep myself and the Grahams out of sight—but I fear I was seen."

"By Red Alex?"

Wesley shook his head. "By another. Red Alex was killed."

Ridley cocked his head consideringly. "Well then. Perhaps it wasn't a complete loss." Red Alex was the plague of the West March—on both sides of the border. He carried on his father's vendetta without his brother's blessing. He'd been put to the horn more times than Ridley could count—only to employ bribery or his silver tongue to have all charges dropped. Ridley only wished he'd been the one to run the bastard through.

"I thought you would be pleased," Wesley said.

"Is that all?"

Wesley shook his head. "Lord Annan gave pursuit as well. We ambushed him and thought it expedient to maim his horses so he couldn't follow. Lord Annan killed the Armstrong messenger—the one who spoke with Caroline's maid."

"So now I am unable to speak with the one man who infiltrated Annancreag."

"Prithee, forgive me. I will do better next time—I swear it." Wesley's eyes burned with far more than the desire to be a faithful and loyal servant.

"Aye, I'm sure you'll manage to murder even more Maxwells and kidnap your sister proper this time—the stone will be of secondary importance to you."

"That is not so."

"Try not to forget that I hold what you want."

A muscle ticked in Wesley's jaw, but he made no reply. Once Fayth was wed to Carlisle, Ridley meant to have the old laird and his heir killed. Wesley would then be given the administration of Fayth's inheritance. Wesley loathed Carlisle nearly as much as Annan. Strange, how he was not opposed to *that* match. Greed made men so easy to use. He wished women were so easily swayed. For though Fayth would rather kill herself than wed a man not of her choosing, she was for some unfathomable reason opposed to ridding herself of an unwanted husband through foul means. Ridley knew Wesley had tried to make her see reason but she was forever mouthing platitudes about sin and hell—most tiresome. She was beginning to sound like Caroline.

"Leave me," Ridley said. "I will consider my next move . . . and hope relations with Lord Annan are not irreparable."

Thank God for Caroline. She would smooth the way. She would convince Lord Annan that Ridley was not involved—and who could argue with such cool, calm logic? Ridley'd spent his life trying! Lord Annan didn't stand a chance.

Wesley opened his mouth, as if to say more, then seemed to think better of it and left. Ridley paced absently to the fireplace. He had feared he would be forced to utilize Fayth, and if so, he wanted to do it on his own terms. But Wesley had brought him nothing, and now his sister was his only hope of doing this covertly, without revealing himself. He did not know if his hold over Fayth was strong enough. Two weeks ago he would not have trusted her, but now that he had promised to give her some say in her future, she had become a different person. He still kept her under tight guard, but she made no escape attempts and her manner was agreeable.

He was loath to use her; yet, he could see no way around it. Lord Annan would accept none of Caroline's servants—no Grahams but Father Jasper had been the agreement. But if Fayth showed up unannounced, surely Lord Annan would not turn her away. Fayth would have to make a show of hating Ridley, sobbing not to be separated from her sister . . . yes, this could work. Of course, there would be problems, after—when he wed her to Carlisle anyway. But he would worry on those when they occurred.

The decision made, he sent his steward to fetch Fayth. He lowered himself into a chair before the fire. How to go about it? She knew some of what he planned—but not all. Surely, she would shrink from deceiving her own sister. They'd always seemed so close—to him at least, being forever on the outside. How to make her see reason? And quite suddenly, it all came together. Wesley's affection for his sisters. Fayth and Caroline's stubborn belief that they should have some say in their futures. Both Fayth and Wesley's fury at him for marrying Caroline to a Maxwell. Both imagined her miserably unhappy and abused. All of this could be used to his advantage.

A smile curved Ridley's mouth and he stroked his beard, pleased at his own cleverness and resourcefulness.

Oh yes, this proved him the worthiest man to possess the Clachan Fala. Who else could exploit its full potential?

The door opened, but he didn't rise. His chair faced away from the door. He waited.

"You wished to see me?" Fayth said loudly.

"Aye. Prithee, come sit and talk."

She sat in the chair opposite from him, her expression wary. She seemed smaller than ever; her narrow shoulders hunched submissively in her shapeless gown, her pointy face shadowed with weariness and pain. She did not smile, but neither did she regard him as if he had horns and a forked tongue.

Ridley arranged his features into a sympathetic frown. "Did you speak with Wesley?"

Fayth nodded.

"And he told you how miserable Caroline is?"

Again, she nodded. Judging by the angry flush now darkening her skin, he'd pinpointed the source of her sleepless nights. Fayth had always been so much easier to read than Caroline or Wesley.

Ridley shook his head, pursing his lips together as though holding in great emotion. "It grieves me that I am the master of this horrible situation. I truly thought marriage would agree with her—but what do I know of women and love, eh?"

Fayth didn't answer, her eyes narrowed with suspicion.

"Aye—I admit now to knowing nothing of women. I thought I knew what Mona was about, but it seems both Father and I were wrong . . . and look where it's gotten me."

Fayth frowned in consternation. "You speak in riddles—be plain."

Ridley sighed. "I am ashamed to admit my folly, but confess, I must." He rested his elbows on the chair arms and leaned toward his sister. "I did not wed Caroline to Lord Annan merely to secure peace. The legend of the Clachan Fala indicates that a marriage between an Annan Maxwell and an Eden Graham must take place. This marriage signals the keeper of the stone to retrieve it and present it to the couple." Ridley shook his head sadly. "It seems that it truly was nothing more than a legend."

The silence ticked by. Fayth's whiskey-colored eyes never left his face. Ridley grew increasingly anxious, though he didn't show it. He took heart from her expression—still cautious, but she was considering all he'd said.

"How can you be so sure you were wrong?" Fayth asked finally. "Wesley said the messenger was killed and that he didn't speak with anyone of import—merely a maid. Besides, they've only been wed a fortnight. I know you believe Mona is the keeper—but methinks not. What if it's someone else? And if that is so, then mayhap they've yet to learn of the marriage. But when they do, they will fetch it. So you must needs be patient and find a way to plant someone in the castle to inform you when this occurs."

He'd not expected her to be so forthcoming with ideas. He leaned back in his chair and considered her. "You've been thinking about this."

She shrugged. "And why not? It may be nothing more than fancy, but if it buys me marriage to a man of my choosing, I'll aid you in any way I might."

This was going to be easier than he'd thought. She would take no convincing at all—in fact, by the set of her little jaw, she seemed determined to convince him of something. Apparently, she and Wesley already had a plot brewing—which explained Wesley's earlier reticence. He'd probably instructed her to speak not a word of their little plan until he'd hammered out all the details. And here the ever impulsive Fayth was, hurtling heedlessly forth, unable to restrain her nature. Wesley would be most displeased, but then this was to Ridley's advantage. He must allow Fayth to believe he was reluctant to send her into danger—that his plans for her had been something else entirely.

"Tell me—have you a plan in mind?"

She sat forward on the edge of the chair, her eyes bright. "You expressed concern over Caroline's unhappiness. Suppose you send me to visit her under the pretense of training me for my upcoming nuptials? I will insinuate myself into the household, find out if the stone is already there, or send you word when it arrives—as well as instruct you on the best manner of taking it."

"That's a fine idea, but . . ." Ridley said, his voice laden with uncertainty. He gave her an aggrieved look. "What about Caroline? She will suffer for our rash acts, we cannot allow that."

Taking the bait, Fayth grinned. "Fash not—for I'll not leave her behind. And since Lord Annan still has not her dowry, you can buy her way into the finest convent, far away from here and the Maxwells' reach!"

"This is most dangerous. What if you're discovered?" He sighed worriedly. In truth, if she were discovered he would deny knowledge of her doings—claim she acted independently. But she must be brought to think that was her own idea, and that would take some time and skill. Her idea needed work—though it was good.

Fayth's hands were clutched in fists; she looked ready to burst with reassurances, but perhaps didn't want to appear overeager.

Finally, Ridley stood with a sigh. "Let me think on it. We'll talk more later."

Fayth stood also, her narrow shoulders stooped in dejection, and started for the door.

"Sister, don't go. Please, stay and sup with me. Perhaps some gaming afterward."

Fayth turned with a dubious frown.

He gave her a self-deprecating smile and shrugged. "I find myself minus one sister, and about to lose another. And until now, I had not realized all I was losing. Please, indulge me—let me have this short time with you."

She shrugged and reluctantly rejoined him by the fire.

14

After more than a week spent fruitlessly scouring his lands, as well as Liddesdale and the debatable land, nothing looked so fine to Robert as Annancreag. He climbed the dirt track at the head of his men, their horses courtesy of Lord Maxwell. The village was already rebuilt. Robert was not surprised—this wasn't the first time the village and his lands had been raped. Because of the frequent raiding, border hamlets were of necessity as quickly constructed as destroyed. New cottages stood in place of the old ones, roofed with fresh green thatch. The black expanse of his fields still stretched outward from the village, but men and women worked steadily, turning the soil. It was too late in the season to plant again. It would be a hard winter.

A mule-drawn cart passed, full of bread and casks of ale. Caroline was feeding the village. He had fretted some about his people—worrying whether they had food and such. He'd told himself Caroline would see to it all, and if she didn't, then surely his steward would. But Henry, though a good-hearted man, was often preoccupied and forgetful.

Father Jasper walked beside the mule, staff in hand. He raised his hand to Robert in greeting. "It's good to see you back and well!"

"Thank you, Father!"

On the ramparts, men waved. Dirt-faced children bounded up the hill from the village to run alongside them. Robert's entire body ached from days spent in the saddle. He'd worried endlessly about Wesley Graham's involvement in the raid—wondering if he'd ever see Patrick again. It frustrated him that he couldn't see who was behind it. Did Ridley truly mean to cozen him? Or did Wesley act independently with a group of broken men—like Alex? And what about Caroline? Had she known of the raid? Was that the true reason for her visit to the village?

In the courtyard he passed his horse off to a servant and headed for the keep. The oak and iron studded double doors stood open and, as he reached them, Alex stepped outside.

"Well? Did you catch them? I cannot believe you didn't send me word! You leave me here like some invalid woman. I was coming after you—today if I heard nothing."

Robert stepped back, inspecting his younger brother. He looked in fine health, though Robert noted he held himself rather stiffly, his right arm to his side.

"There was no word to send. They just disappeared. How are you?"

"Fine. Caroline promised to remove the stitches soon, but she seems to be avoiding me. Think you Ridley Graham had aught to do—"

"Where is Caroline?" Robert interrupted, peering over Alex's shoulder. He had no interest in speaking of the raid any more today. He'd thought of nothing else for days—the messenger he killed, his murdered men and horses, the mysterious Clachan Fala. Tomorrow he would discuss his next move with Alex, but for now, he wanted to be left alone. The most important question right now was Caroline's involvement.

Alex shook his head, a grudging smile cracking his stern demeanor. "As soon as your party was sighted, she was off! To the kitchens first, instructing Cook to prepare something special, next to your chambers where she directed the servants like a damn general."

Robert pushed past his brother. "Well . . . ? What think you of her?"

Alex still smiled. "She's not what I expected, but you've certainly cornered yourself a good woman."

Robert grinned like an imbecile, flushed with pride.

"But . . ." Alex continued, "she likes me not."

Robert turned. "It's just her way." He struggled to explain her manner as Alex stared at him expectantly, eyebrows raised. "It's very difficult to know the true Caroline . . . she pretends to be in control of her emotions—but there is storm boiling beneath that iron composure."

Alex grimaced. "A storm, eh? Why, you've become a poet!"

"She healed you, did she not?"

"Nuns must perform good works—one cannot allow unpleasant emotions to interfere with duty to God."

Robert glared at his brother. "I told you—she is not a nun!"

Alex laughed and held up his hands. "Peace. It was but a jest—the nun part. But truly, she doesn't speak to me unless I force her to, she doesn't laugh at my jests; I showed her my scar and she was most unimpressed." He nodded sagely—as if that proved it. "You shall see. And yet, she still manages to treat me with perfect respect. Good works, I tell you!"

"No one cares about your scar—and I don't think your jests are amusing, either." His eyes narrowed as a he recalled Father Jasper's tale about Ridley. Robert would not tolerate reminders of her brother's cruelty. "What kind of jests? You did not make mention of her being horse-like, did you?"

A voice behind him said, "No, my lord, he did not."

Alex's jaw dropped, his eyes wide—a second later his mouth snapped shut. Robert wanted the floor to swallow him—immediately after he thrashed his brother. This was all Alex's fault—he only said such stupid things when his brother was about. He turned, full of explanations and apologies.

The woman before him was not the same one he'd left behind. Her demeanor was the same—the tranquil smile, the pale, wintry green eyes. Her stance was unchanged, hands folded calmly at her waist. But now, golden curls brushed against her hands. Braided with ribbon in the front, her hair cascaded over her shoulders. The partlet had disappeared. Creamy skin and the tantalizing swell of breasts were visible.

"Caroline." His voice sounded weak, guilty.

"Greetings, my lord." She inclined her head. "I've a bath ready for you. A meal will soon follow." She started for his chambers and, stiff legged with shock, he followed.

Alex, who had been pretending fascination with the floor rushes, grabbed his shoulder. "I didn't say anything! It's not my fault!"

Robert shrugged his hand off, annoyed that he was right, but unwilling to admit it. "You'll pay . . . later."

Alone with her in his chambers, he found he could think of nothing to say. All his explanations for what she overheard seemed poor and inadequate. She was so cool and formal, even more so than she'd been before. The words lodged in his throat since he knew they'd be met with the hated empty smile, the patronizing "of course" she would mouth—all the while thinking what a lout he was. He wished she'd rail at him . . . or cry . . . anything but this calm disinterest.

"You look different . . . you're wearing your hair down."

"Yes," she said, testing the water, checking the towels and soap. She turned partway to him, as if something just occurred to her. "Did you bring back any linen or soap you would prefer to use?"

He stared blankly at her. "What?"

"Plunder. Were you not on a hot trod?"

"We did not recover the goods lost—or anyone else's goods."

She was at his desk now. "You received a letter from Lord Johnstone." She held a ledger up for him to see. He recognized the thin volume—the household accounts. "I've been going over the accounts. I've brought them up to date and found areas of unnecessary expenditure. I thought we could discuss them later. I'll join you for dinner."

He found himself nodding at her like a half-wit, unable to form an intelligent thought. He was reminded of all his misgivings. She'd received a letter from Wesley just before she went down to the village. . . . Robert had read the letter and found nothing suspicious, but there were many ways to convey messages secretly. The Armstrong messenger had been with the raiding party—had attacked Robert. He could have given Caroline a message, instructing her to journey to the village where Wesley would rescue her. All these thoughts had bombarded him for the past week, but he'd fought against them—wanting to trust her, reminding himself she'd been trying to escape from the raiders—and that she had kissed him and not pulled away, but stayed in his arms as if she'd let him have his way with her. And he'd almost won the battle. But now . . .

She'd been going through his accounts? Why? What

else had she rifled through in his absence? Had she been searching for a means into the castle, too—a secret way to let raiders in? And though her hair was down, she did not seem any more approachable than she ever had. In fact, she seemed more than ever an exquisite marble statue, beautiful, statuesque, and ultimately hard and unbreakable.

She strode past him, to the door. "If you should need anything—"

He caught her arm, loath to let their reunion end in such a fashion, wanting something in her manner to convince him his suspicions were unfounded. "Where are you going?"

She met his eyes boldly, one eyebrow slightly raised in question. Nothing remained of the woman who had melted in his arms, who had set his blood on fire with her kisses. This was the venerable Mother Caroline. Or a spy, pretending.

"To change."

"To change . . ." he repeated.

Her words not only displeased him, but also increased his distrust. What was this he'd come home to? His wife comely as a girl, hair down and beribboned, partlet lost— as if out maying. And now she intended to return to her nun's habit. Was it because of his foolish words to Alex? Or had his arrival simply taken her by surprise and she hadn't time to change? He stared into her clear green eyes, but he could fathom nothing there but a cold void.

"Do not change. Your hair and dress please me."

"As you wish," she said. "You're hurting my arm."

He didn't release her, though he loosened his grip. "I also wish you to stay. I've missed our talk, our myths. Please, entertain me while I bathe—tell me of all that has gone on in my absence."

He let her step away. "Very well, my lord." She returned to the desk and slid behind it, her eyes resting patiently on him.

He obviously intended her to see him naked. To what end, she could only guess. Did he expect her to be so inflamed with lust she would throw herself at him? She couldn't blame him if that's what he thought. She'd certainly acted wanton before he left. Or perhaps he simply wanted to embarrass her, force a reaction from her—just like Ridley. Well, she thought confidently, he would be sorely disappointed. It wasn't as if she'd never seen a naked man before. She would simply pretend a fig leaf or some such covered his privates.

She'd had much time apart from him and she'd used it well. She'd gone over and over every encounter, every touch, every kiss, to determine what it was she'd felt. And why. Clearly, she didn't love him. Lust, absolutely. She'd been tempted to give in—to experience it. She'd even taken Celia's advice about losing the partlet and wearing her hair down. She'd missed him—hadn't realized how much until she'd been notified of his approach and become frantic with excitement. And when she saw him, standing there, talking to his brother, she'd hoped he would greet her with a kiss. At the time, lust seemed heavenly.

You did not make mention of her being horse-like, did you?

Her throat tightened again, her chin quivered. It was still a game to him. And she had deluded herself into believing that perhaps . . . just perhaps . . .

Lust would fade—she must only resist it. If Father Jasper could do it, then so could Caroline. He had told her once, when one is called to the Lord's service, He would seek to test her. That's what Robert was—a test of her faith and resolution. Of her strength and will.

"Have you written in your book?"

Robert's words jolted her from her thoughts. He removed his leather jack.

Her composure was tenuous. She didn't know whether to burst into tears, or to rail at him. She wanted to do both. She did neither. "Yes, I have."

"Will you read it to me?"

He dropped his jack on the floor and strode toward the desk, working the ties on the leather vest he wore over his shirt. He deposited that on the floor as well. Caroline made herself remain seated, resisting the urge to gather his discarded garments.

"It would be of little interest to you, my lord." That was a lie. He would exhibit more than a little interest in the love scene between Orpheus and Eurydice she had written. Why had she written such wickedness? She would destroy it this very evening.

"I beg to differ. Everything about you interests me. Such as, why have you stopped addressing me as Robert?"

He was untying his shirt. Crisp brown hair grew on his chest. He did not remove his shirt, letting it hang open, revealing a glimpse of his hard chest and belly, ridged with muscle, like a ladder she thought, fighting to tear her eyes from the exposed skin. He'd asked her a question, she thought wildly, her mouth dry, her mind confused.

"You would not be interested in what I've written."

He regarded her oddly. "Aye—I believe you just said that."

A slow heat crept up her chest.

His hands moved to his belt. *Fig leaf. Fig leaf.* She didn't want to look, and yet if she purposefully averted her eyes he would know she was discomfited. So instead her gaze darted up and back—from his clear gray eyes to his hands—now discarding the belt and untying his breeches. *Fig leaf!*

She stood abruptly. The chair scraped loudly across the floor. "I'll call someone to wash you."

"I want you to wash me."

She had already rounded the desk and was halfway across the room—trying not to trip over her feet in her rush. His words halted her and she turned.

He stood there, large hands dangling by his side, his shirt hanging open, exposing more muscular, furred chest than before. His breeches gaped at the waist, giving her a view of how far the narrow line of hair extended, over strong stomach and further. . . . Her imagination sparked to life, wondering just what she might catch a glimpse of if his breeches slipped just an inch . . . *fig leaf!*

She forced her gaze back up to his, swallowing with difficulty. She could not do this! The hair tingled on her scalp, her skin prickled.

He waited. The bath waited.

"What's wrong, Caroline?" he asked, taking a step toward her, so knowledgeable at his little game, and she so ignorant.

She tried to look brisk. There was nothing untoward in his request. As a wife, she *should* wash her husband. And until the peace collapsed, she *was* his wife. "Not a thing."

She went to the tub and stood beside it. It was bigger than Lord Maxwell's tub—big enough to sit down in if you wanted. At the tub, he stepped out of his breeches. Caroline busied herself with the soap so she didn't have to look at him, feeling foolish and inept. She'd never washed a man before! She'd seen it done, however, and could certainly manage without fainting.

She heard him step into the tub and turned. She'd felt his body, in bed beside her—but her imagination did not prepare her for *this*.

She gasped and dropped the soap. No fig leaf would

cover that! How had she never seen it before? Even with his clothing on? And he wanted to put it inside of her? Her belly tightened, her face on fire.

"Caroline?"

She bent down and fumbled with the soap, mumbling something about it being slippery. Thankfully, the bucket was behind him and she circled the tub. The view from behind was not nearly so alarming, but equally arousing. His legs were thick with muscle and very hairy, but the dark hair thinned at his thighs, and the smooth pale skin of his buttocks was completely hairless.

"Caroline?" he said again, and when he turned, the muscles moved, cutting lines in his thigh and bottom.

The bucket. She lifted it—it was full of hot water. "You'll have to kneel, my lord."

He obliged. She felt his gaze on her the whole time, but she couldn't meet his eyes. She knew her cheeks were ruddy as if she'd been running, even her eyes burned. She poured the water over his head. His hair was so short— like warriors wore it, so it didn't interfere with the helm, or blow into their eyes.

She rubbed the soap over her hands and then buried her fingers in his hair. His ears were small and neat, close to his head. Her hands glided over neck and back, pausing at each scar. Two on his right shoulder, one that looked like a burn on his biceps—must have been cauterized by some incompetent surgeon—and a particularly ugly, jagged one that traced his bottom rib from his back to his front. He'd seen his share of battles. He was silent, but his muscles were hard and tight.

She moved to the front of him, refusing to look down, and so looked into his face. His eyes were black, but then she saw the rim of pale gray circling the pupils. She put her hands on his face, shadowed by a week's growth of whiskers. It scraped against her palms.

Soap. She'd forgotten the soap. Still her hand slid down his neck, over his shoulders. She'd never touched a man before—not like this. Something shuddered inside her, warm and liquid. He caught her hands between his and brought them to his mouth.

"Maybe this wasn't such a good idea." His voice was thick. He pressed a kiss against her palm. "Go. I'll finish."

"But . . . your supper . . ." she heard herself saying. She couldn't look away from his head, bent over her hands, his hair wet and spiky. His warm breath blew against her hands. He kissed her other palm and this time she felt the tip of his tongue. Her knees nearly buckled.

He set her hands away and stood. Water sluiced down his body and she looked away, realizing suddenly that he was giving her a reprieve. She backed away.

"Come back in half an hour," he said, "And we'll finish."

His eyes were dark with promise and she said nothing as she rushed to the door. She made her way through the keep in a daze—up to her tower room. Safe inside, she leaned against the door. Her body trembled. Her belly ached, wanting. She slid to the floor.

She'd had it all figured out until he returned. She'd been sure she could control her emotions. She no longer knew what to do. When she was with him, she *wanted* to lose. She'd never had to fend a man off before—she'd always managed to repel them naturally.

A half hour passed, then another quarter. She was late for dinner. Still, her thoughts circled, indecisive. Was there truly no way to discourage him? Did she want to discourage him? She sat on the bed, trying to find the courage to go downstairs and share a meal with her husband. She could still feel his skin beneath her hands, the kisses in her palm. The warmth spread through her belly again, flushed her chest and neck.

He'd let her go—sent her away. He'd known she wasn't ready for it, that it had overwhelmed her. He could have won then. All her planning, all her resolve, burned to ashes when she was with him. She stood and took herself downstairs. She would not run from him again. There was no reason to fear Robert—only herself. And she was tired of burning. She would fight it no more.

She knocked briefly on the door to his chambers before entering. The tub was empty, water sloshed all over the floor. The food had arrived and was arrayed across his desk. She made a circuit of the room, gathering up his clothes and towels scattered on the floor.

The door to the bedchamber opened. Robert stood in the doorway, dressed in shirt and breeches, barefoot. His wet hair had been combed back, but chestnut locks fell across his forehead. He'd shaved. The smooth skin of his jaw bulged as if he ground his teeth. Arms folded across his chest, he glared at her, eyes the color of cold steel, mouth set in a hard, grim line.

She faltered a moment, quailing at his obvious displeasure. What had she done? Then she realized he'd been in the bedchamber, must know she'd vacated it, moved to the tower room. She'd been quite self-righteous when she'd done it—but now . . .

She set the clothes aside and gestured to the desk, hoping he would follow. "Come. Eat."

He crossed the room, lowering himself into his chair. She dragged another chair over and sat across from him. He didn't eat. He leaned back in his chair, skewering her with his eyes. The falling collar of his shirt was open, exposing a strong tan throat.

"What is it, my lord?"

"Your trunk is gone from the bedchamber. So, I then went to your chamber. Would you care to venture at what I discovered?"

"Your brother was sorely wounded. I gave him your bed and thought it best not to move him."

"He seemed fine to me—I see no evidence he's still sleeping in *our* bed."

Caroline nodded, trying to smile pleasantly, as if this were a minor matter—nothing to get upset over. "Yes, my lord. He is sleeping in the gatehouse now, but I found the west tower so agreeable, I decided to remain."

"The west tower. That's Patrick's room."

"Oh. No one told me."

"That's because Patrick hasn't been here in some time—he's been rotting in a dungeon."

Caroline did not know what to say to that, so she said, "If you wish me to return to your bed, I will." When he only continued to glower at her, she gestured to the food. "Please, my lord, eat. You've journeyed hard."

He slammed his fist onto the table. Every platter and bowl jumped at least an inch. Caroline sat back hard. Robert leaned over the desk, following her movement, his lip curled.

Caroline met his angry gaze, trying to keep her own expression calm. She'd never seen him in such a rage and didn't know how to proceed. "You are vexed?"

He pointed a long finger at her. "You consulted me not on this move."

"You weren't here. Must I defer every decision until you are present? If so, nothing will get accomplished."

"The day of the raid—why did you go to the village?"

His change of subject disconcerted her, as she couldn't see where it led. "You asked me before I left and I told you—to bring blankets to Agnes. Her daughter—"

"Aye, had a wean, I remember. Now I want the truth."

"I am not lying."

He leaned back in his chair, hands fisted on his thighs. Would he become violent? Hit her? She braced herself in case it came to blows. If he thought he could beat submission out of her, he would finally discover just how unsuitable a wife she was. He would beat her dead before she bowed to such treatment.

He shoved out of the chair and summoned Henry, who appeared moments later.

"My lord?"

"Henry—to the west tower with you to fetch Lady Annan's letters." Robert turned to her. "Tell him where you hide them. Henry—wait."

Henry had already turned to leave, but turned back, hands clasped in front of him, head tilted inquiringly.

Caroline's mind whirled. *Hide?* Why would he assume she'd hide anything from him? She told Henry where she kept her correspondence, all the while trying desperately to grasp the source of Robert's anger.

Robert returned to the desk. "Did you speak with the messenger—the one who brought Wesley's letter?"

"Yes."

"What did he say?"

"I remember not . . . I asked him if he'd like ale, he said 'aye' . . . only trivialities. What do you think we spoke of?"

Robert said nothing for a very long time. Caroline sat quietly, enduring his scrutiny with her chin tilted forward. She was innocent of whatever wrongdoing he suspected her of and she would not cower before him, begging forgiveness for something she didn't do.

"The messenger is dead. I killed him."

Caroline gasped. Her hand flew to her mouth.

His eyes narrowed at her reaction.

Her stomach roiled, and at first, she could think of nothing to say. "I . . . I'm sure it was done out of necessity—"

He flew to his feet, shoving platters of meat and bread and cheese, bowls of fruit and nuts crashing to the floor. Caroline pressed backward in her chair, heart hammering in her chest. He planted both palms on the desktop, leaning forward to scowl down at her. He was a giant. He would crush her. Weak limbed, she stared back, unable to mask her unease any longer. If he meant to strike her, she wished he would get it over with.

"Three men are dead, Caroline. Dead! Look what comes of my peace. Death!"

Caroline shook her head. "What has the messenger's death to do with your peace? He was an Armstrong."

"An Armstrong in Ridley's employ. An Armstrong in alliance with Johnstones and Grahams to raid my land, kill my men and horses, and steal my wife!"

Caroline held herself very still, waiting for what he would do or say next, never taking her eyes off him.

After a moment, he sat back down. "What know you of that, Wife?"

"I know nothing."

The door opened and Henry returned. He set the carved wooden box containing Caroline's letters on the desk—looking anxiously at the carnage of dinner covering the floor—and quickly trotted from the room.

Robert opened the lid. "Get me a candle." When Caroline only blinked at his terse order, he said, "Now!"

Her shock could not have been more profound had he struck her. Though only married a little over a fortnight, she'd believed she knew her husband. And she'd thought he was a good man. Not a man to place blame lightly. A slow fury simmered in her heart. This wasn't fair! She'd done nothing to deserve this suspicion—he was looking for a scapegoat and instead found a Graham.

Well, if he expected her to jump from her seat to do his bidding, he would be sorely disappointed. She rose slowly, never taking her eyes from him. She brought him the candle, picking her way through the rubble, and set it before him.

"Your candle, my lord," she said in her iciest voice, holding his gaze, daring him to look away from her.

He did not. Nor did he thank her as he always had in the past. He opened the box. "Stand back, will you?"

Teeth clenched, she took several steps away from him and turned slightly away, since her presence appeared to irritate him.

He removed a letter and held it above the candle flame, frowning at the glowing parchment. He brought it closer to the flame and after a moment wisps of smoke rose as a hole burned through the center. He dropped it on the table and slapped it until the fire was out.

Caroline could only stare at the ruined letter in disbelief. Her body shook with the rage she fought to contain.

Robert took another letter from the box.

"My lord—what are you doing?" Emotion choked her, made her voice thick.

He scrutinized her, then returned his attention to the letter, holding it over the flame as he had the last one. "Intelligence is oft conveyed in such a manner—concealed in the guise of normal correspondence. But there is a secret message written in lemon juice, or perhaps urine. When held to the flame, the message is revealed."

The second letter burst into flames, revealing nothing. Robert put the fire out.

Caroline's voice shook, but she could not stop it. "As you can see, my lord, no such thing has occurred. Prithee spare my last letter, so I have something to read in the lonely days ahead."

After destroying her third letter, he sat back and stared at her.

She trembled, her face hot, her jaw locked. She knew it all showed, but could not conceal it. Found she no longer cared if he knew. "Well?"

He raised an eyebrow. "Well what?"

"Have we established my innocence? Or need you to destroy more of my possessions—just to be certain?"

"Wesley Graham was the leader of the raid. The goal of the raid was to kidnap you. Why?" He scratched his temple in mock thought. "Had it been successful, that would have been fortuitous for you, eh? What with your handfasting and signed statement from me. It would have been as if this distasteful little incident never occurred— you could move forward with a future more *suitable* to you." His brows lowered, his face grew dark with anger. "Though I'm certain it had naught to do with a convent!"

"I did not know about Wesley!" If she had, she certainly wouldn't have run! She'd be in a convent now—not subjected to his beastly tirade. And as for the rest—she'd never meant it like that. What he said was the truth, and yet so twisted and ugly. But she'd always meant to be a nun. She'd not lied to him!

His expression remained skeptical.

Caroline forced her spine to bend. From the ruined feast littering the floor she grabbed a leg of lamb and a loaf of bread.

"What are you doing?" He sighed heavily. "God damn it—"

She surged to her feet. "Do not swear at me!" She hurled the food in her hands. The bread sailed over his shoulder, but the lamb slammed squarely into his chest.

She laughed, triumphant. The shock on his face was worth the beating she would surely endure. Her lips pulled into a gleeful smile and she grabbed more food, flinging it wildly at him. He rose from the desk, ducking the flying food, and came at her. She lurched to her feet—slipping on the greasy floor and cracking her knees.

Fear mixed with her anger. She tried again to stand, but he was on her, dragging her to her feet. Part of her wanted to cower, cover her face—but that would encourage him. She was a big lass—he must learn administering a beating to his horse-like wife would be no simple task. She clawed at his face, kicked at him, used her weight to throw him off balance.

He was a rock—she couldn't move him or hurt him. His mouth moved, but she couldn't hear over the roaring in her ears. He grasped her shoulders and shook her until her teeth rattled. Then he crushed her against his chest, both arms encircling her like an iron band, smashing her face into his chest. She struggled, a deep terror gripping her. He held her hard, forcing her to be still, just to catch her breath.

And still she couldn't breathe—shuddering sobs choked her, seized the muscles in her throat. With no other outlet left, scalding tears sprang to her eyes. *Wrong that he should see this!* In her mind, she saw her mother, weaving endlessly in the solar, sobbing, sobbing . . .

"No," she moaned, but it was no use, a lifetime of hurt poured forth and there was no damming it.

15

Robert knew not what to do about the sobbing woman in his arms. He'd not anticipated his plan to determine what she knew about the raid would meet with such success. He'd known that if he approached her as he always had she would reveal nothing. He hadn't wanted to play games, but she left him no choice. She sagged against him, weeping silently, her face buried in his shirt. He slid his arm under her knees and swung her into his arms. Her eyes flew open, hands clutching at him. Tears clumped her lashes together, emotion blazed in her cheeks.

He'd wanted her to weep or rail at him. Somehow, it wasn't nearly as satisfying as he'd expected. He carried her across the room and into the bedchamber. Her face crumpled, her head dropping onto his shoulder. Tears wet his neck. He laid her atop the bed. She turned away from him, curling into herself.

Robert sat beside her, hand on her shoulder. "Caroline, listen to me." She made a violent move, as if to shove him off. He pushed her firmly onto her back.

She had stopped crying, though tears still streaked her

face. She glared up at him. "If you must rut on me now, please, do me the kindness of being quick about it—and no kissing."

Though he couldn't blame her for either her assumption or her anger, her words still bit deeply. "I'll never rut on you, sweetheart—mark me." Her expression didn't change. "And when we do lie together as man and wife, be assured you'll not lack for kisses."

Her face reddened, but she didn't look away. Stubborn and hateful now. Well . . . he'd wanted emotion, after all . . .

He sighed. "I believe that you knew nothing about the raid."

His admission was met with heated silence.

"But I had to know—I lost two men and much livestock. We'll lose more before the winter is over. We lost an entire oat crop . . ." He shook his head. "I can make no more peace—at least until next year. I'll be forced to raid my enemies just to get through the winter."

"How is this my fault?"

"It's not. I had to discover if you were involved—if you were, well . . . the mission failed, so you'd be sure to try again."

"What have I done, that would cause you such mistrust? Was it necessary to destroy my things? When you had no proof? Only suspicion?"

"The letters I burned—they weren't yours. That's why I wanted you to move away—so you wouldn't notice."

She blinked. "What . . . ?" A series of emotions played over her face, confusion, understanding, and then relief. But the disappointment was still there, the resignation.

"Henry had instructions to switch the letters with some of my old correspondence. Your letters are still in the tower room."

"A trick?" she whispered. The green of her eyes was

darker, mossy from weeping. Her lips parted almost in disbelief, as if she longed for him to deny it, golden brows drawn together. She looked like a child—a child betrayed by one she'd trusted.

"Not like Ridley," he said and when her mouth dropped open in horror, he added, "Father Jasper told me."

She let out an astounded breath. "He told you? Why would he tell you that?"

"Because he wanted me to understand why you're this way."

"What way?" Before he could answer, she said, "Unsuitable, you mean?"

"No!" He was becoming exasperated—she was even more difficult when emotional. He stood and paced about the room.

"How can you say you want peace and be so mistrustful?"

"My brother is still a prisoner! I'm beginning to fear he's never coming home—that he's dead and Ridley's trying to hide it! I want peace—but I'm not a fool."

"I can see now that there will never be peace between Maxwells and Grahams—just let me go."

The defeat in her voice angered him. "There will be—so long as your brother hasn't killed Patrick!"

She pushed herself onto the edge of the bed. "And what if Patrick is dead? What then? Will you turn on me again? As the only Graham within reach, will I pay for Ridley's misdeeds?" She walked to the ewer and basin. "This feud has become so twisted that it can never be made straight. I have no place here."

"I did not turn on you—I have explained it already!"

"Of course, forgive me. I'm but a woman, unable to understand the great doings of men." She had regained her composure, though she was different. No cool mask, no poise. She splashed water over her face and just stood there, leaning over the basin, as if looking at her reflection in the water.

He did not want to leave with her like this—and damn it—he was beginning to feel like bastard. He liked her bitter sarcasm even less than her coldness. He crossed the room, pulling her around to face him. Her jaw hardened and she glared up at him—as if she wanted to strike out, but restrained herself.

"I want this peace. And I *am* coming to trust you—"

She averted her eyes in obvious disbelief.

"Damn it, Caroline!"

Frustrated with her stubborn willfulness, he pulled her against him, hard, and kissed her. She stiffened, tried to turn her head away, but he held her fast. He could take her—now, force her and end this bloody farce. He started to pull away, sickened by the turn of his own thoughts even as his body quickened to them, when her lips softened and he felt her tongue slide tentatively against his mouth. He pressed his advantage, fixating on the idea of making love to her. Now. As if somehow that would prove what his poor words couldn't.

She made no attempt to stop him, her tongue dueling with his, her hands clutching at him. His anger quickly dissolved into piercing desire. He'd never tasted anything so right and fine as her mouth—and he wanted so much more.

Caroline was lost. There was some reason why this should not be happening—but she had forgotten—and for now was content to remain ignorant. Something inside of her was frantic, trembling for expression. She kissed him harder, pulling herself closer, and he made a low growl, though he never took his mouth from hers. His tongue delved deeper, seeking, tasting. She chanted his name in her mind, in her heart, blocking out all other thoughts. And then his hand was on her thigh, bare and warm and dangerous. Longing shuddered through her. She tore her mouth away.

They were at the bed. Her back was against the thick bedpost. His hand slid upward, to her bottom, his fingers brushing the cleft between. He kissed her chin, her ear. Her body throbbed, tight with want. If this continued she would soon be his wife in deed. After what he'd done to her—after his mistrust and trickery, she could not let that happen. She twisted away, pushing at his hand.

He caught at her, scowling and pulling her back. "Caroline—"

She swallowed hard, her body still feverish and weak, and said, "Unless there's some other Graham offense I must make reparations for, I want you to leave."

His eyes narrowed to slits, his breath hissed between his teeth. She steeled herself against the explosion, but it didn't come. He thrust away from her and slammed out of the room.

Caroline dissolved onto the bed, wishing for Father Jasper to take her away.

Caroline did not know where Robert was—and didn't care. She hadn't left the bedchamber or granted anyone admittance. She'd sent for Father Jasper and now sat on the bed, fingers knotted in her lap, waiting impatiently. The incident with Robert played itself out over and over in her head. Had she really thrown food at him? Burst into paroxysms of weeping? Pawed at him like a wanton? It was disgraceful. She was becoming something else here, something she did not know, did not like.

It hurt terribly that he didn't trust her, that he'd tricked her. So much more than it should. Her throat tightened again and she grimaced, fighting the tears. She'd shed more tears for her fool husband than for any man! He was unworthy—he was just like Ridley. Were all men just like Ridley? Tremors gripped her and she closed her eyes, longing for the solitude of a convent. To be surrounded by women. To have every day predictable and calm. And she'd been so close to freedom. Wesley had come for her! If only she'd known.

The door opened. Caroline jumped off the bed. "Father! You must help me. I want to leave, to escape. Take me to a convent. There's one here on the border. Elcho. A day's journey, perhaps two. I'll—I'll take my vows immediately—once I do, he won't be able to touch me."

Father Jasper roused himself from his amazed stupor and hurried across the room, finger to his lips. "Be still, child! There are others in the next room!" He took her hands and looked into her face. "What has happened?"

"I can't bear another moment of this farce!"

"If it's a farce, then it's one of your making."

"No! He is the one making this impossible!"

Father Jasper looked so confused. "How? You must tell me or I cannot help you."

She yanked her hands from him. "And you! You gave him all the information he needed to execute his little drama."

Distressed, the priest made another play for her hands. "What did I do?"

"You told him about Ridley—how he used to tease me—did you tell him about the false letter? Perhaps that's why he pretends to desire me? Is it all a ruse?"

Father Jasper took a step back, but didn't release her hands. "You've never spoken to me in anger." When she didn't respond he said, "My child, please believe me—his feelings for you are no ruse."

Caroline slumped on the bed. "I don't know what to

believe anymore. I feel like a fool." She looked up at Father Jasper, tears welling in her eyes again. "I threw food at him. Can you believe it?"

Father Jasper stared down at her and as he did, the lines on his forehead disappeared, his eyes softened. "What is so wrong with that?"

How could he not see what was wrong with dissolving into mindless violence and weeping? She stood again, wiping her eyes resolutely. "Will you help me?"

"No. You are being cowardly. It does not become you. You made a promise, before your husband, the Lord, and myself. If you truly wish to be a nun, I cannot believe you would enter God's house with that on your conscience."

Caroline didn't know what to say. His words shamed her and yet still her heart cried out, *So? He made a fool of me!*

"And furthermore," Father Jasper said in a tone that brooked no opposition, "I expect you to be a better wife to him."

Indignation heated her cheeks. "I have been a fine wife! He has nothing to complain of!"

"Oh? What about waiting until his back is turned to creep away to your own little corner of the castle to hide?"

"I'm not hiding. Alexander must sleep somewhere!"

"Then why not fix the tower room for him?"

"Because he was wounded—he shouldn't have to climb all those stairs! I was being thoughtful!"

"Thoughtful of yourself."

Caroline felt doubly betrayed. First by Robert, now by her own Father Jasper. "We're not really married! It's a handfasting—a promise to marry in the future."

"A promise you have no intention of keeping."

"But I do it for him—if we consummate he will have to divorce me! This is the only way we can both be free. No annulment, no divorce."

Father Jasper threw up his hands. "What makes you so certain that is how it will end?"

Caroline stared at him in shocked disbelief. "I'm a Graham! He'll never trust me. How else could it end? With me weaving grisly tapestries, singing odd songs to myself, and looking straight through everyone who speaks to me?"

Father Jasper drew in a deep breath. His smile was one of long-suffering patience. "Your mother was one woman. You are another—a different woman."

"But you always say I'm so much like her . . . before."

"Yes—yes, but you twist the meaning. You will never end up like your mother." Father Jasper placed an arm around her shoulders. It surprised Caroline. Other than her hand or shoulder, he rarely touched her—had never embraced her. It felt right, comforting. "You've only been married a fortnight. I know that in some ways it feels like forever—and so it should, for I think there is a chance for you and Lord Annan to be very happy, and when it is good and fine like that, you feel as if you've known each other always. But trust takes time to build—and yet so quickly can be shattered. Don't give up."

Caroline gave him a dubious look, folding her arms across her chest.

"You so love storytelling—let me tell you one." The priest gazed across the room, as though seeing the scene before him. "Instead of misery, why not happiness? You and Lord Annan grow to love each other, have children, live long lives, reading to each other."

"He doesn't read very well."

"Then you read to him and write him stories—and he will love them, I'm sure."

"Stop, Father!" Caroline couldn't bear to listen. Perhaps if he'd said these things yesterday, she would have listened, but now, she could see no happiness with Robert.

Father Jasper led her to the doorway. "Alexander waits for you. He cannot play wind ball with sutures. Take care of your brother and think on what I've said."

He opened the door and left. Caroline wandered into Robert's chambers. Alexander sat behind the desk, eyes fixed on her. One hand rested atop an inflated bladder perched on the desk. She wondered how much he knew, how much he'd overheard. His expression revealed nothing.

She put on her calm like a mask—but it was brittle and false. She derived no comfort from it. "Let me get my shears and we'll—"

He held up the silver shears. *Snip, snip.* Then placed them on the desk. He untied his shirt.

He was so smug and arrogant. Men like him had always ignored her—but he did not. He didn't seem to be making the best of an unfortunate situation either. He challenged her constantly and was amused by her reactions. She'd never understand the Maxwell men.

She went to him reluctantly and inspected the wound—no swelling. Though leaner than his brother, he was still broad and muscular. The reddish brown hair on his chest was darker than that on his head. The sun had lightened it, threading it with copper and blond.

"If I remove these stitches—no wind ball. You must not use your arm strenuously for three days, at least, or you will rip it open again."

He smiled. "As you wish." He would probably play wind ball as soon as he left the room and she'd be stitching him back up in an hour.

He didn't speak to her as she carefully clipped each black thread. As she removed the stitches her mind whirled with thoughts of Robert and all Father Jasper had said. Alexander and his love of feuding reminded her so much of Wesley and Fayth. With such hate brewing on the border, could Robert afford to place complete trust in anyone he'd known for a short time? Perhaps there was some logic to his actions.

She pulled a long length of thread from Alexander's wound. He hissed with pain.

"Sorry."

"You did that on purpose."

She looked up at him, surprised. "I did not."

He studied her through narrowed eyes. "I see why Robert finds you so vexing."

"Do you?" Caroline yanked the last stitch free.

He gasped, twisting slightly. *"That* was on purpose."

She only smiled serenely, causing him to laugh. He stood, tying his shirt closed, and she moved away.

"I'm leaving in two days. I'll take you to Elcho."

Stunned, she met his steady blue stare. "Why?"

"Because this marriage is wrong and will ruin us. Robert cannot be made to see reason."

Caroline found herself hesitating, annoyed Alexander would question his brother's decisions and go behind his back in such a way. "I don't see how this marriage is particularly ruinous to the Maxwells."

"I will confess, you seem to be different from other Grahams. But you may unwittingly aid the enemy. It's dangerous for you to even be here."

She wanted to reproach him. If Robert couldn't trust his own brother, whom could he trust? Her heart ached at the tangle. Could she truly blame him for what he'd done? When he had a brother willing to secret his wife away? "Robert would be very angry—at us both."

"He's always angry with me. He'll get over it. He'll marry a woman more suitable, and you can marry God and your books." He raised a quizzical brow. "If that's what you want, that is."

He was offering her exactly what she wanted. Father Jasper had refused to give her aid, Wesley had failed to rescue her—nothing was left except running away alone, or waiting it out. Or accepting Alexander's offer. Why did it sound so horribly empty when he said it? And why should it make her heartsore to think of Robert marrying again? This was what she wanted, she reminded herself yet again, then wondered why it was necessary to forever remind herself of these things.

But she had vowed before God and Father Jasper . . . and Robert, to give it a year. Blast Father Jasper for laying that on her conscience! How could she be a proper nun if she broke such a promise?

Caroline turned away from her brother-in-law, her heart in turmoil. She needed time to think. "Tomorrow I will give you an answer."

16

"I wish ye'd wait, my lady, at least until tomorrow. I'd go with you then." Celia followed Caroline about the room, holding a plate with bread, cheese, dried dates, and an apple so Caroline could eat as she dressed. Last night, she'd returned to her tower room, needing to be away from Robert, to think. Apparently, he was still angry—well, so was she. Once the hurt and humiliation faded, she'd understood why it was necessary for him to be suspicious. Nevertheless, she was innocent and he claimed to believe her. So, why had he still not apologized for doubting her? She would not return willingly until he did.

And then there was Alexander's offer . . .

She'd spent half the night knelt in prayer—or rather, trying to pray—until her knees ached. Waiting for some sign to tell her what to do. Of course, it was entirely possible the sign came and she missed it, since her mind wandered always back to Robert. She'd finally given up and fallen into an exhausted sleep.

She slipped one of her simpler gowns over her head— no stays. She had a long day in the saddle and the last thing she wanted was the bone cutting into her chest and hips. She paused. Perhaps she *should* wear the stays—to mortify herself for God. She dismissed the idea immediately—how could she think if she were in pain?

Caroline took a bit of cheese from the plate and slipped her feet into her shoes. "I want to go alone."

That was a lie. Oh, she knew she should want to be alone. She had a great deal to think about, a very weighty decision to make. She wanted to have an answer for Alexander when she returned this evening, but part of her would give anything for a distraction, anything to put off having to decide whether to go or stay . . . indefinitely. And she knew what she should be feeling. Perhaps if she tried very hard, she could make herself have the proper feelings. But she would never do it here at Annancreag, with Robert. She had to get away from him, this place, or she would lose herself.

"I know. I'll simply ask Geordie to tell Sim I'll be back—"

"No," Caroline said firmly. She started to braid her hair but Celia thrust the plate into her hands and took over. True to her word, Celia had done her best to prove to Caroline that she was a good maid. And she'd been as vicious in her Graham-hate as anyone. Certainly, if Celia could change her mind, others could.

Caroline picked thoughtfully through the dates. "You should be here today. This is the last time you'll see Sim before the wedding. You should spend time with him— you might change your mind."

"I'll not change my mind."

"I just want you to be sure." She grabbed Celia's wrist. "You do have a choice." Any woman ever under her power would have a choice, Caroline vowed.

"He has much to recommend him," Celia said, her

voice thick with pleasure. "I'll be the lady of my own house—oh, nothing so fine as Annancreag, but it's a good size tower house. He's not fat, nor old. And he has all his teeth!"

Celia's betrothed had sent word yesterday he was passing through and stopping at Annancreag to call on her. Caroline would not be here to meet him. She was off this morning to visit the old Maxwell woman, Bess, Agnes had told her about. She was purported to be eighty years old or more and could tell Caroline much about the history of the blood feud between the Maxwells and the Grahams. Since Caroline's intense curiosity about the origins of the feud had not lessened, it was the perfect task to take her far away from Robert and temptation.

Celia followed Caroline to the courtyard where Heather waited patiently with four mounted guards. The horse nodded at her, nickering softly. By the time Geordie helped Caroline onto Heather, a blanket of melancholy had settled over her. At the gate, Caroline turned in her saddle to wave at Celia. The maid stood in the courtyard, frowning after her. She felt as if she weren't coming back, which was silly—her guards would never let her out of their sight—but the feeling was unpleasant.

It was fine weather for riding. Not a single cloud marred the cerulean sky. They descended the hill at a slow trot. The sun warmed her and she longed to remove the velvet hat pinned to her head and feel the heat against her skin. They were almost to the village when someone shouted for them to halt. Caroline reined in, turning back to the castle. Robert galloped out of the gates atop a huge bay horse. He looked as if he'd dressed in a hurry—his jack was not fastened correctly and he wore no hat or gloves. Whiskers shadowed his jaw. Her heart fluttered. What did he want? She didn't want to see him again until she'd made up her mind. She couldn't think with him near.

When he was beside her he said, "Where are you off to?" The wind blew chestnut hair back from his tanned forehead. The gray of his eyes was colorless as ice in the bright sun.

"To visit Bess Maxwell. She lives at the southern edge of your lands."

"This should be interesting." He spurred his mount forward. Caroline's mare strained to follow. Dismayed, Caroline caught up with him. The guards had fallen behind, following at a distance.

"I thought you had rents to collect."

He slid her a sidelong look. "They'll wait."

She'd come to understand her husband was not a man who shirked duty for play. Since he'd already put off collecting rents for over a week, he must view this excursion as duty. Did he think she would attempt a secret rendezvous with Grahams? Give them intelligence they could use to sneak into Annancreag and massacre the Maxwells in their sleep?

"It's not necessary that you neglect your duties. Your men will surely see that I behave myself."

He rode his horse closer, eyebrows raised. "Did it ever occur to you that perhaps I simply enjoy your company?"

She tried to shrug with nonchalance, but knew her façade was gone. She couldn't seem to muster the energy for it.

As they rode through the village, children ran after them and the women called out, "Bless you, sweet lady!" Caroline waved back. It pleased her to see the people smiling and laughing, to know how resilient they were. The raid did not ruin them. Even Agnes's grandchild thrived. Agnes stood in the doorway, baby on her hip, waving as they passed.

"They love you," Robert said.

"Today," Caroline said. "But if the Grahams misstep tomorrow they'll hate me with equal passion."

He studied her for a long time, hand braced on his thigh. "But you're a Maxwell, too, now."

"No—I'm neither a Graham nor a Maxwell. I'm nothing."

"You're my wife, therefore you're a Maxwell."

It appeared he had no intention of apologizing. That she was to pretend as though yesterday didn't happen. Caroline didn't know if she could, so she ignored his declaration.

He scowled and faced forward again. Once past the village, he said, "Why do we visit Bess Maxwell?"

"She lives so far out and all alone. I wanted to be certain she is well."

"You are a kind lady to your people. And here I thought it had to do with the Clachan Fala you've been questioning my servants about."

He grinned at her and she looked away, fighting the urge to smile back. "Well, yes, that does have a bit to do with it."

"Well? What have you discovered?"

"Not much more than you told me, except there really is a Clachan Fala." At his doubtful look she insisted, "Agnes saw it with her own eyes. And Sandy remembers much the same things as Agnes. But they were both children. Bess was a grown woman."

"Do you hope to begin your own quest for the stone?"

"No . . . it's just that nothing about this legend is as it seems. What if I discover the truth about the massacre? What if it were all a mistake . . . or a misunderstanding? Maybe this whole feud could be fixed for good."

His mouth tilted wistfully. "Too many men and

women have died. Too many men—like my brother Alex and my father before him—thrive on the feud, feed on the bloodletting. Do you think any of them care anymore about what happened three score years ago? It's no more than an excuse to kill with honor. But there is no honor in murdering people who've done naught but be born a Maxwell, or a Graham."

"Then why this marriage? Why bother? You could spend your money and time other ways—building your defenses."

He laughed softly. "Why indeed? Like you, *mo cridhe*, I need a happy ending."

Mo cridhe. Caroline did not understand the other Scots' language—much. But she knew this. She'd heard it used before, as an endearment. It rolled off Robert's tongue, the deep timbre of his voice infusing it with hidden meaning. *Mo cridhe.* My heart. She wanted to look away from him, to pretend it meant nothing, he meant nothing—but he knew when she was false and would force the truth from her. His eyes held hers and in them, she saw possibilities. Things she hadn't dared to dream of before.

"What is it, Caroline?"

She shook her head, breaking the spell at last, and looked to the forest growing thick beside the path. Something surged inside of her—something he'd set loose, that now fought for expression. It was too much, too soon. She hadn't time to think about it, to consider the consequences, to plan. Oh, but shouldn't she have planned for this all along?

After a time, she glanced back at him beneath her lashes. His gaze was fixed ahead of them, his mouth grim and hard. She let herself remember the feel of his mouth on hers, the beauty of his gray eyes, gazing down at her, wanting her. Would she spend her life wondering, *What if . . . ?*

"What are you thinking?" he asked.

Heat stole over her cheeks.

He raised an eyebrow, smiling. "You blush! Now I must have it—tell me."

"I was only thinking I should like to stop and rest." That was somewhat true. They had been riding awhile and she needed to stretch her legs.

"A burn runs through the wood not far from the path. Come." Robert reined in until the guards clustered about him. He instructed them to wait by the road. He led his horse off the dirt road and into the trees. Heather followed with no prodding. Inside the shelter of the wood, it was a different world. Light broke through the canopy of trees in golden shafts. Leaves and fir needles crunched under the horses' hooves as they picked their way over the rocky terrain. Caroline removed the pins from her hat and swept it off, delighting in the cooler air along her neck and brow.

It was not far to the stream; Caroline heard it bubbling before it was in sight. Robert dismounted and led his horse over for a drink. He gripped her waist before she could protest and lifted her down. When she was on her feet, he did not remove his hands from her waist, though he held them loosely, as though he expected her to walk away. And normally, that's just what she would have done. But she found herself unable to move away from him. As the seconds crept by unhappiness took over; she couldn't even look at him! Her gaze fixed on his chin, rough with whiskers, and the muscles cording his neck. What good was this? She stepped away, and just as she did, his fingers tightened, as if to draw her near, then released her.

She looked back, but he had turned away, his hands fisted at his side.

What if . . . ?

The water collected in a small pool beside a rowan tree. Caroline knelt beside it, splashing water over her damp and gritty skin. *What was she doing?* It seemed the changed Caroline was attempting to enter the love game that forever played out between men and women. What a fool! How could she play when she didn't know the rules? This wasn't like her stories, she chided herself, or anyone else's. They all seemed ludicrous now, faced with the solid wall of her husband. He was nothing like the knights in her stories—pretty men, full of flowered words. He was so much . . . more.

She looked up at the tree, at the white blossoms and young fruits. She wondered if she should gather some branches—rowan protected against witchcraft. There was movement behind her. She looked down at the pool. In the dim forest light, the water was a dark mirror. The long reflection of Robert stretched behind her. His head was bent—he stared down at her. The skin on her neck quivered. The wind sent ripples over the water's surface, distorting him. Leaves rustled overhead. She shivered. He knelt beside her. *Leather and sweat.* Her nose tingled and she inhaled deeply.

She couldn't look at him, though she watched him in the water. Neither of them spoke, but he, too, gazed at their reflection. "Look at us," he whispered.

She had been looking at them, kneeling together— what did he want her to see? She spied movement near their knees. Then she felt his hand, taking hers, enfolding it. She didn't pull away. It was somehow easier to imagine the girl in the water doing this, not really Caroline. They sat that way for a long time, Caroline watching their reflections, wondering what he thought. Then she remembered his words to his brother yesterday—*You did not make mention of her being horse-like, did you?*

The conquest—that's what this was. That's *all* this was. Stricken, she turned her face away from the couple in the water, twisting her hand free of his. Before she could stand, he caught her hand again, pulling her back down.

"What is it?"

She let her hand go limp in his grip. "Nothing."

"Liar." His voice was low, harsh, beside her ear. "What are you afraid of?"

"I'm not afraid of you." He was right, she was a liar. He terrified her. He made her understand her mother's grief, understand that she, too, could be broken by a man.

"Then you're afraid of her."

Her gaze went to the pool, where he nodded. There she saw him, looking at the girl in the water. Her hair had come loose from her braid to trail beside her cheeks. In the dark glassy surface her face didn't seem so long, her eyes not so large. She was almost pretty. But it was an illusion—distorted. She didn't really look like that.

"You don't trust her," he said.

"What nonsense!" Her voice shook. She wanted to close her eyes, but could not. "Perhaps you should be the one penning tales."

In the pool, the man moved closer to the girl; his hand brushed the hair from her cheek. He didn't look at the water anymore, his gaze intent on her. His palm slid around to the other side of her face, cupping her cheek and turning her toward him.

She swallowed hard, letting her eyes drift shut.

"Look at me," he commanded.

She couldn't look at him and do this. She wanted him to kiss her, to hold her again. Her body ached for it, trembled in anticipation. Her mouth thirsted for the taste of him. Oh, she was a wanton, would never be a nun—and she didn't care.

"Caroline. Open your eyes."

She shook her head, trying to pull away from him, miserable that she couldn't do this. But he did not let her go, his arm snaked around her, pulling her against his chest, into the V of his thighs. She opened her eyes. Her hands pressed against his shoulders, but she didn't struggle. She stared at his neck again, frightened—exhilarated—something fluttered deep inside her, begging for release. His other hand grasped her braid, pulling her head back. She met his eyes and they ensnared her, holding her still. His curved lashes lowered as he studied her face. His pupils were wide, the silver gray a thin ring about them.

"*Mo cridhe,*" he whispered and she thought her heart might burst. The way he looked at her, the roughness of his voice, as if the same emotions boiled inside him. "You're so beautiful."

It was like letting the air out of a bladder. The spell broken, she tried to wrench herself free. Disappointment, sharp and bitter, forced tears to her eyes. She was many things, but she was not beautiful.

He would not let her go. "What?" he demanded, holding her fast. "Tell me what distresses you. I'll not let you go until you do."

She held her body still, her face turned stubbornly away. "You're the liar—and you almost fooled me again."

"I seek not to fool you, Wife."

"We're not really married and you know it. This whole thing is a sham."

"It's not a sham. I meant what I said that day—I mean to marry you before God."

She pushed at him, trying to get some space. He was too close, overwhelming her again. She couldn't think, couldn't breathe. "Why? I am so unsuitable!"

"You keep saying this and I've yet to see it. You suit me in every way."

She met his eyes—knowing she would see the lie in them and yet all she found was earnestness and determination. She shook her head slightly. "I don't understand. I'm not . . . a beautiful woman, I'm too long, too strong of mind, too forthright, too unmanageable, too . . ." She couldn't go on—it was difficult to admit these things. Easier to pretend she didn't care.

He smiled, gathering her closer. " 'Tis a good thing I'm a greedy man and want too much of everything." He looked to the water again. "I wish you could see the Caroline I see—she's strong and clever. When I'm with her I forget all I must do, wanting only to be near her, to talk to her. And aye, she is bonny to me." His arms tightened around her, as if he expected her to struggle. She didn't. His words were the sweetest she'd ever heard. She believed him, and somehow that was the strangest and most wondrous thing of all.

He kissed her, gently, his lips exploring hers. His hand circled her neck, strong fingers sliding up to turn her head. She needed no encouragement, but parted her lips, welcoming him inside. Their breath mingled, his tongue found hers, stroking sweet and deep, sapping her strength, her will. Disoriented from his kiss, she felt as though she were falling—then her head pressed against something solid, the crunch of leaves beneath her body. He was going to take her, she realized, make love to her. She didn't care—she only wanted this to go on and on. She slid her arms around him, holding him tightly.

He broke the kiss off. Slowly she became aware of how they lay—Robert on top of her, one thick thigh pressed between her legs—his forearms beneath her shoulders, his palms cradling her head.

"Mo cridhe," he breathed, his mouth moving along her jaw to her ear. "I want to make you my wife."

"Yes," she said, her voice strained as if she'd been running. "Please."

He growled, a sound deep in his chest that rumbled through her, and kissed her again—hard, possessive. Her body arched closer to him, her thighs gripping the leg that pressed against her—anything to ease the deep throbbing in her lower body.

His arms were gone from beneath her. Then she felt his hand at her waist, sliding down over her hip to grip her bottom. He pressed her hard against him and she gasped into his mouth. The ache between her legs became sharp. She moved against him, to gain some relief, but each movement only succeeded in agitating her more.

He tore his mouth away, burying his face in her neck, holding her tightly against him. "You must stop," he said, his breath panting in her ear. "We'll not get far if you keep at that."

A haze clouded her mind, rendering his words meaningless. Her whole world had shrunk to this moment, this man. She stroked her fingers through his hair, turned her face to kiss his ear. His hand swept over her waist, up her ribs, cupping her breast through the material of her gown. And she felt it between her legs—everything he did seemed to center there—stoking the burning ever hotter.

He muttered something about her wearing no stays as his hand worked at the lacings of her gown.

"Robert," she pleaded, her hands pulling at his clothes.

His mouth covered hers again, hot and probing. His hand slid into her bodice, covering her breast, searing her through the thin material of her shift. He dipped his head, pressing kisses to her throat and chest. She arched herself, shivering in anticipation. He pushed her shift off her shoulders, then down farther until the cool air caressed her. Her breasts felt swollen, tight.

He did nothing for a moment, holding her breasts. She was afraid to open her eyes, but unable to stop. Fearfully, she let her eyes drift open. He leaned over her, his hands overflowing it seemed with her breasts. Her pale skin was flushed pink, the nipples puckered—his dark hands a stark contrast, so large and rough and powerful. The sight inflamed her. He stared at her breasts as if they were a thing of beauty. His eyes traveled up her neck, to her face, their gazes tangling. The desire inside her became a living thing, clawing to burst free. His thumb brushed across one taut nipple, wrenching a whimper from her throat.

His eyes darkened and he lowered his head again. She wanted to watch him—to see his face as he did these things to her, but then he licked her. Her head fell back and her eyelids drifted shut. Small sounds came from her as he pulled at her nipple with his mouth. Her fingers curled into his silken hair, holding him to her, urging him. All he did only made it worse, made her frenzied. She needed him *there*—the place between her legs that ached to be filled.

She thought she might sob with relief when his hand reached down, bunching her skirts up in his hand. He was kissing her again, their mouths and tongues melded. She fumbled with his jack, the ties on his shirt, until his skin, feverish and damp, was beneath her palms. His hand moved between her thighs, stroking, brushing against the hair that curled there. She felt a moment of panic and writhed against him, closing her thighs.

His hand moved inexorably upward. "Open your legs for me." She did as he bid. He touched her gently, caressing, and her fear dissolved as something built inside her, as if every sensation in her body was gathering, pulling taut. His fingers were wicked as they thrusted and rubbed. She gasped and panted, her hands clutching at him. Her body moved independent of her mind, her hips thrusting. And she could feel it peaking, this thing that had swelled inside her since he kissed her, and as his hand played her like a harp, it broke free, spilling over her in waves.

His mouth covered hers, muffling her cries. Her body throbbed as the aching ebbed away. It was pleasant, to be engulfed in his embrace, her body singing. His hand was gone and distantly she realized he was unlacing his breeches. She couldn't believe that all this had happened and they still hadn't made love. Her belly fluttered again in anticipation. His thumb touched her bottom lip.

He kissed the corner of her mouth. "I—"

A yell cut his words off. Someone crashed through the trees. Caroline's eyes flew open, but Robert pulled her tight against him, shielding her nakedness. "What is it?"

"Uh . . . er . . . naught, my lord. Your horses wandered into the road. We thought we heard the lady scream . . . forgive." Leaves crunched as the guard backed away.

Hot with embarrassment, Caroline kept her face buried in Robert's chest.

"We're fine," Robert said. "Just go—we'll be right there."

When the footsteps faded, Robert's arms relaxed. Caroline opened her eyes, but kept them fixed on his throat.

"No, no," he said. "We'll have none of that. Look at me."

She looked up at him from beneath her lashes.

"We'll go now—but we will finish this later. Understood?"

Caroline nodded, her motions jerky.

"And you'll not turn strange on me—aye?"

"I know not what you mean."

"Aye, you do. You become cold and distant." He tilted

her chin with his finger. His eyes burned into her. "You're no nun, Caroline, and you're going nowhere."

Caroline swallowed, accepting his words. A weight lifted from her shoulders and she nodded again.

He smiled, the lines of worry smoothed from his forehead. She didn't even try to stop her answering grin. He kissed her, once, hard, and hugged her tightly. He helped her stand and after he'd laced himself back up, helped her fix her gown.

"No stays," he murmured again, his hands wandering over her waist, a hot light in his eyes.

She blushed, but it was with pleasure that such a simple thing pleased him.

He took her hand and led her out of the forest.

17
ॐ

They'd been riding for some time; it was well past noon. They'd have to take shelter with this Bess person, or camp in the wood—neither option appealed to Robert, as this was a particularly dangerous area, being near Johnstone lands.

Johnstones. Laird Johnstone had professed ignorance of Bean's doings, but Robert had expected as much. Robert's letters were merely a formality and they knew it. A warning. Next time he wouldn't waste the ink, but raise the Maxwells and ride on their lands with fire and sword. He'd also sent his own messenger to Ridley, asking after his brother and informing him of Wesley's raid. All he could do now was wait. If he didn't hear back from Ridley within a reasonable amount of time, stronger measures would be taken. Alex had been furious, of course, wanting to ride on Graham Keep immediately and take Patrick back at sword point.

And then there was the matter of this visit . . . Caroline's interest in the Blood Stone legend. The Armstrong messenger's dying words came back to him. *Blood Stone.*

He couldn't let himself think of it—couldn't let the doubts rear their ugly head again. He wanted to be fair. He wanted to believe she knew nothing of her brother's perfidy. He watched his wife, remembering how she'd felt in the woods, her body quivering with pleasure, her eyes glazed and rapturous. God, how he wanted to believe. She'd donned her hat again, though it sat askew, dipping low over one eye. Robert said nothing, as he thought it charming.

"Tell me," Robert said, "why you really wanted to enter a convent."

"I never lied to you."

He gave her a skeptical look. "You truly thought you'd make a good nun?"

She shrugged. "Well, yes. I'm not what you'd call . . . a fine specimen of womanhood."

"Oh, I think ye are."

She tried not to smile, but her right cheek dimpled slightly. "Well, you're the first. I'm huge—and not just my height. I'm wider than most women, through the hips that is, and well, my father always said I acted very manly. And Father Jasper thought I would make a fine nun . . . or he used to."

"You have never once reminded me of a man."

The dimple deepened. Her gaze was riveted to Heather's mane.

"And as for width," he continued. "What man wants a woman with hips like a lad's?"

"That's easy for you to say," she said. "But when a man is so long, it's seen as power . . . a handsome thing. When a woman is huge, she's an oddity. Certainly not an object of desire."

Robert laughed. "It's clear you've not met my brother Patrick."

She raised a blond brow quizzically. It was one of her

old mannerisms, but now, with the slight smile curving her lips, it became warm, inviting confidences.

"Compared to Patrick, I was neither powerful nor handsome."

Now it was her turn to look skeptical, which pleased Robert greatly. "By the time I was fifteen I was near as tall as I am now—taller than both my brothers, who are not small men. Patrick is the shortest of the lot, but he was always bulky—heavy shoulders and chest—from the time he was a lad. He was surefooted and born with a keen fighting skill. And me—well, I was reed thin, with these enormous hands and feet." He held his hands out in front of him. "I was utterly without grace—awkward, always tripping. I have scars from sword work; I cut myself more than aught else!"

Caroline laughed. "What happened? For you're not like that now."

Robert shrugged. "Twenty years, I suppose, for it certainly didn't happen overnight. I never knew what to say to a lass—and never got the chance to try with Patrick about."

"What about Alexander?"

"Alex has always been different . . . he never cared much about the lassies—oh, he likes them fine—but he was always too busy for them. Still is. He's more like Patrick. Never had to work hard for much of anything."

"But you did?"

"Aye. Everything takes me years and years of practice just to get right—and then I'm no more than competent; I never quite perfect it." Robert lifted his shoulders thoughtfully. "My father always said it would have been better if Alex had been born first."

"Why not Patrick?"

Robert shook his head, sighing. "Patrick doesn't

care . . . about much of anything. And Alex cares too much."

Caroline smiled, her eyes soft. "Then it seems to me that you're the perfect laird—more than competent."

He grinned, sitting straighter on his horse—a new mount, and one he'd not yet gotten used to—and spied a cottage in the distance. He pointed. "That must be it."

He gestured to his men and they urged their horses forward, galloping into the narrow valley where the cottage nestled. A cow tied to the corner of the building bawled at their approach. Two pigs were penned adjacent to the cottage. A small shaggy dog ran out of the house, barked twice, and ran back inside. Robert only vaguely recollected hearing about this woman—knew he did not collect rents from her. His father had told him once that the land had been a gift and she'd lived on it for many generations. When she died, it would revert to Robert.

They dismounted in the dirt yard. Robert took Caroline's hand as they cautiously approached the open door. "Good day! Is anyone about?" he called.

There was movement inside. Robert stepped over the threshold. A figure shuffled toward them. It took Robert's eyes a moment to adjust, but when they did he saw it was a very old woman—hunched over, a plaid wrapped about her bony shoulders. Her long white hair was braided down her back, escaping to bush about her narrow face. The dog barked again, then ran behind the old woman, peeping out from behind her skirts.

"I've nothing—get ye—and leave me be!" She had most of her teeth, though they were in poor condition. She hit Robert with a stick. The blow glanced off his arm.

Robert caught the stick when she tried to hit him again—this time with surer aim. "Bess Maxwell? We're not here to raid you—only to talk."

She yanked the stick out of Robert's hand and stepped back, squinting at him. Her face was like a dried currant, enfolded in wrinkles and dark from the sun.

Caroline stepped around from behind Robert. "Mistress Maxwell, I'm pleased to make your acquaintance. I've heard so much about you. Allow me to introduce my husband—"

"Lord Annan," the old woman breathed, eyes wide. During Caroline's little speech the old woman's gaze had remained fixed on Robert, slowly registering recognition—which was impossible—he'd never seen this woman before.

"Why yes," Caroline said, edging closer to the woman. "And I am his wife—"

"You're English."

"Yes. I'm a Graham, Lady Annan now—oh, Robert, help me!"

The old woman's eyes had rolled back in her head. Caroline caught her, holding her up. Robert stepped forward and swung the old woman into his arms. She was thin and bony, but surprisingly long. "She's as long as you," Robert muttered, turning about, looking for the bed.

"There," Caroline said, leading him across the room to a narrow bedstead. The dog ran to the bed and sprang onto it, turning in ecstatic circles, tongue curling out.

The woman's eyes opened as Robert carried her across the room, locking on him again. She raised a weak hand toward his face and whispered, "Malcolm . . ."

Robert placed her gently on the bed. Caroline covered her with blankets and adjusted a pillow behind her head. The dog curled in the crook of her mistress's arm. Robert stepped back, surveying the cottage. It was a fine home for a borderer—no bastle house, but still, a large cottage. She had a bed, with pillows and linens. And the livestock, though not a great deal, was still a good bit for a woman of her age to have kept hold of. It was most unusual. Someone must provide for her. It was dangerous for any woman to live alone—borderers made no distinctions between sexes when they wanted plunder.

"What do you want?" the woman asked. She still watched Robert, hardly sparing a glance at Caroline.

"Are you Bess Maxwell?" Caroline found a stool and brought it beside the bed. Once sitting she folded her hands primly in her lap, as always. She had changed, and yet she hadn't. The thought brought a smile to Robert's face. He hadn't wanted her to be different, only to feel different—to feel something for him.

The old woman nodded. "A Graham . . . you're married to Lord Annan here, you say?"

"Yes. *Robert* Maxwell, Lord Annan," she clarified, watching Bess closely.

Bess looked from Robert to Caroline. "Is this about the stone?"

Caroline glanced up at Robert, eyebrows raised. "Well, yes. But how did you know?"

Bess sighed. "That's why they all come."

Robert returned to the bed and squatted down beside it. Bess gazed at him, something strange and sad in her eyes. "You called me Malcolm before."

She nodded, her smile tremulous. It softened her leathery face, gave him a glimpse of what a comely lass she once had been. "You look like him—the seventh Lord Annan."

Robert was the tenth Lord Annan, so she spoke of the Malcolm who had married the Graham, the begetters of the blood feud.

"You knew him?" Caroline asked.

Bess's hand went to her dog, stroking. "Aye, I knew him."

Caroline leaned forward. "Were you there, the night of the massacre?"

"Yes."

Worry drew Caroline's brows together. "Did you lose someone that night?"

Bess's eyes closed. "Yes."

The silence drew out until Robert became uncomfortable. Perhaps they should not probe this woman's memories, causing her pain—but he found himself as eager and intrigued by the mystery as Caroline. He suddenly wanted to know.

"Bess," Caroline said, petting the dog. "I want to know about Malcolm and his bride."

The old woman raised her eyes to study Caroline, smiling slightly. "You would." Before they could inquire as to what this curious remark meant, Bess said, "What wish you to know?"

"Who was to blame for the massacre?"

"Who was to blame?" Bess repeated softly. "We all were. We should have known . . . should have seen . . ."

Robert rubbed his chin. He didn't think Bess was in possession of all her wits. He didn't remark on this since Caroline leaned forward, eager, hanging on every word.

"But you want to know if his bride knew." Her blue eyes were sharp now, darting back and forth between Robert and Caroline. "As I said, she should have known—but no. The marriage was more than a truce—it was a love match. But in truth, Elizabeth was no more than a tool used by her kinsman, all for greed. All for that hell stone."

"Was it the Graham laird?" Robert asked.

Bess shook her head. "No, he knew nothing. It was a younger son with grand plans. Plans that failed. He was eventually killed by a Maxwell; his throat slit in the night as he slept."

"What happened to Elizabeth?" Caroline asked softly.

"Dead. Her brother killed her—right through the heart."

Caroline looked down, at the hands clasped in her lap. Robert covered her hands with his. "Thank you, Bess," he said. "Know you what became of the stone?"

"The Musgraves have it—guard it with their lives. I wish it were gone. Destroyed. It's an evil thing." Her wrinkled face crumpled into itself with disgust. "Supposed to bring prosperity, bring an end to the fighting, they said. It brings death and misery."

"It's just a jewel, is it not?" Robert asked.

"It's more than a simple ruby—though I couldn't tell you how or why." She surged forward, covering Robert and Caroline's joined hands with her own. "When it comes to you—and it will—destroy it!" When they both stared back at her, astonished, she said, "Your future, your happiness, depends on it."

"Why?" Caroline whispered.

"There are those who will stop at nothing to possess it."

Robert was chilled, uncomfortable, and hunched his shoulders to rid himself of the grimness that possessed him. Bess lay back and closed her eyes, her hand leaving theirs to rest on the dog's head.

"If you love this man," she said, her voice weak now, rusty, "you'll destroy it, the moment it's placed in your hand. And be wary of all kinsmen—even those you trust. It possesses the soul, the heart."

The silence drew out and though Robert longed to break it, he remained quietly holding Caroline's hand. She stared meditatively at the old woman. Robert squeezed her hands lightly and when she looked at him, he moved his head, indicating they should go.

"Wait," she said, then, "Bess? Why were you at Annancreag during the massacre?"

Bess didn't answer. Her chest rose and fell gently in sleep.

"Should I wake her?" Caroline asked.

"No—I think she's had ample excitement today. I fear we weren't the most welcome of guests." He removed the small purse of coins from his belt and placed it on the pillow, next to the woman's head. Taking Caroline's hand, he led her from the cottage.

"You should send men out to check on her . . ." She looked over her shoulder, at the empty doorway. "Or perhaps we could move her to the village?"

"I'll see to it the moment we're home."

She was pensive on the return ride. Dusk fell and with it came the fog, rising from the moor and swirling around them like a veil. Annancreag was still several hours ahead. They gathered beside the road, its packed and rutted dirt visible only a few feet before disappearing into the shrouding mist. Though the sky was obscured, the air had become thick, pressing down on them. Rain. They couldn't continue.

"There's an abbey not far," Robert said. "It's abandoned, mostly ruins, but it should offer some shelter."

He led them off the path, and so they followed, single file, as he picked his way across the mossy ground. Though this wasn't as rugged as his lands to the west, it was little traveled. A small village resided here once, when the abbey prospered, but the people, along with the monks, had long disappeared. He led them across the moor until the skeletal arches were in sight. Robert had never particularly liked this place, even when he was a child, though his brothers had loved it. Some of the buildings were intact and would provide shelter from the elements, but the cathedral had been gutted, courtesy of the English. Blackened trees, dead and bare, twisted around the ruins. The arches that had formed the apse, part of two ivy-covered walls, forming a sheltered corner, and strangely, the stone altar, were all that remained. The rest of the stone had been scavenged.

They took shelter in the chapter house, the only building that retained its roof. They huddled about a small fire, the horses snorting and stomping in the next room. A thick tapestry of moss furred the walls. No one spoke and the quiet became oppressive. Robert would have almost preferred to sleep outdoors, but the air was heavy—rain would soon add to their discomfort. One of the guards made oatcakes to accompany the dried meat and cheese Caroline brought. They ate in silence, all affected by the subdued atmosphere of the abandoned house of God. When they finished, Caroline rose. The guards all stood with her, but Robert motioned for them to stay and followed her out of the chapter house.

She took his arm and they wandered about the ruins, stopping every now and then so she could examine something closer. Robert could almost imagine that the hooded figures still wandered the grounds, just out of sight, hidden in the fog.

"What is so interesting about a ruined abbey?" he asked.

She looked away, toward the altar, standing sentinel over the ruins. Fingers of fog swirled around it, obscuring, then revealing it. "Do you think God abandons people, like he does buildings?"

"No," Robert said firmly. "If God were truly contained in a building, or a piece of paper, then He would have deserted the borders long ago."

"Why is that?"

"Aye—oh some twenty years ago, the Archbishop of Glasglow cursed the borders. He issued a commination, condemning us all to the deepest pit of hell." He grinned at her. "As far as I know, 'tis never been retracted."

His attempt at lightness failed. She looked around the abbey with new horror.

"Caroline, it is the people who bring God. This is nothing more than stone. The Almighty cares not about stones—only about people."

"Father Jasper told me he was not called to be a priest." She looked around her and sighed. "Nothing is as it seems."

Near one of the walls, Robert stopped and turned to her. "How long has Father Jasper been a priest?"

Caroline looked upward thoughtfully. "He told me once he took his vows when he was twenty—he's six-and-fifty."

Robert gazed down at her. The mist dewed her skin, made it glow. Was it a Graham resemblance between Caroline and Jasper, or something more? And if it was something more, Robert did no one any favors by digging it up. For then Caroline would be illegitimate and her mother an adulterer. Father Jasper surely kept silent so Caroline would be raised as a lady—and he remained a priest so he could be with her. And yet, she loved Father Jasper. It seemed wrong that she remained ignorant of all he must have sacrificed for her.

He touched her face, traced her brow with his thumb. "You seem sad."

"This place reminds me of Father Jasper. He's always been with me . . . it seems I don't even remember much before he came to Graham Keep. But he stayed to instruct me on how to be a nun." She shrugged and smiled, but it was melancholy.

"You think he'll leave now that you're a wife?"

"I don't know . . . he liked to wander, before."

Robert urged her backward, until she leaned against the wall. "Oh, I think he'll find reasons to stay. I need a chaplain and he suits me fine."

Her smile was sweet, tender. He framed her face with

his hands, stroking his thumb across the velvety skin of her cheek. She didn't look away, holding his gaze. She wore her heavy gray cloak, but he could feel the heightened rise and fall of her chest. It seemed as if he'd waited forever for her. He wouldn't waste another second making her his.

He kissed her. She did not resist—her head fell back against the wall. Her mouth opened under his, sweet and artless, eager for him. She was pinned between his body and the wall, and he was free to do with her as he pleased. She made no protests at his seeking hands, hungry to touch every inch of her body and thwarted by the heavy garments impeding him.

Her mouth became slick beneath his lips. He raised his head. Heavy drizzle fell. Her skin was wet, the droplets beading on her long lashes.

"Robert," she whispered, her eyes opening slowly.

He took her mouth again, his hands sliding inside her cloak, pulling her tightly against him. It was too cold, too wet to remove any clothes. His body urged him to take her, here against the wall—but his mind grappled with the fact that she was a virgin and such an act would be too violent for her. Her arms wound around him, her fingers digging into the leather of his jack—and the thought was lost, only to resurface when his hands pulled up her skirts, were sliding up her thighs, warm and dry and smooth as silk.

He tore his mouth away, panting, looking about at the ground around them. It was raining lightly now. His jack protected his upper body, but his hair and face were damp.

"Robert," she said, her voice breathless, pleading. "You'll do it this time?"

His head jerked back, the ground forgotten. Her lips

parted, the drizzle wetting them, shiny and inviting. Rain slid down her face. Her hair was wet, dark. She raised herself up from the wall and kissed him.

Aye, he'd do it this time. He wasn't sure if he'd spoken the words. He removed her cloak and pulled her to the corner where the two walls joined. The ground was soft and mossy there, and the two walls provided some shelter from the rain. He spread the cloak and pulled her down beside him. She came into his arms, her body fitting perfectly to his. Her hands were in his hair, touching his face. He lowered her onto her back, pushing her skirts up about her waist.

"This may hurt, *mo cridhe.*"

She nodded. Her hands stilled, resting on his arms, watching him. She was not afraid—but he was, his heart raced, his body hot and urgent. By all that was holy he didn't want to hurt her—and yet he knew once inside her, he would be mindless—a beast.

He leaned down, kissing her as he unlaced his breeks. His hand slid between her legs. She moved against him, gasping into his mouth, her hips rocking. He willed himself to wait, to bring her closer to her pleasure. When her hips jerked and her head fell back, he pushed into her. Oh, she was ready—her body took him, her hips still moving, bringing him deeper.

Her eyes flew open and she watched him, jaw clenched as he buried himself slowly inside her. She was tight around him. She frowned up at him and swallowed.

He leaned over her, elbows braced on either side of her head. "Am I hurting you?"

Her legs had moved up, thighs sliding over his hips. She was born for this and he could barely restrain himself from driving into her repeatedly to end this sweet torture.

"No, it doesn't hurt . . . much."

He moved inside her, gently at first, and she gasped, her eyes widening. He slid his hands under her, grabbing her bottom, and rocked against her, again and again. She kissed him. Her hands clutching at him, her body straining. She was so fine and sweet and warm, he thought he might die. When release finally came, he cried out, crushing her against him.

They lay there for some time listening to the rain patter against the wide ivy leaves. The rain increased, the wind driving it sideways so their corner did little to protect them. Robert sat up, pulling her skirts down. Her face was wet—was it from rain or tears?

"Did I hurt you?" he asked.

She shook her head, standing and gathering her cloak. She studied his expression and finally smiled. "Why, you're really worried." She reached out hesitantly, touched his hand. "I'm fine—better than fine."

He slid his hand behind her neck and pulled her close, kissing her hard. He pressed his forehead against hers. "You're mine now. No more talk of ending this marriage."

She nodded. "Maybe we should get out of the rain." Her body shook with shivers. He released her neck and was about to lead her back to the chapter house when she said, "Unless you wanted to do it again, that is."

18

❧

Fayth sat in Annancreag's kitchen with the other Grahams, eating the meal set before them. The security was much tighter than she'd anticipated. The Maxwell servants stared, hard frowns permanently marring their features. They were all the same, Maxwells. Hard. Treacherous. Murderers. Fayth was glad for her disguise, glad their piercing eyes couldn't really see her. She was naught but a lad, sent to deliver Lady Annan's personal items from England. Thus far, that's exactly what they'd seen. She was good at it—had the mannerisms down. She knew how to be a man. Simply behave as an obnoxious, foul-mouthed boor.

It had seemed a good plan at the time, as no one seemed to pay overmuch attention to her when she was in disguise. But now, as she surveyed the four guards circling the table where she and her companions sat, she could see she would never get away with it. And Caroline was not here, for some reason—neither was Lord Annan. She would be forced to leave with Ridley's men and they would have to formulate a new plan.

Or she would be wed to Carlisle. If this failed, Fayth

didn't know what to do next. She certainly wouldn't go willingly back to Ridley and let him marry her to Carlisle—but Ridley's reach was long. Papa'd had many enemies on the border, but Ridley was working hard to mend the rifts—and those he kept as enemies feared him. No one would take Fayth in, no one would shelter her— no one but Caroline. But Fayth wouldn't live among Maxwells. Even Wesley had become Ridley's creature, urging her to wed Carlisle. She couldn't even trust him anymore.

Someone entered the kitchens and the guards came to attention.

"Are they finished yet?" The commanding voice was directly behind her.

Fayth chanced a look over her shoulder and found her gaze level with a set of leather clad thighs. Her gaze traveled up, up, past belt and broad shoulders, until it met the hard blue scowl of a man who, judging by the coppery hair swept away from his face and secured at his neck, could only be the notorious Red Alex. Her blood turned to ice. She could not look away. *Dead*—Wesley had said he was dead.

Jack's murderer—the author of all her current problems—was not dead. The knowledge held her transfixed, disbelieving. If Jack were still alive, she would be wed, having babies and not worrying about some stupid stone or being raped and mistreated by an old man.

"What are you looking at, boy?" Red Alex said. He looked away from her, his gaze encompassing the whole table. "All of you—eat and leave. No lingering for the fine conversation."

Released from his stare, Fayth turned back to the table. But she could not eat. *Jesus God.* Red Alex. He had captured Jack in a raid some seven months ago. He'd demanded ransom, but when Wesley responded to the missive, the only reply was a curt note from Red Alex informing them that Jack was no longer alive. Hate and grief boiled in Fayth's belly, fogged her vision. *He* was the reason her future was so bleak. *He* was the reason there was no other way for Fayth to help her sister but to became Ridley's puppet.

She would never get in to see Caroline, not with Red Alex here. Her stomach cramped, her mind whirled. She forced a piece of bread into her mouth, but it stuck in her throat. A sip of ale sent it on its way.

What to do? Her companions all eyed her warily, aware of the dilemma she now faced. Red Alex said, his voice low, "Aye—I'm heading out. You tell him when he's finished playing husband and wants to save us all from massacre he can send me word."

He strode from the hall, his spurs scraping the stone. The air whooshed out of Fayth. *Leaving.* Red Alex gone. So maybe there was still a chance. Caroline had only to see Fayth for this to work—Caroline would not send her away.

"Come on!" The guard behind her shoved the back of her head so hard her forehead smacked into the tabletop. "Eat!"

Maxwells. Satan's offal, the lot of them. Fayth stifled the rage the guard's abuse brought simmering to the surface and resisted the urge to rub the knot surely forming. She looked over her shoulder, meeting the guard's stare—marking him. Black beard, blue eyes, puckered scar under left eye. She would bide her time. Before she left here, he'd pay for handling her so.

He bared his teeth at her and laughed when she turned back to her meal. There was only one way Ridley's plot could end. She'd balked at that knowledge in the past, but now it gave her a measure of satisfaction.

As she mindlessly forced her meal down her throat, a plan began to form. She looked across the table, at the men Ridley sent to aid her in this endeavor, and winked.

Caroline had never been so relieved as when they finally returned home to Annancreag. Her clothes, saturated from the night's rain, hung from her gritty body like a sack. All traces of rain—except the water permanently logged in Caroline's garments—had disappeared by morning. The sun had burst through, burning away everything but the muddy puddles in the road. It was a fine day, one Caroline normally would not have wasted. But unfortunately, she couldn't smell the after scent of rain, or the wildflowers blooming beside the road. Wet wool and leather, horse sweat and dirt, encompassed her like a cloud.

The remainder of the journey had been miserably uncomfortable, not to mention the embarrassing soreness in her thigh and groin area that made riding a horse decidedly unpleasant.

Robert seemed equally uncomfortable—pulling at his collar with a grimace, and finally unhooking his jack until it hung open. There was little talk, everyone seemingly preoccupied with their personal discomfort. Upon arrival, however, Robert's hand locked onto the back of her neck, steering her to his chambers.

Once inside he shrugged out of his jack, dropping it on the floor with a sigh. "You'll move your things back to our bedchamber."

"Of course," she said. "But prithee—allow me a bath first."

He nodded, lowering himself behind his desk.

"I'll have a bath sent for you, as well," she said as she left. She was surprised she had yet to see Celia. Was her betrothed still here? Keeping her from her duties? Caroline found she could not even dredge up mild irritation. She could certainly understand how one lost oneself in another. In spite of her filth and discomfort, a warmth spread through her at the thought of Robert—and what they did together. And to think—they would do it again— soon. Liquid fire pooled in her belly. This was certainly a benefit of the wedded state she had not expected—she'd thought it would be a chore! Perhaps Ridley had been right about one thing . . .

She ordered Robert's bath, and, humming to herself, hurried up the stairs to the tower and pushed open the door. Her entrance was met by a strangled shriek. A filthy boy had Celia by the throat.

"Shut the door!" the boy demanded.

Caroline did as he bid, recognizing him—her. "Fayth! Release her at once!"

Fayth ignored her. She held a knife to Celia's round bosom, the flat of the blade pressed against rosy skin.

"How did you get in here?" Caroline asked.

Fayth nodded to the open trunk in the center of the room. "I hid in there—your pretty maid just set me free. She thinks me a lad, set on rape." From the wicked grin plastered insanely to Fayth's face, she'd done nothing to dissuade Celia of this notion.

"You know him, my lady?" Celia asked.

Caroline sighed, striding to where Fayth cornered Celia. "Yes—I know *her.*" She grabbed Fayth's wrist, pulling the knife away from Celia. Fayth resisted, but knowing her strength was no match for Caroline's, released the knife and slouched across the room, sprawling on the bed.

Celia edged toward the door.

"No," Caroline said. "Do not speak a word of this until I give you leave to."

Celia gaped her. "But—that's a Graham!"

Caroline went to Celia and took her hand. "She's my sister—please, allow me to tell Robert in my own way."

Celia's eyes boggled and she looked around Caroline to peer at Fayth, who blew her a kiss. Celia shuddered. "What a horrid little creature." She looked up at Caroline, her mouth pursed. "I suppose, as she's your sister, you'll be safe. You'll be telling him soon, though?"

Caroline ushered her to the door. "I promise—as soon as I find out why she's here."

Celia crossed the threshold reluctantly, then turned. "I'll be watching—and listening." She pointed threateningly at Fayth. "I suspect any trouble from you—and I go straight to Lord Annan."

"Not that!" Fayth gasped, her mouth a round O of feigned horror. Celia's fear had fled, however, and her fight had returned. Her eyes took on the familiar heat of resentment and she started back into the room.

Caroline placed a staying hand on Celia's shoulder, urging her back out the door. "Not a word," she repeated, closing the door behind Celia.

Caroline turned on Fayth. "What are you doing here? And why do you come hidden in a trunk—like a common thief?"

Fayth sat up, the mockery vanishing from her expression. "I didn't know what else to do—where to go! He's forcing me to wed Carlisle—I won't do it!" Fayth's face was tight, her eyes wide. Her forehead was red as though she'd been struck. Had Ridley hit her again? "I ran away again—I'll never go back."

Caroline stared at her sister hopelessly. "But you can't stay here!"

Fayth leaned back, her shoulders slumping, as if literally taken aback by Caroline's refusal. "Why? You're my sister, you won't take me in?"

"I can't—Lord Annan won't have it. He trusts no Graham."

"But you're a Graham."

"I'm his wife."

"He trusts Father Jasper."

"No—Father Jasper is guarded at all times."

Fayth's face fell, tears welling in her eyes. "You'd turn me out? Where shall I go? What shall I do?"

Caroline joined her sister on the bed, torn. Uncertainty clawed at her heart, her belly. She could not send Fayth back to Ridley—she knew how he abused and mistreated Fayth—how her life had become a hell. She also knew Carlisle was not an escape from Ridley but a different circle of hell. Mona had told her as much. To send Fayth away would be sentencing her to the kind of horror Caroline was only now realizing she'd evaded by marrying Robert. Having been in the same position, Caroline knew there was nothing else for Fayth, no one who would help her. Her little sister, always so impulsive and reckless, had come to her for succor—her last hope. But what Caroline had found with Robert was so new, so fresh. So fragile. To bring a Graham into his home could shatter it.

"What about a convent?"

"No," Fayth said miserably. "That's only a temporary solution and you know it. I can't stay there forever—I have no desire to be a nun and Ridley will never release my dowry."

Caroline was tempted to ask her why she didn't just join up with the ruffian reivers she was so fond of. This wasn't the first time Caroline had seen her sister attired as a man—at times she'd ridden alongside Wesley, and once even their father, raiding and pillaging. But in her heart Caroline didn't want that. If Fayth were ever discovered while in her disguise, the result would be disastrous.

Fayth stood, utterly dejected. "At least let me slip out . . . I'll head south . . . go to York or London perhaps . . ."

Caroline shuddered to imagine Fayth loose in such corruption. Fayth was a lady, not some commoner—whatever would she do alone in a city?

She snagged her sister's sleeve, pulling her back onto the bed. "Stay—I'll sort this out."

Fayth's smile was brilliant, lighting her whole face. She'd always been thoroughly charming and Caroline couldn't help but return her smile. Acting on her newfound self, she hugged her sister. Fayth went rigid, her arms at her side.

"I'm so glad you're here." Caroline hadn't realized how much she'd missed her family, but the emotional turmoil she'd struggled with for the past weeks boiled to the surface and she was unable to blink back the moisture from her eyes.

Fayth pulled away, studying Caroline's face, a vertical line of worry marring her brow. "You . . . you're crying!" She flung herself at Caroline squeezing so tightly Caroline could hardly breathe. "It's all right now," Fayth whispered. "It'll be all right now."

Caroline suddenly felt that it would be all right and embraced her sister harder.

"What has he done to you?"

Caroline drew back, shaking her head. "Oh, Fayth—it's not like we thought—the Maxwells, they're no different than we are and Rob—"

"How can you say that? Red Alex is here—I saw him! He *murdered* my Jack!" Fayth's face distorted, fighting pain and anger. "Jack probably died here—in this pile of stones."

Caroline fell silent, worried. Coming here must have

been difficult for her sister—bringing back her pain at losing Jack, of losing her future. Did Fayth know Red Alex was Robert's brother? Caroline hoped not. She still had to tell Alexander she wasn't going to Elcho. She would also advise him to stay clear of Fayth—for his own safety.

Caroline took Fayth's hands and squeezed them. It would take time, but she would see that the hate was to blame for Jack's death, not the Maxwells.

Caroline asked, to change the subject, "How long were you inside the trunk?"

Fayth sighed, the tension draining from her. "Not long. One of the men caused trouble at the wagons and I slipped inside the trunk. Another rolled up blankets and covered them—even used my boots, sticking out the end, so it looked as if I'd fallen ill." Fayth stuck out her bare, dirt-streaked feet. "He blamed it on plague—that kept the Maxwells from getting too close!"

Caroline chewed her lip nervously. Robert would be furious—Alexander worse. How to tell them? Would Geordie or the other guards be punished? She wanted to be happy about Fayth's arrival, but already she was causing so much discord.

She patted Fayth's hand. "You wait here and I'll tell Lord Annan."

Caroline had left, grim faced with determination, to tell Lord Annan about Fayth's arrival. She was afraid of her husband, Fayth saw, and this angered her. As Fayth wandered about Caroline's chambers, her heart ached. Poor Caroline, to be sacrificed in marriage. Fayth couldn't remember the last time she'd seen Caroline cry. That Maxwell bastard had driven her to tears. Caroline had never been one to cry, or complain, or even to speak of her unhappiness. Fayth knew she'd done a good thing by coming here. She'd had some misgivings, fearing she was blinded by selfishness—trying to save herself from Carlisle. But she'd be saving Caroline as well. And no one needed saving like Caroline. She was too accepting of her fate. She needed Fayth to champion her.

Fayth folded her arms across her chest, gazing out the window, a slow smile spreading across her face. Her sister's champion. Caroline had been a mother to her when their own became a shell. Caroline had shielded her from Father's anger, Ridley's cruelty. Though Caroline had always been distant and contemplative—confiding in no one but the priest—Fayth had still always known she could rely on her sister. Fayth would not let her down.

She glanced around the room—alone now—and set to searching it, wondering how long Caroline would be. Even if the Maxwells had the stone, it was doubtful that it would be in Caroline's possession, but Fayth wouldn't let Ridley accuse her of not trying.

Would Lord Annan be angry? Would he beat Caroline? Had he violated her yet? Fayth thought not—why else would he exile her to this remote tower room? It was likely he couldn't bear the sight of her. Fury welled up inside Fayth again. He was probably another, like Ridley, who couldn't see past Caroline's size to the heart within. Well, before this was over, Fayth vowed, he'd pay for his oversight. They'd all pay.

19

Caroline slipped through the door, into her old chamber. Light slanted through the narrow window, highlighting the empty place where her desk had once rested. At the door leading to Robert's bedchamber, she paused. Uncertainty would be her undoing if she didn't get herself under control. She closed her eyes, hands fisted at her sides, and breathed deeply, searching for the composure that had once been so easy to command. She feared if he knew how distressed she was about the whole situation he would imagine a deeper reason for her anxiety—would see plots and treachery where there were none. So, she must do this right. She could not let him send Fayth back to Ridley.

She heard movement in the bedchamber and stiffened. He was just on the other side of the door. She touched the carved oak, remembering the night before, in the ruined abbey. She was possessed by a man—his chattel. The prospect was not as repulsive as she'd once thought. She treasured every moment of yesterday—she wanted many, many more such days with him. Perhaps Father Jasper was right; perhaps she would not end up like her mother.

She felt it—the possibility of happiness, contentment, *love*—all within her grasp, if only she could gain his trust.

She rehearsed her speech a few more times, silently testing the mannerisms that would inspire his trust, when the door flew open. She froze, blinking up at her husband standing naked before her except for the bath linen wrapped about his waist. Even after her surprise evaporated she couldn't move or close her mouth.

He turned his head slightly, in question, an arm braced on the door frame. Muscles moved and bunched beneath dusky skin with every motion. The hair under his arms was as dark as that on his chest and belly and forearms.

She wanted to lie with him again. And again and again. Desire weakened her legs, warmed her skin.

"What are you doing?" he asked, a knowing light in his pale eyes.

Aware of how filthy and travel stained she was, she took a step back. "I wanted to have a word with you."

He straightened, serious. "And you've not bathed—it must be important."

Caroline fussed self-consciously with her hair, letting herself smile at him. She'd never realized before how she'd suppressed such natural reactions, a smile, a hug—until she had to consciously force herself to act on the impulses.

He stepped aside. She walked past him, hands held firmly at her waist, shoulders squared. Candles illuminated the room. The tub stood before the fireplace, puddles of soapy water around it. He closed the door, following her into the room. All the ways she planned to tell him about Fayth seemed inadequate, forced—and he would know. She chewed her lip—a habit she'd rid herself of years ago. She strode to the fireplace, stepping around the puddles.

The bath water was still fairly clean, milky from soap. She inhaled, filling her lungs with the damp, soap-scented air. She was taking too long. He moved behind her, placed his hands on her shoulders. Now she could not say it—he would see her difficulty, assign meaning to it.

"What did the letter from Laird Johnstone say?" she asked instead, to buy time, her mind working furiously on her problem. How to tell him? How to make it sound as innocent as it was? Why did Fayth have to sneak in, dressed as a man? It made everything seem so much more sinister than it was! Why could she not have normal siblings who arrived as proper guests?

Her gown laced up the side. His fingers slid under her arm, working at the lacings. "He heard of the raid— claims he had no knowledge of Bean's actions. Swears Bean will be properly punished."

Caroline tried to move away, but Robert's other hand slid around, in front of her, pressing against her stomach, so she was flush with his back.

"My lord," she said, breathless. "You're clean—I'll soil you."

"I'll wash you, then."

Caroline's gaze darted to the tub. Images from the night before flooded her, of his rain-slicked lips moving over her mouth and face, the sweet taste of rain mingling with his own, purely male flavor. She should protest—it was unseemly for a husband to bathe his wife. He gathered her skirts in his hands, pulling the gown up, over her head. She raised her arms to aid him.

"Do you believe him?" she asked.

He tossed her gown aside, his hands skimming over her linen clad shoulders, sliding beneath her arms. She could feel him behind her, his heat, his arousal. His head was bent, his mouth near her ear.

"Mmm?" His warm breath tickled her.

"Laird Johnstone," she said. "Do you believe him?"

"I don't know."

He started to gather her shift, as he had her skirt, but her hands stayed him.

"What are you doing?"

"I told you." And he yanked it up, over her head.

She closed her eyes tightly, hands clasped at her waist. She felt ridiculous, huge. She fought herself though. Robert didn't think she was ridiculous, or huge. It was a difficult battle and before either side could claim victory, his hand slid down her arm, grasped her hand. He pulled her toward the tub. She had to open her eyes or stumble. She focused on the tub, refusing to look at him—or to look down at herself.

"Get in," he said, holding her hand as she stepped into the warm water.

She wanted to hide herself from him. Her breasts were tight, heavy. "I can wash myself," she said, reaching for the cloth hanging over the side of the tub.

He caught her braid, pulling her up straight. She didn't resist, resigning herself to fighting him no more. He obviously wanted to do this—she must bear it with dignity. She straightened her shoulders and lifted her chin, motionless as he unbraided her hair, combing it through his fingers. Her scalp tingled from his gentle ministrations. She closed her eyes.

When her hair was arrayed down her back and over her shoulders, he stood before her. She opened her eyes, her discomfort returning. He stared at her for a long time. She said nothing at first, but hot embarrassment flushed her chest, her neck, and she finally pleaded, "Robert?"

One corner of his mouth tilted up. "You must accustom yourself to it, *mo cridhe*—I intend to look upon you at every opportunity."

Intense pleasure mixed with her mortification—her cheeks burned, but she smiled back, feeling silly and beautiful.

He took the small bucket beside the tub and filled it with water—then dumped it over her head. She gasped, pushing the sopping hair from her eyes, but not before another bucketful sluiced over her. She crossed her arms over her breasts and stood shivering as he wet her down. She knelt and he rubbed soap over her hair.

Water lapped about her belly, partially covering her, and she was able to relax, the scent of rose enveloping her. Her head fell back slightly as he gently but thoroughly washed the long length of her hair. It was no small task. Unbound, her hair nearly reached her knees.

Unexpectedly, his hands, slick with soap, slid over her shoulders and arms, then around to the front of her, cupping her breasts. She stiffened.

His mouth was beside her ear. "Peace. I seek only to wash you—nothing more."

True to his word, his hands moved over her almost impersonally, inflaming her nonetheless. When finally he rinsed her clean and she stood, she'd forgotten why she'd come. Her mind was a fog of aching desire. She only wanted him to kiss her and carry her to bed. He held a bath linen out for her as she stepped from the tub. He rubbed it briskly over her hair, then draped it around her shoulders.

He started to turn away, but she placed a hand on his chest, wet from bathing her, but hard and smooth with muscle. His heart thudded beneath her palm. His eyes were hazy, hot—the hand that covered hers shook slightly.

"Where are you going?" she asked, taking a step closer.

He blinked as if he couldn't remember. "A comb . . . for your hair."

She released the linen she'd been holding closed over her body. It fluttered to the ground. She touched his shoulders, ran her hands over the warm power of them, the cords of muscle leading to his neck. "That will take too long," she whispered, raising herself up to kiss him.

As if released from a trance, his arms wound about her, pulling her against him. His mouth slanted over hers, his tongue stroking, hot and knowing. Somehow they were at the bed and she was on her back, his weight pressing her down. His mouth left hers to cover her nipple. She arched toward him, fingers in his hair, nearly purring with pleasure.

"Who'd've thought," he murmured, his mouth against the underside of her breast, kissing, licking.

"Hmm . . .?"

"That you and I . . . a Graham and a Maxwell . . ." He moved lower, down her belly. His words cut through the blanket of desire, reminding her why she was here. Not for bath and pleasure—but to tell him about Fayth.

"Robert," she said, then gasped when he kissed the inside of her thigh. "Robert!" She scooted backward. He followed her movement on all fours like some predatory beast.

His smile was wicked, ravenous. "What? Don't be afraid—it won't hurt—I promise."

She laughed nervously. "That's not what I meant." He was kissing her again, his mouth sucking at her thigh. She quivered, falling back against the bed. What would it hurt, to wait until after?

He was still talking to her, she realized, murmuring against her skin, his hands sliding up under her thighs, stroking her bottom. She could hardly breathe—unable to believe what he was about to do to her, unable to protest since her body wanted him there. Again, he whispered something.

"What?" she said.

He raised himself up, over her, and kissed her—a long drugging kiss that left her limp, clinging to him. When he raised his head he said, "I can think of nothing but you, day and night, *mo cridhe*." He kissed her again, working his way back down her body. "Of doing this . . ." He embraced her suddenly, his face pressed against her belly.

Her heart tripped over itself. Her breath, harsh and erratic already, caught on a sob. To know that he was also consumed by this was more than she could bear. He looked up, his chestnut hair rumpled from her fingers, his eyes dark with concern. She reached for him and he came to her, wrapping his arms around her, holding her against his chest. She had to tell him now. If she waited any longer, if he found out from someone else, he would misconstrue it.

"Robert, I must tell you something, before another moment passes."

He frowned, brushing her wet, tangled hair from her face. "Have I hurt you?"

She touched his jaw. He turned into the caress, rubbing his rough whiskers over her palm. Her heart ached with tenderness for him. "No . . . but I fear you will be very angry with me."

"Impossible."

She gazed at him, the words trembling on her lips, her heart hammering in her chest, and as he watched her expectantly, his frown became wary.

He drew away from her slightly. "Out with it, Caroline, you're frightening me."

"My sister is here."

His arms fell away. He sat up.

Caroline did too, snatching the bedcovers to hide herself. "I didn't know—I swear it. She—she's dressed as a man. She does it oft, dresses like a man, that is. She came with the men who brought my things—she concealed herself in a trunk."

"Where is she now?"

"In the tower room."

He swung off the bed, secured the linen about his waist, and strode to the door.

Caroline hurried after him, struggling to keep hold of her blanket. "What are you doing?"

"Having her apprehended."

"No!" Caroline caught his arm. His other hand remained gripping the door latch, but he didn't open it. "I swear she's not here to cause harm—please listen to me, Robert, hear me out."

Pensive, he stared down at her. Oh, she'd ruined everything! Why had she not just blurted it out the moment he'd opened the door? She wanted to cry and strike something—but this was too important. Fayth's future was about to be decided and she could not fall apart as she had taken to doing of late. The thought gave her a measure of calm and she released his arm, straightening. "Please."

He dropped his hand. His jaw clenched, a muscle ticked beneath his skin. He crossed to the bed and sat on it. "Explain."

Caroline followed him. "There's so much about me— us—you don't know, or understand."

"Make me understand." He was hard, implacable, his arms folded over his chest, the muscles taut. She'd been afraid of this. If only she'd been able to gain his trust first, this would be a simple matter. *Oh, Fayth! Could you not have waited another week!*

She went to the other side of the bed, pulling the blanket closely about her nakedness. His gaze followed her, gray ice. She sat down, taking a deep breath and meeting his eyes across the now great expanse of the bed.

"Ridley has ever been cruel to us both . . . though he never hit me, he found other ways to inflict misery. Unfortunately, Fayth is a very different kind of woman. She's wild, reckless, given to act on thoughtless impulse—"

"And she's here?" By the disbelief in his voice she knew that had been the wrong way to go about it—he was horrified—thought Fayth a beast.

"In spite of it all," Caroline continued as if he hadn't spoken, "she's a sweet child with a good heart. Ridley could never see that and sought to beat the defiance from her. He kept her like a prisoner, mistreated her when she spoke to him with sarcasm—which is just her nature, it means naught. So, she ran away. She had nowhere else to go."

His mouth, which only moments before had been hot and passionate against her skin, was a thin grim line. It shook her, this change, and that she had caused it. She wanted their closeness, their friendship, back, but did not know how to obtain it.

"She sought succor with a Maxwell?" he said, his voice skeptical.

"Not with a Maxwell—with her sister." She looked down at her hands and repeated, "She had nowhere else to go."

"Why didn't you tell me immediately? Why did you let—this—happen?"

Her cheeks were hot—she kept her gaze on the bed. "I meant to, but I was afraid you wouldn't believe me, that you would think this is some plot . . . I was trying to find the right words, but you kept touching me . . . I couldn't think."

She burned with shame. She should have told him—her excuses sounded so poor.

He sighed deeply. She glanced at him. His elbows were braced on his knees, his face buried wearily in his hands. After a moment he rubbed a hand over his face, raked it through his hair, and met her questioning gaze, a shadow of a smile on his lips. "I cannot turn your sister away, I suppose."

"Oh, Robert! Thank you!" She wanted to embrace him, but was afraid of her reception, and so just smiled gratefully.

"Is that all the thanks I get?"

She scooted across the bed to hug him.

He held her tightly. "She'll be watched at all times, understand?"

She nodded vigorously against his shoulder, deliriously happy that he wasn't angry with her, that nothing had changed.

"Oh Robert, I . . ." His arms became crushing. She lifted her head, met his intense gray stare, and her breath caught. The darkness in his eyes held her.

"You what?" he asked, his voice low.

She'd been about to tell him she loved him, but was glad she'd held her tongue. He looked dangerous—threatening almost. As if he knew what she'd been about to say. And didn't believe it.

"I . . . I wanted to thank you."

"You did."

She looked away, shy.

"Oh . . ." he breathed. His hand came up, hovered by her cheek, then his thumb whispered across her eyelashes. Shivers danced over her skin.

"Then thank me."

His tone was still odd, but when she looked at him, she knew he wanted her and it set her heart racing. His hand settled on her shoulder, his thumb tracing circles on her neck. She leaned toward him, then smiled slightly when she noted that he watched her eyelashes, as if fascinated. His gaze moved to her cheek and his thumb brushed over her dimple.

Oh, she couldn't say it, but she did love him. Her heart nearly burst with it. She moved her lips over his, slowly, her tongue darting out to tease, just as he did to her. She wound her arms around his neck, wanting to show him all she couldn't say. Her sheet slipped away and the hair on his chest tickled her breasts. He was strangely still as she did this, as though coiled and waiting. She slid her tongue between his lips and he snapped, dragged her against him, onto his lap. Her thighs straddled him as his tongue plunged into her mouth, stroking deep. There was a wildness to him, a threat of violence in the mouth that ravaged her, in the arms imprisoning her. Her blood roared in her ears, her heart thundering.

His hands roved over her body, stroking, cupping, pressing, enveloping her in his heat. She could feel him, hard, between her thighs. She moved against him and gasped as shards of pleasure pierced her. When she did it again, he groaned and lifted her suddenly, turning as if to lay her on the bed.

"Don't," she said, clutching his shoulders.

He held her tight, one hand beneath her bottom. "Why?"

"I'm too big."

He bounced her up as if she weighed nothing, resettling her in his arms. As if to prove her a liar, he braced her against the bedpost. Before she could protest, he was kissing her again, his hips rocking against hers until she was frantic. She forgot her size—only knew that he was bigger, stronger. She hooked her ankles together, behind his back, trying to get closer. His sheet was gone and she felt the hot length of him, urgent against her. She held his face between her hands, caressing the whiskers on his jaw, the damp skin of his neck, the silken steel of his shoulders. She couldn't get her fill of kissing him, of his body against hers.

He hitched her up again, only this time, sliding her down onto the length of him. Her fingers dug into the muscles of his shoulders, her breath ragged. His eyes held hers, smoldering, intense. He drove into her harder, faster—the bedpost rubbed her back and she reached behind her, to steady herself. The action pushed him deeper and she gasped. Her head fell back, pressed against the post as she writhed and strained. His mouth was on her neck, licking away the sweat. He loomed over her, the muscles bunching and cording in his arms and neck, filling her, expanding her until she thought she couldn't take anymore.

It broke over her like a wave, crashing through her, senseless. He captured her mouth again. His arms left her, gripping the bedpost behind her as he drove into her the last time, his body shuddering with the force of it. Her belly and thighs still shivered deliciously when he laid her on the bed, collapsing beside her.

Caroline drifted to sleep, utterly spent, wrapped in his sweat damp arms. After a time, she woke, remembering her sister. She sat up, meaning to slip out of bed quietly and go to Fayth without waking Robert. But he was awake. She gazed at him, troubled by his closed look.

"You'd best get your sister settled," he said, rolling away and sitting on the edge of the bed opposite her. His broad scarred back faced her, his shoulders hunched slightly. When she didn't move, he said, "Go on."

She left the bed and poked at her filthy shift and dress wadded on the floor—she did not want to put them back on. He tossed his dressing gown at her. She pulled the heavy velvet around her, tying it shut. It smelled like him.

She smiled to herself, as if he still held her in his arms. At the door, she looked over her shoulder. He still sat on the bed, staring after her, and the line of worry between his brows had returned.

When she was gone, Robert quickly threw on some clothes and summoned Henry. When he appeared Robert told him to fetch Geordie. There was a sickness inside him. Suspicion. Distrust. Doubt. He needed to rid himself of it.

He paced his withdrawing room as he waited for his master of guard, going over the events in the bedchamber. When she'd come to him, it had been obvious she was preoccupied. She'd said she was afraid he'd be angry with her. It made sense. As a child, he'd been hesitant to confess some misdeed to his father. But she was not a child—she was a self-possessed woman. And why did she ask about Laird Johnstone's letter? In fact, she'd wanted to know if he believed Johnstone's excuse. Why was that significant? A test of how easily he was gulled?

He stopped before the fireplace, bracing his hands on the mantel and staring down into the flames. He'd lost his judgment. He was so completely besotted with her he could not see his way in this. He'd looked in her eyes— thought he saw her. He wanted to trust her.

Alex would surely berate him for his indecision. Everything was simple for Alex—he cared about nothing so much as his feuding and raiding. Robert pushed away from the fireplace.

And how did that damn stone factor into all of this? Could someone—Wesley or Ridley—really believe the legend? Was Caroline or Fayth a plant—to see if the stone was delivered as the legend claimed? His head throbbed. He hated this—hated that she'd wanted to visit that old woman. What was her interest in the stone?

Why did she wait until he'd blathered his mindless words of passion before she told him? Idiot! Knowing of his infatuation, she must also know he would deny her nothing. But how would she know that? She was an innocent, a virgin, destined for the cloister until he'd snatched her away.

Memories of the abbey assailed him. He'd been afraid of hurting her—breaking her maidenhead. But could not remember feeling a maidenhead and she'd not seemed in any great pain—no more than discomfort—easy enough to fake. And this evening she'd certainly been willing enough. What was this contradiction he'd wed? The freezing Mother Caroline one moment; passionate, writhing wife the next. Or was it more simply explained by "accomplished actress"?

He stormed into the bedchamber. Her clothes were still crumpled on the floor—the same she'd worn last night. They'd lain on her cloak, but surely there would be blood on her gown. He inspected every inch like a madman—finding nothing. Then, heartsick, he pressed his face into her gown, inhaling the scent of her.

Oh, he was lost.

He heard a knock in the other room. He laid her garments across the bed, returning to his withdrawing room as Geordie entered. "My lord?"

"Have the Grahams left?"

"Aye, my lord."

"Did you realize one of them remained behind?"

Geordie started, his mouth opening and closing. He shook his head. "Forgive—I shall flog the men guarding them myself."

Robert held up a hand. "That can wait. Our Graham guest is Lady Annan's sister, Fayth Graham. She will be residing in the tower room. I want her guarded at all times—never is she to be unattended."

"Aye, sir."

"Go to her now. Tell her I wish an audience when she has made herself presentable."

Geordie turned to leave.

"Wait."

Geordie turned back expectantly.

Robert gritted his teeth, wishing it weren't necessary, then said, "My wife, too—she is not to be left unattended."

"My lord? We always—"

Robert shook his head. "No, I mean within the keep, as well as without."

Geordie's eyes passed no judgment, though Robert felt as conniving and disloyal as he suspected his wife of being.

When the guard was gone, Robert slouched behind his desk, brooding. He didn't want to feel this way—doubting Caroline and himself. But there was simply no way around it. Until he was assured of Patrick's safety, he would take no chances. Nothing promised to Robert in the marriage contract had been delivered. He could not make excuses any longer. Ridley meant to deceive him somehow. For sixty years and more the Maxwells and the Grahams had set a precedence by cutting each other to collops at every opportunity, by lying, stealing, raiding, raping, and tricking each other. There was nothing to do but wait and see how this played out—if indeed, it played out at all.

And, of course, never drop his guard.

20

⟲

"There," Caroline said, tying a golden ribbon to the end of Fayth's pathetically short braid. Her sister had shorn her hair on numerous occasions in order to pass as a boy. It was finally starting to grow long again. The reddish brown tresses waved just past her shoulders when loose.

Fayth shrugged restlessly in the borrowed gown. Of course, Caroline thought, slightly exasperated, her sister had not thought far enough ahead to slip some garments into Caroline's trunk and so had nothing but the men's clothes on her back. So, she wore one of Celia's gowns. Caroline's clothes were far too large for Fayth. Even Celia was larger than Fayth—the skirt dragged the floor and the bodice, though laced as tightly as possible, hung like a sack about Fayth's midsection. Caroline tried to hide her concern over her sister's diminished appearance. She'd always been small, but now she was painfully thin as well.

She moved in front of Fayth, adjusting the partlet that hid her modest bosom—as well as the rack of ribs and jutting collarbones stretching her translucent skin. Fayth's eyes were on Caroline's chest and she said, "Don't let me take your only one."

"I have others."

Fayth's eyebrows rose. "Then why do you walk about bare chested?"

"I'm not bare chested—and because Lord Annan wishes me not to wear one."

"If he doesn't like them, why must I wear one?"

Caroline sighed. "I'm trying to make you look as mild and innocent as possible. Not an easy task."

Fayth grunted.

"You're in a gown now—please conform your behavior to your attire."

Fayth just scowled and for the first time Caroline silently bemoaned the fact their father had raised them in such a loose manner.

Fayth squared her shoulders and took a deep breath. "What does he want to talk to me about?"

"Well—Wesley led a raid on Annancreag recently. Do you know anything about that?"

Fayth shook her head—wide-eyed. "I haven't spoken to Wesley in weeks. Ridley wouldn't allow it."

Ridley was a beast! Caroline was appalled at how he treated Fayth—couldn't blame the poor thing for running. "Tell him that and I'm certain everything will be fine. He's waiting, so we should go."

Fayth caught Caroline's arm. "What if he sends me back?"

"He won't—I promise."

"How can you be sure?"

"He . . ." Caroline started to tell her sister how wonderful Robert was, but it would only begin an argument and remind Fayth of Jack. Caroline did not want Jack's murder on her sister's mind when she met Robert. Fayth would soon see for herself that Robert was a good man.

"You'll see," Caroline said. "Lord Annan is different."

"But he's a *Maxwell*." Fayth's lip curled as though the word was foul. "Jack thought he was coming home, too—I wonder if I'll share his fate?"

"Oh, Fayth!" Caroline stared at her sister hopelessly. "Jack was a victim of the feud—a feud Lord Annan seeks to end. That's why I'm here, remember?"

Fayth shook her head incredulously. "You believe that? He must tell you nothing."

Unease snaked through Caroline's belly. "What mean you?"

"The Maxwells still raid our land! Why, just last week they burned the village, killing women and children."

Caroline shook her head. "That's impossible . . ." But was it? Robert was gone all last week. Could he have been on a raid of retribution? Why wouldn't he tell her? And if all this were true—why was Fayth here, of all places? Caroline had never thought her sister a liar, but now her eyes narrowed suspiciously. "Why hasn't Ridley released Sir Patrick? Or sent my dowry?"

"I know not—but he has his reasons. He's dealing with Maxwells, after all. You can never be too careful."

Caroline stared at her sister incredulously. "Mean you, he has no intention of releasing Sir Patrick?"

"Sir Patrick! Sir Patrick! Who cares about that piece of Maxwell waste?"

"I care! Lord Annan—and most especially his brother, Red Alex, care! They will not stand for this much longer."

There was a knock on the door.

Fayth's face went nearly purple at the mention of Red Alex.

Caroline didn't go to the door. She asked, her voice hushed, "What do you know about Sir Patrick? Has Ridley murdered him? Or maimed him?"

"I know nothing! Ridley only tells me what he wants me to know—you know that."

The knock came again—louder, more urgent, followed by Geordie's voice. "Lady Annan, open the door, or we'll force it."

Force it?

Stunned, Caroline went to the door and opened it. Four men-at-arms, including Geordie, waited just outside the door, hands on sword hilts. Geordie said, "Lord Annan requests Mistress Graham's presence."

Caroline nodded distractedly and started out the door, beckoning Fayth to follow.

Geordie held out his hand, stopping Caroline. "Alone."

Caroline blinked, but said nothing as Fayth passed her. Fayth paused at the top of the stairs and glanced over her shoulder at Caroline. Her eyes were wide with apprehension. Caroline knew she didn't want to face him alone. Caroline tried to give her sister a reassuring smile.

Geordie and another guard followed Fayth down the stairs. Caroline didn't close the door, waiting for the other two guards to leave. But they didn't. They just stood there, eyes averted. Guarding her.

Very slowly, her heart heavy, Caroline shut the door.

Fayth returned a short time later. Caroline was writing in her book. She had changed her mind about her story and was anxious to record the new ending. Perhaps the story wasn't so unacceptable in its original form. It certainly reflected the reality of marriage better than her story did. Of course Orpheus would look back—he wouldn't trust Eurydice to follow him, he would be compelled to check up on her. Such lofty concepts as loyalty and honor based on love were alien to feebleminded women. Only men could grasp such things. She scribbled gleefully, a rictus of satisfaction fixed to her face, until Fayth's grousing forced her to set her book aside.

The catharsis she derived from her writing soon dissolved as Fayth told Caroline about her audience. "He was rude and suspicious, insisting I'm here on Ridley's orders. He tried to intimidate me with his size." She gave Caroline a sympathetic look. "It grieves me to see you wed to such a beast. That such a good woman should come to this. It's disgraceful. Your life was to be so fine—the best of nuns, you would be, with all your books."

Caroline didn't respond. How could she contradict her? His actions proved his lack of faith in her. Any words defending his behavior sounded poor even to herself—she did not intend to voice them. Her faith in the future was shaken. It had been a fragile faith, formed in an abbey's ruins and in her lover's arms, but it had been warm and precious nonetheless.

The more she thought about it, the angrier she became. He'd been false with her. She'd assumed by allowing Fayth to stay—not to mention the passionate lovemaking—that he was giving this a chance. But he'd been suspicious all along. After he'd finished rutting on her, he immediately set guards on her, believing she had something to do with Fayth's appearance—that it all indicated some impending massacre she'd plotted from the beginning. True, they'd only been together a few weeks, but had she not proved herself trustworthy? Enough to deserve better than this?

By the time the brief knock sounded, followed by

Celia's entrance, Caroline was nearly fuming with indignation. "What is it, Celia?"

"Lord Annan wishes to know why he dined alone this evening."

This information incensed Caroline, though she struggled not to show it. "As he set guards on me, I assumed I was confined to my chambers."

Celia cleared her throat. "Lord Annan also wants to know why you've not vacated the tower."

"Tell him that since I'm his prisoner, I thought the tower a more appropriate lodging."

Fayth's eyebrows shot up.

Celia leaned close to Caroline and whispered, "He's most vexed, my lady. I would not continue antagonizing him. He might decide to punish you."

"Your concern is misplaced. I have the situation in hand." Caroline smiled at Celia and sent her away. This act of defiance somehow settled her. She felt a measure of her old composure return.

"Oh—he'll be in a lather!" Fayth seemed to find the situation humorous, then her brow creased with concern. "Will he beat you? Perhaps you shouldn't be so defiant."

"No," Caroline said and fetched a deck of cards from her trunk. She did not want to speak of it. She had hoped to prove to her sister how good and fine the Maxwells were—her husband in particular—but he was acting like a heathen. "Shall we?"

Fayth had only just dealt the cards when someone pounded on the door so hard it shook.

"Caroline!"

Caroline's heart seized. She'd not expected him to come for her—to confront her! The door flew open, revealing her husband—furious, his shirt hanging open and out of his breeches as if he'd been disrobing. His gaze sought her, impaling her.

Fayth was on her feet before Caroline, moving between them. She whipped a short knife from her bodice and brandished it at him. "Don't you touch her!"

Robert gaped at her, then swung around, bellowing for the guards. They hurried into the room. "I thought you searched her!"

Caroline tried to dislodge her tiny sister as the guards stammered that they had searched her, but didn't think to check her bosom. Fayth was surprisingly firm, knife waving madly through the air. She held an arm out, to keep Caroline behind her, her gaze locked on Robert. "Stand back, Sister. I've stuck meaner brutes than him before."

"You haven't!" Caroline said, appalled and embarrassed. "Stop this before you get hurt."

When Fayth refused to relinquish the weapon, Robert strode forward and grabbed at her. Fayth hopped back, jabbing at him with surprising skill. Caroline grabbed her sister's shoulders, holding her still. Fayth squeaked in alarm. Robert grabbed her wrist, jerking her around so her back was against him. Fayth struggled wildly, but the knife clattered to the floor. He thrust her away—at the guards—then turned on Caroline.

Caroline barely managed not to cower under the heat of his anger. She tilted her chin—determined to hang onto the shredded dignity she still possessed. "Is there a problem?"

He took a menacing step toward her. "Why are you still lodged in this chamber?"

"I assumed these new orders—of having me guarded—rescinded the old ones."

He smiled but there was no humor in it. "You assume too much."

"If you order me to vacate these chambers, of course, I will—"

"Don't." He grasped her arm, hauling her close. "You will not turn into Mother Superior on me again. I will—not—have—it."

She let her arm go limp in his grasp and averted her eyes stubbornly. She had nothing to say to him until he apologized, or at the very least, explained himself.

He released her arm and stood back, breathing deeply. "Get your cloak."

She hesitated. "Why?"

"Get it."

Oh, not this again! She would not cry. *She would not!* She walked stiffly to the cabinet and withdrew her cloak, trying to detach herself. It used to be so easy! She would pretend she was someone else, watching all this. It couldn't be happening to her.

Fayth fought against the guards—yelling threats at Robert, who ignored her. His eyes remained on Caroline, unwavering. She stopped in front of him, as though waiting for her next orders. He waved his arm for her to proceed.

Caroline gave Fayth a reassuring smile before she led Robert from the room and down the stairs. At the foot, she stopped. "Where to now?"

His hand clamped onto the back of her neck. "My chambers."

As he urged her along her confusion mounted. Then why did she need her cloak? Once in his chamber, he didn't stop, but led her straight through to the bedchamber, closing the door behind him and finally releasing her neck. She stood in the center of the room, unmoving, waiting, trying to tamp down her apprehension and unhappiness.

He circled her, hands folded behind his back—prowling. After several unbearable moments of this, he took her cloak. She blinked at his back as he went to the bed and spread the cloak, inspecting the lining. Was he looking to see if she concealed something? Intelligence? But no, he didn't touch it as though feeling for something, he merely scrutinized it. Then he crumpled it into a ball and tossed it across the room. This had to be another game—to force some unknown confession from her. His behavior was too bizarre to account for aught else. He turned back to her, glowering, his ice gray eyes slits through heavy dark lashes.

"I expect your plan has succeeded," she said.

He straightened. "What?"

"If you meant to drive my sister away, I assure you, she'll not want to stay another night under your rule. She might as well stay with Ridley—after all, there is some comfort in the familiar."

"You think I'm no better than Ridley."

She shrugged lightly, looking away with a deep sigh.

"I want to trust you. I want to help your sister."

Caroline smiled, meeting his eyes. "Of course you do."

He came at her, grabbing her arms. She started, unable to stop the intake of surprised breath. "I mean it, Caroline—I will not play along anymore." He shook her slightly, rattling her composure. "I will have the truth from you."

"Or else? What?"

His fingers dug into her arm, his mouth thinning. "Or else I send your sister and Father Jasper back to Ridley—tonight."

The pressure built behind her eyes, burning. She clenched her teeth and stared back at him. "I have not lied to you, my lord. I know not what you want from me."

His gaze held hers, searching, then he said, "Were you a virgin—before last night?"

The air whooshed out of her. Baffled, she stumbled

over her words. "Of course I was—what kind of question is that?"

He released her, retrieving her cloak, and to her astonishment, the garments she'd worn before he bathed her. He approached her slowly, watching her, clothes held in front of him like evidence of a crime. "No blood."

She stared blankly from him to the clothes. "So?"

"I felt no maidenhead either, when I pushed into you that first time."

The implications of what he suggested horrified her. Her face slackened with shock. "Robert—you must believe me. I've never even kissed another man. How can you believe otherwise?"

"It's certainly what I was meant to believe."

Her hands flew to her mouth, her gaze fixed on him. Her purity had never come into question—one had only to look at her to know she was untouched. "No man has lain with me but you . . . yet I know of nothing I could say to convince you."

His hands crushed the fabric of her garments as he stared at her. He seemed so torn, so upset. She could read the indecision in his eyes. He wanted to believe her. And yet he was a Maxwell—born and bred to hate Grahams. She began to doubt her assumption that this was some form of foolery.

Cautiously, she said, "Not all maidens bleed when deflowered. And I've heard a maidenhead can be broken in other ways . . . after all, I'm four and twenty. Not a young maiden. But that is something you must discover on your own, as I'm certain you'd never take my word for it. Please—talk to Celia or Agnes." She looked away. "But I could always be lying. You'll never know, will you?"

She looked back. His jaw was rigid, his gaze never wavering from her face, knuckles white from gripping her clothes. She took a step toward him. "You have only faith to go on. What you know and believe about me." She bolstered herself. She could see it now—he wanted to believe her. Tenderness sent her to him, closing the distance between them. "Do you believe me untrustworthy? Have I shown myself disloyal? Without honor?"

He dropped her clothes, shaking his head. His hand trembled slightly as he touched her cheek. "No, *mo cridhe,* but I have." His arms came around her, pulling her against him. Warmth flooded through her, relief, happiness. The tears did come now, pricking the corners of her eyes. She held him tightly, praying they could make this work, that they could overcome all the barriers their surnames put between them.

His face was buried in her neck. She turned, so her lips pressed against his ear and whispered, "Take me to bed, Robert. I'm so tired."

He made love to her slowly, silently, and his reticence troubled her. Afterward, he stared down at her in the candlelight. The slight frown was back, marring his brow. She smoothed her hand over it. "What troubles you?"

He smiled, one-sided. "When I'm with you, nothing truly troubles me."

"And when you're not?"

He sighed, shrugging one shoulder. "Everything."

She slid her arms around his waist, pressing close. "Then I shall endeavor to be always close at hand."

His kissed her, pressing her back onto the bed. It amazed her that she could be inflamed, ready for him again so soon. His lifted his head, frowning into the shadows. Then she heard it, someone knocking on his chambers. He was barely out of bed, breeches yanked over his hips, when the knock started on the bedchamber door.

Robert swung the door open. A man stepped inside, filthy, his face soot blackened. Before Robert could speak, the man said, "I come from Red Alex." He glanced at Caroline, who clutched the blanket to her breasts. "Perhaps we should speak elsewhere."

Robert glanced at her, then said, his voice firm, "Nay—out with it."

"Well, we've been sticking close to Annancreag of late—Red Alex thinks there's a Graham plot hatching. He gets the idea they might be hiding in the moss—as it's verra dangerous and most Maxwells go around it. And there they are—Johnstones, Armstrongs—Grahams. They've set up camp. We attacked them—killed one. Red Alex is pursuing them now. They outnumber us and he wishes for your assistance. He says Wesley Graham is among them and he means to kill the lad."

"Aye." Robert snatched his discarded shirt off the floor and shrugged into it. The man left. Caroline stared at Robert as he quickly dressed. Fear for Wesley left her speechless—but she must say something. He came to the bed and leaned over her.

"I know not how long this will take. Alex has a gift for making a muck of everything. If I don't get there quickly, our marriage will have been for naught."

She nodded.

He pressed a kiss to her forehead. "Do you regret it—now?"

"Regret what?"

"Lying with me? It seems you might have had your convent, if only I'd kept my hands off you."

"No," she said solemnly. "I . . ." He was motionless, leaning over her, eyebrows raised in expectation. She wanted to tell him, needed to, but the words wouldn't come.

"Yes?" he said encouragingly.

She stiffened her spine, determined not to waste another moment in this useless fear. "I love you."

He smiled down at her, rubbing his knuckles over her jaw. "And I you, *mo cridhe.*"

He kissed her gently and sweetly, and started to rise, but she caught his arm. "Robert—you won't let Alexander kill Wesley?"

"I'll do what I can," he said and was gone.

21

By the time Robert arrived at the remote tower in the debatable land, Alex's siege was well under way. Alex had managed to separate Wesley and a handful of his men from the main body. He'd pursued them through Robert's lands—as well as the estates of several other clans—across the Sark and Solway Moss with its stinking swamps, right into the heart of the debatable land—the area disputed by Scotland and England. He'd caught Wesley and wounded him, but the Graham lad had escaped and taken shelter with other reivers who made their nest in the debatable land. The tower, standing lonely on the banks of the River Esk, surrounded by rich, arable fields that no one bothered to cultivate, belonged to the Grahams. The Grahams reigned supreme in the debatable land and no one challenged them for long; they could call up more men than any other clan on the borders to crush their offenders—be they Scot or English, they made little distinction.

It was a modest tower, Robert noted on his approach, constructed of red stone and surrounded by a barmkin wall—which Alex had already breached. Several lairds, whose land Alex had traversed, had joined the sport. The bailey milled with activity. Nearly three score men (many more than Alex commanded) rushed about, piling every piece of kindling they could find outside the great double doors that barred the entrance.

"Rob!" Alex called, striding across the bailey from where he'd been directing labors. "I've got him—like a rat in a trap! I'll burn him out, then string him up for the buzzards!"

"This is a Graham tower."

Alex looked up at it, hands on hips. "Och, aye. They gave him sanctuary, knowing it was me they'd give account to. They'll pay for their gall."

Several cheers of support went up—one from Robert's closest neighbor—Lord Bell. He was busily hacking at a tree branch with his sword and throwing the pieces onto the soon-to-be bonfire. Alex, like Red Rowan, always inspired love and admiration in men, so understandably he'd gained an entourage and audience in this endeavor— all thirsty for Graham blood. And unfortunately, in the debatable land, most actions, criminal or otherwise, were free from reprisal, as neither country took responsibility for policing it. Alex had not been exaggerating when he called Wesley a rat in a trap.

But the trap could close both ways.

"You'd better move fast—once the Grahams hear about this, they'll descend in force, and you'll be the rat." Robert gazed upward, at the top of the tower, shading his eyes from the sun. "Have they lit a signal fire?"

Alex shook his head, frowning in consternation. "No—that's what's strange."

Robert's gaze swept over the revelry around them. "Well . . . looks as if you don't need my men any longer."

"The rest of Wesley's men could show up at any time and you know they'll scatter as soon as Graham reinforcements arrive. And if this happens to last a few days, they'll all get bored and melt away. Nay, I need you here, Brother."

"Oh, I'm not going anywhere."

Alex slid him a suspicious look. "Why is it I dinna like your tone?"

Robert crossed his arms, not relishing another battle with his brother. "I can't let you kill Wesley Graham."

Alex leaned forward, so their noses were inches apart, frigid blue eyes that knew no mercy piercing him—so like their father. "I plan to send the little bugger back to Ridley Graham, piece by rotten piece, until he releases Patrick—and you can't stop me."

Robert lifted his shoulders, inhaling deeply. "I'm still bigger than you."

Alex leaned back, smug grin in place. "But not half as quick."

The crackle of fire distracted them. The men had lit the pile of wood before the doors and fanned at it. The flame caught, eating its way through branches and leaves, and though it burned right up against the door, the thick oak remained unmarred.

Alex turned back to him. "Did Lady Wife send you after me with orders to keep her brother alive?"

Robert only smiled.

"You're here as deputy warden?"

"I'm afraid so."

Alex swore, swinging around to stare at his siege, hands on hips. "Your jurisdiction doesn't extend to the debatable land, Brother."

"No . . . but once you step foot off it, I'll have you for murder—and your honeyed tongue works not with me."

"That's assuming you catch me, of course. In the unlikely event you do, I'll take up the matter with Lord Maxwell. What care he if another Graham dies—all the better if I take along a few Armstrongs."

Alex was right. He would get away with murdering Wesley—no one would care—not even the English, as Graham reivers such as Wesley gave the English warden as much trouble as the Scottish warden. And if Wesley did act independently of his brother, even Ridley might not complain overmuch.

"If Patrick still lives . . . and I'm beginning to doubt it—rash acts like this do him no good!" When Alex ignored him, Robert grabbed his arm, turning him around. "I'm still awaiting an answer from Ridley. If I do not hear from him in a sennight—we'll take stronger action."

Alex's lip curled. "Do what you must—and I'll do what I must. I'll not allow Wesley Graham to go free."

Robert ground his teeth in frustration. "May I appeal to you then as a brother? Caroline will be heartbroken if you kill him."

"You've given her your trust."

"Aye."

Alex snorted, derisive. "You lovesick fool." Before Robert could take umbrage Alex rushed on. "Twice I have discovered Wesley Graham and his broken men— men surely in the employ of Ridley—sneaking about Annancreag—as though waiting. Waiting for what? And why? If it were merely a raid, they would do reconnaissance, then leave—coming back for their attack. But they loiter, biding their time. There's no other explanation, Rob. Someone in your household is waiting to give them a signal—or give them entrance!"

Robert refused to give in to the doubt his brother

dredged up. It was unfair to Caroline. She was not here to defend herself—and damn it—until he had some kind of proof it shouldn't be necessary for her to! Her sister's visit, however, might not be as innocent as she'd led Caroline to believe. But it wouldn't do for Robert to accuse Fayth without proof. And Robert certainly wasn't about to share that information with Alex—to do so would only invite more insults.

Alex studied Robert, shaking his head. "How did she do it, I wonder? The nun fiction? She was untouchable—something you couldn't have. Clever, clever. Men always want what they can't have and here she is, right under your nose, daring you to take it."

Robert's temper surged. Damn Alex! Why must it always come to this?

"The nun persona was useful in other ways, too. Such as establishing her trustworthiness; after all—who would call a nun a liar?" Alex rubbed his russet whiskers. "It amazes me that the same ploy could work twice, but alas, it has. We've shown ourselves not very clever, haven't we? You've lost your head—all reason—over a woman. Just remember—Malcolm was parted from his head permanently. Dinna let the prospect of a tumble part you from yours."

Robert grabbed the gaping front of Alex's jack, yanking him forward so they were eye to eye. "Our shared blood will earn you little tolerance if you keep at this. I will not hear another word against her. Until you can show some respect, you are no longer welcome in my home."

Robert shoved his stunned brother away. Alex stared at Robert, obviously so offended his poison tongue was rendered mute. *A cause for celebration.*

He turned on his heel and joined his men. Geordie had

stayed behind to oversee Fayth's activities. Robert had dropped the guard on Caroline—other than as protection if she left the castle. He trusted her. She would not betray him. It irritated him that it seemed like a credo he must intone in order to make it so. Alex's words cut too deeply—and too close to the truth. But damn it! He loved her. He *did* trust her.

"My lord," one of his men said. "Should we assist?" He looked eagerly at the siege in progress. Such bloodlust—and for what?

"Nay," Robert said, leaning against the barmkin wall. "We watch and wait."

Robert had been gone only a day when the messenger Caroline had sent to Bess Maxwell returned. Bess had tried to beat him with a stick and when he was finally able to relay his message—an invitation to visit Caroline—the response had been a curt "Go away!" and a sharp whack. And so, with Celia in tow, Caroline had set out to visit Bess Maxwell again.

Caroline had been avoiding her sister. She didn't want to tell Fayth where Robert had gone—to stop Alexander from killing Wesley. And she couldn't face Fayth and withhold the truth. Wesley and Fayth were very close—the best of friends. So, after putting Fayth off repeatedly yesterday, Caroline thought it best to be gone. Hopefully by tomorrow Robert would return with good news.

The ride was oddly exhilarating for Caroline, bringing back heart-stopping memories of her last outing with Robert. *The abbey was that way—across the moor—and there, that's where he took me to the burn, and the reflecting pool.*

Caroline set a brisk pace and by noon they spotted

Bess's fine little cottage. The dog dashed out, barked an alarm and returned inside. The guards waited outside while Caroline and Celia followed the dog. The interior was dim, lit only by two open windows and the fire. "Bess?" Caroline called. It took a moment for her eyes to adjust, but when they did, she saw the old woman, sitting at the table, watching them.

"Why did you come back?"

Caroline went to the table. "This is Celia, my maid." The old woman nodded at Celia. "May I sit?" Bess nodded again. Caroline sat across from the old woman.

Bess shelled peas, her gnarled fingers quick and sure, blue eyes fixed on Caroline. "Well?"

"Why did you refuse to move to the village? Surely you realize how dangerous it is, living out here all alone."

Bess laughed. "I've managed this long—what do I need your protection for?"

"Well . . ."

"I'm old and all alone—how sad for me," she said mockingly. "You will be too, lassie. Perhaps, when this is finished, you'll have a cottage of your own . . . oh, I forgot—you're the Pious Graham Mare, you'll just retire to a convent."

Caroline was having trouble keeping up with the old woman. What did she mean? And how did she know Caroline's nickname?

"Unless he's put his seed in your belly . . . ? If so, you're in more danger than I thought. They'll want you dead, too."

"Mind your tongue, hag," Celia said from the door.

Caroline held up her hand to still her maid. Though her lips twisted with scorn, Bess never looked at Celia, her gaze moving between Caroline and the peas.

"Who are you?" Caroline asked. She had her suspicions, which had contributed to her decision to make today's journey, but it seemed too incredible to be true.

"Don't you know? Haven't you figured it out? And I was sure you were a clever one."

"Elizabeth Graham . . . or . . . wife of—"

"Widow," Bess corrected harshly. "Of Malcolm Maxwell, Lord Annan."

"What . . . ? How . . . ?" Caroline couldn't form a thought, let alone a coherent sentence.

Celia had approached the table, wide-eyed, and asked, "How did you survive the massacre? Or did ye survive because you're a conniving betrayer? Your life in return for the lives of the Annan Maxwells?"

"Evil shrew!" Bess threw a handful of peas at Celia.

Celia yelped in surprise, shielding her face.

Bess laughed. "I knew your mother's mother and she could shred a suit of armor with her tongue! Blood runs true, aye?"

Celia retreated a few steps, nonplussed.

Bess turned back to Caroline. "I survived because it was my brother that did the killing. He might not shrink from torturing helpless women, but murdering his own sister, for some reason, was distasteful to him." Bess's hands stilled over the peas, her eyes far away. "I couldn't go back, though. Never again. Malcolm's brother, William, didn't trust me completely." She grinned wryly, showing darkened teeth, sharp eyes focusing again on Caroline. "But he surely wanted to swive—so he set me up here, kept me fed and clothed— trying to lift my skirts all the while." Her smile faded and she shook her head firmly. "But I saved myself for one man—and my own blood took him from me. You're looking at the oldest virgin alive who hasn't given herself over to God."

"But . . . why?" Caroline asked. "Surely if you never meant to marry, a convent would be the safest place for you."

"Because there is no God."

Celia crossed herself and backed away, to the door. Though unsettled by Bess's pronouncement, Caroline could sympathize with the woman's lost faith. She'd suffered a horrible ordeal, lost her only love—taken by her greedy brother. Enough to shake the strongest faith.

Bess shrugged. "Besides, I'm a Maxwell and a Scotswoman—have been for three score years. This is where I belong." Her gaze fixed on Caroline, steady. "History repeats itself, lass. Mark me. You be ever watchful. Blood does not always run true—but love does."

A seed of terror was planted in Caroline's heart. Fayth. Wesley. Such hatred. But Caroline *loved* them. She leaned forward, surprised to find she trembled—that her hands were icy and stiff. "Who killed your brother?"

Bess smiled complacently and went back to shelling her peas. "Why, I told you, lass. A Maxwell slit his throat. He got his, he did."

Caroline sat back.

"Hate makes a person strong. Vengeance gives a body purpose. Together—they're unstoppable."

Caroline didn't know what she referred to—the feud or herself. Perhaps both.

Bess looked over her shoulder, out the window. A cloud had passed over the sun, darkening the room. "You'd best be getting back. You shouldn't be out and about at night with only two guards and that termagant of yours."

Celia crossed herself again and left the cottage.

"I can't just leave you here."

"Why?"

"It's just not safe!"

Bess's voice lowered. "Think you it's safer at Annan-creag? With that Blood Stone on its merry way to you? No thank you, Lady Annan. I'll stay right here."

And so Caroline left. They rode hard on their return, as if demons licked at their heels, returning to Annan-creag hours before dusk. Still covered with road dust and sweat, Caroline sought out Father Jasper. He was in the great hall, speaking with Celia's daughter, Larie, who had a natural ability for letters. Caroline stood back a mo-ment, her heart softening, reminded of her own youth, spent bent over books with Father Jasper, who had always been so kind to her. He had loved her just as she was— something her father, though she could not deny he'd held affection for her, could not do. His love had always been conditional.

Father Jasper glanced up and spotted her. He said something to Larie, who gathered up the flat board and coal she'd been writing with and hurried past Caroline, issuing an obedient greeting as she passed.

Caroline joined Father Jasper at the table, sitting across from him. "I've discovered some most distressing news—and I know not what to do with it."

Father Jasper folded his hands together on the table. "Tell me."

She filled him in on her visit to Bess Maxwell—on all that had been said, stumbling over the blasphemy— which didn't appear to faze the priest in the slightest.

"Elizabeth Graham . . ." he whispered. "Well, that's certainly unexpected. She claims the Clachan Fala is real and on its way to you?"

Caroline nodded. "Do you think she's right? Why does Wesley continue to harry the Maxwells? Could he be after the stone? Do you think my marriage was noth-ing more than a ruse to bring the stone into the open?"

"I know not. But this woman is very old—perhaps her mind is feeble. Maybe she only imagines herself a great lady. And as for Wesley—well, the lad wouldn't know what to do with himself if he stopped raiding and reiving."

Caroline wasn't swayed. Bess's mind was not feeble. And knowing Ridley and her father, Caroline felt there was truth to Bess's warnings. Father's obsession with Mona had always been puzzling—and now Ridley's. Didn't Bess say that Musgraves were the keepers?

Her thoughts went to Fayth's unexpected arrival at Annancreag. "But . . . what about Fayth?"

The priest's gaze sharpened, moving to something over Caroline's shoulder.

"What about me?" Fayth asked.

Caroline's stomach knotted, sickened by the position she now found herself in. Like Bess, she was no longer a Graham. Her loyalty lay with her husband and his family. Though she loved her sister, she must proceed with care. She'd had years to hone her acting skills—planning every response and rehearsing it to perfection. She never thought she'd employ them to deceive Fayth—but she vowed she would not become Bess Maxwell.

She looked over her shoulder, a false smile fixed in place.

Fayth's eyes narrowed suspiciously.

"I was simply wondering what we're going to do with you. Such as, would you like to marry? Or live with me as an old spinster? Or . . . ?"

"Marry? Who could Lord Annan possibly scrape up that I would wed?"

"It wouldn't have to be a Maxwell," Father Jasper said. "Lord Annan has other allies, other friends. Why not a Scott? Or a Kerr?"

Fayth scowled, shrugging her narrow shoulders resentfully. "Why does it have to be a Scotsman?"

Caroline reached across the table, covering Father Jasper's hand with her own and squeezing it. "Thank you, Father—we'll talk later." She stood and said, "Tonight, Fayth, we shall dine together and you can tell me all your requirements for a husband. But for now—I must speak with Cook." And she was off before Fayth could protest.

22

Wesley sat motionless at the top of his tree where he'd wedged himself into the upper branches, eyes trained on the distant castle. The wide oak leaves shielded him from sight, should anyone chance by—which was doubtful. His position afforded him a good view of the battlements of Annancreag—the rock that this particularly malignant branch of the Maxwell family crawled from under. Dusk was falling and soon, even with the torches lit along the walls, he would be unable to make out movement from this distance.

He waved away the insects buzzing about him. One flew into his cheek and he winced. He fingered the long ragged cut on his cheek. It was feverish and swollen. When he pressed it, thick liquid oozed from it.

He should have known an unholy demon like Red Alex would not die so easily.

Red Alex would pay for scarring him. Black fury enveloped him again, bringing a cold smile to his face. The curving of his lips made his wound ache—fire pulsed within, as if it had a heart of its own. Red Alex was probably still there, at the tower in the debatable land, trying to flush him out. The fool.

Wesley'd been in the tower no more than a few minutes—long enough to make it to the cellars, down a tunnel that led him a quarter of a mile away, reemerging in a scrub of bramble and bush. He'd left two men behind, to show themselves through the arrow slits and gull Red Alex into believing he was still in the tower. Then he'd met up with the rest of his men and returned to Annancreag. This time they kept their camp mobile, staying farther away, deeper in the forest. But thus far, Red Alex had not returned. Wesley's only regret was that he wouldn't be there to see Red Alex's face when he finally breached the tower's defenses and found Wesley gone.

He'd been worried their plot had failed when Red Alex had came upon them and chased them away. He'd been waiting for a sign from Fayth—informing him she'd discovered the stone. They both knew Lord Annan would never leave her unguarded and so they devised a signal that she could give him, even in the presence of Maxwells. All she must do is get herself to the battlements while wearing something red over her hair.

He noted movement at the wall and tensed. It was too far away to distinguish if it was Fayth, but the time was right—late afternoon. His shoulders slumped. Whoever it was did not wear red.

He waited until it was too dark to see, then climbed down to move his camp.

The siege was over in short order, less than two days. The tower's inhabitants were not inclined to put up much of a fight. The door had resisted burning and they'd had a skirmish with some reivers who happened to be passing by.

Through it all, Robert had grown increasingly irritable, wanting to return home, wondering if a letter from Ridley waited for him, or if Geordie was having problems with Fayth, or what Caroline was doing. Last night, while trying to sleep on the hard ground, he finally understood what he must do to rid himself of the suspicion or distrust. Immediately when he returned, Caroline would wed him proper—with Father Jasper's words and blessing, and the kirk's approval. And she would destroy the statement. Only then would he feel secure.

It was with immense relief that he dashed after his brother when the tower doors were finally battered down. Robert climbed over the rubble, chasing Alex up the stairs to where he stood, sword drawn, over a woman and her child.

"Where is he?"

"Who?" the woman asked, clutching the boy to her. "Just take what you came for and leave us!"

"I came for Wesley Graham—where are you hiding him?"

Robert shoved Alex, who swung around, sword ready.

"Put that thing away and leave her be!"

Alex sheathed his sword and pushed past him, sprinting from room to room, searching. His men subdued the few occupants—far fewer than they'd anticipated. Other than two of his broken men, Wesley Graham was nowhere to be found. Frustrated, Alex grabbed one of the men, hauling him to his feet. "Where is he?"

"Gone."

"Impossible! Where? How?"

The man just grinned. Alex flung him away and turned in a circle, eyeing the tower's occupants, blue eyes narrowed dangerously. Robert tensed, ready to stop his brother if his fury got out of hand. Red Rowan had not been above killing women and children. Though Alex had yet to stoop to such levels, Robert feared he was capable of it.

Alex's gaze fixed on the little boy, clinging to the woman's skirts. He approached them slowly and crouched in front of the boy. "What's your name?"

"Patty, sir."

"Patty. D'ye hear that, Rob?" Alex never looked away from the boy. "Why, I've a brother named Patrick. We called him Patty when he was but a lad."

"Does he carry a big sword, too?" Patty asked.

Alex laughed. "Och, aye—bigger than mine."

The boy's eyes grew round.

"I've a question, Patty-boy."

Patty nodded expectantly.

"Did you see a man with a cut on his face?" Alex drew a line down his own cheek with his finger.

"Oh, aye—he was here."

"Hush," the woman said, trying to pull the boy away.

Alex clamped a hand on Patty's shoulder. "Let him go."

The woman gripped the boy's arm. "Please—he's just a bairn, please spare him." Her whine turned to a sob when Alex's men dragged her away.

Alex led the boy away from the woman and crouched down again, so they were at eye level. "Where did the man go?"

Patty pointed to a door in the floor that led to the cellar. They'd already been down there and found nothing. Alex stood, taking the boy's hand. "Show me."

Robert grabbed a torch from the wall sconce and followed Alex and Patty as they descended the ladder. Once down there, Patty pushed a barrel aside, revealing a hole. Robert thrust the torch inside. The tunnel was dug into the earth, like a cellar. Roots dangled from the walls and wooden slats had been nailed into the earth as a ladder.

The *plop plop* of dripping water told him the bottom was flooded.

"It leads to the moss," Patty said, smiling at Alex. His two front teeth were missing.

To Robert's surprise, Alex smiled wryly, shaking his head. He turned to Robert and gestured to the hole. "It leads to the moss." He swung back around to the boy. "How long has the man with the wound been gone?"

"He was hardly here at all."

Alex laughed, shaking his head again. Robert watched his brother worriedly. He'd expected an explosion, violence—not amusement. But before long Alex was bent over, clutching his sides as though in pain. Robert slapped his brother on the back.

Alex straightened, wiping his streaming eyes. "Here I've been, thinking he's trapped—"

"Like a rat," Robert offered.

Alex snorted. "Aye, like a rat. And all the while he's been . . ."

Alex's smile faded as he met Robert's gaze.

Robert finished his sentence. "He's been back at Annancreag." He shoved the torch at Alex and climbed the ladder. Fear drove him from the tower, shouting to his men to saddle up.

Alex caught up with him as he tossed the saddle over his horse's back. "What if this was his plan all along—what if—"

"No," Robert said. "No 'what if.' If something were wrong, they'd have sent word."

"But would we have received it? Do they know where we are? We've only been gone four days."

Robert shook his head, refusing to give in to panic.

"If you think naught's amiss—why then do your hands shake?"

Robert stopped trying to buckle the saddle, hands fisting against his horse's withers. He could not tell Alex about Fayth—not now. "Because, though I trust Caroline—I do not trust her brother." He turned his head, meeting Alex's gaze. "I don't want to think that you might be right—I can't think it. But I must go. Now."

He yanked the buckle, tested it, and swung into the saddle. He raised a quizzical brow at Alex, who stared up at him, hands on hips.

"I thought I wasn't welcome."

Robert could use his brother's sword arm if his worst suspicions proved true. But he wasn't about to beg—not when an apology still wasn't forthcoming. He shrugged and tapped his horse's side, leading it out of the bailey.

Behind him, Alex called, "I'm right behind you, Brother."

23

They arrived in the wee hours of the morning. The weather had turned. Rain scudded about them, drenching them and slowing their progress. The men had wanted to stop, but Robert refused. Alex didn't complain, but rode beside him through the torrent.

The battlements of Annancreag were dark. Robert tried not to panic—after all, it was a downpour. He pounded on the gate for a quarter of an hour before the window opened and Geordie's face peered through the grating.

"My lord!" he cried. "I didna realize it was you at first, what wi' all the thunder."

Moments later, with much assurance from Geordie that the castle was secure and there hadn't been the slightest mishap in his absence—and still no word from Ridley—the portcullis was raised.

They went straight to the fire, shedding their cloaks and jacks. Hot, spiced ale was served. Robert's chamber door opened and Caroline glided out. Golden hair streamed down her shoulders, nearly reaching her knees. She wore a simple gown over her shift and her arms were filled with linens. The sight of her hurt his eyes and yet he couldn't look away.

"Robert—you're soaked." She flung a linen around his shoulders, then turned and threw another around Alex. Robert thought he heard her mumble something to Alex—". . . answer is no" or some such. His gaze sharpened when a grin broke over Alex's face.

Before Caroline could turn away, Alex caught her up, lifting her off her feet. "Welcome to the family, Sister!" He kissed her cheek with a resounding smack and set her on her feet. Dazed and unsteady, she looked from Robert to Alex. Robert caught her arm, laughing, as Alex—who had tried to set her free—now found his fingers tangled in her hair.

"Well," she said, smiling warily—then wincing as Alex yanked his hand free. "Thank you, Alexander."

Alex burst out laughing. "Oh—I do like her."

Robert slung an arm around her shoulder and pulled her close, beneath his towel. She shivered. He pressed his mouth against her hair, where it hid her ear. "I missed you." She made a little sound in her throat that sent desire curling deep in his gut.

Celia appeared and hurried over, Henry right behind her.

"My lord," Henry said, smoothing down the dozen or so blond hairs that covered his shiny pate. "Would you care for a meal? The stew is still warm, I'm sure. I'll have Cook fetch some."

"That sounds fine," Robert said and Henry disappeared.

Robert was weary suddenly—he'd slept little, spent his nights in torturous thought, alternating between love and doubt and trust. To return home and find all well was like a tonic, sweeping his suspicions away, making them seem foolish and petty. How small he'd been. The thought was startling, but he could see now how the feud had endured, festered. If such unfounded suspicion resided in every Maxwell and Graham's heart, how could it not? And though he'd believed himself to be peace loving, he was as guilty as the rest for harboring hate and mistrust, for attributing the worst kind of motives to a person, simply because of their surname. Caroline was not responsible for Patrick's imprisonment or for his lack of release. He must stop regarding her with caution and look on her as his ally.

He hugged her closer to his side. She turned her face to him, meeting his eyes. His breath caught. Though she hadn't said it, he saw it in her eyes, large and pale and warm—she'd missed him. Her hand slid tentatively around his waist, returning his embrace.

"Anyone seen Wesley Graham?" Alex's pointed question saved him from drowning in his wife's eyes. Robert tensed, waiting for someone to mention Fayth to Alex, ruining this fine moment. But no one—not even Celia—uttered the name.

"We received word just yesterday," Celia said, a teasing note in her voice, "that you had him trapped in a tower. What happened?"

Alex shook his head, that bemused smile returning to his face. "I laid brilliant siege to an empty tower! The lad's a wily opponent—I'll give him that. Slipped through my fingers thrice now!"

Robert felt the tension immediately drain from Caroline's shoulders, her body leaning more fully into his. How thoughtless of him—she'd been worried about her brother. He should have told her as soon as he saw her that Wesley was still alive.

"That little man—her brother—" Celia pointed at Caroline, amazed. "Has escaped the black hearted Red Alex—thrice?"

Alex shrugged, rubbing the linen vigorously over his hair, wet and roan dark. "Aye—I've no excuse. He's clever for a Graham."

Celia crossed her arms under her chest, her brow furrowed. "He with the curly hair and the big brown eyes—aye? Such a fresh lad! Such passion!"

Alex scowled. "He's a Graham, Celia—dinna even think of it."

Celia nodded at Caroline. "She's a Graham—and no cloven feet—I can attest to that!"

Robert was well pleased that Caroline's presence was mending the rift between the clans—but he knew if the conversation continued, Fayth would be introduced into it and Alex would explode. He cleared his throat—ready to send them all back to bed—when Alex said, "She's no Graham—not any longer. She's a Maxwell."

Rather than inciting further argument, Celia nodded in thoughtful agreement, and Henry, who had returned with Cook and two bowls of steaming stew, said, "Aye—Master Alex has the right of it!"

Cook nodded vigorously, his bulging neck trembling. "Aye, aye! She be a Maxwell."

Robert looked down at Caroline. Her cheeks had colored softly, imperceptibly, but her eyes shone and the curve of her lips was warm with pleasure.

Robert whispered, "I'll take my stew—and my wife in my chambers. Wait for me there?"

She left his side, retreating to his chambers with the bowl of stew. When Celia started to follow, Robert called after her to wait.

"Cook, Henry—all of you, gather 'round." He put his arms around Alex and Henry's shoulders, huddling them together. "I wish to plan a surprise for Caroline—tomorrow. I shall marry her again, more than just statement before witnesses. This time Father Jasper will say the words and give us the blessing of the kirk."

Never in his life had Robert planned a celebration himself. Oh, he'd given vague directions for festivities— but always he'd left the logistics to someone else. But this was to be perfect. He gave everyone their instructions and told them to report back to him in the morning. Celia had special orders—given to her after sending everyone else to bed—to keep Caroline and Fayth away for most of the day.

In the privacy of their bedchamber, he changed into dry clothes, listening to Caroline relay news from the village. A child had been born, but was sickly and not thought to live long. The parents were certain it was a changeling and Caroline feared the child would be left somewhere to die. She'd approved a marriage between two of the villagers— but now the parents were in dispute over the tocher. She seemed distracted throughout, her mind elsewhere.

He joined her at the fireplace, rubbing his hands over her shoulders. "What is it?"

She lifted her gaze to his, solemn, heavy. "Nothing."

Though he suspected she wasn't being completely honest with him, his body would wait no longer for their reunion. His hand circled her throat, his thumb brushing against the hollow where her pulse thrummed. Her eyelids drifted shut. He'd imagined that he would make love to her slowly, initiate her into all the ways a man could give pleasure. When he brushed his lips against hers, her lips parted on a caught breath, her heart jumping beneath his thumb—and he was lost.

He kissed her forcefully, his hands buried in her hair, twisting the silken ropes about his fingers and wrists. Her hands were on his face, fingers trailing over his skin and hair. He slid his hands up and down her back—no stays—

and groaned. He loved the feel of nothing but Caroline beneath her gown.

His restraint vanished—he wanted her, in the bed, with nothing but her hair, wrapped about them like a web. He pulled at her gown, yanking inelegantly at the lacings, as he propelled her backward.

"Robert," she said, her voice breathless. Her fingers fumbled over his, trying to help him. "Am I a Maxwell, now? Truly?" She loosened the lacings enough for him to pull the gown over her head. He pushed her back onto the bed. He kissed the hollow of her throat, licked it. Her pulse skittered beneath his tongue. So sweet and fine.

"If you're not now," he murmured against her skin, his hands sliding under her shift, "you soon will be."

Caroline scooted back on the bed, wondering what his odd words meant. He crawled after her, stalked her. Desire clawed at her, insisting she leave the conversation for later. "What do you mean?"

His hands were on her breasts, shaping and molding them through the linen of her shift. He wedged her thighs apart with his knee. "I don't mean anything."

He was making no sense! And sending her away as he had—to take his stew to his chambers—stew he never touched. When Celia didn't follow, she'd looked back out the door and saw them huddled together. Why? Was he reminding them she was not a Maxwell and not to trust her? It had warmed her when they pronounced her one of them—even Alexander had finally accepted her. Was Robert warning them not to trust her so readily?

She didn't want to have these thoughts. Not now.

He pulled at the ties of her shift, exposing her breasts to the cold air. She shivered, but was soon warmed by his mouth, moving over the sensitive skin. She fell back on the bed—abandoning talk. Later, she would puzzle it out—but now . . .

She'd never known anything could feel this way—never imagined a man's mouth—this man's mouth—could ignite such an intensity of sensation. His hand was between her thighs, his fingers brushing over the damp hair. Her hips jerked in response, her breath hitching. It was agony—the desire, a pain she couldn't bear, yet needed more of.

"Robert," she pleaded. He loomed over her, hard between her legs, pressing against her. *Yes.* Her hips surged upward, taking him. He met her, driving deeply into her. She strained against him, needing him deeper, faster, until the throb inside her shattered. His body continued stroking her, drawing out the pulsing heat. His mouth moved over her neck, fever damp. *"Mo cridhe."*

Later, swaddled together under the furs that covered their bed, he said it again, pushing her hair off her forehead and placing a lingering kiss at her temple.

"My heart," she whispered.

It was dark in the room, the fire had died to embers, and the candles that flickered across the room left them in shadows.

"So you've known—all along."

"Known what?"

"That I love you."

She reached out, her hand meeting a wall of hair and muscle. She stroked her hand over his chest, the skin smooth and warm. "No—you called me a horse's ass and Mother Superior, too—am I to take everything you say as truth?"

He groaned, clasped her against him. She smiled to herself, but said nothing to alleviate his embarrassment. His breath was warm against her neck. "Do you not believe me then—that you have my heart?"

"I believe you. But part of me expects Ridley to jump out at any moment, laughing that this was his greatest jest ever—to make Caroline fall in love."

His arms tightened around her. "Never doubt me, Caroline—this is no jest. You're mine now and you never have to see Ridley again. I swear."

She laid her head on his shoulder, feeling beautiful and protected and loved with his great arms about her.

As she was drifting to sleep he asked, "Have you written me a story?"

She smiled and laughed softly. "Yes, and I will read it to you. Tomorrow."

24
꙯

When Caroline awoke the next morning, Robert was gone and Celia was digging through her trunk—gowns were everywhere, draped over chairs, stools, and the end of the bed.

"What are you doing, Celia?"

Celia jerked around guiltily. "Och, just picking out a gown for you to wear."

Caroline swung out of bed, feeling light and refreshed and happy. "I'll wear my green."

Celia scowled. "Not the green. You wear that one all the time. Something different today. Lord Annan has returned. You must be beautiful for him."

Caroline smiled to herself, warmed by the thought that she already was beautiful to him. She didn't feel like arguing, so she shrugged and sat quietly while her maid draped gown after gown across her shoulders.

"Ah," Celia said, standing back to admire the lavender silk. "That's a fine gown and it brings out the creaminess of your skin, makes your eyes glow. That's the one!"

Caroline regarded her maid strangely, but made no

comment. It seemed amazing that there had once been such animosity between them, for now Caroline was very fond of her.

But Celia did not allow her to linger over idle thoughts. "Hurry—let's get you into this, you're needed in the village posthaste!"

Caroline stood when Celia pulled on her arm and was docile throughout Celia's ministrations—but when she forgot the stays, Caroline said, "Celia! What's wrong with you? You forgot my stays."

Celia hesitated, then said, "Why, my lady—you don't need them, being so tall and slender. Forget the stays—you've some walking to do, 'twill make you most uncomfortable."

"Are you not accompanying me?"

"Oh, aye, I'll be there."

"Then why are you wearing stays?"

Celia stared at her blankly then said, "Well, I canna very well go without them—being so round."

Round? Rounded perhaps—but certainly not round! "What are you talking about? What is so pressing in the village that I must be there?"

Before Celia could answer, the door burst open and Fayth sailed in wearing one of Caroline's gowns that she and Celia had altered. Stunningly pretty in clothes that fit—her tiny waist curved into narrow but well-proportioned hips, and her breasts, though small, filled the embroidered bodice out nicely. The gown was a pale blue, the bodice and skirt embroidered with tiny gold and pink flowers—Celia's handiwork. Fayth twirled around, looking down at her skirt. Her smile was brilliant, rarely seen dimples denting her cheeks.

Caroline couldn't help smiling in return. "You look like a butterfly!"

"It's beautiful, Caroline, thank you." Fayth gave Celia a look of grudging admiration beneath her eyelashes. "My thanks—you're a fine seamstress."

Celia nodded briskly, pushing Caroline onto a stool so she could dress her hair. Caroline felt swelled to bursting with happiness—perhaps she'd been wrong about Fayth. Thus far, her sister had been perfectly pleasant, if not a little annoyed that Caroline spent so little time with her. She didn't even complain about the constant guard.

Fayth poked about Caroline's chamber, opening boxes and cabinets, rifling through Caroline's letter box.

"Have you decided what you'd like to do?" Caroline asked her sister, relieved she didn't have to avoid her anymore. Wesley was alive—no Maxwell had murdered him. "Should I ask Lord Annan to find you a husband?"

Fayth plopped on the bed. "Can I not think about it—at least for a while?"

"Of course—but you must think about it some time."

"Not today! Geordie told me I'm to go with you and Celia to the village. I just want to enjoy my day of freedom!"

Caroline nodded, feeling awful suddenly. Since Father's death, Fayth's life had been confinement. First Ridley and now Robert. It didn't seem fair. And though Fayth was allowed to leave the castle with them, she would be well guarded.

"I'm sorry about the guards, Fayth—but they follow me everywhere, too. It's just for protection."

"Geordie didn't follow me this morning!" Fayth said. "He told me I had my liberty so long as I was within the keep!"

Caroline turned, yanking a hank of hair out of Celia's fingers. "Really?"

Celia swore. "Be still, my lady!"

Caroline turned back, holding her head very still, but her gaze was riveted on Fayth. Caroline couldn't believe Robert had done this for her—was deeply touched at the gesture. "I know, since you've been here, what you've seen of Lord Annan hasn't been . . . pleasant. But truly, he is a good man—you will see."

Fayth didn't say anything, but averted her eyes. It would take time and now that Robert was back, Fayth would see them together, see how well he treated his wife. And then everything would be fine. Perhaps Fayth would even agree to wed a Scotsman and be nearby!

After a moment Fayth stood, wandering about the room, opening and closing cabinets again. She even dug through Caroline's wardrobe.

"What are you looking for?" Caroline asked.

"Do you have something red? For my hair?"

Caroline didn't but Celia did and fetched it as they left the keep. To Caroline's surprise, when they left the castle, only two guards trailed after them. Fayth tied the red kerchief over her hair and grew quiet and watchful. Of course, it would make her nervous, surrounded by Maxwells. For all Caroline knew, she might have participated in a raid on this village. Caroline pushed the distasteful thought away, determined to enjoy the day, the newfound lightness in her step, the pleasure that became easier to infuse into every smile.

The pressing business in the village turned out to be surprisingly commonplace. The babe, who'd been so sickly a few days ago, was recovering. Father Jasper had baptized the child, but the parents hadn't bothered to christen him. Now that it appeared the child would live, the parents wanted Lady Annan present for the christening. Father Jasper, however, was nowhere to be found. They waited, chatting with the parents, until out of breath, flags of scarlet on his bony cheekbones, the priest appeared in the doorway.

Caroline stood. "Father? Have you been running?"

He tried to answer, but couldn't catch his breath.

Caroline went to his side. "You shouldn't be running at your age! What was the rush?"

He shook his head, straightening. "Good for the heart," he wheezed. "I'm fine, truly." He went quickly through the ceremony and then was off again. Caroline peered through the window after him. He jogged back up the road to the castle, hand clutching his side. What was wrong with everyone today?

The rest of the day seemed equally odd. Every time Caroline attempted to return to the castle, she was way-laid by villagers, insisting she taste their ale, take some flowers, eat some haggis. It was a bit bothersome, as she was eager to see Robert. She had no particular reason to see her husband, though she would offer to write or read for him. She simply wanted to be with him, to sit with him, to talk to him, to look upon him. But everyone was so kind she could not refuse.

It was nearly dusk when Caroline, violets threaded through her hair, Fayth, and Celia trudged back up the hill. They had just passed through the gates when Geordie stopped them. "Mistress Graham hasna taken her walk on the battlements yet. Lord Annan wants her to do it afore dark."

Fayth had taken to walking the battlements in the evening—probably for no other reason than to annoy her guards. Caroline glanced at her sister. "We've been walk-ing all day, surely you don't want to tonight?"

Fayth chewed her lip, as if she couldn't decide. Earlier, she'd removed her red kerchief from her hair. She stared down at it, crumpled in her fist, with a strange intensity.

When Fayth didn't answer, Celia said, "Oh, let's all go! I could use some fresh air!" She hooked her arms through Caroline and Fayth's, turning them toward the battlements. Geordie gave a slightly hysterical laugh and nodded his head enthusiastically.

Caroline pulled away, staring at Celia in consternation. "We've been out in the fresh air all day! What is wrong with everyone?"

Fayth looked from Celia to Geordie, suspicious. Then, resolute, she replaced the kerchief on her head. "Let's just walk, Carrie. Something strange is going on around here and it's making me nervous."

Caroline certainly couldn't argue that point and, with a sigh, allowed Celia to lead her to the battlement steps.

Fayth's heart pounded in her ears as they left the battlement, returning to the keep. She'd done it. She'd worn the red kerchief, given Wesley the signal. Now she must somehow slip away and unlock the postern door. It would be guarded of course; Lord Annan always ran tight security. She chewed her lip, oblivious to Celia's inane chatter.

She shouldn't have done it. The timing was wrong. She still knew nothing about the Clachan Fala—or if there even was one, which she doubted. Ridley, however, would not be so easily convinced and her punishment for botching this would be marriage to Carlisle. She closed her eyes, gritting her teeth. She'd think of that later—not now.

She'd been so certain this morning. She'd overheard the servants whispering together, saying Lord Annan planned to make this union "real" tonight. They'd stopped talking the moment they saw Fayth, but she'd heard enough to send her into a panic. Wesley had assured Fayth that Caroline was still a virgin, but Fayth hadn't really been concerned, since she intended to rescue her sister whether she'd been debauched or not. Wesley, the *man,* saw Caroline's fate as sealed if she'd been deflowered. Fayth would not abandon her sister just because she'd been forced to have relations with her husband. Besides—she'd read the statement Caroline kept in her little wooden box. It said that the consummation had been faked and Lord Annan had signed it. Caroline was keeping it for only one reason. And after what the servants said, it appeared Lord Annan meant to rectify the oversight tonight. Fayth simply could not let that happen. She'd taken the statement when Caroline and Celia weren't looking and hidden it in her bodice. Her sister would surely need it where she was going.

Caroline looked exhausted, limp flowers dangling from her golden braids. She'd not seemed terribly unhappy today—in fact she'd been in high spirits this morning. But then Caroline didn't know what Lord Annan planned for her. Perhaps she'd resigned herself to this life because she assumed Lord Annan would not force intimate relations on her. She ran the castle with efficiency and apparently took pleasure in it. These thoughts gave Fayth a moment of misgiving. Caroline was different here. But then she remembered Lord Annan bursting into the tower room roaring like an angry bear, then afterward Caroline avoided Fayth, treating her with the same cool detachment she'd formerly reserved for Ridley. No, something was very wrong.

Caroline halted just inside the great hall and Fayth bumped into her. Rather than apologize or explain her sudden stop, Caroline stood still as a statue. The few people who had been left in the bailey streamed into the hall around them, excited smiles fixed to their faces. Fayth backed up, realizing all eyes were on Caroline. She moved aside, peering around her sister, and gasped.

The entire hall was decked in flowers—the scent was intoxicating—mixed with the heady aroma of roasting meats. Lord Annan stood at the far end of the hall on the dais, decked out in his finest—which wasn't nearly so fine as Ridley's daily attire—Father Jasper by his side. The priest wore his best green vestments.

Panic and indecision assailed Fayth. Now was the time—she must act quickly while everyone was gathered in one place. This was perfect. Wesley's men could circle the hall, trapping everyone into inaction. They could strike rapidly and few people would get hurt.

Fayth backed away, into the crowd. No one noted her; all eyes were on the spectacle, waiting to see what Caroline would do. Fayth knew what Caroline would do. She would hide her horror and confusion behind a mask of politeness, accepting her fate. *Poor Caroline.*

Fayth slid around the wall, behind the partition that hid the door to the kitchens. She pulled the red kerchief from her hair and kept her head down, pushing through the press of sweating bodies until she exited the back door. Thank God Lord Annan had relaxed the guard on her—otherwise she'd have a sentry trailing her. The timing of Lord Annan's unexpected foolishness couldn't have been better.

She paused just outside the kitchen door, scanning the area. She was alone. What now?

A weapon. She had no weapon and she had to overpower the guards. Her first thought was seduction—all men were led by their loins. She'd tease him to distraction, then take his weapon and incapacitate him. But most of them knew who she was—certainly the guards. *Damn!*

She slid along the wall—surprised at how deserted the bailey was. She noted two figures on the battlements ahead of her, but no one below. They passed near where she stood and then out of sight. She raced across the bailey and into the shadows of the castle wall. She panted with fear. She'd done many stupid things before, but never anything this dangerous. If some angry Maxwell caught her—her end would be ugly.

She continued down the wall. Only one guard was posted at the postern door. He didn't look terribly alert. He wandered about in idle circles, drawing in the dirt with his lance. She would pretend to be looking for a tumble—he would believe her of course. Even the most suspicious man had such overblown conceit when it came to his prowess with the ladies that such a lie couldn't fail to work. She'd heard it for herself, when disguised as a lad, what men truly thought of women. Women were valued for the secret place between their thighs and nothing more. She'd seen proof of it, from her father and brothers—from Jack, even. The esteem she commanded as a boy disappeared the moment she donned a gown. Respect turned to lust.

A jingling froze her and she turned her head. A tall man approached from the keep. The sentry heard him as well and straightened. Before the man reached the postern door, he stopped and lifted his head, like a wolf catching a scent. The tall, broad-shouldered, lean figure could only be Red Alex.

Fayth thought she might expire from horror when he began to walk toward her. She couldn't move, couldn't run. She stared at him, caught, as he approached with catlike grace. She was hidden in the shadows—how could he have seen her? She wanted to bolt, but reason intervened, reminding her that he didn't know who she was—had never seen her—as a girl, that is. He stopped in front of her. A set of keys hung from his belt and in one hand, he held a jug. She caught a faint whiff of whiskey from him.

"Well, well . . ." he drawled, his gaze skimming over her.

Her lip curled in disgust. He was drunk—and wouldn't you know it—probably looking for some lass to maul. This could benefit her—if only he didn't revolt her so. *Murderer. Destroyer of dreams.*

"What are you doing, little one, sneaking about?"

She licked her lips, gazing at him from under the sweep of her lashes. "Only looking to keep yon guard company." She would continue her pretense as a wanton. Even Red Alex couldn't deny the pull of sex.

He inhaled sharply, straightening. "I know you."

She shook her head. "Nay, sir—I've never seen you before."

He grabbed her arm. She thought he would drag her to the guard and ask him to identify her—and then it would all be over. But he only pulled her to the nearest torch. He pushed her against the wall and stepped back, staring at her. He took several long drinks of whiskey. And as he inspected her, her fear fled—he didn't know. That's the way it always was—men who'd tried to grope her as a woman would treat her with friendship as a lad. They simply couldn't reconcile it—their opinion of women was too low to believe they could possibly be fooled by one.

She smiled, looking him over provocatively. "Like what you see? It's yours, but I'm not cheap."

He went still, jug halfway to his mouth. He lowered it slowly. "You're a whore?"

The way he said it—full of contempt—nearly made her wince. But she only raised her brows suggestively, licked her bottom lip.

He exhaled, still regarding her. "Mayhap that's from whence I know you." How typical—he thought he might have rutted on her—yet couldn't remember for certain.

He glanced at the guard, farther down the wall, then said, "Stay here."

He strode purposefully to the guard and conversed with him briefly. The guard hurried across the bailey and into the keep. Red Alex leaned against the gate that protected the recessed door and crooked a finger at her.

Her stomach clenched with renewed fear. What if she couldn't find a way to overpower him? What if she was forced to rut with him—to act like a whore? *Never.* She'd never killed a man before—hoped to never have to. But she'd kill Red Alex before she allowed him to touch her that way—or die trying.

Stiff legged, she walked down the wall, trying desperately to look seductive, but fearing she looked like a half-wit. He didn't straighten from where he leaned lazily against the door, his eyes scorching her.

"You don't look like a whore," he said when she stood before him.

What to do with her hands? She placed them on her hips, thrusting her chest out and shifting her hips forward. "That's why it'll cost you."

He snorted. "You're so costly because you look like a little girl playing at being a woman."

Her face flamed. "I'm two-and-twenty!"

His brows rose appreciatively and he took another drink, never taking his eyes from her.

She made her mouth turn down in what she hoped was an enticing pout. She took a step forward and said, her voice low, throaty, "You don't want me? You don't think I'm worth it?"

He frowned and shifted uncomfortably.

She smiled, letting her gaze drop to the evidence of his arousal. He was a dog, just like all men. And even better—he wanted her. For some reason she'd thought Red

Alex was different. Her imagination had turned him into some invincible fiend. But he was just a man and no different from every other man she'd known—ruled by the organ between his legs. Made them so easy to understand—and use. She took another step. Their bodies almost touched. Heat seemed to emanate from him.

She tilted her head back—he was so tall—and met his gaze. Blue fire. "May I have a drink?"

He handed her the jug. As soon as her fingers curled about it, she wanted to hit him—but he was too tall. He would duck as soon as she swung. Then he would be furious—and merciless. When she hit him, she would have to bring him down with one blow. She took a drink, her mind working furiously at her problem.

The whiskey burned its way down. She gasped and coughed. Red Alex pushed away from the wall and reached for the jug. She took a step back. "I'm not finished," she rasped, her eyes watering.

He smiled indulgently and gestured for her to drink again. She did, taking several long swallows.

"Whoa-ho," he said, and lifted the jug from her hands, spilling some down the front of her.

Damn! She stared at the jug now back in his possession, then at her bodice. "Look what you've done!" she said, wiping the whiskey off her chin.

He snagged her wrist, dragging her against him. "I dinna want ye soused." His Scots burr thickened with alcohol and desire. He held her wrist firmly. His other hand still held the jug, but now it snaked around behind her back.

What had she gotten herself into? Panic bloomed in her chest. She fought the urge to twist away and run—or to scratch his murdering blue eyes out. She might not get another such opportunity and she realized, as he bent near her, that if he kissed her, his head would be low enough to bash in. And he would be suitably distracted not to notice.

But he didn't kiss her. His cheek, rough with a shadow of coppery whiskers, brushed against hers, and he whispered in her ear, "You smell fine, lass." For some reason, his voice, the feel of his breath stirring her hair, sent shivers across her skin. She reached behind her, trailed her fingers over his arm until she found the jug. He released her wrist, using that hand to pull her tightly against him, and moved the jug out of her reach.

"You want this?" he asked, holding it to the side of them.

He was making this too hard. She forced herself to smile, though it was difficult, pressed against him as she was. His hand burned through her gown—she could feel the imprint of each long finger where it splayed on her lower back.

"Aye," she said—then had an idea. She raised herself on tiptoes. "One drink, for one kiss."

"God's wounds, you're not only a whore, but a sot, too."

Fayth barely kept her temper in check. Let him think she was a sot—that she bartered her body for drink. What did she care? When she didn't reply, he leaned down and took what she offered, his mouth molding over hers, his tongue insistently parting her lips. It was no courtly kiss—nothing tentative or uncertain about it. He bent her over his arm, his mouth ravaging her senses, muddling her thoughts. He tasted wild—whiskey and man—and God help her, she wanted more. No one had kissed her in such a manner—his hunger was raw, unleashed. There was only one place such a kiss could lead.

When he tore his mouth away, he was breathing hard. She clung to his arms for support, dazed. Her skin tingled where his whiskers had abraded her. He still held her with one arm and pushed the jug at her.

"Here," he said, his voice thick. "Have the whole thing."

She took it in shaking hands and drank deeply. The warmth spread through her, making her limbs loose. She must end this—it was going on too long—someone would discover them. He looked around, urgent.

"When the guard comes back, we'll go somewhere," he said.

His words conjured visions of him kissing her like that again—someplace dark and secluded. Her knees nearly buckled. She had to act fast. She moved close to him, her free hand sliding up his chest and grabbing the front of his leather jack. He seemed surprised, but lowered his head to kiss her readily enough. With all her strength, she swung the jug around. It slammed into his head, just above his ear, with a resounding *thunk!* The blow vibrated up her arm. He grunted and stumbled against the wall. He had a handful of her skirt clutched in his fist and dragged her along with him.

He grabbed his head with his other hand, moaning. He wouldn't let go of her, even as she pried at his fingers. He was trying to stand, his eyes refocusing on her. She grabbed the jug in both hands and brought it down again. This time it shattered on impact and he toppled over, drenched in whiskey.

Fayth shook violently as she stared down at him. Blood poured from a cut in his temple. He didn't move—she couldn't tell if he was breathing. Had she killed him? She'd never killed a man before. Hysteria choked her, but she forced it down. *He murdered Jack.* If she had killed him—he had it coming! *For Jack.* She kept telling herself that and by the time she'd removed the keys from his belt, she felt better—indignant, even. How dare he handle her so? Kissing and mauling her like a common whore? As she stared down at him, she noticed the gentle rise and fall of his chest. Not dead. Relief sighed through her.

She hesitated before opening the postern gate. Why should she feel relief? He was a murdering bastard! A knock over the head wasn't vengeance enough for all he'd done to ruin her life. But time was wasting. She settled for kicking him, hard, and spitting on him—for Jack—before opening the door to the Grahams.

Caroline couldn't shake the dream-like fog that had descended on her. Celia dragged her forward until she stood beside Robert. She could only stare at him.

He took her hand, smiling. "Will you wed me again—with the kirk's blessing?"

She looked around slowly, taking in the smiling faces—pleased with themselves for having kept the secret—then back at him. "You did all of this . . . for me?"

His smile grew.

She choked on a sob and leaned forward, pressing her face into the silk of his doublet, stretched over wide shoulders. He put an arm around her, gesturing with his other hand, and the musicians began to play. Soft conversation rose around them.

"I'm sorry," she said, her voice muffled by his doublet, but she couldn't look at him or anyone else. Her hands were fisted against his chest, her body pressed close—stupid, silent sobs shaking her. She wasn't sad—why did she cry? Never had anyone made her feel so important, so deserving. When finally the tears stopped flowing, she leaned back, looking up at him. "Why did you do this?"

He ran his thumbs over her cheeks, wiping away the wetness. "Because I wanted all to know this marriage is binding, not to be torn asunder by any man—or woman. Not even you."

She couldn't speak, could only gaze at him, over-whelmed by how much he'd come to mean to her, how he'd changed her life.

He frowned. "I had hoped the surprise would be a pleasant one—am I mistaken?"

She shook her head, another tear sliding down her cheek. "No, Robert—it's the finest surprise ever."

He caught her face in both hands and kissed her hard. Then with his arm around her, he turned to address the hall. Henry, who'd been standing at the ready, silenced the musicians. Before a word could be spoken, someone shrieked at the back of the hall.

As one, the assembly turned toward the voice. More screams. Robert swore, shoving her toward Father Jasper, who placed his hands on her shoulders.

"What's happening?" Caroline whispered, watching her husband stride across the hall. Perhaps it was just an altercation between two villagers? The dispute over the dowry had become rather heated—she wouldn't be at all surprised if the fathers had come to blows. She started to relax when the crowd surged back toward her, stamped-ing, screaming. Robert stumbled back a step, then pushed purposefully through the crowd. And that's when she saw them. The raiders who had tried to kidnap her in the vil-lage—and Wesley, his face red and swollen.

The Maxwells shed their shock and attacked. Sur-rounded by women, Caroline was propelled out of the hall. The press of bodies was suffocating. She could smell the panic, the fear. She craned her neck. Robert's tall head was visible, his sword slashing.

"No!" She couldn't leave, had to see.

Then Fayth was there. "This way." She took Caro-line's hand.

"What's happening?" she asked, letting Fayth lead her

from the hall. Father Jasper was behind them. In the bailey, Maxwell women dashed for cover—taking their children and hiding them.

Caroline pulled her hand away. "What have you done?"

Fayth grabbed Caroline's elbow and yanked forcibly. "Come on! We must hurry!"

"I'm going nowhere with you!" Caroline cried, wrenching herself free.

She whirled and, lifting her skirts, ran back into the hall. She was halted in the doorway. A Maxwell man fell at her feet, dead. Caroline stared down at him, mouth agape, as his murderer lifted his sword as if to strike her, then stopped himself. She didn't know this man—he was dirty and scarred—one of Wesley's broken men. He grabbed her arm, pulled her forward.

Caroline struggled, terror in every movement. A burst of heat beside her sent her stumbling against the man, covering her eyes. A tapestry caught fire. The flowers blackened. The blaze spread rapidly, devouring the beautiful decorations.

The man dragged her through the fighting—stopping every so often to hack at someone. Caroline stopped struggling, stopped trying to escape. Her situation was far too dangerous—all around her men fought and fell and died. One of the raiders crashed into her. She would have fallen beneath him had her captor not held her up. The man tumbled to the ground, knife through his neck, blood foaming at his lips.

And then Wesley was there. He grabbed her. "Caroline! Are you hurt?"

She shook her head.

Robert loomed up behind Wesley, his face twisted in rage. He was going to kill Wesley.

"Robert, no!" she screamed. He hesitated and Wesley swung around, slashing his sword at Robert's side.

Caroline couldn't scream—the sound locked in her throat—stuck there. Pain and horror seized her, rooted her to the spot. Her mind insisted that this couldn't possibly be happening—wouldn't accept it—and yet it was before her—undeniable proof. Robert stumbled back, holding his side. But he didn't look at Wesley—his eyes were on her—filled with stark disbelief—betrayal. Wesley moved forward, as if to finish Robert off.

Caroline found her voice. "No!" she screamed, rushing forward. "Wesley, no!"

Wesley caught her about the waist, dragging her backward. Wesley was very strong—he'd always been—but the sheer force of Caroline's grief propelled her forward, regardless of his hold on her, dragging him along behind her.

"Robert!"

The Maxwells closed ranks around Robert, hiding their laird from her eyes, protecting him. Wesley yelled at her. Many hands pulled her away, back out into the bailey. She'd lost all reason—cared only about Robert—he'd been wounded. He needed her.

She fought and struggled and screamed and cried. Wesley barked questions at her about Mona and the stone. She clawed at his face, trying to escape. When shaking her violently caused no change in her behavior, Wesley struck her and the world went black.

25

Alex paced the floor in his brother's chambers, impatient to be gone. His head ached and throbbed where that bitch had beat him over the head. He'd woken some time later—long after the raiders were gone—drenched in whiskey, covered with broken glass, and bleeding copiously from a gash on his forehead.

He'd wanted to kill her—until he found out who she was. Fayth Graham. As soon as he'd been informed the manner in which she'd gained entrance to Annancreag, it had all fallen into place. He remembered where he'd seen her before—the fair lad in the kitchen—the one who'd been staring at him.

"When I get my hands on her—death is too good—too easy!"

Robert didn't reply, maintaining the stony quiet that had descended on him since the raid. Alex was minus a sword and a horse, but he wouldn't let that stop him. There were horses to be had—the March was filled with his enemies—and they all had mounts.

"I will kill Wesley this time—do you hear me, Rob?"

Robert raised his gaze, not quite meeting Alex's, and nodded shortly. He was shirtless, sitting on the hearth while Celia sutured the wound in his side. It was in much the same place as Alex's had been—Alex's scar ached in remembrance—but luckily not mortal.

His brother's pensive mood was no surprise. Alex couldn't begin to fathom what Robert must be feeling—to be betrayed by his own wife! It had been obvious to Alex that Robert was thoroughly besotted with Caroline—had put her before everything. Though Alex still had his doubts, he'd set them aside, seeing that his mistrust was causing a rift between them that could not be mended. Alex wanted to punish her for trifling with his brother.

"And as for your *wife*," Alex said, stalking over to stand in front of Robert. "This is treasonous—to sacrifice her new family—to sacrifice you."

Celia, who knelt beside Robert, swiveled around and glared up at him. "I don't think she knew a thing about it!"

"She knew. She's as fine an actress as that—that . . . sister of hers." He couldn't think of Fayth Graham without the rage exploding afresh.

Celia shook her head. "This was Fayth's doing—not Lady Annan's." She turned to Robert and began wrapping the linen bandage around his chest. "You don't believe it, do you, my lord? She is your wife. I know she cares for you. You must go after her."

"Oh, I'm going after her," Alex said, striding toward the door.

"Hold," Robert said.

Alex gritted his teeth and paced back into the room. He was only honoring Robert's wishes because of his wife's involvement, but he was fervent to be after them. If they hurried, they could catch them! His mind was swollen with thoughts of revenge.

Robert stood, turning his body stiffly, testing his range of movement, and grimacing in pain. Hands on hips, he faced Alex. "Prithee, tell me again, how she overpowered you and took the gate keys. For I have seen this woman and she's but a wee elf."

Heat crept up Alex's neck. "Not an elf—a troll!" Robert's dubious frown shamed Alex and he burst out, "She pretended to be a whore."

Robert frowned harder. "And you believed her? Did you not take note of her attire?"

Alex shrugged, averting his eyes. "I'd been drinking."

"Drinking." Robert paused, pacing around Alex thoughtfully. "Think you I would bring whores to my wedding? And if I were so disposed, where would I find aught but a toothless village trull?"

"I don't know!" Alex yelled, furious at himself. "I don't know what I was thinking."

"Oh, I ken what you were thinking," Celia muttered.

Alex took a step toward Celia. "What was that, Celia?"

Celia stood—that haughty manner of hers that so annoyed him slipping into place. Hands on hips, she walked right up to him. "You heard me. You were thinking with your cock, you stupid ass. Don't try and pin the blame on Lady Annan—you let them in!"

Alex folded his arms over his chest and stared over her head, refusing to acknowledge her. The women about this place were far too impudent for his tastes. She made some rude hand gesture at him that he caught in the periphery of his vision and stalked from the room.

"Now that she's gone," Alex said, "we can decide what to do."

Robert pulled his bloody shirt over his head. "We're going to Graham Keep—that's where they're headed now that they have what they want. Ridley's game has gone on long enough. He will hand over Patrick and my wife—or I will take them."

Alex smiled. "Aye, that's good. But Wesley and the lass are mine."

Robert's shoulders slumped and when he looked at Alex his eyes were bleak. "Just let it go, would you? Celia's right—it was your fault. You gave her the advantage. Accept it—punishing her won't change the part you played."

His disgrace seared him anew and Alex looked away. Robert was right. This was all his fault. The men who had fallen today—their deaths rested on his conscience. Their wives' and children's grief was his creation. He was sickened by it—it choked him.

"Forgive," Alex said, his voice rough. "I . . ."

Robert clamped a hand on his shoulder. "You made a mistake—now rectify it. Help me."

Alex nodded. "You love her."

Robert's gaze was fixed on him, but Alex could see he'd withdrawn again. After a long pause, he said, "It feels as though my heart has been ripped out."

Alex gripped his brother's wrist, hard. The driving compulsion for revenge seized him, made him frantic for action. "I swear to you—I will find Caroline and set things to rights. I will have vengeance."

Robert's gaze focused on him. He shook his head and turned away. "Sometimes, Alex, I think that's all you'll ever have."

When Caroline woke, they were on the banks of the Solway Firth, waiting for a boat to take them across. She blinked—the pain throbbing in her head. She groaned and a face appeared above her. Fayth.

Caroline struggled to sit up. She was numb, empty.

She looked at her sister, not knowing her. "How could you do this?"

Fayth was back in her male clothing, a cap pulled low over her eyes, hiding her hair. Her face was strained, her eyes bleak. She didn't answer.

Footsteps crunched on the rocky shore, approaching. "Carrie!" *Wesley.* "Tell her you're happy—tell her this is what you wanted."

Fayth's eyes narrowed, her lip curling. "You said no one would die!"

Wesley kicked his booted foot at her, sending a shower of pebbles at them both. Fayth cowered in time, but the stones struck Caroline's face. She winced.

"Witless fool!" Wesley sneered. "You think I can pull off a raid of this size without one death? Jesus God! I lost men, too. You're such a little girl, Fayth."

Fayth turned away, her jaw hard, but her chin quivered slightly.

Caroline looked up at Wesley, shaking her head. "I didn't want this—I love him!"

Wesley's face froze—he seemed to have stopped breathing. He stared at her in speechless horror.

Caroline moved forward, crawling almost, and the pain and loss washed through her fresh, raw. "Did you . . . ? Is he . . . dead?"

He looked down his nose at her. "So you've both turned traitor?"

Fayth turned violently, sending stones tumbling across the beach. "I haven't turned traitor! My feelings haven't changed—but you didn't have to kill anyone! It was perfect—they were all in the hall—there was no reason for what you did!"

Wesley grabbed the front of Fayth's doublet and yanked her to her feet. "Where is the stone? Why did you give me the signal and let me in when you didn't have it?"

"There is no stone, fool! It's a story!"

Wesley shook her, hard. Her cap fell off. "You'll tell your story to Ridley—for I'll not take the blame for this one."

Fayth spat at him and his hand drew back as if to slap her.

Caroline scrambled to her knees, grabbing at Wesley's arm. "Stop it! Stop it!"

Fayth swung her leg, her boot connecting with Wesley's knee. He released her and stumbled backward. He glared at them both, then spat on the ground and stalked off across the beach.

Fayth sank back down, beside Caroline. "No one was supposed to die," she whispered, her gaze fixed on Wesley's back.

"Why are we here?" Caroline's voice was as dull as the throb in her head. Her mouth tasted like sand.

"We're crossing the firth. We're taking you to England. Once there, Wesley will find a way to get his hands on your dowry, then we'll take you to France . . . or Venice or Florence—to a convent. You pick."

Caroline shook her head. "No. I'm not going."

Fayth just stared at her, her expression unreadable.

"Is he dead?" Caroline's voice caught and she covered her mouth.

Fayth shook her head. "No—Wesley just wounded him." She looked away, across the water, at the fog rolling in, cloaking the world in damp gray. "He won't let you go back, you know."

Caroline's composure broke, tears welling in her eyes. "Robert wouldn't have me back after this. It's over." She covered her face as sobs shook her body. She'd been so close to something so wonderful, so fine—only to have it ripped away.

Fayth did not attempt to comfort her. "This isn't just about you, you know."

Caroline wanted to hit her, to shut her up. She couldn't stand another moment in their presence.

"Wesley will force me to go back to Graham Keep and marry Carlisle—and I knew that. But I did it for you, Carrie."

Caroline dropped her hands, incredulous. "Who asked you to? I asked you for no favors!"

Fayth looked away, mouth flat and tight.

They sat in silence for a long time. Caroline tried to decide what to do. She couldn't go back to Robert. Not now. Not yet. Not until she knew how he felt—if he hated her. If the Maxwells hated her. But never would she go back to Ridley. "Why are we at the firth? Why not travel southeast—through the debatable land?" That was the quickest route to Ridley's estates—and with horses, the best way.

"Because that's the way they'd expect us to go." Fayth's voice was hard, her gaze remote. "Wesley sent a group of men that way with the plunder. Lord Annan's sleuth dogs will pick up the scent and divert them from us. In the meantime, we'll get you to England and safety."

Caroline pushed the hair out of her eyes with shaking hands. "You said I could choose the convent I wanted to go to."

Fayth looked at her then, her head cocked quizzically. "Yes?"

"There are several nearby—one to the north, another to the east."

Fayth didn't say anything.

"I know you and Wesley are arguing, but you'll make up, you always do. Please, for me, convince him that a convent nearby is the best thing. That the sisters there will take me in and keep me safe. Tell him they have the means to get me into a convent on the Continent."

"Why? So you can go back to him?" When Caroline didn't answer, Fayth asked, "How can you want to go back after the way he treated you? I saw how he treated you!"

"I love him! You'll never understand—you only see what you want to, and twist everything contrary to that into something ugly."

"They killed Jack."

Caroline grabbed Fayth's arms, shook her. "Jack is dead—and I'm sorry—but it was his own fault. He went on the raid—no one forced him! Stop blaming everyone else!"

Fayth pushed her away and stood. She looked around, at the firth, now obscured by fog. "We're not going anywhere tonight." She looked down at Caroline and shrugged, her face set in lines of resignation. "I'll see what I can do."

The Maxwells descended on Graham Keep en masse. Put to it, Robert could raise nearly one hundred men, mounted and armed to the teeth—with promises of reinforcements from the warden, Lord Maxwell. It was no surprise to find Ridley's castle closed up tight. The Maxwells formed up outside the main gate, banner snapping in the breeze, and waited.

Other than shouted orders, Robert hadn't spoken throughout the journey south. His mind was occupied, calculating his utter failure at peace, remembering his father's countless diatribes on how Grahams couldn't be trusted. What had he accomplished? He'd not gotten his brother back—and he'd lost his wife in the effort. His fury simmered, ready to burst forth at the nearest foe.

Graham Keep held a high position, overlooking a desolate moor to the north and lush fields to the south. The keep rose above the thick curtain wall, the original tower structure identifiable by the gray-black ashlar. But it had been expanded by generations of Grahams so that it sprawled high and wide. Conical, crenellated towers framed the old square tower. Decorative turrets jutted out at random. An ornate gallery wrapped the west side of the keep. It was an old whore, trying to hide her age with paint and baubles.

The portcullis rose halfway and a group of knights trotted across the lowered bridge—Lord Ridley Graham at the center. Robert spurred forward, flanked by Alex, Geordie, and half a dozen men-at-arms.

"Not a word," Robert said to his brother.

Alex didn't reply but his stallion was in a nasty temper—snorting and pawing, chewing the bit. Ridley and his entourage stopped at the foot of the bridge and waited. When Robert was a dozen yards away, he reined in.

"Lord Annan," Ridley shouted, riding to the head of his men and no farther. "This is most unusual—when I see this many Maxwells at once, my keep has been stripped bare and my kine lifted."

"Och, he's a pretty one, isn't he," Alex said under his breath.

Ridley Graham had a soft, pampered look about him. His golden brown beard was trimmed close to his face and his clothes were some of the finest Robert had seen: brushed velvet doublet, a deep blue, trimmed with gold braid. Lace peeked out from his sleeves and he wore a ring on every finger. An elaborate studded codpiece drew the eye to his lower body. His crushed velvet hat was adorned with bright green and blue plumes. Even his horse jingled with tassels and bells. Were this a true raid, Robert would strip Ridley to his underclothes and sell the garments for a fine bit of coin.

"I'm here for my brother and my wife," Robert called out.

"Sir Patrick is on his way home, I expect. Or perhaps he's dead—a victim of witchcraft. Who can know?"

Alex started forward, hand on sword hilt.

"Wait," Robert said, his voice low, staying his brother. He yelled, "Explain yourself!"

"Sir Patrick escaped—with my stepmother. I haven't a clue to their whereabouts. She's a murderess. She poisoned my father and I will see her burn for it, mark me."

Alex frowned at Ridley, his mouth flat and grim.

"What do you make of it?" Robert asked.

Alex exhaled loudly. "It wouldn't surprise me if Patrick did escape, he always has before. But I don't trust Lord Graham. I don't like his eyes."

Robert peered across the empty space at Ridley—who stared back, seemingly calm and unbothered. After a moment, Ridley raised his hand. "I'm coming forward, Lord Annan—alone." He trotted to the empty space between the Grahams and the Maxwells.

Robert shot a look at Alex before spurring forward to join him. They faced each other silently—horses stamping and swishing their tails.

"There," Ridley said, rubbing his gloved palms together. "That's better. We shouldn't face each other like enemies. We are friends, yes?"

"Where is my wife?"

Ridley dropped his hands to his thighs. He shook his head, wide-eyed. "This is the first I've heard of her absence—though I must say it doesn't surprise me. She fought me on this, begged to enter a convent." Ridley shrugged, waving a hand at Robert to indicate his great length. "I thought a man of your size would convince her otherwise, or at least, control her."

Robert ground his teeth together. "She did not leave me willingly. Do not pretend you know nothing—Wesley and Fayth Graham kidnapped her."

Ridley's eyes gleamed but his mouth turned down thoughtfully. "I know nothing of this. Fayth ran away some time ago and Wesley has been unmanageable for years. I have no hand in his actions. Indeed—when I get my hands on him, I'll flog the skin off his back for jeopardizing such an important truce." Ridley's gaze jerked to something behind Robert, his eyes pale blue slits. "What's this, eh?"

Robert looked over his shoulder to where Alex aimed a loaded crossbow at Ridley's chest. He waved.

"Pity you're not even wearing mail," Robert said.

Ridley ran a hand over his fine velvet doublet. "I've met you here, outside the protection of the castle walls, as a friend. I expect you to honor that!"

Robert shrugged helplessly. "I cannot help you—Alex is completely unmanageable. I take no responsibility for his actions."

Ridley held Robert's gaze for a long moment before laughing shortly. "And here I thought all Maxwells were violence-crazed dullards." He held up a gloved hand, then turned it in a gesture of friendship. "You think me false. Well—I suppose I cannot blame you. But we have both been duped. I fear Caroline has conspired with her siblings for her freedom. This situation is most difficult, but I believe we can come to an understanding. Let's put this behind us and move forward."

"I'm agreeable—but I still have no brother and no wife. Our situation will only become more difficult until they are produced."

Ridley was beginning to look a trifle put out. His gaze darted back to Alex—then a smile slid across his face, placating and false. "I cannot give them to you because I do not have them. All I can do is extend an invitation for you to search my home yourself."

Robert frowned at the unusual offer. "Very well." He paused—smelling a trap. He did not want to find himself imprisoned like Patrick. "How many men will you allow me?"

Ridley scanned Robert's men, assessing. "A score—no more."

Ridley was being generous—which made Robert's heart sink. Clearly neither Caroline nor Patrick was here. Robert rode back to Alex, who still trained the crossbow on Ridley. Robert placed his hand on the bolt and aimed it at the ground. "Gather nineteen men and join me at the bridge. We're going to search Graham Keep."

"He must know we'll find nothing."

"Aye," Robert said. "But that won't stop me from looking. Perhaps we'll find a clue to Patrick's true fate." Robert looked back at Ridley, waiting expectantly at the bridge. "He knows something about Caroline—of that I'm certain. I've an idea how to force his hand."

Robert had split his men—seven to search the ground floor, seven the above floors, and seven to the dungeons. Robert was impressed by the size of Graham Keep's dungeons. Annancreag's were nothing more than a hole in the ground. These dungeons were a series of vaulted tunnels that led off into heavily barred rooms. Torches affixed to the walls lit their way. It took an hour for Robert to search every room—and still he felt as though he were missing something, as if the dungeon continued deeper, but he could find no other passages. Ridley accompanied him, mostly silent, except when giving a brief history of some portion of the dungeon, arms folded across his chest.

Finally Robert returned to the curved stone staircase and looked around, hands on hips.

"You see?" Ridley said, rubbing his beard. "I have not lied to you. Yet can you be certain Caroline hasn't?"

Robert turned on him. "Why was my brother down here at all? He is a knight of good family—deserving better than this!"

"You find my methods crude."

Several Grahams stood guard near the stairs, and gathered around, as if they expected a fight. Robert's men, who were still poking about in some of the rooms, abandoned their search to stand behind Robert.

"I find you lacking honor."

Ridley went still, his gaze locked on Robert, who stood significantly taller. Robert had noted that Ridley avoided standing too close, so he didn't have to crane his neck to look up.

"Your brother caused me much trouble. He destroyed several rooms trying to escape and cuckolded my steward. My steward is a man of mild temper and yet he beat his wife severely for her indiscretion and vowed to kill Sir Patrick—attempted to on one occasion and came out of it maimed. I moved Sir Patrick for his own safety—as well as the safety of the women. I simply could not have him among my household. He caused too much discord."

That certainly sounded like Patrick. Those were the very reasons Patrick had finally run off to fight on the Continent. He'd tired of listening to Father berate him for being shiftless, inconstant, apathetic.

Robert pointed to the cell across from the stairs. "This was his cell, you say?"

Ridley nodded.

Robert took a torch from the wall and entered the cell again. It was a small room. There was no bed—not even a straw mat. Filthy rushes were scattered across the floor and as Robert crossed the room, bones crunched beneath his boots. The only items in the little room were a blanket wadded in a corner, a foul-smelling bucket, and a candle burned down to little more than a lump of wax.

Robert left the cell just as Alex bounded down the stairs two at a time. Robert's heart pounded at the intensity in his brother's eyes, but Alex only shook his head.

"I found nothing."

He was lying. Robert could tell and was suddenly anxious to leave. Something about Caroline, he prayed. Emotion flooded him and he fought it. He wanted the anger, or the emptiness—not this aching loss. He looked again to the tiny befouled cell where Patrick had been imprisoned for months, remembered how poorly Ridley had treated Caroline, and the rage returned, sustaining him.

Ridley watched him with sharp eyes. He approached, his footsteps echoing. "So, you are convinced?"

"I'm convinced he's not in Graham Keep, aye," Robert said. "But if I discover he died in your care, I will come back and cut your lying tongue out so you cannot scream when I peel the fat from your bones."

Ridley's eyes were flat and cold, his lips white in his beard. "Do not threaten me. I am not friendless—even in Scotland." His expression relented as he smiled slightly. "I understand your frustration, Lord Annan, and I value this alliance—let us come to some new arrangement. I have another sister; you'll surely find her more appealing. She's . . . pretty in her own way—and full of spirit. Caroline really was very unsuitable, but I thought she would at least be easier to manage."

Unsuitable. Robert clenched his fists, fighting the

need to choke Ridley. This was the opening he'd been waiting for—the only way he could induce Ridley to return Caroline to him.

"You are certainly anxious to wed me to a Graham—why is that?"

Ridley paused. "You have no sisters or daughters, else I'd offer for one."

"Really?" Robert said in mock surprise. "So, it has naught to do with the legend?"

Ridley frowned, confused. "Legend?"

"Of the Clachan Fala." When Ridley shook his head blankly, Robert elaborated. "According to the legend, a union between an Annan Maxwell and an Eden Graham will bring the stone forth."

Alex had moved away, into the shadows, and watched Ridley closely.

Ridley snorted. "What nonsense! You believe that, Annan? Really! How fanciful of you."

Robert hadn't expected Ridley to admit to it. In fact, Ridley's reaction was just what he'd hoped for. "No—but many do. I did think it odd, however, and a most unusual coincidence, for that old hag to appear." He shrugged and started for the stairs.

Ridley caught his arm. His grip was hard, strong. "What old hag?"

"Oh, it was naught—probably someone's idea of a jest."

Ridley's mouth stretched into a smile and he didn't release Robert's arm. "I love a good jest. Do tell."

Robert stared down at the restraining hand. Ridley dropped his hand and took a step back. Robert started up the stairs, Ridley right behind him.

"Well, some old woman arrived at Annancreag, claiming to have a gift for us—only for the laird and lady's eyes. But when she heard Caroline was gone and why, she said there'd been a mistake. I was most distressed by my wife's kidnapping and was not to be disturbed—so my men didn't fetch me immediately. By the time I heard of it, she was nowhere to be found." Above ground, in the tapestried corridor, Robert raised his brows speculatively. "Verra odd—wouldn't you say? For some reason, it made me think of the legend."

Ridley's smile was brittle. "Indeed."

"I suppose we'll never know now," Robert said. "If she were the keeper, she's taken it back into hiding."

In the hall, Robert's men gathered near the door, waiting. Robert turned to Ridley. A tension seemed to have sprung up around him, the lines of his face deeper, his actions quicker.

"I thank you for your cooperation, Lord Graham. But I must be off. Perhaps I can locate your brother before he gets far with my bride."

Ridley placed a companionable hand on Robert's arm. "My Lord Annan—don't fret another moment. I can see you care for my sister and therefore I will do everything in my power to assist you. I will begin a search for Caroline on my side of the border. I will send you word the moment I discover her whereabouts. I give you my word, both Wesley and Fayth will be punished severely for this act of defiance."

They weren't far from Graham Keep when Robert asked his brother, "What did you find?"

Alex unhooked his jack and reached inside. He dropped a small leather pouch into Robert's outstretched hand. Robert opened it and poured the contents into his palm. Nail parings, a lock of hair tied with a string, and a large stone bead with strange carvings on it.

"What is this?"

"Look at the hair," Alex said.

As Robert lifted the tuft of dark blond hair his heart caught. "Patrick."

"Aye—I ken not how much of Ridley's blatherings are true—but I found this in the witch's chambers."

Robert met Alex's gaze, incredulous. "So he *has* escaped."

Alex nodded. "Looks as if he caught the dowager's eye—perhaps these were part of some love philter."

"What now? There is naught we can do but wait for him to turn up." Robert stared at the hair a moment longer before replacing it in the bag with the nails. He held the small bead a moment longer.

Alex took it from Robert's fingers. "I'm not so sure about that."

Robert braced a hand on his thigh and viewed his brother quizzically. "What mean you?"

"You think this is some sort of runic stone or bead, aye? Something used in witchcraft. No doubt Ridley has dismissed it as such, too." Alex shook his head, eyes strangely fevered. "But I recognize it." Alex closed his fist around the stone. "It's a landmark."

"A landmark."

"The dowager Lady Graham is a Musgrave, aye? And a witch. The keeper of the stone is supposed to be a Musgrave witch. Only she knows where the Clachan Fala is hidden." Alex held the stone out again, but rotated it, so it was standing on end. "It is a standing stone. I've seen it— far north, in the Highlands. Near the coast. There is a group of them—all shaped like this, with markings."

Robert regarded his brother and the stone silently. He'd never been to the Highlands and he had to admit, the bead was unusual—slightly oblong with a wide hole through the center. But Robert was tired of this legend. He cared nothing for the stone—only for finding his wife.

"If we go to this stone," Alex said. "We'll find Patrick—or perhaps the Clachan Fala."

Robert looked away. It was too shaky a theory for Robert to pursue. Patrick was in control of his own destiny again and needed Robert no longer. Patrick could take care of himself.

Caroline, however, was a victim of the feud. It had become a living thing, this hate, ruining lives and leaving misery in its wake. Robert was more determined than ever to end it—through violent means, if necessary.

"Do what you must," Robert said, digging his spurs into his horse's sides. "I'm finding my wife."

26

Father Jasper trudged up the hill to Annancreag with a heavy heart. The villagers, as always, had recovered quickly from the raid. The day after, he'd said blessings over many graves—Maxwells and raiders alike. But the memory of it lived on, as it always did, in those who'd lost loved ones. He'd spent this morning enjoining a young lass to eat. Her husband had been killed. Her family, and her husband's, would take care of her, so she needn't worry for her future. She knew this and yet still had no will to go on. Thankfully, by the time he'd left, she'd eaten several of the sweetmeats Lord Annan had sent down for her.

The priest didn't know what to do now. Caroline had been gone nearly a fortnight. Lord Annan had scoured the West March to no avail. He'd even made forays onto the English side, but had been run out by Wharton and his men.

Jasper couldn't stay here—not without Caroline. She was the only reason he'd come, the only reason he'd stopped his wanderings. The Maxwells didn't hold him responsible, regardless of his Graham surname, and strangely no one blamed Caroline either. They all directed their ire at Fayth. Wesley was a man and a known reiver, and therefore his actions had not been unexpected—unnatural. Fayth, however, had become anathema. When her name was spoken in the village it was in the vilest terms and usually followed with an excess of expectoration. Jasper did not try to defend her, though he knew, in her wrong-headed way, she'd only been trying to help. Something festered in her soul, poor child, and it was changing her.

The priest stopped outside the gates, mopping his brow. The castle seemed empty without Caroline, devoid of life. The guards were engaged in a bit of sport, roughing a man up. Bush-bearded Geordie stood at the gate, lance in hand, ignoring the man's mistreatment.

He watched Jasper's approach, his mouth grim.

"What's this?" Jasper asked, waving at the man, now on his bottom in the dust.

"Graham messenger," Geordie said. He held the leather packet. "No Graham steps foot in these gates again—ever."

Jasper sighed. He didn't remind Geordie that he was a Graham, as they all seemed to have forgotten. "Is he waiting for a response?"

Geordie nodded.

"I'll take Lord Annan the missive."

Geordie gave him the leather packet and moved aside so Jasper could enter. The castle's inhabitants were subdued. Everyone felt Caroline's absence, though she'd only been here a short time. At Lord Annan's chambers, Jasper scratched at the door. It swung wide. Lord Annan stood before him, unshaven, dark circles beneath his eyes. He grabbed the priest and dragged him into the room. He'd been drinking again, Father Jasper noted, averting his face.

"My lord," Jasper said, trying to disengage the hands

from his robe, but Lord Annan held fast. "You've received a letter—from Lord Graham."

Lord Annan released him and snatched the leather packet away. His eyes burned feverishly bright as he tore at the leather straps, muttering to himself.

Jasper watched uneasily. Lord Annan had been acting very strangely since he returned from his search—holing himself up in his chambers, refusing to speak to anyone.

Robert opened the letter and flattened it on the desk, palms holding it down. He stared at it, then thrust himself up. "I can't read it fast enough." He pointed to the letter. "Read it to me—now!"

Jasper hurried over to the desk. The letter was from Ridley. Jasper rushed through it, summarizing the main point—which was that Ridley had located Caroline. "She's in a nunnery—north of Crossraguel Abbey." He looked up hesitantly.

Lord Annan's shoulders slumped, "A nunnery?"

Jasper went to him. "It means nothing—where else would she go for safety?"

Lord Annan's pale eyes fixed on him. "She could come home!"

"Wesley would never bring her back."

"Why hasn't she written?"

"You know how she is . . . she probably feels responsible—thinks you blame her."

Lord Annan faced him, hands on hips. "She took the statement. I searched her chambers and the tower room. It's gone."

Jasper didn't know what to say. He'd been so certain that this was right for her, that Lord Annan was right for her. And it was obvious Lord Annan loved her. Where had he gone wrong in directing her? Why would she do this? He covered his mouth, paced away from Lord Annan.

He turned finally. "You must go to her. You'll never know unless you confront her—she keeps much to herself—so any doubts she had, any worries, she might not have given voice to."

"Not even to her father?"

Jasper gave him a puzzled look, but Lord Annan's gaze didn't waver. "Hugh Graham?"

"No—I mean you."

Jasper's heart seemed to stop. He clutched his chest until the pain receded. "What did you say—I misheard you."

"No, I think not. I think she learned much of her behavior from her father. Perhaps if you were more forthcoming, she would be, too."

Anxiety gripped Jasper. He tried to deny it, but saw in Lord Annan's face that he knew and that, more than anything, convinced Jasper that their union was right and good. No one had ever suspected before. And yet, Lord Annan *knew*.

But what would this mean for her? Jasper turned away, went to the chair behind the desk, and slumped into it without Lord Annan's leave. Lord Annan thought he'd married a gentlewoman, not the illegitimate child of a priest. No man liked to be cozened so.

"What do you mean to do?" Jasper asked. "It was my sin, and her mother's. She's nothing to do with it and so shouldn't suffer. Hugh Graham raised her as his own—so far as I know, never suspected. Do you mean to repudiate her because she's a bastard?"

"No one need ever know but you and I . . ."

Jasper heaved a sigh of relief, wondering what was next—would Lord Annan send him away, knowing he'd fallen from God's grace?

"And Caroline."

Jasper's head jerked up. "No, no. I cannot tell her—she mustn't know—"

Lord Annan flung the door open, waving the priest's stammered protestations away. "You can explain it to me on the way."

Jasper stared at the empty doorway Lord Annan had just disappeared through. His gaze turned skyward and he whispered, "Thank you."

The convent was a mile north of Crossraguel Abbey—an impressive and wealthy order of Cluniac monks. A dozen nuns inhabited the old, run-down priory where Caroline currently resided. None of them could read or write, so they were well pleased with Caroline's arrival. Though their life was routine and structured, Caroline found it lacking the spirituality she had expected. She supposed it was due to the nuns' illiteracy, but a priest from the nearby abbey visited on occasion, to see to the sisters' religious instruction. It was truly a sorry state of affairs.

Caroline spent her days writing letters for the abbess to the queen of Scotland, the pope, and other such authorities who might aid the convent with grants or endowments. The brothers from the abbey were apparently too busy for such things and a scribe was not to be found locally. And if one were to be found, there were no funds to pay him with.

Released from her writing duties for the day, Caroline had retreated to the chapel. She should be taking a meal with the sisters, but found she had little appetite. There were no benches in the tiny chapel, not even in the front for the local nobility—not that any local nobility came here to worship. Caroline walked slowly up the aisle, stopping before the altar and gazing up at the stained glass picture of Saint Margaret.

She knelt. She'd never been good at worship and, of

late, it was useless. Her prayers all dissolved into wishes
to turn back time, to change the past, to tears and regrets.
Caroline lowered her head, her heart empty and aching.
She should at least send him word, let him know where
she was and beg his forgiveness. But then she'd remember the betrayal in his eyes—the disbelief—and knew it
would not be enough. He would never trust her again.

She looked back to the stained glass, the red and yel-
low light blurring together. "We're not so different," she
whispered to the dead queen. "You, too, were an Englishwoman who wished to be a nun. You, too, were sent to
wed a Scotsman, against your will." The tears slipped
down her cheeks. "You, too, came to love him well."

She heard something behind her and quickly wiped
her tears away. It wouldn't do to be caught in such folly.

"Did she also write such . . . interesting tales?"

Caroline whirled, trying to gain her feet, but stumbling. Robert started forward, holding her book—the one
he had gifted her with, the one she had written such wanton stories in. *Dear God!* He'd read it! Caroline covered
her face, horrified, overcome, delirious.

"Caroline . . ." There was such an odd timbre to his
voice that she lowered her hands. He stared back at her
with eyes full of haunted questions. She searched for the
condemnation, the anger, and found only worry.

Her gaze traveled over his body—unable to believe he
stood before her. There was a roaring in her ears and she
feared she might faint. He seemed bigger, broader than
before, filling the room. He'd not shaved since she'd last
seen him. Long, dark whiskers, sprinkled with silver,
covered his jaw and cheeks.

She couldn't speak, her lips trembled. He was simi-
larly reticent, regarding her cautiously. She looked at the
book. "Did . . . it disgust you?"

His frown smoothed and his mouth tilted slightly. "Ah . . . no."

She took a step closer. "Did you like it?" Her skin tingled—she felt lightheaded. He'd come for her. He wasn't angry. She dared to let herself hope.

"Did I like it?" He looked at the ceiling, nodding vigorously. "Oh, aye."

A flush crept up her neck.

"I like the ending," he said, taking a step closer. "When Orpheus didn't look back."

The tears started again and the words she'd been holding back burst forth in a torrent. "You must believe me—I knew nothing . . . I suspected Fayth might be up to no good—but I didn't tell you because if I was wrong, I didn't want to sour you against her. But I never thought she'd do something like that. I swear it."

"I believe you."

She came at him then, propelled forward by her need to make him understand. "I don't want to be a nun—I hate it here. It's horrid—all the praying and the silence and the cold cells and horrible food. Take me home, Robert! I can't bear another moment!"

Robert gathered her in his arms, laughing. "I always knew you'd never be a nun."

He kissed her, gently at first, then hungry, his arms and mouth punishing. She tasted her own tears on his lips, relished the rough beard abrading her skin, the smell of road dust and horses. She could almost forget. Almost.

When he raised his head she said, "I've been writing you a letter, trying to explain it all."

"Well, I'll not let you scribe for me anymore, if that's the fastest you can write." His voice was rough, raw. He touched her face, tucked her hair behind her ear.

"I was afraid you wouldn't believe me, would never trust me again."

"I never lost faith."

"I'm so sorry the peace has failed." She laid her head on his shoulder, relief and happiness making her weak. "I know not where Fayth and Wesley went after they left me here."

"Alex is determined to have revenge—I hope, for your sake, he never meets up with them again."

"They thought they were rescuing me—they didn't understand. They still don't."

"I know. I'd do the same for my brothers." He took her face between his hands and said forcefully, "Let us hope they don't try it again!"

Caroline shook her head. "They won't. Fayth took the statement." She removed it from her bodice and handed it to him. He didn't open it.

He moved past her, to the candles burning on the altar. Holding the folded paper over a candle, he asked, "May I?"

Caroline nodded. The paper caught and blazed. They both watched it burn to his fingers. Then he dropped it and stamped out the flames. He stared down at the ashes.

She went to him, slid her arms about his waist, and whispered, "I don't want to return to Annancreag until we've said the words, before a priest. So there's no more question."

He smiled down at her. " 'Tis a good thing I brought a priest."

Father Jasper appeared in the doorway, smiling broadly at them.

Robert leaned close and whispered, "Are you ready? I cannot promise you an easy life, perhaps not even a safe one. But I'll protect you with my life, give you my heart—and never look back."

Caroline slid her hand into his. "And I promise to be a most suitable wife."

Father Jasper married them with the church's blessing and before witnesses, and together they returned to Annancreag. Caroline had never been so happy to be home. She lay on her bed, exhausted and content. Robert, freshly shaven and washed, joined her.

"So, what do you think of my story?" he asked. "That was very clever, how I tricked Ridley, aye? He never would have helped me otherwise."

He leaned over her, arms braced on either side of her head. She smiled, loving that Robert was so indignant over Ridley's treatment of her and wishing she could have seen her brother's face when Robert told him the story of the old witch.

"Very clever," she said, putting her arms around his neck and pulling him down for a kiss. "But that can only mean one thing."

He pressed his knee insistently between her thighs, settling his weight on top of her. "What is that?" he asked, distracted, sliding his hands under her shoulders.

"That this isn't over. Ridley thinks the stone is coming to us. . . ." She tried to think, but Robert's mouth on her neck was making it difficult. "He said Mona was gone . . . he must think she's gone for the stone . . . you must have confused him with your hag story."

"Mmhm."

She shuddered as he bit her ear, then licked it. "What will we do if he's right?"

He lifted his head, meeting her questioning gaze. "You mean, if the stone from Excalibur's scabbard manages to find its way to us?" He didn't believe the legend—even

after she told him about her last visit with Bess
Maxwell—and was only teasing her.

"Well, yes. What will we do?"

He made a face as if he were actually considering it,
which made her laugh. "According to the legend, we're
only to keep it safe, for our son."

"But we don't have a son."

He smiled down at her, wicked and knowing. "I mean
to remedy that, *mo cridhe,* right now."

SONNET BOOKS
PROUDLY PRESENTS

TAMED BY YOUR DESIRE

JEN HOLLING

Available July 2002
from
Sonnet Books

Turn the page for a preview of
Tamed by Your Desire. . . .

The litter, piled high with pillows and blankets, creaked and swayed as the horses made their way inexorably west—to Lochnith and Fayth Graham's betrothed, Lord Ashton Carlisle. It was late August and the weather was mild; even so, Fayth was sweating, stifled by the closed curtains of her litter. But they shielded her from the sight of the heavily armed guard surrounding her. The guards were more than protection. They ensured she'd never escape her fate.

Fayth leaned back against the pillows, loosening the laces of her bodice, untying the throat of the linen shift and spreading it wide. But that brought no relief. The air was thick. The stench of unwashed men and horse sweat permeated the heavy brocaded curtains. Fayth's eyes drifted shut as fatigue washed over her in heavy waves. A strange lethargy had settled over her of late. She discovered a refuge in sleep that couldn't be found in wakefulness. Her mind became blissfully blank. No thoughts of her brothers, who forced her into this union; no thoughts of Jack, the man she almost married, or his murderer, the black-hearted Red Alex; no thoughts of her sister, Caroline, whom she'd betrayed and hurt . . .

Caroline. No, even in sleep Fayth could not escape what she'd done. The memories oozed through the thick haze of her mind. Fire eating through tapestry and flowers, blood spilling, bodies twisting in agony. Fayth's head jerked, as if to flick away the visions like an insect—but they gripped her. Caroline screamed and screamed. Arms imprisoned Fayth, stifling, suffocating. Fayth fought his embrace, struggled for air as he squeezed. But he was too strong for her.

She gasped, forcing her eyes open. Sweat stung them. Icy fingers trailed down her spine, even as her body swelled with an inexplicable restlessness. Vomit soured her throat and she pushed a curtain back, securing it open. The cool breeze couldn't sweep away the lingering feel of Jack's murderer, holding her like a lover. They were in a wood, sunlight streaming through the branches like shafts of gold. She searched the trees, looking for a means of quick escape when the body of an enormous—and gaudily arrayed—stallion blocked her field of vision. Fayth's gaze rose until she met Ridley's pale blue eyes and bearded face. His plumed helm rested on his knee. Sweat plastered the thinning golden brown hair to the sides of his head

"Cover yourself," he hissed.

Fayth was not inclined to obey any order of his. He'd flogged her himself when she refused to marry the Scots laird, Ashton Carlisle, and still he'd been unable to wrench an agreement from her. But once Carlisle's representative assured Ridley her acquiescence was of no import, Ridley had wasted no more time on her. He was escorting her to Carlisle himself. He intended to drag her gagged and bound to the altar if necessary.

It would be.

Fayth glanced down at her gaping bodice. The tops of her breasts were visible almost to the nipples. An angry red welt, the skin broken and crusted over, snaked around from her back to mar the skin of her collarbone. When she looked back at him, he was staring at the welt with remorseful eyes. But Fayth knew he felt no regret for the pain and humiliation he caused her; he feared Carlisle might be displeased with damaged goods.

Ridley glittered like a jewel. A fur trimmed velvet surcoat covered his heavy mail sark. The surcoat was deep green, liberally embroidered with gold threat. A thick gem encrusted chain spanned his chest, holding the ermine lined cloak in a graceful fall off his shoulders. He'd not forgone his passion for indecently short breeches. The slashed green velvet barely covered the tops of his thighs. The white silk of his undergarments was pulled through the slashes. An obscenely large codpiece covered his groin. His thighs and calves, usually fully exposed but for the tight stockings encasing them, were covered with greaves today. White plates bearing a green serpent protected his shoulders and thighs.

His horse was no less adorned—its mane and tail braided with ribbon. Feathers, tassels, and bells jingled and bobbed with every step.

"What's the matter, Brother? Are you afraid Scratchton Carlisle of Louseland won't take a marked bride? Surely he's used to scurvey-ridden women, being a Scot."

"Cover yourself or close the curtains," he repeated through gritted teeth.

Annoyed that he ignored her baiting, Fayth pulled a

kerchief from her bodice, further dislodging her breasts. They were pushed high by the stays constricting her breathing. She dabbed her forehead and then her chest. She smiled slyly at her brother, aware that behind Ridley, the guard's gaze was fixed on her bosom—waiting for the horses to misstep and her breasts to spring free.

"Make me," she said.

Ridley's lips curled back from his teeth. He leaned forward and shoved her—his thick leather gauntlet scraping her forehead. She tumbled back into the litter. Metal hissed as he drew his sword and cut the tie holding the curtain back. It fell into place, closing out the sun and the air and his hated face. Fayth didn't move from her sprawl on the pillows.

She laughed softly—the unfamiliar sound bubbled up from her chest like a sob, shaking her shoulders.

"Laugh now, Sister," Ridley said. "But your defiance will only make it worse."

She laughed again—loud and forced—but Ridley said nothing more. It was too uncomfortable for such antics and soon she lay still, staring up at the swaying ceiling of her litter and contemplating her fate. Ridley was right. Defiance would only earn her more lashes— along with her husband's anger. Her stepmother, Mona, said he was a cruel man.

Fayth turned her face, ashamed at the weak stinging in her eyes. She would not give up—he could beat her dead, but she would never marry Carlisle voluntarily. And yet . . . she could see no escape.

This was not how she'd imagined her life. Once there had been love, joy, friendship, family. Now there was nothing in its place. Fayth squeezed her eyes shut, pushing the memories away. Nothing would be gained by dwelling on what could not be changed . . . for now. But there was still hope . . . there was always hope.

Sleep pulled at her again, but she resisted, reluctant to relive that night, when things had turned from bad to unbearable, when Jack's murderer had groped her like a whore. She could still feel his hands on her—no amount of bathing washed them away.

Fayth opened her eyes; her gaze finding the golden slit of sunlight that wavered between the fall of curtains. How far to Lochnith? And if she could escape from her brother and her betrothed, where would she run? She closed her eyes—refusing to dwell on how everyone who ever loved her was either gone, or had turned away. Nothing was gained by thinking on it. She repeated these words—again, and again, until the aching loneliness and regret ebbed away. Perhaps in sleep, an answer would present itself.

After much searching behind tapestries and rugs, Fayth found the door connecting her chambers to Carlisle's, disguised as paneling. She pushed a heavy trunk in front of it, knowing that wouldn't keep him out. The sky was already darkening, though full night was still some time away. Fayth scoured her room, hunting for some weapon to use against her betrothed when he arrived. There was nothing. She emptied the juice from the small glass vial she'd thought contained poison and broke off the top, so she had a sharp edge. She could ram it into his eye or throat.

Fayth sat on the bed, waiting, alternately chewing her fingernails and stroking Biddy. The anxiety was making her ill, but for some reason, the dog helped to calm her. She'd almost fallen asleep when she heard shouting— not one voice, but many. It sounded like fighting.

She rose from the bed and looked out the window. The bailey was alight with torches—and she was not wrong. Lochnith was being raided! Carlisle's men poured into the bailey, engaging the raiders.

Fayth ran to the door and swung it open. The guards were still there.

"What's happening?" she asked.

"Red Alex has attacked."

"Are you just going to stand there? Or help?"

"I have orders, Mistress Graham."

She slammed the door and returned to the window, peering down at the fighting below. Maybe Red Alex would take the castle—but then her circumstances would only be worse. If Red Alex got his hands on her . . . She shuddered, remembering all too vividly that last time his hands had been on her—all over her. He was not the kind of man to be tricked twice.

She pushed those thoughts away. It seemed her worse fears would not be realized, tonight, at least. Carlisle and Graham men dominated the fight and the raiders were retreating. Fayth saw her betrothed, wearing a leather jack and wielding a huge sword. She turned away from the window—knowing he would be randy when he was finished. Men always were after battle.

Her eyes went to the rug where the door to his room was hidden. If he was out there, then he wasn't . . . She ran, pushing the trunk away and throwing the rug aside. She pushed on the paneling until it popped open. The narrow stairwell was unlit. Fayth felt along the wall until she reached the bottom, the dog snuffling at her heels. She was faced with a wall. She ran her hands over the surface before her until she encountered a lever. The wall sprang open.

She found herself in a bedchamber, even more elaborate than her own. The bed was enormous and hung with heavy brocaded curtains. A bust of Carlisle stood beside the bed. There was a small room, just off the bedchamber where Carlisle's attendants slept. Fayth rummaged through their meager belongings until she found an extra set of clothing. She shed her gown and shift. She slipped into the hose, abandoning all but the most strategically placed points. When she was fully dressed, her hair tucked into a cap and pulled low over her eyes, she slipped out of Carlisle's chambers.

Carlisle's device was sewn prominently on the shoulder of the tunic she wore, so she wasn't worried about being mistaken for a raider. She was, however, worried she would come across one of Red Alex's men who would slay her with no questions. The keep was fairly deserted and those not fighting were too busy hiding the valuables to take much note of her. In the kitchen, a man filled a sack with food. Fayth's heart stopped when he turned around—but then she saw the device on his arm, matching hers. He came after her—to shut her up with his fists no doubt—and she ran into the bailey.

She was just outside the stables when the man grabbed her and shook her. "Ye tell no one what ye've seen."

Fayth shook her head vigorously—she didn't care that he was pilfering his master's larder. But she was afraid he would recognize her as a woman. A figure loomed behind him. Fayth's mouth dropped open, but before she could say a word, her attacker was struck in the back of the head with a sword butt. The man crumpled to the ground.

Fayth shrunk against the wall. Her rescuer's broad, heavy shoulders were encased in chain mail, covered with a leather jack. A small, light crossbow—a latch—and a bundle of quarrels hung from his belt. He carried an enormous two-handed sword—that he wielded with one hand. His metal helm had no nose guard, so his face was visible. It was a face she'd never forget, one that had been branded in her memory by his hands and his mouth.

Alexander Maxwell—better known on the borders as Red Alex.

She was in the shadows, so she prayed he could not see her face—for if he did, he would run her through right where she stood.

"Carlisle's bride," he said, his dark eyes freezing with purpose. "Where is she?"

He thought she was a servant. She pointed to the castle and started to edge away. His scowl was fierce as he came after her.

"I know she's in there—*where?*" He grabbed the front of her tunic, dragging her out of the shadows. "Take me to her."

She fought him, kicking, scratching, punching. But he was a rock. Her cap fell off in the struggle. His breath hissed between his teeth. "Well, if it isn't the wee whore herself." He leaned over, pulling her onto her toes by the front of her tunic. His face was inches from hers. "In yet another disguise." His eyes were dark, dark blue. She had noticed that before, but then they'd been hazy with drink and desire. They froze her now, made her bowels watery. This man would kill a woman without a single ounce of remorse. Her gaze went to the ugly wound on his temple, the one she had inflicted, healing now.

Fayth knew the price for that bit of work would be heavy. She was rarely at a loss for words or a plan of action, but she found herself scared to immobility, her mind frozen with fear. He sensed it, his eyes roving over her face. He picked her up under his arm, as if she were no more than a sack of grain, and carried her into the stable.

She squirmed and bucked silently. She didn't scream. Carlisle might come to her rescue. She didn't know whom she feared more—Carlisle or Red Alex—though both meant to punish her. She'd left her broken vial in her gown and had nothing but her wits to save her. Biddy wasn't even growling, trotting silently along beside them.

Lanterns were lit inside. He pushed her against a wall and ripped off the band sewed around the sleeve of her shirt, removing Carlisle's device. Biddy sat at his feet, Fayth's cap in her mouth. Red Alex took it from the dog.

"Good lass," he said, scratching the dog between the ears. He put the hat firmly onto Fayth's head, pulling it low over her face and stuffing her hair under it. Biddy sat beside him, panting.

Fayth stopped struggling, confused. "Biddy knows you."

He stepped back, keeping a hand on her, but looking her over. "I cannot believe ye almost fooled me again—you look nothing like a lad." He met her gaze. "Biddy?"

"My dog—Biddy."

"Och, Biddy, eh?" He looked down at the dog, one corner of his mouth lifting. "That's what they're calling ye these days?"

The dog's tail swished vigorously through the dirt.

He looked back at Fayth and shook his head. "You're a stupid, stupid girl, out here, alone, dressed like a lad."

"What will you do to me?"

"Right now we're getting out of here—once we're

away . . ." He stared down at her, hands hard on her shoulders. "I dinna know. Kill ye, mayhap."

Fayth said nothing—her mind speeding forward. She'd been working on how to get out of the gates unnoticed and he just solved that problem. If she left with him, as a raider, she knew he'd get her out safely. But what then? At least Carlisle didn't plan to kill her—not right away, that is. And who knew what Red Alex had planned before he murdered her? Torture? Rape? She still recalled the last time they'd met—her skin burned at the memory and she glared back at him.

Once outside the walls of Lochnith she would be free—all she must do was escape from Red Alex and run. He'd never catch her on foot, encumbered with his armor and weapons. Red Alex was one man—Lochnith contained scores of men-at-arms—and Ridley. The odds of her living and seeing Mona again were far better if she let Red Alex kidnap her.

"Are ye going to scream?" he asked.

She shook her head.

"I didn't think so."

He took her wrist and dragged her out of the stable. He moved swiftly along the wall until he neared the gatehouse. Fayth saw that the raiders were gone. Only Red Alex remained. Her heart sank. He'd never get out alone—without a horse! Carlisle's men were gathering near the keep entrance, Carlisle at their center. Fayth spotted Ridley, just stepping outside, his armor unscathed, having missed the entire battle.

Red Alex whistled, low and musical. A moment later a horse appeared from the shadows, reins trailing the ground. Red Alex mounted, with Fayth under his arm, and flung her across his lap. She tried to sit up, but he was loading a quarrel into his latch on her back.

"I can't ride like this—what are you doing!"

"Shut your mouth and keep your head down." His helm dropped onto her head. She quickly secured the strap under her chin. His thighs tightened as he spurred the horse forward. Fayth closed her eyes and held on. Men began to shout. Fayth heard arrows whoosh by, pounding feet pursuing. She heard the click of Alex's latch releasing the quarrel, followed by a scream of agony. And then there was the hollow clop of boards beneath the horse's hooves. Moments later, the horse was in a flat run, Red Alex's hand firmly on her back, arrows filling the air around them.

Fayth thought she might vomit. Her stomach and chest and thighs were battered from the ride. When the arrows stopped, he didn't slow the horse, though he slid his arm around her waist, lifting her so she could swing her leg over the horse's withers.

They sped through the darkness, his arm a solid band around her waist, pressing her hard against chest. If he was going to kill her, she reasoned, she'd be dead now. So it was punishment he had in mind. She refused to even consider how he planned to extract vengeance from her hide and focused instead on the advantages this gave her. Escape was possible.

After a time, he slowed the horse to a walk. Where were his men? Why had he no plunder—except her? Then she remembered the question he'd asked when she thought she was a servant. *Where is Carlisle's bride?* This was no chance meeting—he had come for her. Her heart dipped down to her toes, urgency and desperation filling her again. She had to get away from him.

Full dark had fallen. The moon rose high above them, huge in the cloudless sky. They rode for an hour before he finally stopped. Fayth had been cataloging all the ways she could escape from him and none of them seemed likely. After the last time, he would be too diligent, too suspicious. He dismounted, dragging her down with him, never releasing her. They were at a burn. The horse's hooves crunched on the stony bank as it went to drink.

Memories of their last encounter flooded Fayth. It had been a fortnight ago, at Annancreag. She'd given Wesley the signal and had been sneaking about the shadows of the bailey, trying to find a way to let Wesley into the Maxwell stronghold. She'd met up with Red Alex, Lord Annan's brother, and pretended to be a whore. He'd been only too willing for a tumble. His mind fogged with lust, she'd managed to smash a jug of whiskey over his head, incapacitating him. She'd stolen his keys and let in the Graham raiding party.

He must hate her—not only for tricking him and wounding him, but for making him the weak link that let in a swarm of raiders. Raiders who murdered his people and stole his sister-in-law.

Fayth unhooked the strap under her chin and dragged the helm from her head. Her cap fell off with it. She kept hold of the helm—it was a good weapon. She felt no remorse for what she did to Red Alex. She'd never meant for it to become a massacre—for that she was sorry. She'd never meant to hurt Caroline—for that she was filled with regret. But wounding and humiliating Red Alex was not payment enough for what he did to Jack— what he did to Fayth. She would never have been at Lochnith about to be wed to Carlisle if Jack had been alive.

Fayth was significantly shorter than Red Alex—who was a giant of a man. The top of her head barely reached his shoulder. Her eyes were currently trained on his leather-clad chest. His hands dropped away from her shoulders. He began to remove his gloves. Fayth let her eyes trail upward, over wide shoulders and a neck thick with muscle. His chin was dark with whiskers, his mouth a hard, unforgiving line. His hair appeared brown in the moonlight, but she knew it was roan-dark and threaded with blond and copper. His gloves off, he held them both in one hand, and folded his arms over his chest.

Fayth met his eyes finally, a fist squeezing her heart. His gaze was steady and thoughtful.

She swallowed hard. "Well . . . what now?"

"I believe, the last time we met, we were transacting some business."

She blinked up at him. "What . . . ?" *Transacting business . . . ?* She'd been pretending to be a whore . . . Her eyes widened and she took a step back. "You can't mean . . ."

His mouth curved wickedly.

"You know I didn't mean it . . . it was a ploy, nothing more."

He followed her, the smile softening the hard line of his mouth. "Ah little one—that was your first mistake. You don't play games with me. You started it and I mean to finish it."

Return to a time of romance...

SONNET BOOKS

Where today's

hottest romance authors

bring you vibrant

and vivid love stories

with a dash of history.

PUBLISHED BY POCKET BOOKS